A TASTE FOR LIES

THE APEX KINGDOM BOOK 1

LC WHITEHOUSE

Printed in the United States of America

First Printing, 2025

Published by Lauren Whitehouse

https://www.laurenwhitehouse.com

Edited by Shavonne Clarke, Editor In Chief, Motif Edits

Interior map art by Eileen LaGreca

ISBN 979-8-89694-147-7 - Paperback
ISBN 979-8-89694-146-0 - eBook

AUTHOR'S NOTE

A Taste For Lies is a seductive, adult fantasy romance, set in the unequal world of Valenrae. It is intended for readers who are 18+ and includes elements regarding forced servitude, racism, spying, lying, stealing, hand-to-hand combat, perilous situations, blood, intense violence, brutal injuries, death, death and injury to minors, poisoning, graphic language, and sexual activities that are shown on the page. Readers who may be sensitive to these elements, please take note, and prepare to be stolen away to Valenrae...

LET'S CONNECT

Villains deserve love too. Join my email newsletter list and get an exclusive copy of the prequel to *The Apex Kingdom* series. This novella takes place a few decades before the events in *A Taste For Lies*, and follows the love match between the capital "R" rake King Elias Nyxley and the innocent courtier who falls for him and becomes queen. *A Heart For Sacrifice* can be enjoyed before or after *A Taste For Lies*, and is exclusively available to newsletter subscribers.

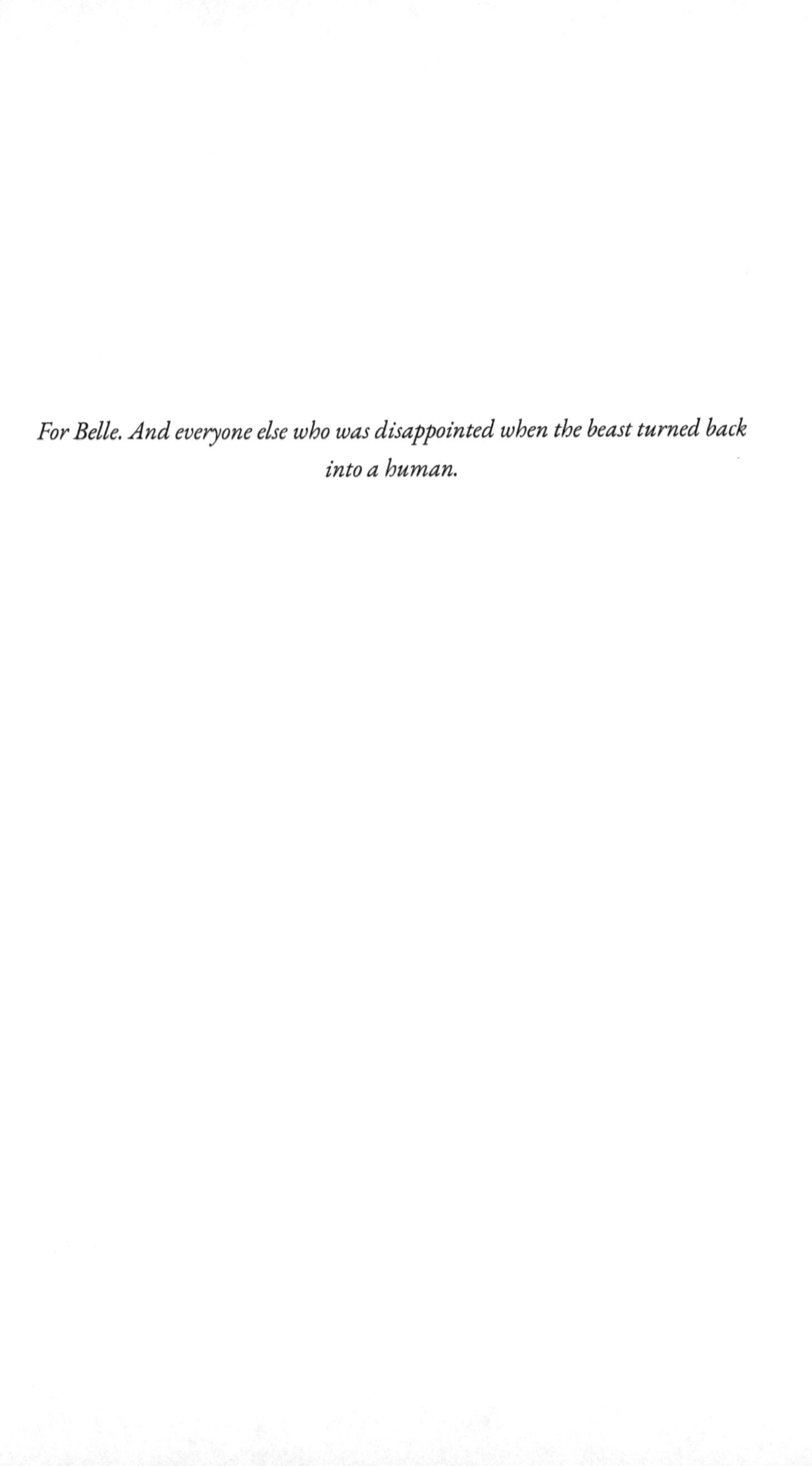

For Belle. And everyone else who was disappointed when the beast turned back into a human.

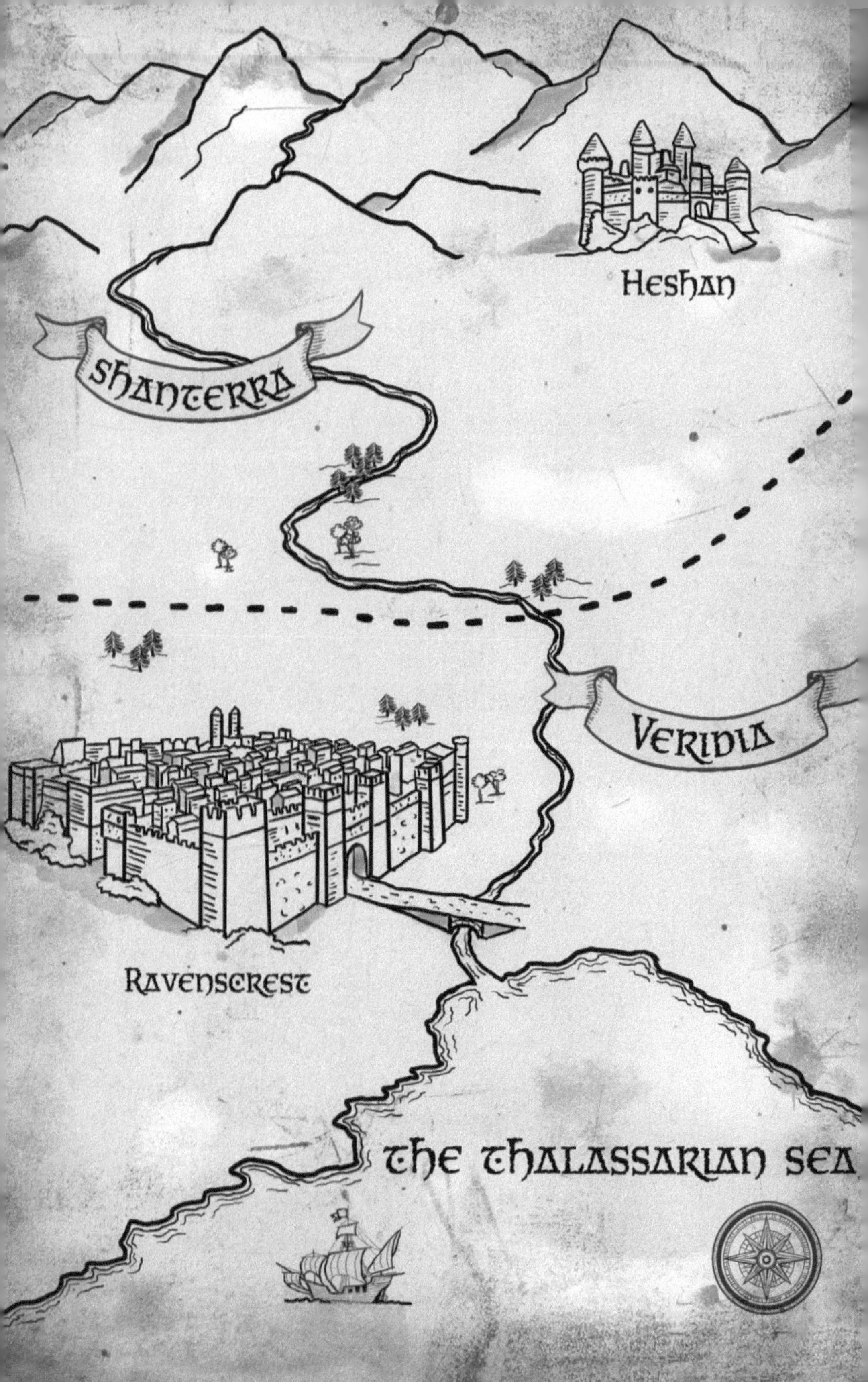

Heshan
Shanterra
Veridia
Ravenscrest
The Thalassarian Sea

The Guild's Ten Rules for
Spy Craft and Thieving

1. Trust in the Guild. And no one else.

2. The first thing is first.

3. The best lies are mostly true.

4. Everyone wants something.

5. Secrecy is your most valuable asset.

6. Plan thoroughly, act swiftly.

7. Information is power.

8. Stay silent and observe.

9. Leave no trace.

10. Maintain control.

Chapter 1

ALORA

I've been staking out the Elite's mansion for over three weeks when I finally, *finally* catch a break.

Twenty-two nights of minimal sleep huddled under the hood of my cloak on the windy neighboring rooftop. Twenty-three days of listening to mind-numbing chatter from Count Zhao's household below. Too many meals of jerky and nuts and dried fruit.

It has been six days since I ran out of bread.

When the count's own Apex guardian makes the mistake I've spent all these days and nights waiting for, it feels like the sun coming out to warm me from behind Heshan's constant cloud cover.

Even in fall, the bite of the mountain wind is harsh. But I swear the whipping wind gentles by my ears, a softer touch, whispering at me to listen closer.

"Mark my words: after tonight, we'll finally be rid of her," the massive Apex promises.

"Who—the countess?" As usual, the human gatekeeper is a little slow on the uptake.

A snarl erupts from the Apex guardian. The gatekeeper and I both start. "No, you idiot. The daughter. She's been angling for a proposal, and the count has plans to secure her match tonight."

I pop another piece of walnut flesh into my mouth, riveted by the drama. It's clear, to me at least, that this guardian carries a torch for his lord's daughter despite the strict laws forbidding Apex and human relations that extend to every country in Valenrae. Apex *serve* the human Elite, they don't marry them.

But the brute's obsession has turned to resentment the longer the girl continues to ignore him. I hope for the young Lady Zhao's sake this really is her chance to escape this guardian's oversight. He practically breathes violence, and it has nothing to do with his species.

"The girl's gone three seasons with no suitors. What's different about tonight? And what would a dumb animal know about Elite proposals anyway?" the gatekeeper retorts.

Like the rest of the human populace, I maintain a healthy fear of Apex myself. You never know when they might go feral and unleash all that power on anyone unfortunate enough to be nearby. But I still can't help but wince at the vulgar slur, no matter who it's directed at.

"Let's just say that when all the eligible lords arrive for the ball tonight, the spoiled brat will be showing off the very reason they should make their proposal posthaste," the Apex replies in a derisive tone that demonstrates exactly what he thinks of the young lady's plot to secure a husband.

And that's just what I need—a confirmed location.

Reconnaissance is strange work. It's a little like reading a good book—you get so sucked into the characters and the tension and the stories that when it finally ends, it's downright wrenching to come back to your own reality. But the burn of my wind-battered cheeks as I pack up my bedroll and gear is enough to bring me most of the way back. The wafting smell as I dump the bucket that's served as my chamber pot these past three weeks does the rest.

The life of a thief is not as glamorous as the tales make it out to be.

Numb fingers prickling painfully on the iron bars, I make my way down the townhouse fire escape on the opposite side of Count Zhao's luxurious mansion.

The second my boots hit the ground, I'm moving away at a slow and steady pace, my gear in a pack on my back. My hopelessly tangled hair is tucked into the hood of my cloak. Even the long braid can't hide how my normally warm chestnut locks have turned dull and dark with grease.

For nearly the entire walk to The Spinning Top, I fantasize about the bath I'll order at the inn—the Shanterran Guild's base of operations. I swear I can practically smell the expensive jasmine soap. It's a long walk, too—from Count Zhao's estate in the Elite northern district, with views of the surrounding mountains, to the southern valley where the plebeians live.

With every step, my shoulders relax a little more. The dull tension headache that's been my constant companion these past weeks from straining to hear through the howling wind begins to fade. Warmth spreads through my muscles as I move, the stiffness melting away.

Feeling nearly peaceful, I let myself savor the win. Tonight, I steal the Pearls of Azure.

They're an almost mythical artifact, said to have been worn by the sea goddess herself and imbued with mysterious power. I'm fairly certain it's just an ancient necklace, but the story drives up the price, so who am I to argue?

I've no idea how they ended up in the count's hands. This job is a *blind commission*—Guild-speak for a job where neither Xinlei nor I know the buyer's identity. All we had to go on was a vague location. Last I heard, the pearls were snatched by an infamous pirate captain, the Sea Serpent, and assumed lost to Thalassarian waters. How the buyer discovered they'd ended up with the count is anybody's guess.

Maybe the Sea Serpent himself wants me to steal them back for him. He'll get his wish. But I'll make damn sure everyone knows it was the Lynx—not the Serpent—who pulled it off.

Too soon, I arrive at The Spinning Top. The wooden sign swinging wildly out front is carved with the eponymous whirling top, the sigil of Jinai, god of tricksters and liars. A sign not just for the inn but for any traveling guild members looking for respite.

And I am in dire need of respite.

Sadly, it's going to have to wait until after I make my report.

I swagger into the tavern, pausing by the bar to let Shenmi know I'm back.

"Gods, Alora!" The guild steward starts coughing theatrically. Rui and Haoran, perched on stools nearby, physically recoil, their faces scrunched up in disgust.

"It's not that bad." It probably is that bad. I'm at the point where I can't really smell myself anymore, thank Jinai, but I imagine my stench is downright revolting. The corner of my lips twitch with the effort to contain my smile.

I slide a gold coin imprinted with Jinai's seal across the bar. "Can you have a bath sent up for me?"

Shenmi pinches her fingers over her pert nose, so her answer comes out muffled and nasal. "Fine. You're in the green room."

My jaw drops. She's offered me the smallest room in the inn. "What happened to the red room?"

Shenmi's dark eyes narrow. "You've been gone for nearly a month. It's occupied."

The Spinning Top is a revolving door of thieves and spies passing through Heshan on assignment. I'm one of the few who always returns. Since the day I appeared in this country at fifteen, with no memory, this inn has been my only home.

Apparently, not even a decade is long enough for Shenmi and everyone else in the Shanterran Guild to accept my Veridian heritage. It's not enough that I speak every dialect in this country—and there are many—as well as a native. It's not enough that I'm the most notorious thief in the guild, raising our reputation with every high-profile heist. All they see is the olive tint to my skin, the light amber of my eyes. With the exception of Xinlei, the people of Shanterra take every opportunity to treat me like the foreigner I appear to be.

The gnawing ache in my chest that never really goes away makes its presence known. My fingers reach automatically for the tiny golden lynx charm on my necklace.

I'm just out of practice dealing with their prejudice. "Xinlei's in his office?"

Shenmi is aghast. "You're going in there before bathing?"

I send her a mocking half-smile. "Rule Number Six." *Plan thoroughly, act swiftly.* Once you have your plan, put the pieces into place immediately.

It's possible I swing my smelly cloak a *little* more than necessary as I spin towards the guild master's office. Gagging sounds echo behind me, and my lips curve higher.

For a nearly full inn, the rest of the tavern is deserted. The Spinning Top's guests tend more towards the nocturnal, so the low couches and battered wooden tables won't start to fill again until supper.

I stride past the large fireplace to an unassuming door tucked beside the staircase. The pattern of quick knocks is specific to me, so when Xinlei finally opens up, there's no surprise on his wrinkled face. Just the wide smile he reserves for his most profitable guild member.

"Alora! Come in, come in." Xinlei has only a human's sense of smell, and even that is probably compromised due to age, but he'd have to have lost his olfactory sense completely not to notice my stench. He hides it well, though.

Removing my hood, I confirm what he's likely gathered. "I came straight from reconnaissance."

He bobs his head of white hair. "Rule Number Six." The guild master is already turning back to his workbench, drawn irresistibly to whatever new project he's tinkering with now—some kind of silver plate with a weighted spring mechanism.

Tiny screwdrivers, pliers and tension wrenches are scattered haphazardly on every surface, mingling with delicate lockpicks and oddly shaped files. Shelves line the walls of the small office, bowing under the weight of jars filled with brass tumblers, old lock mechanisms and keys of every size and shape imaginable.

The faint metallic scent of oil and brass lingers in the air, mixed with the dusty smell of old wood. It's comforting. I used to fall asleep curled up in that leather chair after late-night planning sessions. But it's been a long time since I relied on anyone else to plan my heists.

Xinlei, his eyes like black coal, peers up from the silver plate, a fat ruby in one hand and a simple rock in the other. "Do me a favor. Try to replace the coin purse on this plate with one of these."

"Without setting off the alarm?"

"Naturally."

I take the rock in one hand and the ruby in the other, eyeing the purse critically to assess its weight. With a shrug, I pocket the rock, then use one hand to snatch the purse and the other to slide the ruby in its place.

The resulting alarm is so loud, I have to cover my ears. Xinlei leans over and resets the spring. "What was your mistake?"

I suppress a sigh. "I should have chosen the rock."

"They're both the same weight."

My eyes widen and I study the plate with renewed interest. "I don't see the sensor."

"It's designed by the Veridian Guild's key master." Xinlei crouches down and examines the mechanism, prodding it gently with a curved finger. "I think he's using blood magic."

A shudder prickles down my spine. The Veridian Guild is free to do as they please in their own country, but the latest rumor is they've been selling their knowledge to the Elite as some kind of security service. Designing uncrackable holding containers for Elite valuables. If they're using blood magic, an Apex might be involved.

"Then...I suppose my mistake was not asking more questions."

The Shanterran guild master finally abandons his project and smiles up at me, crow's feet crinkling. "Bravo, Lynxling."

Enough time wasted on his never-ending lessons. "I have a confirmed location, and I'll be securing the prize tonight."

Xinlei's white brows furrow. "What's your in?" I must visibly bristle because the old lockpick hastily holds up his hands in peace. "I'm not meddling. I know you're the big bad Lynx who can take care of herself. I'm just asking...one professional to another."

I may be the Shanterran Guild's best thief, but Xinlei is the one who taught me nearly everything I know. We'll never be equal, and we both know it.

"Sure you are." I give my mentor an unamused look, but the conditioned reflex to answer him is too deeply ingrained. "The young lady will be wearing the pearls tonight at a ball in her honor. Her father is trying to use the display to force a proposal."

"A guardian said that?"

"Good as much." I shrug. "He's obsessed with his mistress."

"Big mistake to be gossiping about the security of an item like that," Xinlei remarks neutrally. "Especially for an Apex."

My lips press into a hard, flat line. It's like I'll always be a novice in Xinlei's eyes—the same vulnerable child he took in under the guild's protective wing ten years ago. "You just can't help yourself, can you, old man?"

He tosses me an innocent smile.

"I was out on that rooftop for over three weeks, Xinlei," I bite out through gritted teeth. "Trust me, it's in character for the male. Now, can you let the client know I'm ready or can't you?"

He makes a placating gesture, and I cast about for my trunk—ah, there it is, hidden under a mountain of rolled papers. The locks on it are top-notch, of course, but I still prefer to leave the trunk containing all my worldly possessions in Xinlei's office when I'm out on a job. This inn *is* full of thieves, after all.

I start to drag the heavy trunk by an iron handle towards the door when a wrinkled hand shoots out and grips my wrist in a surprisingly strong hold. My gaze snaps back to the guild master.

"Lynxling—no calling card tonight. I mean it."

I yank my wrist out of Xinlei's grasp, exasperated with the mollycoddling. "The Pearls of Azure are a famous prize. One of the *most* famous. How am I going to maintain my reputation without leaving a calling card?"

"How are you going to maintain your reputation if you're dead?" he counters evenly. "Rule Number Nine. Promise me, Alora."

"Right, right, 'leave no trace.'"

It's not that I'm not thankful for Xinlei—I am, deeply.

He's the one who taught me the guild's *Ten Rules* as a tender child, for Jinai's sake. The old worrywart is the closest person I have to a parental figure in my life. Maybe the closest I'll ever have.

That familiar ache spasms again.

"I want your word, Lynxling," Xinlei insists as I'm making my escape towards my well-earned bath, the groan of the trunk scraping behind me.

"No calling card," I promise.

But in my pocket, where the old guild master can't see, my fingers are crossed.

Chapter 2
ALORA

Sighing, I sink deeper into the tub, soaking away the dirt and sweat of the past three weeks before squeezing fragrant jasmine soap into my hands and starting on my hair. I take the time to massage my scalp with my fingernails and slowly work the lather through the long, thick tresses. The water could definitely be warmer—Shenmi making her feelings known yet again—but it's still divine.

"Lor! You're back!" Eleni's trilling voice, thick with the local Shanterran dialect, interrupts my ministrations. She bursts into the bathing room, then promptly flushes a light pink to the roots of her white-blonde hair upon finding me in the bath. She spins around and faces the doorway.

My lips curve up of their own accord. "Len. It's just a naked body. You've got one, too." I duck under the water to rinse, then, before she can react, surge out of the bath, dripping wet, and make as if to wrap her in a bear hug.

She shrieks and bolts out of the room. Laughing like a loon, I grab a towel and dry off before throwing on my favorite silky floral robe.

The decadent feeling of clean clothes against my clean body is a luxury I will never again take for granted.

Eleni leans against the wall of the green room, arms crossed over her ample chest, big blue eyes narrowed. Still chuckling, I hold open my arms in peace.

Without hesitation, she walks into them, squeezing me tight enough to steal my breath. "I missed you. This place is never the same when you're gone."

"Oof, I missed you, too."

One final squeeze and she steps back. Though not without giving me a pinch. "That's for teasing me."

"But you make it so easy." I grin. Whenever men get a look at Eleni, they make assumptions about the curvaceous knockout. But at twenty-two, she's still innocent as a girl, with the heart of a hopeless romantic. "Any romantic liaisons while I was away?"

Eleni bites her lip. "I'm thinking of approaching Bowen Sun."

I jolt backwards. "Absolutely not."

"Come on, Lor." I would never describe someone with a voice as sweet as Eleni's as whining, but this comes pretty close. "I have nothing exciting in my life. I create beautiful clothes so other people can go off and have adventures in them. Including you! I need my own adventure. A *romantic* adventure."

Unlike the rest of us criminals, Eleni isn't a spy or a thief or a cutthroat. She's the guild tailor, a talented seamstress who constructs all our disguises. Costumes designed to look as good as the real thing, with silhouettes made for stealth.

And pockets. Lots of pockets. Never underestimate the power of a beautiful garment with pockets.

I wrinkle my nose. "Not Bowen Sun."

"Why? You think he wouldn't be interested?"

I snort. "Bowen is interested in anything on two legs. He's too experienced for you."

She rolls her eyes. "They're all too experienced for me."

I huff a laugh, kneeling to sort through my trunk for this evening's disguise. "You're not wrong. But Bowen is a notorious rake." My attention flicks up to meet my best friend's gaze. "Is that really who you want for your first romance?"

"Maybe?" Eleni falls to her knees at my side, helping me sort through the layers of folded fabric. "Lately I've been wondering if I might be tired of waiting for the perfect man. Maybe a more experienced partner is just what I need."

Eleni is nearly my opposite in every way—the innocent sunshine to my jaded darkness, physically fair to my dark hair and bronzed skin.

But the one thing we share has built an unbreakable bond between us: our foreign heritage and resulting outcast status in the guild. With her silvery hair, Eleni is easily recognized as a daughter of the Thalassarian islands. In Shanterra, where all the locals have dark hair and eyes paired with ivory skin, she stands out more than I do.

I pause my digging and catch Eleni's small hand. Eyes as deep as the Thalassarian sea collide with mine. "The right person is always worth waiting for, Len."

She squeezes my hand—a silent acknowledgement. As a young guild member aching for acceptance, I made a very different choice. Eleni's romantic life is hers to navigate, but I will be damned if I let someone like Bowen Sun hurt her that way.

"Besides"—I drop her hand and go back to sorting through the fabrics—"everyone knows Bowen is terrible in bed."

"Lor!" She smacks my shoulder. "Have you slept with him?"

I shudder. "Absolutely not." I wish Bowen was the worst man I'd slept with.

"Then how do you know?"

I waggle my eyebrows. "Girls talk."

Like it always does, Eleni's bubbly laughter eases the ache in my heart. Not completely, but somewhat.

"This one," she declares, unearthing a black-and-burgundy masterpiece. "Go ahead, try it on."

"I need to eat first."

"Well, it's a good thing I came prepared." Eleni jumps to her feet, pausing to hang this evening's gown to let the wrinkles out. Before she can fully turn around, I'm already elbow-deep in the grease-covered paper bag she brought.

"I wuv you," I tell her earnestly around a mouthful of flaky dough.

Her trilling laughter chimes again. "You're always dying for pastries when you finish reconnaissance."

I swallow a too-large bite. "You would be too if you'd been surviving on nuts and jerky for the better part of a month."

Her smile dims. "Well, I don't think surveillance is in the cards for me."

I pause my rabid chewing. "You're a goddess at tailoring, Len. No one else can do what you do. Trust me, the last place you want to be is up on a freezing rooftop, peeing in a bucket."

She sighs. "No, you're right. I don't really want to be a thief. No offense."

I wave her comment away, stuffing more of the heavenly goodness into my mouth.

"But I meant what I said earlier. I need some adventure in my life."

I eye her with suspicion. "Is Shenmi giving you a hard time again? Because everyone knows how important you are to this guild, and Xinlei would be furious if he knew she was devaluing your work."

"No." I give her a hard look. "*No,*" she insists. "It has nothing to do with Shenmi. I'm just...ready for something more. And if that something isn't going to be Bowen Sun—"

"It's not."

"Right. But I'm tired of not having a partner. When you're not around, which, let's face it, a lot of the time you're gone on a job, I'm bored out of my mind around here." Eleni sits on the small bed, twisting her hands in her lap. "I want to see the fashions in different societies. Expand my craft. Someday, I'd even like to visit Thalassar, but I would settle for Veridia. At least they're a coastal country with trade and different cultures." A place where her silvery hair wouldn't mark her as other. Where she might have a better chance of finding that elusive partner she's always wished for.

I finish off the final bite with relish, wiping my hands on the bath towel. I've been anticipating this conversation for the past month, and I don't want to have my mouth stuffed with pastry while I have it. Joining Eleni on the bed, I take her small hands in mine. She meets my gaze with trusting ocean eyes.

"I think we should go." Her mouth pops open. "To Veridia," I add, in case that wasn't clear.

"Lor," she breathes. "You've never been open to leaving before. What changed?"

I drop her hands and rub at my chest. "It's getting worse."

"The ache?"

"Yes. It's always been there, but lately..." My heart pangs as if it's been squeezed. "When I was up there alone on that rooftop, the hole was so gaping sometimes I felt like—" I don't need to finish. Since she joined the guild eight years ago, Eleni and I have been close as sisters. She knows the piece that's missing.

"What do you think Xinlei would say?"

I rub the aching spot again. "I don't know. I've never broached it with him before. I feel guilty just asking. But I think, I *hope*, he'd understand. It's not like I'm running off to join the Veridian Guild. I just need time to find some answers."

"And you're sure Veridia is the place to find them?"

"I'm not sure of anything, Len." And damn if that doesn't sting more than the constant hole inside my rib cage. "I don't remember anything before Xinlei found me wandering around Shanterra when I was fifteen. Do I have parents out there? A brother? A sister? A best friend?"

She clasps my hand again, lacing our fingers. "Your best friend is here."

I smile back half-heartedly. "I speak fluent Veridian. I *look* Veridian. If I'm going to find answers, they'll be in Veridia." I reach for the charm on my neck with my free hand. "You know that I was wearing this lynx necklace when Xinlei first found me. I've been thinking, the Elite record every Apex that ever emerged, along with their inner creatures. Maybe my parents were Apex in Veridia. Maybe one of them had a lynx for their inner creature. Maybe that's why they...abandoned me."

Eleni squeezes my hand. "I'm sure they didn't want to, Lor."

No one knows why certain people emerge as Apex when they hit puberty. There doesn't seem to be any rhyme or reason to it—it's certainly not passed down in families. I suppose a priestess would call it a blessing from the goddess Faunera. Doesn't sound like much of a blessing to me. But it does mean that my being human doesn't necessarily mean my parents were.

I push out a frustrated breath. "It's not that I miss my family, whoever they are. The ache, it doesn't feel like a missing memory. Or the feeling when you long for someone who's not there. It feels like a piece of my *soul* has broken off. It's getting so I can hardly breathe around it.

"I'm going to ask Xinlei tomorrow after I bring him the pearls." Saying the words out loud feels right. "Will you come with me?"

Eleni's eyes sparkle. "*I'm* the one who told *you* that we should go to Veridia!"

"You don't think your family will mind?"

She scoffs. "They'll hardly notice. Giselle is too busy with her own family, my mother is too busy with her grandbabies, and my father's head is always buried in his work." Eleni's father moved his entire family here from Thalassar when she was a baby for a position tutoring the Elite Shanterran nobles. They all believe she's a regular seamstress, picking up odd jobs for the local Elite.

"It's going to be dangerous," I warn her. "And Xinlei's not going to want to lose both of us at the same time."

Eleni brushes my concerns aside with a wave of her hand. "You'll need a tailor if you're going to pull this off. Shenmi and the rest can make do with the many disguises I've already made for them." A sly smile that is very unlike my friend pulls at her mouth. "And perhaps while I'm gone, they'll learn just how valuable a good tailor really is."

A few hours later, as Eleni is helping me tie the last of the ribbons on my gown for the evening, I silently promise that I, personally, will never forget the value of a skilled tailor.

Like everything she makes, the work is exquisite. The structured bodice is black with a sweetheart neckline and drooping off-the-shoulder straps that give the illusion of feminine charm without restricting movement.

The deep burgundy skirt has light layers that make a delicate swishing sound when I walk. More importantly, they hide my soft suede work leggings and boots.

"Let me do your hair and makeup," she suggests, and I give in immediately.

I could say it's because she's more familiar with the styles worn by the Shanterran Elite. The truth is, I'm feeling a little nostalgic on the night of what could be my final job in town for the foreseeable future. I want to shut my eyes and let her pamper me.

She starts by sweeping kohl on my lashes, smudging it at the edges. Powder lightens my skin and covers the freckles that sprinkle the bridge of my nose from too much time spent outdoors. A deep burgundy lip stain matches the skirt and finishes off the dramatic effect.

Shanterran Elite fashion is in a theatrical mood at the moment, and I can't say I mind it.

Eleni pulls out the ribbons twisted in the bottom of my long, blessedly clean hair, revealing loose, bouncy curls.

"Pull back at least the top half so I can add the hairpin, please."

She nods and begins weaving many intricate braids from my temples, drawing them together at the back of my head, where they will fade into the curls down my back. She slides an ornate golden hairpin—a backup stiletto—into the braid. Nearly as precious to me as my custom lockpick set, it was a priceless gift from Xinlei on the eve of my first solo job.

There. That will hold it out of my eyes and still be in keeping with the tousled look the Elite are so fond of. I tug a few fine strands out of the braids. Just enough so the look appears effortless.

That's the trick. To appear as though you spent mountains of coin and countless hours to look this way, and simultaneously none at all. It's the height of absurdity, and I can think of nothing else that better defines what it means to be Elite.

"All done." Eleni squeezes my shoulder. I should probably get going. It'll take a while to make my way back uptown, and I need to stage my arrival at the perfect time.

"Now, off with you!" She makes a shooing motion. "Go steal those pearls so we can get on the road and get you some answers!"

A skilled tailor may be valuable. But they've got nothing on the worth of a best friend.

Chapter 3
TARAN

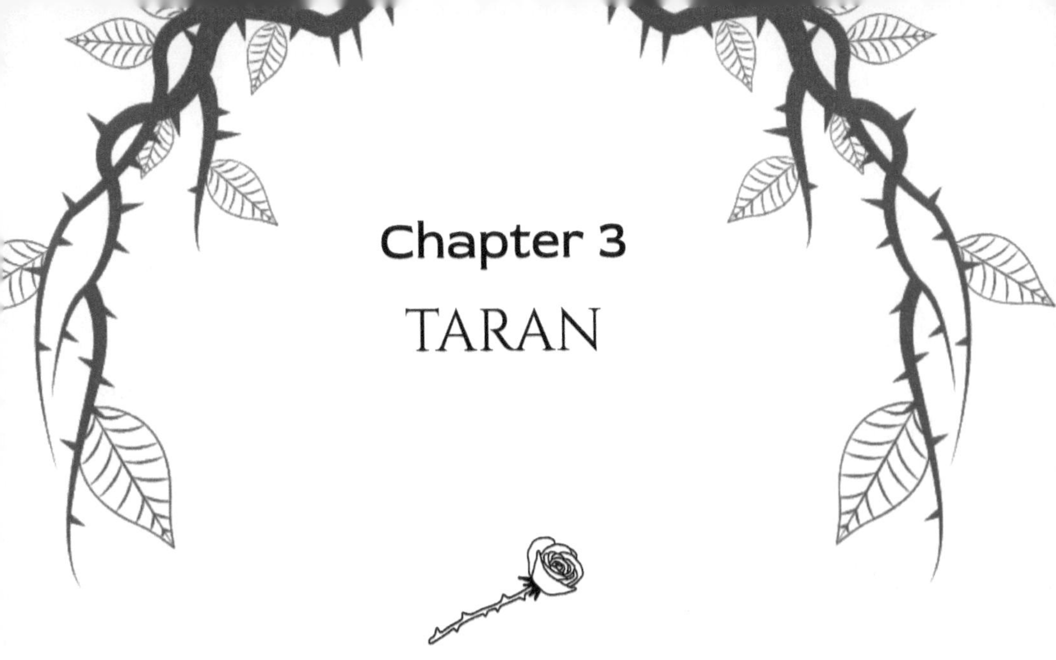

Carter blinks rapidly. "Gods, the smell of those lilies is making my eyes water. How are you bearing it?" He glances sideways at my nauseated expression and answers his own question. I'm not.

Maeve casts an unimpressed look around Count Zhao's ballroom. "White lilies are on the Shanterran royal crest. They're a staple at every Elite revel in this country." She sniffs delicately, and her emerald eyes widen. "Although they appear to have overdone it tonight. Perhaps we should have informed our hosts that the Elite Veridian prince and infamous Apex olfactory would be in attendance?" She waves a bejeweled hand pointedly in my direction.

We all glance over at the count and his wife, holding court with their guests across the ballroom. I offer them a polite, princely smile and they both blanch as if I snapped my teeth at them instead.

I wish I could claim I'm immune to that reaction, but you never really get used to it.

"No," I bark for the umpteenth time. In most political matters, I'll defer to Maeve, but not this. "It would have tipped off the thief," I mutter under my breath, conscious of the Apex guardians posted around the room, obvious in their uniforms marked with Faunera's sigil, even if I couldn't sense them.

Only a few are auditory and with low power levels besides, but it's still best to be cautious.

"How do you even know she'll choose tonight for the heist?" Maeve murmurs back. Sometimes, I find my cousin's stubborn need to be right endearing. Not often, and definitely not right now.

"She likes to make a scene." For months, I've been poring over everything my spies can gather on the Shanterran thief known as "The Lynx." Ever since I realized we'd need to bring in a professional if we're going to have any chance of pulling this job off. I can't stop berating myself for not coming to that frankly fucking obvious conclusion much earlier.

Since the mark's high profile makes contracting with the Veridian Guild impossible, and given we're now facing an increasingly urgent timeline due to my own stupidity, the Lynx isn't just *a* choice for the job—she's *the* choice.

Notorious for targeting Elite houses, she was the clear pick to take the pearls commission. The Lynx ticks every box: female (which is unusual enough), foreign, and a reputation for successfully completing every job she accepts, no matter how impossible it appears.

She'll need to be the best thief in Valenrae for this to work.

I gesture to the younger Lady Zhao in the far corner of the ballroom as she accepts compliments on the stunning pearl necklace draped around her neck. Despite the overpowering lilies, an undercurrent of brine still coats my tongue from the ocean scent emanating from the artifact. The Pearls of Azure are just as tantalizing as promised. "And she couldn't be sure the count really had the pearls until this evening."

"Do you think she's an Apex?" Carter wonders aloud, not for the first time.

Maeve brushes a hand through her vivid red mane. "Unlikely. Apex in Shanterra are conscripted to serve the Elite the day they emerge, same as back home. The odds of one escaping servitude, much less a notorious criminal with a bounty on her head, are minuscule."

"Either way, we'll know soon enough." If she is an Apex, I'll be able to scent her power level, inner creature and unique gift the second she walks into the mansion. That's *my* gift. Even with all the guardians around, and my own standing beside me, I have a feeling the Lynx's power would stand out.

"Her alias is a creature name," Carter insists.

A frustrated huff escapes me. "I told you already, that's typical. Nearly every member of the guild goes by an Apex creature name, and probably all of them are human. Just trying to make themselves sound more impressive." And lynx are sneaky wildcats—just right for a thief looking to bolster her reputation.

Not that it needs much bolstering, I silently acknowledge. There's a reason we traveled all the way from Veridia to make this proposal in person.

I do wish she had less of a flair for dramatics, though. Leaving an amber lynx carving at the scene of all her crimes? Taunting. It's a bold move and unusual for the guild, whose members are surprisingly professional despite the unscrupulous nature of their services.

Carter's tawny brown eyes scan the crowded ballroom with his enhanced Apex sight. "Is she already here, do you think?"

"Hard to say. Just keep your sight trained on the pearls."

"She hasn't even gotten a proposal yet," Maeve grumbles. Carter and I exchange equally bemused looks before turning to my petite cousin. She makes an exasperated sound in her throat. "You two are hopeless. The girl is clearly wearing the pearls to attract a match."

"You Elite with your matches and your revels and your marriage marts." Carter tosses her a crooked smile—the kind that usually makes most females, and a fair number of males, swoon. As always, Maeve remains unaffected. "I'm just a guardian," he continues. "I don't need to know about all those...games."

"Taran does," she shoots back.

"Well, that's a conundrum, isn't it?" His teasing grin widens. "The only Elite to emerge as Apex in a world where Apex and human relationships are forbidden. However is the beast prince meant to make a suitable match?"

The infamous moniker—one that never fails to enrage me whenever it comes from anyone else's lips—slides off me like water out of the mouth of my best friend.

Maeve raises her voice. "There's a *rumor* going around that Their Majesties intend to make an exception for Prince Taran. If the gaggle of Elite women of marriageable age arriving in Ravenscrest every day is any indication."

Excited whispers ignite around us, leaping across the ballroom like wildfire. A smug smile plays on Maeve's rose-tinted lips.

"Lucky me," I deadpan.

Carter gives me a bracing clap on the shoulder—he's one of the few who can reach. "And where is *your* match, Lady Ashbourne? Surely the king's niece warrants her own attention."

Maeve waves a delicate hand dismissively at my guardian. "Yes, yes, eligible Elite men are arriving as well. They all want to take advantage of the upcoming revels and annual masquerade."

"As do we," I murmur quietly, my gaze still fixed on the young Lady Zhao and her spectacular necklace.

"As do we," Maeve concurs. "Now do you think—"

But I never hear what Maeve wanted to ask because at that moment, I'm hit so hard by the explosive scent of jasmine that everything and everyone else falls away.

Chapter 4

ALORA

The beauty of Heshan, for someone like me, is that all the Elite houses are nestled high in the mountain, perfectly situated for their privileged inhabitants to admire the sweeping views. This means arriving on foot as an Elite is not just typical, it's expected. They spend their evenings at whichever mansion is hosting that night's revelry and their days sleeping it off.

What *would* be unusual is showing up alone. The Elite are obsessed with personal safety. Most nobles have a personal Apex, trained from the moment they emerged in puberty to be that Elite's guardian. The two are usually of a similar age and typically the same gender, the better for the Apex to stay close to their charge.

Count Zhao's ostentatious mansion looms before me, its wrought-iron gate guarded by a figure I recognize from my lengthy reconnaissance. The uniform catches my eye: the Apex guardian for the count's younger son.

My pulse quickens the moment my brain processes the implications. The male's charge is too young to attend the ball, so they must have thought to put his guardian to better use at the entrance. All my plans for sweet-talking a human go right out the window.

I have no way of knowing what this male's gift is or whether his Apex sense is auditory, olfactory, or sight. His inner creature could be a venomous viper or an eagle-eyed hawk.

I hate unknowns. Especially when it comes to Apex.

But the male is already looking past me with narrowed eyes, clearly wondering where my own guardian is. An automatic smile forms on my lips as I rack my brain for how to manipulate the situation to my advantage.

The Apex doesn't return my smile. "My Lady."

And just like that, his accent in the common tongue jolts a memory from my reconnaissance. I can speak this Apex's hometown dialect. My shoulders dip with relief. Now I know exactly what to do.

"Excuse me"—I address the guardian in the unique vernacular of the Yuelains, my accent pitch perfect—"could you direct me to the main entrance?"

He blinks, looking taken aback by my unexpected use of the humble language, especially dressed as I am in Elite style. My elaborate dress is covered, but my cloak is thick and rich, my hair is artfully arranged, and, thanks to Eleni, my makeup is flawless.

The cognitive dissonance plays out over his face—I look like an Elite, but I sound like him.

"You're from Yuelai?"

I pretend to be caught out, forming my mouth into a round "O" before clapping a hand over it. "I cannot believe I just did that," I say in the common tongue, with precise Elite elocution. "Please, *please* don't tell anyone."

"How do you speak...?"

It takes barely a moment for fake tears to fill my eyes. Crying on demand is a surprisingly useful talent in my line of work.

As expected, the guardian's gaze darts to and fro, looking anywhere but at the Elite woman breaking down on his lord's doorstep. "Oh please don't cry, My Lady. It's not my place to ask."

"My Apex"—I sniff loudly—"she taught me. And now she's gone. At events like this, I suppose I just want to feel closer to her. She should be here."

He draws a sharp intake of breath. Another Apex from his hometown, lost while protecting the Elite. "Can I... Could I perhaps ask...her name?"

I shake my head vehemently. "I can't, I can't. It's just too fresh."

He rubs the back of his neck, no doubt filling his own narrative into the empty space I've conveniently left.

Peering up at him from under kohl-darkened lashes, I murmur, "Would you keep this little indiscretion between us? My parents are already furious with me for my continued attachment to her. They keep pushing me to find another guardian, but I just..."

His gaze softens. "Of course, it will be our secret. Lady—?"

"Lightfire." I manage a tremulous smile. "Just come to town."

"May I accompany you to the door? It wouldn't do for you to arrive without an Apex."

"Oh! That would be lovely, but—don't you need to be here for the other guests?"

He glances over my shoulder. "You're likely the last to arrive. And it will only take a moment."

I sigh in genuine relief, patting my eyes dry and ensuring my makeup is still intact. "Thank you. I don't even know your name."

He puffs his chest up a bit at an Elite lady paying him attention and gestures up the path. "It's Jei, My Lady."

As we stroll up to the mansion, my entrance assured, my mind is already whirring towards the next step in the plan.

Jei guides me inside and departs with a deep bow, leaving me in the foyer. Resigned, I pass my fine cloak to the waiting servant. I would really prefer to hang onto it—odds are, this is the last I'll see of it.

The opulent ballroom envelops me in a haze of extravagance. As usual, the air is laced with the strong perfume of Shanterran white lilies. I wrinkle my nose. Quite strong tonight.

Crystal chandeliers cast a dazzling array of light upon the polished marble floor. The chatter of guests echoes against it, creating a symphony of whispers, a melodic backdrop to the event. My ears catch fragments of conversations—the intrigue, the scandals, the delicate alliances that define Elite society.

Through the throng, my eyes snare on the young Lady Zhao, and something settles in my stomach. Because around her neck, just as I'd known they would be, gleam the Pearls of Azure.

The luminescent orbs glow with a blue-green-tinged simmer, casting a radiant aura upon the young Lady Zhao's face, making her appear otherworldly, mysterious. Having seen the lady myself in the unflattering dawning light of day—stumbling her way home from the past night's revelry—I can say with great certainty, this is not her natural state.

It appears I've arrived at the perfect time. The other guests have already noted the pearls and moved on, though surreptitious glances linger.

The stage is set.

My gaze drifts to the brute guardian from earlier, the one who unwittingly gifted me this opportunity. He's now standing sentinel behind his charge's daughter. His stoic demeanor betrays nothing, but to me, it's clear—he guards a treasure he both cannot stand to be without and resents to his core.

I subtly shadow Lady Zhao's steps as I wait for my moment, pretending to sip from a glass of sparkling wine I swiped from the refreshment table. I don't drink while I'm working as a rule, but it helps me blend in.

Rule Number Eight: Stay silent and observe.

A different kind of reconnaissance... My lips kick up involuntarily. I suppose it *can* be glamorous sometimes.

Something distracts me—a prickle of awareness, the unmistakable weight of eyes on the back of my neck. But a furtive glance behind me doesn't reveal anyone watching.

What does catch my eye is an enormous man in a tailored black suit, towering over the other revelers. He's bigger than the count's brute, only nearly matched in height by the more slender Apex in a guardian uniform at his side. The Elite's back is to me, but the guardian's tawny eyes are fixed on Lady Zhao and—I frown—the pearls around her neck.

Are they thieves posing as an Elite and his Apex in an attempt to steal my commission?

Before I can ponder further, a young Elite man about Lady Zhao's age approaches her, his own guardian in tow. I'm close enough to listen in on their conversation as they exchange bows and pleasantries. I recognize the lord from other nights spent among the Elite—a second son from a less prosperous family. Exactly the kind of suitor Count Zhao thought to attract for his daughter with this display.

"My Lady, I find myself compelled tonight to ask you a question..."

Rule Number Two: The first thing is first. When faced with multiple challenges, concentrate on solving the most immediate one first.

I can't afford to be distracted right now, or these interlopers really will take my prize. As the Elite bumbles through his proposal, the lady's dark eyes shining, I keep my gaze trained on her father's guardian. He's close enough to hear every word. A red flush begins to creep up his neck, his jaw clenching harder with each word exchanged.

I set down my drink and thread through the crowd on silent feet to stand directly behind them, all the while monitoring the proposal. My fingers find my lynx charm as my heart beats a little faster, anticipation fizzing through my veins.

The young Elite barely finishes his speech before the lady squeaks, "Yes!" The absolute picture of Shanterran Elite propriety, she clasps his hand demurely, attempting to restrain the excitement on her face.

The guardian may be much larger than me, but he's entirely focused on the events unfolding in front of him. A strong, unexpected push from behind and he stumbles right in between the newly engaged couple, shoving them apart.

My hand moves to the small dagger concealed against my thigh, easily accessible through the custom slit in the right pocket of my skirt. With a fluidity born of repetition, I deftly sever the necklace string. The pearls glide like magic into my palm, then right into another hidden pocket.

I let out a loud, theatrical gasp, and more heads crane to glimpse the spectacle. But by the time they're focused on the scene, I'm already standing on the other side of the room.

"Did you see that?" I stage-whisper to the Elite now standing next to me. "Lady Zhao accepted the lord's proposal, and that Apex went mad with jealousy!"

Excited twittering starts up around the room. A blush stains the lady's face as she quickly puts space between her and the brute.

"Lady Zhou"—the new fiancé is staring daggers at the guardian, who is more than twice his size—"is this *animal* bothering you?" I flinch automatically at the slur, but no one in my radius so much as bats an eye.

"Oh!" Her hands flutter anxiously as she steps to the Elite man's side. "I can't imagine what's come over him…"

Count Zhao, his cheeks red from drink, barrels through the crowd. "Hua? What's the meaning of this?"

"Lady Zhou has accepted my proposal to wed. This *Apex* seems to think he's entitled to an opinion about it." The fiancé says "Apex" like what he really means is strider dung.

The guests recoil, forming a ring of empty space around the guardian, lest any drop of this scandal touch them. I use the natural shuffle of bodies to slip towards the exit.

Hua is baffled, trying to simultaneously assuage her new fiancé and her father. The guardian starts defending himself loudly, and my lips tip up. Wrong move. His protests only serve to enrage the Elite men further. A surge of exhilaration courses through me. Almost complete.

I throw the final log onto the bonfire I've built.

"The Pearls of Azure! They're gone!" I cry out, pointing to Lady Zhao's now-bare neck. "That Apex must have taken them!"

As the shouts grow louder and multiple guardians rush forward to restrain my patsy, I chance a glance towards where the huge Elite and his guardian were standing…only to find them carefully navigating their way through the rambunctious crowd in my direction.

Time for my exit.

But instead of heading to the front door and my waiting cloak, I slip up the stairwell. On the third floor, two doors await me. According to my research, the one on the left leads to the count's private study. Pausing, I press my ear to the wood. No sound. Perfect. With a few deft moves, I pick the lock, silently thanking Xinlei for the excellent lockpicks, made of his own design. The door clicks open, and I slide in.

The count's study exudes masculine luxury: heavy wood furniture, dark textiles. And...there! Across the sumptuous room, the moonlight from the window reflecting off it, is a glass case where the pearls would typically be on display.

No need to break into an empty case. Instead, I slide a tiny amber figurine of a lynx from another hidden pocket and place it gently on top. My calling card.

For a moment, I admire the beautiful symmetry of the amber lynx atop the empty case. But the sound of footsteps coming up the stairs jolts me out of my reverie. Just one set. It has to be one of the rival thieves.

Forget letting me go to Veridia with Eleni. Xinlei will *murder* me if I get caught because I was leaving a godsdamn calling card.

In less than a second, I determine that the hushed footfalls are too close and too fast for an escape. I'll have to hide.

Throwing the window wide open to stage a false exit, I duck under the count's massive wooden desk. My hand instinctively moves the pearls from the pocket in my skirt to the more secure one sewn into my bodice. They're almost...thrumming, like tiny bees are trapped inside. My fingers tingle from the brief moment they touched my bare skin.

The footsteps are heavy—maybe the big man. My heart pounds double-time.

There's no reason for whoever that is to open the shut door and come into this room. Even if I'm right and those men were thieves, why would they expect me to hide here?

The door creaks open anyway.

My breath stills. They should see the open window and assume I'm long gone.

But no. As if in a nightmare, the owner of the footsteps (alone for now, but I can hear two more sets start up the stairs) beelines straight for my hiding place under the desk.

I mentally curse in four different dialects. What the hells is happening right now?

Two black trouser-clad legs ending in surprisingly utilitarian boots stop right at the opening to the desk.

Then a rich male baritone in a cultured Elite Veridian accent says, "The Lynx, I presume?"

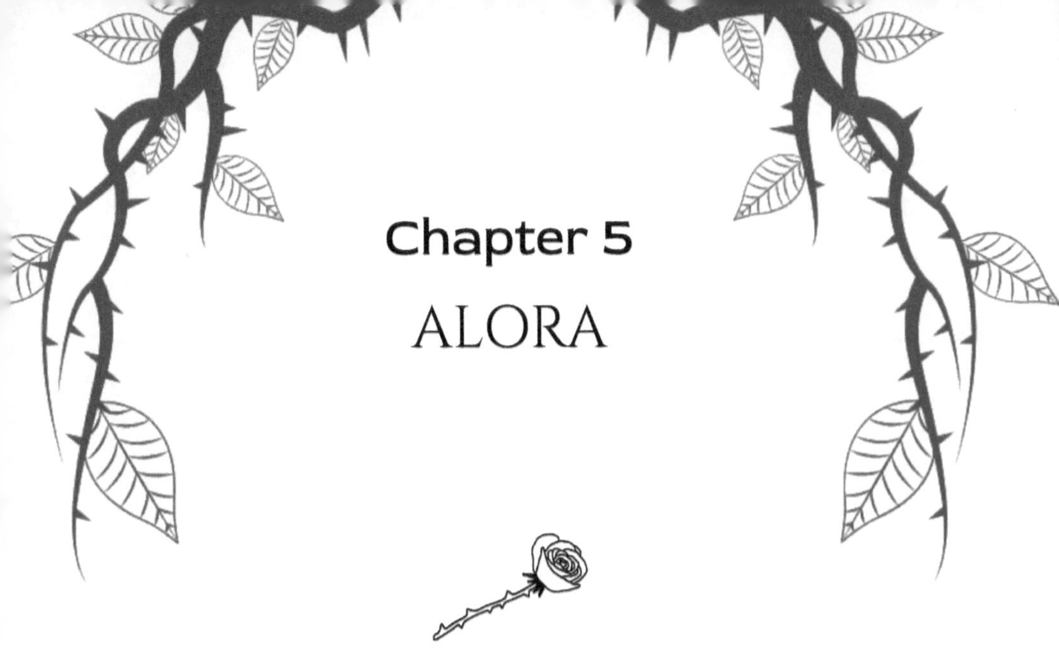

Chapter 5

ALORA

Every part of my being comes alive at the rumble of that rough voice.

The man squats down to my level and deep-set, silver-gray hunter eyes framed by dark brows peer at me through the opening of the desk frame.

"Your reputation precedes you."

Instead of answering, I study the huge man from downstairs who, regrettably, knows my name—or at least my alias.

As I'd noted earlier, he's dressed like an Elite, in fine clothes, all black. But the rest of him... His tousled hair, a mixture of ebony and dark browns threaded with a few tiny braids, sweeps past his chin. Stubble dusts his strong, square jawline, and the unkempt hair paired with the shape of his nose—long and slightly curved at the bridge—lend a ruggedness that seems to suit his muscled frame far better than his polished attire.

And then there's his eyes.

We stare at each other...

I jerk back so quickly, I knock my head on the bottom of the heavy desk frame, hard. But I barely notice the throbbing pain.

He's an Apex.

But that's not the scary part.

The truly scary part—the part that has me pulling my knees up to my chest and pushing back as far away as I can get from him in my semi-crouch under the desk—is that I can sense his inner creature looking out at me.

A savage stoneclaw stares out from behind that mesmerizing blend of silver and stormy grays that seem to shift and darken in the short time we hold each other's gaze.

I'm well and truly shaken now, trying desperately to keep it from showing. My hands curl into fists to hide their trembling. I've *never* instinctively known someone was Apex before, much less sensed their inner creature—I didn't even know that could happen.

The eyes of any Apex can glow with a luminant, animal-like sheen—when they're excited, when they're expending an inordinate amount of power. This stranger's seem to be brightening by the second.

But even if I could guess his species from his eyes, I should have no clue what his creature is. No less *feel* it looking at me, for Jinai's sake. My chest squeezes, and I can't get my breath down.

He cocks his head to the side, a gesture that feels less human and more...predatory. It's like his ruthless creature is studying me, too.

"Lady Lynx?" He extends a big hand towards me.

Rule Number Seven: Information is power. When you're the one at the disadvantage, take your cues from your adversary.

I force my breathing to even out and make a solid attempt at a nonchalant shrug—decidedly less believable following my hasty retreat under the desk. His hand remains steady, so I take it, and he helps me up from my crouch as though I'm some delicate maiden who needs assistance. If he knows I'm the Lynx, we both know that's the farthest thing from the truth. Our twin calluses scrape against each other as if to prove this absurd charade.

"There," he says, all false courtly politeness and exacting Elite pronunciation in a low, gravelly voice. The combination is jarring but not in an unpleasant way. Not by a long shot. It wakes something sleeping deep inside of me.

I find myself holding his gaze—and his hand—a few seconds too long, pulling in a sharp inhale of his rain and pine scent. Once I get a lungful, it's all I can do to drop his hand and take a deliberate step back, revealing far more than I wanted to.

A slow curve starts up the right side of his full mouth. This close, I have to crane my neck to meet his unnerving gaze, even though I'm considered tall for a woman. Every inch of the male screams raw strength, from the powerful curve of his tree-trunk-sized arms to the solid stance of his muscled legs.

And now that I'm paying better attention, there's this...energy rolling off him. A faint hum in my ears, like a vibration. Like power.

For the first time in a very, *very* long time, I have no idea how to play this.

Luckily for me—or unluckily, depending on how the next few minutes turn out—the owners of the other two sets of footsteps burst into the room. They come to an abrupt stop on the other side of the desk, breathing hard from their race up the stairs.

I assumed they'd be more Apex, but while the male looks the part in his guardian uniform, the woman is petite and dressed in an evening gown herself. Her eyes are a startling shade of emerald green set in a heart-shaped face. A brief glance is enough to guess that she's actually Elite—not...whatever this costumed male in front of me is.

I eye the guardian warily, the more likely threat, after the enormous stoneclaw beside me, of course. He's lankier than the giant, but his bare forearms are still corded with muscle covered by rich umber skin. The close military crop of his tight black curls and his uniform tells me he's probably Apex, too, or at least trying to appear like one. But I don't have any sense of *his* inner creature. Thank Jinai for small favors.

"Tare, you should have waited for us." The guardian addresses the giant by my side in Veridian rather than the common tongue.

"You should have kept up," Tare replies in the same language, then turns to me, but I'm already backing away, closing the distance to the window.

He raises his hands non-threateningly and switches back to the common tongue. "That was an impressive performance downstairs."

I take another quick step towards the window. "I have no idea what you're talking about," I reply in my Elite accent.

"You misunderstand. I'm here to speak to you about a different precious artifact. One I'm hoping you'll steal for *me*."

I pause my retreat but stay on high alert. This is some kind of job offer? *Rule Number Four: Everybody wants something.*

"Forgive me for cutting right to it, Lady Lynx, but I believe we are all short on time tonight. There's an amulet I require, and I need you to secure it for me."

Despite myself, I'm intrigued. This Apex knows my alias and my reputation. And they're foreign Elite who I don't recognize, which means they likely traveled from Veridia for this meeting.

"Come now, can we stop pretending?" The stoneclaw speaks in Veridian this time, directed at me. Does he know I speak the language, or is he testing me? "Sooner or later, they're going to realize that guardian doesn't have the pearls on him."

I'm not willing to drop my cover, but against my better judgment, I do ask in the common tongue, "Where?"

He hesitates. "Ravenscrest."

"No." I'm not stupid enough to turn my back on the trio, but I do start shuffling backwards again.

Tare lunges forward, his massive size overwhelming me, and snatches my forearm in a firm hold. "Wait."

My skin erupts into goosebumps at the touch. "I'm not interested."

His lips kick up into a wicked smirk. "Not even to steal from the Veridian king?"

I can't help it. Despite everything in me screaming not to, my eyes still widen at such a prestigious mark. Of course, the stoneclaw presses his advantage.

"That's what you do, right? Steal from the Elite? Well, what greater heist than to steal the king's own amulet right out from under his nose." He gestures with his free hand at the glass case and my calling card atop it. "You can even leave your little token." His voice lowers. "Matches your eyes."

It's tempting. Extremely tempting. A legacy-defining heist that would put me right where I want to be anyway—the capital city of Veridia. The Elite would surely keep their records of emerged Apex in the palace...

But at the thought of the palace, I reluctantly shake my head, a stray curl flying loose from Eleni's arrangement. The Apex's silver eyes track the movement. "Doesn't matter what I want. It's an impossible job."

"I thought impossible jobs were your specialty."

This dangerous stranger knows far too much about me. I tug at my trapped arm but he holds fast. "*Nearly* impossible jobs. Only an idiot would take a job where the odds of failure are one hundred percent. Which is any job located in Veridia's palace."

"Why?" he challenges.

How stupid is this male? Despite my earlier dread, I find myself glaring up at his too-close face. "*Why?* You know why. The beast prince. He'll sniff out anyone who's not supposed to be there faster than Faunera herself, and we'll all end up on the execution block."

Yet incongruently, the biggest smile stretches across the stoneclaw's whole face, practically lighting up the room. His eyes crinkle into slanted slits; his strong cheekbones stand stark above straight white teeth. It leaves me a bit dazed, which is the only excuse I have for not making the connection myself before he says—

"I think he'll be alright with it. You're looking right at him."

It all becomes clear in a rush. Speaking in Veridian, dressed as an Elite because he *is* one. Finding me so easily when I've never even come close to getting caught before. "Tare," his guardian called him. And no one knows what inner creature lends the notorious beast prince his Apex power, but a deadly stoneclaw certainly fits the bill.

My stomach drops three stories to the ballroom below.

I've been caught stealing a priceless artifact by Prince Taran Nyxley. The one Elite I can never outrun.

He's going to devour me whole.

The panic must be written across my face because the beast's smile drops, and then, so does his hand from my arm. I don't wait. Spinning on my heel, I make for the window. Fuck not turning my back on him—my priority right now is getting the hells out of here.

"Wait. Wait!" he calls out to my back. A muttered curse and then, "If you run, I'll chase you."

I freeze, one hand on the windowsill, my shoulders tense. Slowly, I turn my head to meet the intense, glowing eyes of one of the most powerful Apex in Valenrae.

And I truly don't know what comes over me at that moment, but I say back, "You'd have to catch me first, Your Highness."

The burning silver darkens to molten gray, and his next words come out in a low rasp that curls my toes. "I think we both know how little effort that would take."

The silence drags out. I remain frozen at the ledge, afraid to make a move.

Finally, the glow of the prince's eyes recedes, replaced with what I think is determination. "You can have the pearls." My breath catches. Behind him, the Elite woman grumbles a protest under her breath. "Take them back to your guild master. Collect the commission. But only if you agree to help us in Veridia."

My teeth sink into the inside of my cheek. He's letting me escape with the pearls when he could just as easily throw me in chains? "Why me? You could have gone to the Veridian Guild with this."

"I could not," he counters.

And, fair enough, he is attempting to steal from his father, *the king*. It's smart to go outside the local guild.

But that brings up its own issue. "I can't operate in Ravenscrest without the Veridian Guild's approval. I'll be excommunicated for that."

"You're the Shanterran guild master's protégé, practically his adopted daughter. You'll figure it out."

I stiffen at yet another confirmation that this royal Apex knows many things he shouldn't.

The woman saunters forward and stands at her prince's side. Her delicate frame is dwarfed by his hulking presence, but she shows no alarm at being so close to the beast.

"You'll walk out of here tonight, free, with the pearls." She negotiates evenly in a melodic Veridian accent. "We'll provide you with every assistance you could need to secure the amulet by Samhain. *When* you manage it, you'll be free to go. We will inform no one that you are the Lynx, or of your service to us."

"And, of course, you'll be well compensated," she adds, almost as an afterthought, then names a figure so high it leaves me spinning. It's more than I've ever earned—likely more than even *Xinlei* has ever received.

I'm speaking before I can stop myself. "What if there's something else I want?" Like the Apex records for their entire country.

"Name it, and it's yours," Prince Nyxley vows with zero hesitation. The redhead's stunning eyes thin.

Before I can push further, a muffled shout rises from below, followed by the undeniable sound of more footsteps pounding up the staircase. The time for negotiation is at an end.

"I'll consider it."

I simultaneously jump to the window ledge and pull the ribbon on my burgundy skirt. It falls away in a puddle to the floor, revealing the dark suede leggings beneath. Behind me, the prince makes a choked sound—whether from surprise, amusement, or something else entirely, I can't say.

I'm through the open window and halfway down the portico to the ground before the beast calls softly out the window, "Meet us at dawn on the road to Ravenscrest."

I can't stop the rapid patter of my heart, each beat hammering in my chest. My breath comes short and sharp, panic clawing at my throat. When I hit the ground, it takes everything I have not to bolt—running as fast and as far as I can feels like the only option.

But Xinlei's soothing voice whispers in my head. *Rule Number Ten, Lynxling.* Maintain control.

Exposed, with contraband in my pocket and a house full of Elite and Apex searching for it, I force myself to pause. I shut my eyes and take a few deep breaths.

In and out.

In and out.

When I finally open my eyes, I know what to do.

Chapter 6
ALORA

I miss my cloak.

That's my first thought as I rush down the mountain to The Spinning Top. The moon is full and doing its best to shine through the cloud cover, casting enough light that I have to cling to the shadows. Sneaking away from the scene of the crime takes longer than I'd like. My instinctual vigilance kicks in and I pause frequently to listen for footsteps, doubling back and around multiple times to ensure no one is on my trail.

At least I'm dressed in head-to-toe black now. My breath puffs out in white clouds, and I rub my bare arms, desperate to spark some warmth. Maybe the next pull-away skirt Eleni makes for me could have a black underside, something reversible to double as a cloak. I start to design the ensemble in my head, a small distraction from the biting wind—and the lingering memory of a certain beastly royal.

Finally, after what feels like hours, I arrive at The Spinning Top. I spend another good ten minutes shivering outside, scanning the darkened streets and alleys, before deciding it's safe enough to enter.

That's when I get my second shock of the evening.

The entire tavern is empty. No patrons, no Shenmi—nor anyone else—behind the bar. It's late, or rather very early, but the hour is usually never too dark for the guests of The Spinning Top.

Yet tonight, the guild master sits alone by the flickering fireplace, nursing a glass of dark liquid. Shadows darken his deeply lined face and the nimbus of his white hair.

Hesitantly, I join him, sliding into the chair closest to the fire. The welcome heat washes over my bare skin almost painfully as it seeps in.

Xinlei pulls out a battered gold pocket watch and flicks it open with a deliberate motion. His eyes cut into me with a look that says he's not in the mood for excuses.

"I had to be sure I wasn't followed." I clear my throat. "I used every trick in the book—it took me nearly half the night to get here."

"Why is that, Alora?" he rasps softly in Shanterran. "Why were you so worried about being followed?"

I swallow. "So, the heist went perfectly. I have the pearls." I pat the pocket in my bodice. "But, uh, when I went to leave, there was another client there."

Xinlei's brows pull. "Another client?"

"A prospective client. He wants me to do a job for him. I guess he watched me steal the pearls as...an audition, of sorts." I squeeze my eyes shut and decide to just get it over with. "The beast prince. That's who the client was. That's who caught me."

Tentatively, I open one eye and then the other. Judging by his slightly hanging jaw, I've managed to surprise Xinlei—a feat I thought never to achieve in this life.

But, true to form, he moves on quickly. "He let you go."

It's a statement, not a question, but I answer it anyway. "He did."

"And you still have the pearls. He let you take them, too."

"Yes," I answer again unnecessarily. Reaching into my bodice, I pull out the pearls and pass them over. They're cool to the touch, as if they've only just been dredged from deep water. But maybe that's my frozen fingers.

Xinlei weighs them thoughtfully in his wrinkled palms.

"Do you feel the buzzing?" I ask.

He looks up sharply. "What?"

"The pearls. They made my fingers all tingly." I stretch them out now at the memory, but there's nothing left—just the blissful warmth of the fire on my frozen limbs.

Xinlei blatantly ignores my question. "Talk me through the heist. From the beginning."

I give a deep sigh, then launch into my standard debrief. It doesn't escape my notice that Xinlei still hasn't explained why he's sitting here alone, waiting up for me.

"You said you knew he was Apex, dressed as Elite. How?" he interjects.

I shift uncomfortably.

"Alora? What aren't you telling me?"

He's too intuitive for his own good. "I sensed the prince's inner creature."

Xinlei's dark eyes nearly bug out of his head. Alright, I was wrong before. *Now* I've surprised him. "You *what*?"

"I looked into his eyes, and I saw his inner creature looking out at me. This brutal stoneclaw." I shiver. "No wonder he's called the beast prince."

Xinlei's throat bobs. "Has that ever happened before?"

"What do you think? *Of course not.* His Apex guardian came in after him, and I had no idea what *his* creature was, just like always."

I jump up and start pacing, my mind whirring. Up until this point, I've just been following *Rule Number Two: The first thing is first.* Focus on the immediate danger.

But now that I'm out of imminent danger, the bigger picture looms. I need to do what I came here to do. I stop dead in my tracks and turn to face my mentor straight on.

"I want to take the commission." My words come out so fast, it's a wonder he can understand them.

Xinlei's face gives nothing away. "The one the Veridian prince offered you?"

"Yes." I rub my lynx charm. "But...it's in Ravenscrest. In the palace."

"Who's the mark?" he asks in that same neutral tone.

I bite the inside of my cheek. "King Nyxley."

A slight lift of the old lockpick's brows is the only indication he recognizes the level of danger this target represents. "The prince wants you to steal from his own father?"

"So it would seem. Some kind of artifact—an amulet. Does that mean anything to you?"

"No." And that *does* disturb him, I can tell. "Whatever it is, it must be very powerful. The prince is taking quite a big risk attempting to engage you." His eyes narrow. "Let me guess, he doesn't want to contract with the Veridian Guild."

I swallow. "Correct."

"Which means he hasn't told them about the job and doesn't want you to, either."

"Correct again."

Xinlei shakes his head. "No."

My heart sinks. "The commission they're offering is the highest I've ever heard of. And I'd be willing to split it fifty/fifty with the guild." His gaze turns scrutinizing. "Fine, sixty/forty. The guild takes the majority."

He doesn't move, doesn't even blink. We sit in an uncomfortable silence. Xinlei's favorite negotiation trick. Even knowing that, it's still remarkably effective.

"Seventy/thirty."

His white head cocks to the side. "Why are you so keen to take this job, Alora? I know the size of the payout isn't it. And how are you so eager to work for an Apex? They're unpredictable at best and deadly at worst. Especially this one."

I have nothing left to bargain with but the truth. "It's the ache. It's getting unbearable." Xinlei sits back in his chair, a subtle indication for me to continue. "There's this gaping hole. Like an essential piece of *me* is missing. I thought...if I could go to Veridia, I could find some answers."

His eyes soften. "Take it from an old man, Lynxling. Often, when we find the answers we seek so desperately, we discover we only wish to go back to ignorance. There is no reburying the truth once uncovered."

"I don't care. I can't live like this any longer." My throat closes, and I have to clear it before I can speak the next words. "Please, Xinlei."

Another long silence as he considers me. "You can go to Veridia with the prince to find your answers, but"—he holds up a hand to stop the gratitude poised to drop from my lips—"if you decide to take the job, you must first clear it with the Veridian Guild." I open my mouth, and he cuts me off again. "Otherwise, you will be justly excommunicated. And I will not contest it."

Whatever the prince thinks about our relationship, I know Xinlei better than anyone. If the guild master says he won't fight to keep me from being excommunicated, he damn well means it.

Tentatively, I broach my next ask. "Can I bring Eleni?"

"Have you considered that she'll be excommunicated too if you fail to secure a waiver and go through with the job anyway?" My eyes widen. I hadn't considered that. "In any case, it is her choice, as it is yours. You are grown women, capable of making your own decisions."

I nod absently, my mind racing through plans and discarding them just as quickly. I could try to find the answers on my own, but the lynx necklace is my only lead. And now that I'm thinking it through, there's really no chance I can get my hands on those Apex records without the prince's aid. Or at least his willingness to overlook the blatant spying in his own palace. Neither of which he'll allow if I don't agree to steal the artifact for him.

Xinlei's raspy voice cuts through my anxious scheming. "Alora, did you leave a calling card tonight?"

Godsdamnit.

"Did you?"

"Yes," I admit, trained, as ever, to answer him.

He gives me a hard look. As if I'm a stumbling novice again. "When you're in Veridia, Lynxling, you might do well to remember the Ten Rules.

Especially if you're planning on risking your best friend's life as well as your own."

I hang my head, thoroughly chastened.

He clears his throat. "When do you leave?"

"I have to meet them on the road to Ravenscrest at dawn." Not much time left to wake Eleni and pack.

"You'll be needing this then." He leans over and drops the Pearls of Azure back into my hand. The tingling starts immediately.

Dumbfounded, I close my fingers over the buzzing stones. "Don't you have to give them to the client?"

"You might as well do it. Seeing as you'll be seeing him yourself in—" He glances at the window. "A couple of hours."

My eyes widen. "You must be joking."

"Didn't you wonder why I was waiting up to speak with you alone? A very intimidating guardian came in this evening to drop off the commission. She also said you wouldn't have the pearls, but not to worry. That this was just a down payment for the next job." He arches his brows.

"She? Are you sure she was an Apex?"

"If she wasn't, she was doing a bang-up imitation of one." He shudders, then drops a heavy purse in my other hand. "Your cut."

Realization dawns. "The prince was the client all along."

"Certainly seems that way." Xinlei's frown deepens the lines on his face. "When you get to Veridia, before you do anything else, go straight to The Painted Mask. Ask for the Viper—that's their guild master." He shakes his head. "I don't know what kind of reception you'll get."

My mentor looks worried. About *me*. The broken lump in my chest squeezes. Quick as a flash, before he knows what I'm about to do, I drop to my knees and snatch the old man into a tight hug.

"Thank you," I whisper fiercely in his ear. "Not just for tonight, for..."

"I know," he murmurs, patting my back. "Be safe, Lynxling. And remember, Rule Number One—"

"Trust in the guild," I finish, pulling back to meet his gaze. "And no one else."

Chapter 7
ALORA

Breaking into the small cottage Eleni shares with her parents is easier than I expected. Less than a minute with my trusty lockpicks, and I'm through the back door, slinking on silent feet to her small bedroom. Thank goodness her sister Giselle is long gone with a husband and family of her own. Still, I don't want to wake her parents, snoring softly in the adjacent room.

I lay one hand over my friend's mouth and shake her gently with the other. There's a muffled yelp as her eyes fly open, rolling wildly. They finally catch on me in the dim light, and her breathing slows. Cautiously, I remove my hand.

"What. The. Hells," Eleni hisses, clutching her chest. "You scared me half to death, Alora."

"Do you still want to come to Veridia?" I murmur.

"Now?" she whisper-shouts.

"Now or never, Len. Get packed. I'll tell you the rest on the way."

"For Jinai's sake!"

"Do you want to come or don't you?"

She holds my gaze for a beat, searching my face before realizing I actually mean it. "Yes, yes, alright. Hold on, I have to tell my parents—"

"Write them a note." Outside, the sky is beginning to lighten. I locate her pack under the bed and start tossing things into it. Her tailor kit. A couple of gowns I know she favors.

I already completed my own frantic packing at the inn. I'm dressed in a fresh tunic and leggings, a dagger strapped to my hip, another to my thigh, one hidden in my boot, and Xinlei's shining stiletto still nestled in my hair. I probably should have included more than the one black-and-gold gown, given we're on our way to a palace in the company of a prince. But I reasoned that I'm bringing my tailor along with me instead.

Honestly, I might not have packed even the one, but I needed a hidden pocket to stash the pearls. They seemed to glow in the near darkness of my room, as though lit by an inner fire all their own. My calling card went into another pocket. I almost left it behind after Xinlei's lecture, but the prince *did* specifically offer...

Eleni has finished dressing and writing her note. Now she's pawing through my hasty packing job. She rolls her eyes, pulls it all out, and starts over.

"Hurry," I urge. "We need to meet him at dawn."

She freezes mid-fold. "*Him?*"

I widen my eyes and gesture for her to continue. A quiet sigh, and she does.

But by the time we sneak out of the house and make it to the mountain pass, dawn is dusting the icy mountain peaks in a soft rose. The few guards at the entrance to the city ignore us. Even this early, wagons laden with pastries and fruit trundle in, bound for the Elite's breakfast tables. We're just two humble travelers on foot in dark, heavy cloaks.

"We're going to the Veridian palace? With the prince?" Eleni's eyes are starry, her cheeks pink in the morning chill. She's been hanging on to my every word like I'm reciting one of those romantic novels she loves.

"The *beast* prince," I remind her sharply. For some reason, I haven't told her yet about sensing the prince's inner creature. That the mysterious beast is actually a stoneclaw. The whole experience was so surreal, I'm half convinced I imagined it.

Much of what I know about stoneclaws comes from religious texts and dark campfire tales. Massive creatures, bigger than a grizzly bear, with dark-gray fur like a wolf. Their huge canines are as sharp as their formidable hardened claws that give them their name, and two massive horns curl over their ears, equally deadly. The nature goddess Faunera is said to have gifted her human consort, Calyx, two of them as protection. She took their horns for part of her sigil.

So they're basically legends. A fitting creature for the most infamous Apex in the realm.

"I can't believe he's the only Elite to emerge as Apex," Eleni muses as we pick our way through the pass.

"Apex are fairly rare," I counter. "Doesn't seem that strange to me."

"Must be awkward for him. If he was any other Apex, he'd be serving the Elite. Instead, he has his own Apex to serve him." She frowns thoughtfully. "I wonder how he's supposed to find a match when all the other Elite are human."

I groan. "Can we not feel bad for the spoiled prince who's *also* gifted with superhuman strength and the ability to scent anything from miles out?"

She giggles. "You're just mad he can scent *you* out."

"Hmmph."

As though our conversation has summoned him, I spy the prince and his party up ahead, slightly off the main road. I quickly hush Eleni. I know the prince isn't an auditory, but that doesn't mean he doesn't have one traveling with him. "There they are."

We slink through the woods to greet the Veridians. The prince, his guardian, and the Elite woman from last night are all there, dressed in plain traveling clothes, but there's another female as well. This must be the Apex Xinlei met. And now I understand why he was so sure of her species.

Like most Apex females, she's taller than me and broader in the shoulders. She absolutely dwarfs the redheaded Elite beside her. Her brown eyes examine me like I'm a distinct threat, which would be flattering if she wasn't so intimidating. She looks like she could snap my neck in two if the urge struck her. She's also the kind of beautiful that makes you look twice, with olive skin and silken, light brown hair pulled back into a tight ponytail braid.

I count five striders hobbled by a stream nearby, hear their gentle huffs as they nose at the grass around their bits. Five striders, but only four riders. I subtly look around but don't spy anyone else in the royal party.

The redhead has her arms crossed, shooting me an accusatory look that raises my hackles. What in Jinai's name could I have possibly done to her already?

Meanwhile, the prince's guardian scans the surrounding area for anyone following us. A visionary Apex, then. Makes sense—they're usually sharpshooters of some kind, and it would be a natural complement to the prince's own gift.

By the time a threat gets close to the prince, I've no doubt he would just take care of them himself. I suppress a shudder at the thought.

"We're here alone," I tell the male guardian as we walk closer.

"I'll believe it when I see it," he replies, but with a smirk on his lips that tells me he's kidding. Sort of.

"She's telling the truth," the prince announces. Of course he'd know—he'd be able to scent anyone on our tail. He looks more at home in nature, with the pine trees framing him. His strange silver-gray eyes study me beneath heavy dark brows. "I wasn't sure you'd come."

"Neither was I."

"What made up your mind? It didn't seem like you were planning to last night."

I'm not ready to reveal my true purpose for this trip to them—not yet. So I say something different, something that also has the benefit of being true. "I didn't think I could escape you."

That clearly pleases him. Arrogant Apex. "You can't."

"Well aware."

"Sooooo, looks like introductions are in order!" The prince's guardian rubs his hands together, a smile forming. "I'm Carter Belmont, His

Highness's personal Apex guardian and his army captain." He says Belmont in the melodic Veridian way, dropping the "t."

"This is Maeve Ashbourne, His Highness's cousin." He indicates the redhead, who's still staring daggers at me. Then, he nods towards the menacing female at her side. "And her personal Apex guardian, Astrid Moretti. Of course, you are acquainted with our beastly prince already." Said prince slides an incredulous look over to his guardian, who ignores him completely, continuing in a chatty tone, "I, for one, am thrilled to have you join our team."

"Team?" If he thinks I'll be working with them on this heist, he's sorely mistaken. I work alone.

"Yes!" Carter nods encouragingly, like he's happy I'm picking it up so quickly. "The team to steal the amulet. I'm working on a catchier name. Perhaps you two have some suggestions, given your line of work?"

Maeve looks like she's reached the end of what was probably a very short rope to begin with. "What, no one's going to say it?" Her tone is definitely belligerent, and it's accompanied by another scathing glare in my direction. "This is a *secret mission*. What made you think you could invite a friend?"

At my side, Eleni stiffens. Anger bubbles up hot in my chest. How dare this Elite think she has the right to make her feel unwelcome? "You said whatever I need, right? She's my tailor. I need her."

"We're going to the royal palace." Maeve over-enunciates every word, as if I'm slow-witted. "Obviously, we have seamstresses."

"Seamstresses are not guild tailors." I wink, sure it will piss her off.

Her eyes flare, and she makes to lunge at me, but the prince's large hand descends on her shoulder. "Maeve," he chides gently.

She huffs and recrosses her arms but doesn't say anything else. Her Apex guardian is a scary, vigilant presence behind her. Typical.

A charming smile lights Captain Belmont's tawny eyes as he lifts Eleni's hand and kisses it like a character straight out of her romance novels. His long, elegant fingers curl over her small, pale ones. "Pleasure to meet you, Miss…" He trails off suggestively.

A delicate flush suffuses her entire face. "Eleni Katsaros."

I keep my eyes from widening in alarm as she gives him her *real name*, but just barely.

Rule Number Five: Secrecy is your most valuable asset. This is my fault. I should have prepared her better—she's never been out on a job before and isn't trained. Belmont is still holding my friend's hand, eyeing her with an interest I don't care for.

"You can call me Loriella," I cut in dryly, choosing something that will make sense when Eleni inevitably calls me Lor. Eleni releases the captain's grip on her hand as though it's seared her, turning a guilty expression in my direction as she realizes her mistake.

"Wonderful," the beast prince says, even as he frowns a bit. At the name? "You can call me Taran. We need to get back on the road. We can talk more tonight after we make camp."

"Don't we need to wait for your companion, Prince Nyxley?" I deliberately ignore his invitation and use the formal address instead. A muscle feathers in his jaw, and I smile inwardly. He didn't like that.

"It's just us, Wildcat," Carter says cheerfully.

My brow furrows. "You have five striders."

"The last one was meant for you, Lady Lynx," the prince informs me. I tense as he uses that ridiculous title from last night instead of the name I've just given him. A taste of my own medicine, I suppose. "But I'm sure it can carry the both of you. I assume you can ride?"

I nod slowly. The guild trains us to do anything that might be required for a quick getaway, which includes riding striderback.

Ours is a sturdy female, nut-brown in color, with a seemingly gentle demeanor. I hitch our packs to the saddle and am about to mount when I feel a presence behind me. Whipping around, I pull my hip dagger.

"Whoa." Taran raises his hands in the universal sign of peace, my dagger inches from his heart. "I was just going to help you mount."

"I've got it," I reply tersely.

"Clearly."

He's walking to his own strider, a large, dark gray male with antlers, when I call after him, "How did you know I'd come?"

He swings up onto the animal, then glances at me, confused. "The extra strider," I clarify.

I think he's ignored my question. We're all mounted and on our way back to the road, Eleni's hands clasped tight around my middle, when I catch his low, rough voice answer quietly in Veridian, "Maybe I just hoped."

Chapter 8

ALORA

We make fast progress on the striders—far faster than I had anticipated. I'd expected us to be on foot, or at least Eleni and me on foot, trudging along while the Elite rode in a rumbling royal carriage.

The striders, fleet-footed as deer with the steady endurance of cattle, barely need to stop. At this rate, we'll pass the Veridian border the next morning. Carter thinks we'll make the capital by nightfall tomorrow, which makes my stomach squirm.

Our fast pace leaves little opportunity for conversation but ample time for my anxious inner monologue. I brood over the Veridian Guild and the Viper I'll need to somehow convince to let me work in their territory. Over Eleni, who I'm exposing to more danger than she even realizes. And over an Apex prince and his companions, who I know little to nothing about.

By the time Taran finally announces we'll make camp for the night, just shy of the Veridian border, I'm an internal maelstrom of worry. I barely wait until I have the food in my hands (rabbit stew, courtesy of Carter—I was right about the sharpshooting) before blurting out, "So what's my cover?"

There's a lot more I want to ask. Starting with *why is a royal entourage dressed in plain clothes, riding striders, and sleeping on the cold, hard ground* and ending with *why do you want me to steal an amulet from the godsdamn king of Veridia.* But they've been so tight-lipped. I decide to start with a question they won't hesitate to answer.

There's a long moment of silence. So much for an easy opener.

"You're going to have to tell me eventually," I point out reasonably. "The sooner you do, the sooner I can commit important details to memory, and the sooner we can work together to shore it up."

It's infinitely fair, but they still all turn to Taran, their ringleader, for approval. He chews his stew thoughtfully, considering.

"You'll pose as an Elite lady," he finally answers after swallowing, "a friend of Maeve's from the outskirts of Veridia, come to visit the capital. With that accent you used the other night, it shouldn't be too difficult to pull off."

I can poke a hundred holes in this backstory without even trying. I start with the most obvious one. "And why, pray tell, would I just suddenly make the arduous journey to court? Just to visit my *dear* friend?"

The same muscle in Taran's jaw feathers again. But Maeve and Carter break out into matching grins. Astrid has her usual cryptic expression—I haven't heard her speak once. My head swings back and forth between them all, completely lost.

"You'll be in good company." Carter takes pity on me. I'm starting to think he's the only one with manners. "Ravenscrest has been filling up with beautiful Elite women from all over Veridia."

"Because...?"

"Why, to ensnare the eligible beast prince, of course!" Carter looks very pleased with himself. Taran covers his face with one huge hand and lets out a long-suffering sigh.

"I would think I'd be more inclined to snare the eligible *crown prince*?" I venture.

The smile drops off Carter's face. "No."

"He's betrothed," Maeve murmurs. "Since birth."

"And currently the tender age of five," Carter adds around a bite of stew.

Eleni's brow creases. "If your brother's only five, how is *he* the crown prince?" Her attention bounces to the elder Nyxley in our midst, obviously the firstborn.

There's an awkward silence before the prince breaks it. "Don't you know?" Taran's voice is deep and eerie, his silver gaze predatory. Everyone stills, the apprehension practically palpable. "They would never let an *animal* like me ascend the throne." He bares his teeth, and Eleni's throat bobs.

"Stop scaring her," I snap, though my own breath feels trapped in my lungs.

The prince's face tilts to the ground for a long moment, his dark hair sweeping in front and hiding his face. When he finally raises his eyes back up to meet Eleni's, the supernatural glow is gone, and his expression is contrite. "My apologies. That was...unfair."

She nods, wide-eyed, sneaking me a sideways glance that says everything. Like me, she's more shocked by Taran's apology than the intimidation.

"He's my half-brother," he continues in a quieter voice. "The queen is my stepmother."

He leaves what happened to his own mother unspoken. It must have been years ago—perhaps soon after I arrived in Shanterra, seemingly from nowhere. I can't remember hearing about the Veridian royal family then, and I'm certainly not going to ask now.

Maybe that's why the prince wants me to steal the king's amulet for him—revenge for the loss of his inheritance? Or perhaps it was important to his mother.

"If you're not the crown prince, why are all these women showing up to try and court you?" I wrinkle my nose.

Recovered, Eleni pipes up eagerly, "And can you even marry them? Apex and human relationships are forbidden." I inwardly roll my eyes. Of course that's what she wants to know.

Carter's teasing grin is back. "Isn't the forbidden reason enough? Every lady wants a little beast in her prince."

The prince groans.

"The women are holding out hope that Their Majesties will choose to make an exception for Taran," Maeve answers archly. "There's been a rumor going around that they'll announce it in a fortnight at the annual Samhain masquerade. And he's still a prince. Since the gossip started, Ravenscrest has been inundated with young ladies hoping to make a royal match." She tilts her head. "How old are you?"

"Twenty-five," I answer.

She studies me critically. "You could pass for younger with the right makeup."

"Thanks ever so," I mutter. From his appearance, the beast has a couple of years on me, so I'm not sure why I need to appear younger. Must be an Elite thing.

She ignores my griping. "The women flocking to Ravenscrest have been a broad range of ages anyway. Even the widows are coming out of the woodwork." She shudders delicately.

"Hence why you were all thrilled when I suggested this little getaway," Taran cuts in.

"Speak for yourself," Carter snipes. "All the Elite potentials brought female guardians with them. I barely got a chance to survey the land before you hauled us out of there."

"Won't that be strange then? That I don't have an Apex with me?" It's the same hurdle I faced getting into Count Zhao's home. I need an Apex who is required to be by my side at all times.

The group exchanges glances, and flickers of unease cross their faces.

"I could pretend to be her Apex?" Eleni suggests tentatively.

"No," says Maeve. Blunt. "I'm sorry, but no. Pretending to be an Apex guardian is much harder than pretending to be an Elite. And you're a tailor, not a thief used to masquerading as someone else. You're too petite, your eyes won't glow, you have no heightened sense or strength, no goddess-blessed gift—"

"I think she gets it, Maeve," Carter drawls.

I bite my bottom lip. "Why don't I pretend to be the Apex, and Len can be the Elite?"

Taran squashes that idea with a shake of his head. A tousled dark lock falls in his face, and he brushes it back impatiently. "You won't have the same level of access. And Maeve's right. Pretending to be an Apex when you're human is just asking for trouble. Take it from an actual Apex."

I pale, imagining being surrounded by *real* Apex in close quarters while I'm just pretending. This is the most time I've spent with any of them in my life, and it's nerve-wracking enough. Well, in the part of my life I remember anyway.

"Not to mention," Maeve adds, tossing her bright hair over a shoulder, "Eleni is clearly Thalassarian, which would raise its own questions. Such as how and why a lady traveled through pirate-infested waters for a chance to court the Veridian prince who's not first in line for the throne." She flashes me a triumphant look as though her point is irrefutable. "The Lynx, on the other hand, will be surrounded by other Veridian women new to court and will easily blend in until Samhain. We just need an Apex to pose as her guardian. How hard can that be to find?"

"Hard," Astrid answers flatly.

I jerk my head around and stare at the female guardian.

"What?" she asks, but in a bored tone that suggests she doesn't really care.

"I didn't know you could talk." The honest answer blurts out of my mouth before I have a chance to think about how it might sound.

Carter bursts out laughing, tipping his head up to the starry night sky. Eleni and Maeve join him with quiet chuckles, and even the prince's lips twitch.

Taran sets aside his empty stew bowl. "Astrid, may I share your Apex creature with the Lynx?"

I cover my surprise at the royal prince asking an Apex guard for her permission. Like the apology, it feels wildly out of character with what I've heard of the notorious beast. Astrid gives a sharp nod, her long braid swishing.

"How much do you know about an Apex's inner creature?" Taran asks us, leaning forward as though he's about to start a lecture.

I swallow hard. *I know yours is a stoneclaw, and it terrifies the ever-living shit out of me.* "Not much. The few Apex there are work for the Elite. The guild is made up of humans."

The prince shoots a triumphant look at his guardian, who waves his hand good-naturedly in response. Not sure what that was about.

"The day an Apex emerges," Taran starts, "is actually the day our inner creatures emerge into our consciousness. One minute, we're alone. The next, we're not."

"My father says the relationship between an Apex and their inner creature is deeply meaningful," Eleni offers. "Some would say divine."

"Your father must be an educated man."

Eleni's chin lifts a bit at the respect in Taran's tone. "Is it true that you can shapeshift into your creatures?"

Carter flashes a crooked smile that brings a light pink to Eleni's cheeks. "Myth."

"Our creatures bless us with our Apex sense and gift," Taran continues. "They closely mirror our own personalities. Astrid's creature is a snow leopard. She is a fierce guardian but prefers her solitude. She only speaks when she has something to say."

"Noble," I respond. It sounds flippant, but I meant it sincerely. Even with the guild and Xinlei hammering the rules into me, thinking before I speak doesn't come naturally. It's the shadow side of being a good improviser.

"Mine is a gryphon," Carter confides. Combined with the prince's stoneclaw, they make up a trio of dominant predators. I'm struck again by how surreal it is to be surrounded by powerful Apex like this, interacting with them as if we're the same when we're anything but.

"What's your gift?" Eleni asks Carter, then immediately sucks in a sharp breath. "Or wait, was that rude to ask?"

Carter's smile softens. "It was a bit." He doesn't answer her question. And Taran doesn't volunteer his own creature.

I rub my eyes, which feel as though they're stuffed with sand. On top of the extended pearls stakeout, I slept not a wink last night.

Taran's attention sharpens on my wide yawn. "Why don't you head to bed? You're on last watch with me."

I open my mouth to protest, then have to smother another yawn and promptly decide not to. "Alright," I say instead, dropping my empty stew bowl by the pot and shuffling off to my bedroll. We're all arranged in pairs near the fire—the Elite with their Apex, me with Eleni.

Bending down, I stifle a groan. I'm in great shape for normal activities like escaping down a mansion portico, but riding uses an entirely different set of muscles. My whole body aches from a full day on the strider with barely any breaks.

"Which watch is mine?" I hear Eleni ask the prince as I try to get comfortable.

"Only Apex on watch duty," he replies.

"You just said Lor is on last watch!"

"He misspoke," Carter cuts in. "Only those who've been trained to keep watch."

"I'm a guild member too—"

I hate trusting my new reluctant allies to keep watch for any amount of time, but I can't stay up indefinitely, and the exhaustion is starting to burn at my eyelids. Their arguing fades quicker than I would have thought possible as oblivion begins to claim me.

Just before I fall asleep, a stray thought flits through my mind: the prince never asked me for the pearls.

Chapter 9

TARAN

"You're not waking her for watch?" Carter indicates the little thief with an incline of his head. She's fast asleep among strangers, the softened lines of her face limned by firelight.

"Did you see the bags under her eyes? I need the Lynx sharp when we get to Ravenscrest."

Instead of heading for his own bedroll, my best friend drops back down and sits beside me. I glance at him sidelong. "I need you sharp, too, Captain."

He ignores me. "Is that the real reason? Or is her scent still bothering you?"

Bothering me is an understatement. Even out here in the woods, with plenty of fresh air to dilute it, the Lynx's jasmine fragrance wraps around me like a vise. And underneath the jasmine is something distinctly—wild. Something that makes my mouth water. I don't know what I was thinking, putting her on watch duty with me. Pure hubris. There's no way I could sit right next to *that* until dawn.

"Her scent is...an unexpected complication."

Carter snorts. "I'll say. How are you going to link with her? Didn't you say your olfactory sense gets amplified when you connect with your creature?"

"Don't you think I've already thought of that?" I lean my head back against the tree and squeeze my eyes shut. "I'm dreading even being in the same room with her, much less attempting linking."

"But you're sure she's not Apex?"

"Of course I'm sure. I'd be able to scent her creature, her power. There's nothing." Even I can hear the gruffness of my tone. The stress is getting to me.

But Carter doesn't let up. It's not in him. "So then what happens when you scent her? Is it like the lilies in the ballroom?"

It's nothing like the lilies in the ballroom. The opposite, actually. Whatever the opposite of nauseated is. I open my eyes, unsure how to describe it. "It's like my creature is closer to the surface. Like everything is heightened."

He leans back on his hands. "That sounds like a good thing. A good sign for the power sharing at least."

I make the monumental mistake of pulling in a deep breath and regret it immediately. "My creature being close to the surface is *never* a good thing."

The tightness in my voice is enough to make Carter pause. I can tell he's going to tread carefully now, recognizing he's close to pushing me too far. His next words are placating. "Maybe we could find another—"

I cut off my friend's half-formed thought. "I've already considered that. Believe me, if there was any other way, I'd take it in a heartbeat. But we need to get that amulet away from my father and Lord Winters as soon as possible. Every day they have it is another day Veridians are at risk. That we're all at risk. Maeve's already laid the groundwork with the ridiculous rumor about the announcement, so the Lynx will blend in at court. And Samhain is the only night there's a glimmer of a chance we can pull it off."

A familiar feeling of self-hatred bubbles up again as I lay out the precarious position I've landed us all in. "There's no time to engage another thief, even if we could find one as good as her, which we can't. She's the one, Carter."

Both our eyes rest on the sleeping human, the object of all our hope—and my own personal torment. She shifts in her sleep, a loose chestnut curl sliding across her face. My fingers twitch with the inexplicable urge to brush it back.

"At least she's beautiful," Carter remarks. My head snaps to my guardian's, and a warning rumble begins to build in my chest before he continues, "So that'll piss off Victoria."

The growl morphs into a low laugh as I envision my former betrothed's impending reaction to the little thief. But just as quickly, I sober. "We'll have to keep an eye on her. Victoria is as dangerous as my creature when she's riled."

Carter hums in agreement. "Too bad the Lynx didn't turn out to be an Apex after all."

"Why?" I ask warily.

"When she called you *Your Highness* and told you you'd have to catch her first, I thought we'd finally found you a suitable match."

I fucking did, too. Never mind that she was already torturing me with the most tantalizing scent in the realm. When she practically dared me to chase her—I have to adjust myself at the memory. With the exception of Maeve, no females act like that in my presence. They're all either fawning or frightened. To have one boldly taunt me was...exhilarating.

But she is a human. And a thief. Which is exactly why I won't be letting my creature *or* my cock do the thinking. "Even if she were Apex, I can't afford the distraction. This is too important. I need her help to steal the amulet. That's it." *That's all it can be*, I mentally add.

Although it shouldn't, the blinding rage from my stoneclaw catches me unawares. I brace a hand on the ground, fingers curling into the dirt, and pant through the storm as it splinters through me. Since that luscious scent first erupted into our consciousness, my creature has been more than clear. The Lynx is *ours*.

But I know what happens when my stoneclaw gets its way. If anything, its territorial insistence is only more confirmation that the beguiling woman is off-limits. My creature lashes out harder at the thought, and I grunt through the mental strain.

Carter is watching me with a pitying expression. "It's alright to want things, Tare."

"Not for me." My eyes find the sleeping thief again, drawn to her like a moth to a flame. "Not for me."

Chapter 10

ALORA

Taran never wakes me for last watch. Instead, I awake at the time I've trained myself to, just before daybreak. Usually at this point, I would go back to sleep. Like the rest of the guild, I tend towards nocturnal and prefer to sleep away the day when not on a job.

But when I open my eyes, they immediately meet the prince's luminescent silver-gray ones, shining like a creature's in the pre-dawn light. We stay like that, gazes locked, for a long moment, still in the quiet morning.

Carter groans, and I'm the first to look away.

"I can't wait to get back to my bed at the palace," he complains, stretching his arms with a grimace.

Taran snorts from his position on watch, leaning against a nearby tree. "For the Apex guardian to the Apex prince, your inability to sleep in nature always confounds me."

"My creature likes to nest," Carter sniffs.

I shake Eleni awake gently, and she blinks up at me with heavy-lidded eyes.

Maeve lets out her own disgruntled noise from within her bedroll. "Must we start so *early*?"

"We must," Carter answers in his signature cheerful tone. "Ravenscrest waits for no man. Er, woman. Males and females. Humans. Apex. In any case, we've got to get back."

My stiff muscles scream in protest as I drop into an abbreviated version of my daily stretching routine to warm them up. The stretching eases the ache somewhat, but I'm still not looking forward to today's ride. After sleeping on that rooftop for almost a month, then the cold ground last night, I'm nearly desperate for a soft bed myself.

Twice, I catch Taran's eyes trained on me like Carter's creature. Both times, it sends goosebumps prickling up my arms.

As we pack up our camp and make a quick breakfast of hard cheese and bread unearthed from the royal saddlebags, I wonder again why they are forcing Maeve to rough it. This type of travel has to be way outside her comfort zone.

"Why didn't you stay in Shanterra and make your way back as an official entourage?" I finally ask the group.

Maeve spears me with another one of her sharp-eyed glares. A look I am becoming intimately familiar with. "Well, that *was* the plan. But then *somebody* chose to let you make off with the pearls instead of returning them as would have been appropriate. And then Carter thought it better to make the journey incognito."

I scoff. "Like you could have stopped me."

"Oh, I could have stopped you, Lady Lynx." Taran's low purr is like fingernails trailing down my spine. I ruthlessly tamp down a shiver. "Make no mistake about that. But it would have drawn more attention than I wanted."

I've always been extremely cautious of Apex, which is a logical response to a stronger species. So I can't explain why *this* Apex seems to provoke the exact opposite reaction. If I was going to cower from any of them, it should be him. Yet just like the night of the pearls heist, my natural instinct is to challenge him right back. The words spring from my lips without thought. "You go ahead and believe that if it helps you sleep better at night, *Your Highness*."

His response is the same beautiful smile that stunned me in the count's study, all white teeth and hewn cheekbones. I'm a little dazzled, but not enough that I don't notice his hand slipping into his pocket, clutching something there. Interesting.

He removes his hand quickly, as if he doesn't want me to notice. Too bad for him. I may not have Apex sight, but I do know *Rule Number Eight: Stay silent and observe.*

I'm aces at the observe part. Less at the stay silent part. To Xinlei's perpetual frustration.

Gods, I miss him. Mostly I miss not having to constantly be on my guard with my companions, afraid to even sleep through the night. Though I guess I ended up doing just that anyway. I wonder again why Taran didn't wake me for the watch.

"Speaking of the pearls," the prince says, drawing my attention back to the confounding present. "I assume you were just trying to find the right moment to give them to me?"

I have precious little leverage for this impending conversation with the Veridian Guild. To win the waiver, I'm going to need absolutely everything in my arsenal, including the priceless necklace hidden in the bottom of my pack.

Rule Number Three: The best lies are mostly true.

I widen my eyes in mock innocence. "Astrid told the guild you didn't expect me to come back with the pearls. That the commission was a down payment on the amulet job." A low growl slips from Astrid's lips, and it's terrifying. But I'm committed now. "I left the pearls with the guild."

The prince's silver eyes leap straight to my strider and the pack resting on it. Shit. Can he *smell* them? They're only a bunch of stones, not a human or an Apex or a living creature.

But I remember how those stones lit up Lady Zhao's face the night of the ball. The way my fingers vibrated every time they touched them. The prince's gift is sensing Apex power. Maybe that extends to magical artifacts as well.

Yet his eyes leave my pack and come back to rest on mine, his expression inscrutable. My pulse hammers in the silence, every second dragging out. Until all he says is, "Let's go."

Chapter 11

ALORA

We pass the Veridian border without incident, bushwhacking through forest and avoiding the main road to circumvent the guard posts. But even with the extra time that requires, the striders are such exceptional animals, it's clear we're going to make it to the outskirts of Ravenscrest by nightfall as Carter predicted, if not sooner.

By our midday food and water break, I decide I'm done with this silent, grueling ride to the capital. When we get there, Eleni and I will have to head straight to the Veridian Guild, and I'm running out of time to broach the subject with my new clients.

Rule Number Seven: Information is power.

"I need to know more about the amulet."

"Like what?" Carter asks around a mouthful of cheese, but in an open way that suggests he'll actually share the answer.

"Like where it's kept, for one."

"That's why you need access to Taran." Surprisingly, Maeve is the one who responds. "We don't know where the amulet is yet."

I blink. Twice. "You conscripted me to steal this amulet for you and you don't even know where it is?"

"We know it's in Ravenscrest," Carter assures me. "The king—he would never be far from it."

"And Tare can find it," Maeve adds confidently. The tone of someone who trusts her cousin's abilities implicitly with no room for doubts.

"But when he does, we need you ready to pounce, Wildcat," Carter finishes.

My brow furrows. "Didn't you say my cover would only last until Samhain? How can you be so sure you'll locate the amulet by then?"

"Because we have to," Taran answers, and something in his tone makes me shut my mouth with a snap.

I chew on this new information for a little while. It's not so different from the pearls job—starting with a general location and waiting for the right moment to make my move.

Except with the pearls, I was on my own. As I prefer. It sounds like for this job, I'll be dependent on Taran locating the prize. Which makes me want to hiss.

"Have you solved my cover story issue yet?" The others start at the sound of my voice. They must have thought I was done with this interview once I lapsed into silence. "The personal Apex," I clarify.

Taran and Carter exchange a glance. "Well, we think Maeve vouching for you might be enough..." Carter starts.

My eyes narrow. "To explain why I traveled here from Shanterra to court the prince with no Apex guardian?" It's clear from both their expressions they expected this reaction and are trying to manage me. Males.

"We can say something happened to her before the journey—"

"That's not going to work." Maeve shakes her head decisively, saving me the trouble. "These women aren't even bringing their own Apex necessarily. More likely, they're bringing the most impressive one in their family's retinue."

We all lapse into silence.

I sigh. In for a feather, in for the flock. "I can ask the Veridian Guild for assistance. I have to get the waiver from them anyway."

"What?" Taran jumps to his feet and annihilates the distance between us in one huge stride so he's towering over me. "You cannot tell the Veridian Guild about this!"

It happens so fast. One second, we're all sitting in a loose circle, speaking casually. The next, I'm being shouted at by a looming predator. I break out into a cold sweat.

Quickly, I rise to my feet. But he's close, much too close. His expression is the desperate kind of dangerous that has my stomach twisting like a knot. I take a healthy step backwards and raise my hands slowly, my tone measured. "I told you. I have to get a waiver to do a job in Veridia, or I'll be excommunicated."

"It's true. We both will." Eleni's voice is thin with nerves but she still lends her support. Every member of our little troop went still at Taran's reaction, the rest of their meals forgotten in their laps.

Taran's attention snaps to my strider and the pack lying atop it. "You want to trade the pearls to them, don't you? That's why you *lied*."

The air gets trapped in my throat, and I can't speak around it. He *can* smell them.

Taran's glare swings back around to me. His eyes flare like gray ash as they burn down into mine, and a low sound rumbles from his chest. Everyone else's heads have lowered, their eyes on the ground, even Astrid's and Carter's. It's involuntary; the dominance rolling off the prince is palpable.

"Your Highness," I start, but a menacing snarl rents the air, making me jump. Carter visibly winces. I swallow. Try again. "Taran."

The prince's lips stop curling back over his teeth. The suffocating dominance lacing the air lessens enough that I can finally draw breath. Flecks of silver break through the dark gray storm clouds.

"Taran." I say it again, softer this time. Silver overwhelms the gray, and the piercing glow begins to fade. Reason returns to his face. Something else flashes in his eyes—an emotion I can't place—before it's masked by resolute indifference. I only catch it because he's standing so close, and my attention is hyperfocused on him.

He steps back one giant pace, which should make me feel relieved. Instead, I have the strangest instinct to follow. To touch his hand. To soothe the beast.

I clear my throat. "I won't tell them anything about the job. They wouldn't expect me to anyway. I'll just say it's a personal issue and ask for the waiver." It's sort of true. I do have a personal reason for being in Ravenscrest, even in the palace. But if I get caught operating for a client in their territory—my eyes flick to Eleni, and my stomach sinks. Excommunication. For both of us. "I'll, uh, need to offer some kind of compensation, though. To make it worth their while to overlook our presence."

"I'll give you as much gold as you need." The prince's voice is rough, like sand scraping stone. "But you can't trade them the pearls. And I'm coming with you to the negotiations."

"Ahem," Carter cuts in from across the clearing, cautiously raising his head. "You can't go with the wildcat. None of us can, or the guild will know you're involved."

Another snarl, but this one is half-hearted. He knows Carter's right.

"Eleni will come with me," I say. "And...you can hold on to the pearls while we do. As a gesture of good faith." I finger my necklace, holding my breath for his response. His eyes track my hand, and I self-consciously drop the charm.

Taran shakes his head. "It's too big a risk. I've contracted with the Veridian Guild before. So has my father. Any one of them could tell him."

Rule Number Five: Secrecy is your most valuable asset.

"I won't even say the job is for a client." My pulse pounds in my throat, and I worry he can see it. "Eleni and I are here on personal business and need permission to operate in Veridia on a limited basis. Neither of us has ever been there before—there's no connection between us and the mark."

He frowns. "How are you going to convince them to give you the waiver if you've never met them?"

Eleni carefully lifts her eyes from the dirt. "She'll tell him the Shanterran guild master requests their assistance."

"That'll work?" Carter asks.

"It will work," I say decisively, even though I have no idea if that's true or not. The pearls were a backup plan—and a solid one. Without them, this negotiation is going to be much trickier.

Taran paces back and forth, raking his hands through increasingly disheveled hair. "Fine." The prince suddenly stills his frenetic pacing, extending a huge hand to me. "It's a deal."

Tentatively, I slide my much smaller palm into his. His warm grip encloses mine, and when our eyes meet, the ache in my rib cage is so sharply painful, it nearly steals my breath.

"Deal."

Chapter 12

ALORA

Veridia is more beautiful than I imagined.

A vibrant quilt of golden wheat fields, orchards, and vegetable gardens blanket the countryside. Compared to Shanterra's stark mountain climate, it's a veritable paradise. Moisture coats the air, ripe with the sweet tang of dropping fruit, as we descend towards sea level.

Eleni and I are both bursting with excitement to see the ocean for the first time, Len even more than me. She was only a baby when her family crossed over from Thalassar through the Veridian port. But it will have to wait until later. The marina is on the other side of the city from where we'll be entering, and I promised Xinlei we'd go straight to the Veridian Guild upon arrival.

We stop to regroup in the last copse of trees before the bridge—the one main entrance over a sparkling river leading to the high, white stone city walls. Worryingly, it's manned by Apex who could potentially recognize the royals immediately.

The original plan was for Astrid and Maeve to enter as themselves, acting as a distraction. The rest of us would stay tucked into our cloaks despite the more temperate Veridian weather. But after a heated discussion, Carter agrees to accompany Astrid and Maeve and lead the striders. The animals, faster and with superior endurance to horses, are too expensive and too noticeable for Eleni and me to ride one to The Painted Mask.

Taran should quite obviously be going with them, but he insists on accompanying me and Eleni through the city—even if he can't come to the inn. I'd like to argue, but I've already stood my ground against a volatile stoneclaw once today. I'm not eager to repeat the experience.

"What are you planning to tell the guild?" Taran sounds like he's trying to keep the suspicion out of his voice. He's failing at it. Miserably.

I blow out a frustrated breath. "You just worry about staying out of sight and winning us enough time to negotiate before the whole city knows their prince is back. I'll worry about what to tell the guild."

He stiffens. "I might be able to help. I told you, the palace has contracted with them before."

"On what?" I give the prince a sidelong glance. "Don't tell me. Security."

"How did you know that?" A startled expression flickers across his face. "I thought you said you've never met with the Veridian Guild."

I shrug one shoulder. "Lucky guess." So the rumors are true. It's no wonder he sought outside help for this job. If the palace is already working that closely with the guild, the thief would have to be a foreigner.

And I don't see the Thalassarian Sea Serpent sailing into Ravenscrest to assist.

"Taran," Carter interrupts. "Are either of the guards on the bridge olfactory?"

Taran barely glances in their direction before answering. "No. Both auditory. Low power levels, which is why they're posted at the gates and not assigned as guardians. Jaxon and Levi."

Of course, the prince is familiar with every Apex under his employ. Even at this distance, he can scent who they are. "Can you..." I shouldn't ask. But my curiosity is practically a living thing and not easily tamped down, even when I know better. One of my greatest weaknesses, according to Xinlei.

"Can I what?"

"Can you scent Apex creatures too?"

"Yes." He actually gives me a straight answer. "I can scent their inner creature along with their Apex sense *and* the strength and nature of their gift."

He fires back his own question before I have a chance to mull that over. "What was the thing you wanted more than money? That you were about to ask for in exchange for stealing the amulet?"

We both know the exact moment he's referring to. "Does it matter? You've already promised me anything I want."

Dark satisfaction rolls through me at his answering scowl. I'm not used to having the upper hand. Usually, the person across the table is Xinlei. "You should let Maeve do your negotiating in the future." I nod towards the Elite lady, now resplendent in an expensive riding habit. Astrid and Carter have likewise changed into their uniforms. "She never would have offered that."

Taran snorts. "I'd like to refute that statement, but you're spot on. Maeve is much more attuned to political matters and advantageous deals." His eyes narrow. "Let's hope you are, too, Lady Lynx. For all our sakes."

"I certainly seem to be doing well for myself so far," I respond airily, but my stomach clenches at the reminder. My gaze darts over to Eleni, giving our strider a farewell pat. It's her guild membership on the line, too, if I can't pull this off.

I shake my head. *Rule Number Ten: Maintain control.* I *will* pull this off. I've got the favor of the Shanterran guild master and the crown's coin on my side. The hole in my chest pangs fitfully. As well as the proper motivation. If I do this job, the prince will give me access to those guardian ledgers. And I'll finally get some answers. All I need is to win this waiver.

Taran pulls a heavy coin purse from his jacket and places it in my hand. But before letting go, he pauses, grip firm around the pouch. "I'm trusting you not to run off with this."

I reach into my own pocket for the pearls I secreted there when we stopped earlier. They buzz like bees against my fingertips, still cool to the touch. "Here." I drop them into the prince's waiting palm. "Don't ever let it be said the Lynx doesn't hold up her end."

His broad hand douses their mysterious light. As he tucks them in his own pocket, there's the barely perceptible sound of them sliding against an object already there. Whatever he was touching before. His eyes meet mine, noticing where my attention has gone.

"They taste like the ocean in the air," he rasps, his voice a husky timbre that sends chills scattering down the back of my neck. "That's how I knew you were lying."

I bite my lip. "I thought their story was a myth to drive up the price, but..."

"But?"

"But there's something about them, isn't there? The way you can smell them, the way they make my skin tingle—"

He gives me a sharp look. "Your skin tingles when you touch them?"

"Tare," Carter interrupts again. "It's time."

Maeve, Astrid and Carter start off first, Maeve sauntering towards the guards at the bridge as only a royal Elite can. Astrid and Carter march stiffly behind her, leading the striders.

"Jaxon, I thought that was you!" Maeve's trilling voice is nothing but pure delight.

"You honor me, Lady Ashbourne." Jaxon is gruff but clearly pleased the royal lady recognized him.

"And Levi, how is your sister faring?" She's really laying it on thick. I wonder if she actually knows these Apex or if Carter fed her this information earlier.

Either way, it's working. We pass unnoticed, cloaks drawn tightly over our faces, as the guards barely glance our way, enraptured by the dazzling redhead. Dusk lengthens the shadows of the travelers and wagons who rumble across the wide bridge, limiting visibility.

Taran hunches over like a weary laborer, keeping to the other side of a crofter's wagon. In spite of myself, I'm impressed by his ability to transform his formidable presence into something more subdued and unassuming.

Careful to keep my face covered by my hood, I sneak glances of the city in the dimming light as we pass through the high stone walls. I can't get over how *green* everything is here. As we make our way down narrow cobblestone streets, potted plants spill over balconies and crowd the front stoops of the shops and residences. Creeping ivy drapes up the sides of colorful stucco buildings nestled into the shadow of the white stone walls. Even many of the flat rooftops have gardens made of planter boxes.

Just before the entrance to a raucous tavern, Taran ducks into an alleyway. Eleni and I follow close behind.

"The Painted Mask is three blocks up, two to the right, a sharp left, and you can't miss it," he murmurs. "I'll meet you back at this tavern in one hour." He inclines his head towards the building next door. A faded sign proclaims it "Tipsy's."

I immediately start to protest, "That's not enough—"

"One hour, Lady Lynx. If you're not walking through the doors of this tavern in one hour, I'm coming in after you."

"You can't," I bite out.

His silver eyes start to glow under his hood. "Try me."

"For Jinai's sake, fine!" I throw my hands in the air. "Ruin your own heist—see if I care."

Eleni grabs my hand, tugging me back up the alley. "Alright, glad that's settled then. See you soon," she calls back over her shoulder.

As soon as we're out of sight, I snatch my hand back. "What was that about?"

She shudders. "I did not want a repeat of earlier. How can you needle him like that? You're the one who said to remember he's the beast prince!"

I swipe a hand across my face, brushing away road dust and sweat. "I don't know. Because he's wrong! He'll blow this whole operation if he comes striding into The Painted Mask with a stick up his ass."

Eleni snort-laughs but quickly sobers. "I can't understand you. I really, truly thought he was going to *kill* you earlier. And you just stood there, shouting back at him!"

"It's..." I search for the right words and give up. "It's stupid. I won't do it again."

She gives me a too-knowing sidelong glance. "I wish that were true. Sadly, I don't think you can help it."

I'm saved from responding by our arrival at The Painted Mask. It's a grand sight, a large building with plenty of windows coated in a mural of vibrant colors. The ubiquitous flowering plants grace the wraparound porch, lending it a cheerful air. Eleni and I share a confused look. *This* is the headquarters of the Veridian Guild?

It couldn't be more different from The Spinning Top, which looks more like Tipsy's Tavern we passed earlier. An unremarkable establishment, easily overlooked.

The Painted Mask is bold, loud, begging to be noticed. It's a statement. There's no need for hiding here—they're operating in plain sight.

With a jolt, I realize I never told Taran the name of the inn. He already knew.

I swallow hard. Will the prince's gold be enough? Would any amount? I wish I had the pearls in my pocket instead.

"Ready?" Eleni asks, her voice high and reedy.

"Not even a little."

And with that, we walk into The Painted Mask.

Chapter 13

ALORA

The first thing that hits me as we push through the heavy oak doors is the rich scent of incense—spicy, exotic, layered with notes of sandalwood and something sweet, like vanilla. The inn's front room is elegant but understated, designed to appeal to discerning guests. Plush velvet chairs, dark wooden beams, and intricately woven rugs give the space an air of opulence without being too garish. Breezy curtains enclose the space, creating an intimate feeling. Every detail feels intentional.

I glance around, catching the subtle glances exchanged between patrons. Their attire is a study in fine tailoring—a broad array of styles. Eleni's eyes gleam, taking in every stitch and fashion with a tailor's appreciation. By contrast, our dust-covered traveling cloaks, fresh from the road, betray us as outsiders. Quickly, I remove my hood, Eleni following my lead. Together, we march to the long, gleaming bar counter and the steward polishing a glass behind it.

She looks to be in her early forties, with midnight-dark skin and black braided hair circled in a knot on her head. She's dressed in a colorful kaftan with equally bright earrings that hang to her shoulders. Her soil-colored eyes flick to us with a bored expression.

Acting on instinct, I slide a golden Jinai coin across the bar. She pockets the coin with a blank expression, then tilts her head to an open low table.

"We're here to see the Viper," I murmur softly.

Her expression flickers—just for a fraction of a second—before smoothing back into impassivity. Instead of answering, she tilts her head towards the table again.

I press my lips together. "Very well." Eleni and I sweep into the luxurious armchairs, setting our packs on the ground and shedding our cloaks. The steward is already setting ceramic mugs and a pot of steaming tea before us. Expertly, she pours us each a glass of the aromatic brew, then disappears through one of the walls of curtains.

Eleni glances around. "Everyone else is drinking it," she whispers.

My gaze bounces around the room to confirm. She's right—every patron has a similar mug in hand. Though that doesn't necessarily mean anything. Poison could be in the pot or lining the mugs.

But the Jinai coin had felt like a test—one we passed. Without it, I suspect we'd have been politely but firmly escorted back out the palatial doors.

I raise the mug to my nose and nearly groan at the scent—sweet and spicy, with a hint of orange peel. Not letting myself overthink it, I take a tentative sip. Eleni eyes me carefully.

"Waiting to see if I drop dead?" I tease, taking another glorious swallow of the hot liquid.

"Yes." But the scent proves too enticing, and she wraps her hands around her own mug and breathes in. With a little whimper, she gives in, too.

We don't drop dead. Unfortunately, nothing else happens, either. Minutes tick by, the steward eventually returning, only to ignore us completely. My gaze keeps darting to the doors, convinced I'm about to see a raging prince burst through them.

"Len, do you think—" I start, but shut my mouth with a snap. A young man, about our age, with curling russet hair and piercing yellow-brown eyes, appears at our table.

"The Viper will see you now," he says in Veridian.

Eleni and I jump to our feet with alacrity, awkwardly grabbing our cloaks and packs. We follow the man through the curtains, down a hallway, and into what I assume is the Viper's office.

Just like the rest of The Painted Mask, this office bears no resemblance to its counterpart in Heshan. Xinlei's is a broom closet compared to this. In fact, this office bears a closer resemblance to Count Zhao's study but surpasses even that Elite elegance. Eleni's jaw practically scrapes the floor.

Tall, arched windows allow shafts of pale light to illuminate shelves of leather-bound books lining the walls. Here, the scent of the incense is diluted, but the pleasant tang still lingers. On the far wall, a large tapestry depicts a coiled serpent, its ruby eyes glinting as if it's watching my every move.

The desk at the center of the room is imposing, carved from ebony wood, with intricate gold inlays that spiral like vines around the edges. The papers are stacked on top with precision, a far cry from Xinlei's cluttered mayhem. And behind the desk, in a high-backed chair upholstered in black velvet, sits the Viper.

She's every bit as formidable as I pictured someone bearing a name like that would be, with handsome, sculptural features and a regal bearing. The Veridian Guild master appears to be only in her late thirties with dewy olive skin and thick black hair that hangs past her shoulders. She's dressed not as a guild master but as a visiting dignitary, in a white pantsuit with a matching cape. An elegant hand with blood-red nails gestures to the two wooden armchairs facing her.

After exchanging a quick look between us, Eleni and I slide into the chairs. The heavy wood of the door settles into place behind our escort with a muffled thud and he strides to stand against the wall, his arms crossed and a sly smirk on his face.

"So. The Shanterran guild master's most cherished thief and her tailor have come to my doorstep." The Viper speaks in the common tongue, her face and her tone both purposefully neutral. I keep my own mask resolutely in place. Internally, my mind is whirling, trying to determine how she already knows who we are.

"To what do I owe the honor?" she continues in that same, uninterested tone.

And so it begins. I take a steadying breath. *Rule Number Four: Everyone wants something.* I just need to figure out what that is for the Viper. Quickly. Before the beast prince shows up and ruins everything.

"Thank you for receiving us, guild master," I begin in a respectful manner. "The Painted Mask is beyond any guild we have ever had the good fortune of visiting."

The Viper casts a glance over to the russet-haired man. "Flattery," she drawls.

"It's the truth," I insist.

"And how many other guilds have you had the good fortune of visiting, Lynx?"

"None in Veridia," I respond truthfully. That's the thing about lying that most people don't understand. It's better to be honest when the truth doesn't cost you anything. The more you mix in the truth, the harder it is to spot the lie.

The Viper's lip curls. "We do things...differently here."

"I can see that."

"Then you'll also understand my reaction when your guild master sent me a falcon about the two of you requesting assistance." She frowns, the smallest of lines appearing between her brows. "Shanterra keeps to its own, and Veridia does the same. I see no reason to break precedent."

Xinlei tried to smooth the way for us. My fractured heart warms. Even as anxiety licks at its edges.

"No need to break precedent. I come here on a personal matter." I tilt my head to Eleni. "My tailor is assisting me. All we ask is for a waiver to conduct our business."

Her manicured fingers begin drumming lightly on the polished ebony desk. "No commission?"

"No commission." The lie flows smoothly from my lips.

"What is your business?"

"That's personal." My tone is firm, almost threatening.

"Where are you conducting it?"

"Also personal."

"Not good enough," she shoots back. "I need to know if you're going to disrupt one of the many delicate operations *my* people are conducting."

I chew the inside of my cheek. It's more than fair. I don't want to tell her, but I'm already trying to sell an outrageous lie about the prince's commission. I need to skate as close to the truth as possible. *Rule Number Three: The best lies are mostly true.*

"The palace," I finally admit.

A smothered laugh turned fake cough from the man against the wall. The Viper's deep brown eyes narrow. "How are you planning to get past the beast prince?"

"That's why we're here now. Elite women are flooding into the palace from all over Veridia in anticipation of the king and queen's announcement about the prince." I shrug one shoulder. "I'll pose as one of them."

"And I will make sure she looks the part," Eleni pipes up.

Capturing the momentum, I toss the prince's heavy purse onto the desk. It lands with a satisfying thunk. "For your troubles."

The Viper barely glances at the gold before addressing the man leaning against the wall. "What do you think?"

I cover my surprise. I assumed our escort stayed for her protection. Who is this man that the guild master solicits his opinion?

That same smirk is fixed on his face, but no amusement reaches his eyes. "I say let the Lynx get herself skinned. It makes no difference to us. But—" He glances towards the bulging purse on the desk. "She's going to have to compensate us better than that to look the other way."

I really, *really* wish I had the pearls right about now. "What do you want?"

"To start with, double what you brought. And..." His piercing yellow-brown eyes settle on Eleni. She shifts uncomfortably in her chair. "I have need of a tailor."

I don't even have to think about it. "Absolutely not."

He snorts. "Relax, Lynx. I'm not trying to steal her. I only need to borrow her while you're in town. Ours recently met with...an unfortunate end. And I have a sensitive operation that requires a certain level of skill, which your guild master led us to believe this tailor possesses."

"No," I snap, but Eleni's small hand encircles my wrist. I meet her steady gaze. "No," I say again, but to her, my tone beseeching.

Her eyes lift to the Viper, who's examining Eleni with a contemplative look. "I'll be under your protection?" Len confirms.

"Of course," the Viper answers. "As would any guild member staying at The Painted Mask." She leans forward. "And if the key master says he needs you, I'm willing to overlook this *personal* business at the palace. For a set period of time." She looks over at the key master, who nods once, almost imperceptibly.

"We will be here through Samhain." Eleni turns to the key master. "Will that be enough time for your operation?"

His lips curve higher. "Depends on how quick you are, sweetheart. Me, I prefer to take my time with my partners." Eleni's pale skin flushes a delicate pink, and his eyes flare in response.

"Over my—" I start hotly.

"There's something else we need," Eleni cuts in, turning back to the Viper.

The guild master waves her hand, indicating that Eleni should go on.

"An Apex. The Lynx needs an Apex guardian so she can pass as Elite at the palace."

"Done," the key master answers. The Viper purses her lips but doesn't contradict him. This man wields a lot of power. And he's clearly stuck on Eleni.

"No," I protest again. I capture Eleni's attention and speak directly to her. "Forget it. We can come back another time—"

"What other time, Lynx?" Her sweet voice is sure, comforting. "You said it yourself. This is the only time you can breach the palace without the prince noticing." Unsaid is the second part we both know to be true. This is my only chance to have the prince's assistance, without which I'd have no hope of getting those records. And the fact that the key master needs a tailor? It feels too perfectly timed, too fortunate—but it's also impossible to ignore. Still. "I'm not leaving you," I murmur.

The Viper makes a frustrated noise. "Don't disparage my hospitality, Lynx. This is the Veridian Guild in the capital city of Ravenscrest. There's no safer place for her in the country than The Painted Mask."

"Don't worry, Lynx. I'll watch out for her," the key master purrs from his spot against the wall.

"Stop it," the Viper admonishes him sharply. "Or you won't get your tailor, and you won't complete your operation, and then *you'll* be the one who needs to watch out."

He grins back at her, unrepentant. She rolls her eyes, fixing her attention back on me. "The key master will arrange an Apex for you by tomorrow morning. What will your alias be at the palace?"

This is happening too quickly. I shake my head, but Eleni answers for me, "Lady Loriella Thorne."

I reach out and clasp Len's hand. "I need you."

She smiles softly. "You don't, though. You never do."

Grasping at straws, I blurt out, "I only packed one gown."

Her brow furrows. "Why did you do that? You're going to the palace."

"I brought *my tailor* with me."

Eleni looks up at the key master. "I may need to allocate a bit of time for the Lynx, if that's alright."

He holds up a finger. "One gown. She brought one, you can make her one. That should be enough for whatever business you have planned. You'll deliver it, and she can pay you the rest of the gold we're owed. The palace seamstress can handle the rest." He gives me a pitying look. "If she makes it that far."

I'm rising out of my chair, fists clenched, when Eleni's soft hand wraps around my own. I tamp down my frustration with the key master and search her face. Her expression is untroubled, maybe even a little...excited?

"Adventure, remember?" she whispers.

I squeeze my eyes shut for a long moment. *Rule Number Ten: Maintain control.*

"Well?"

I open my eyes to the Viper's red lips curving into their first smile. She knows I don't want this, and that makes her happy. It means she has the upper hand.

This is all the beast prince's fault. If he'd let me keep the pearls, I would have had *them* to bargain with instead of my best friend.

"Well?" the Viper says again. "Do we have a deal?"

Eleni's eyes are shining, her hand still squeezing mine. The key master's attention is on my friend, hungry.

"You promise she'll be safe," I reaffirm with the Viper.

She scoffs as if I've offended her. "As I said."

"From *any* unwanted attention." I send a pointed glare at the key master.

His expression darkens, his smirk vanishing. "I don't know how they do it in Shanterra, but we don't make a habit of hurting women here. Especially not guild members under the Viper's express protection. I assure you, Lynx, any *attention* your pretty tailor receives will be because she wants it." His voice lingers over the final words. Goosebumps prickle Len's forearm where it rests on my lap.

Xinlei's answer from when I begged him to let us come here echoes back to me. *In any case, it is her choice, as it is yours. You are grown women, capable of making your own decisions.*

Not bothering to hide my deep frown, I drop Eleni's grasp to extend my hand to the Viper. "It's a deal."

Chapter 14

TARAN

The bell on the jewelry shop door chimes as I walk in. I've been in here only once before, with Maeve, and I don't recognize the young woman behind the counter. A practiced smile paints her freckled face. "Help you find anything?"

"Uh." I clear my throat, unsure what I'm doing here.

Her smile widens, revealing a gap between her two front teeth. "Something for a special someone, perhaps?" She sweeps her hand towards a glass case. "We have an array of beautiful necklaces."

Necklaces. That's why I'm here. The thief can't stop fiddling with that little lynx charm. Maybe it went unnoticed in Shanterra, where the Elite are less familiar with the guild, but my father will spot it in an instant. And he's not one to ignore something that scratches at his curiosity.

It's unprofessional for her to wear it—just like leaving the calling card. But I can tell by the way she's constantly touching it that she's attached to the charm. It means something to her.

Maybe it was a gift? My stomach sours as the shopkeeper's words replay in my head. *A gift from a* special someone?

The rage of my stoneclaw threatens, but I lock it up tight. I can't afford a scene right now.

"I need a gold chain. A long one. Thin. Something that can be tucked beneath clothes." If she won't stop wearing it, at least she can do a better job of hiding it.

"Of course!" The shopkeeper bolts to the case, pulling out a few options for my perusal. I surreptitiously scent the metal. They all smell of real gold—not that I should have expected any less from an establishment Maeve frequents.

"This one." I point at the most delicate option, nearly translucent.

"Lovely choice, sir. And what about a charm to go with it?"

Before I can decline, she's already laid out a small velvet-lined box beside my chosen chain. My eye catches on a diamond-gilded lily. The mark of the Shanterran royal court. It makes me think of the count's ballroom and the first time I scented her.

Seeing where my attention has gone, the shopkeeper quickly slides the charm onto the chain, holding it up to her own neck so I can appreciate it. I know I'm being handled, but I can't find it within myself to mind.

"Very good. I'll take them both."

She flashes a triumphant gap-toothed smile before busily popping the necklace into a velvet drawstring bag. I pass over the coin, grateful I kept enough back after handing over most of my gold to the Lynx and her tailor.

I thank the shopkeeper, who more than earned her commission, and make my way back towards Tipsy's Tavern to wait for the thief.

The night is just getting started, and it's already raucous, a cacophony of laughter, shouting and clinking glasses spilling into the street. My nose wrinkles at the smell of stale drink. Hunching to hide my size, I slip into the tavern, weaving unnoticed to a darkened corner table. In this part of town, void of the Elite and their constant shadows, it's only humans in here.

I slide into the seat, tugging my hood low to cover my face. Only then does it strike me: I didn't get anything at the store for Eleni.

You didn't buy the thief a gift either, I remind myself brusquely. *It was for the job. So she doesn't get caught before we even get started.*

Maybe the chain, a voice that sounds suspiciously like my creature whispers back. *But what about the lily?*

I need a drink. I flag down a harassed-looking waitress and order a dark ale. She swipes my coin with barely a glance, returning moments later with a brimming tankard. I take a pull and grimace. The aftertaste is so bitter it's nearly undrinkable. I down another swallow anyway.

My eyes lift to an old grandfather clock by the door. Now I'm forced to wait. I don't know what I'll do if they don't show up on time. The little thief was right, of course, the last thing I can do is stride into The Painted Mask like I own the place and connect myself to the Lynx.

But letting her out of my creature's sight was nearly impossible. I had to force myself to stand there in that alley, feet rooted to the dirty ground, while Eleni dragged her away, her bewitching scent finally fading into the overpowering smells of the city.

The minutes tick by. I order a second shitty ale. The hour mark passes. Still no sign of the Lynx and her tailor. It's fifteen past. I've just made up my mind to storm into that overdressed monstrosity of an inn and tear the place apart until I've found her when the tavern door creaks open.

She steps inside. Alone.

Her big amber eyes scan the room, alighting on me in the corner. She looks drained, her lips settled into a thin line, her usual spark dulled. As she walks towards me, I flag the waitress again and order a dry cider plus another ale. I feel no effects from the first two—not surprising. Whether it's a byproduct of my size or my species, my tolerance is impossibly high.

The Lynx slides onto the stool across from me, a distant expression on her face, her eyes listless. A cider drops to the table in front of her, and she frowns at it.

"It tastes like shit," I admit. "But it's strong."

Tentatively, she takes a sip. Her face puckers. But then another. Slowly, life breathes back into her expression.

"Did you get the waiver?" I want to ask where Eleni is, but something warns me not to start there.

"They want more gold." She takes another pull of her cider, purses her lips. "But if we can deliver that...then yes."

"Anything you need."

Her beautiful eyes narrow. "But not the pearls, right? So not exactly *anything* I need."

"No, not them," I agree, confused about where she's going with this. "What about the Apex?"

"They'll give me that, too. Someone will arrive tomorrow at the palace for Lady Thorne."

I shift in my seat. "They know you're working in the palace."

"Yes. There was no way around it." She swirls the remains of her drink. "But trust me, they have no idea what I'm really here for."

Consciously, I control my reaction. "Lady Loriella Thorne." I try for a smile, but the name feels wrong in my mouth. "It has a ring to it."

But instead of returning my practiced smile, her lips curve downwards. She stares at the nearly empty cider glass in front of her. I motion to the waitress to bring another.

"Lady Lynx," I murmur quietly, counting on the mounting din of the tavern to cover the name. I don't want the taste of the false one to linger. "What's wrong?"

Her gaze snaps to mine, her expression murderous. "What's wrong? What's wrong? I just had to trade my best friend, my *sister*, for *your* fucking heist, that's what's wrong."

I suck in a sharp breath. This close, her intoxicating scent tickles my tongue.

"I lied to the guild for you. If they find out, I lose my membership—and now, maybe my friend, too." She buries her face in her hands for only a matter of seconds before her amber eyes are back burning into mine. "And I'll tell you something else, *Your Highness*—we better pull this job off on Samhain because as soon as the night's over, I'm getting Eleni back, and we're getting the hells out of here, win or lose. You get one shot." She downs the rest of her drink in an aggressive swallow. "And before I help *you*, I want what I came here for."

My throat is dry. I take another pull of bad ale. "Which is?"

Her mouth tightens, suspicion mingling with frustration. Even now, when I've already promised to give her whatever she wants, she's unwilling to tell me. The waitress drops off her cider, and she drinks half of it without stopping.

She finally comes up for breath, slamming the glass down, her gaze meeting mine. "I want the Apex guardian records. Going back for at least the last two decades."

Whatever I was expecting, it wasn't that. Lord Winters guards those ledgers nearly as closely as the amulet. "Those records—"

"I don't care. Whatever you're about to say, whatever excuse you're about to give, I don't care. Do you hear me? You promised me anything I wanted. That's what I want. *Before* Samhain."

I study her defiant expression, the way her fingers tighten around the cider glass. Being forced to leave Eleni at the guild has her rattled. She's hiding it behind her fire.

"Anything you want, as I promised." However the hells I'm going to manage that.

She nods, mollified—for now—and takes a smaller sip of the disgusting cider.

After a moment, I dare to say quietly, "Eleni will be safe there. No one would ever touch her under their protection."

"Don't you think I know that?" She sighs, a depressed sound that tugs at my splintered soul. "That's the only reason I'm sitting here with you in this shitty tavern and not knocking that place down to its floorboards."

"We'll get her back, Lady Lynx."

"*I'll* get her back, Prince. *You'll* get me those records, I'll steal your amulet, and then we never have to see each other again."

I fight to keep the strain off my face. Clink my glass with hers. "To getting what we need. And never seeing each other again."

Outwardly, I finish the terrible ale with relish, my face impassive.

Internally, my stoneclaw rages.

Chapter 15
ALORA

The ocean stretches out before me, merging into the dark horizon where the cloudless sky and moonlit water blur together. The soft sound of waves lapping against the docks of the nearby marina fills the quiet air, rhythmic and constant, as if its depths are breathing beneath the night sky. Anchored fishing skiffs and impressive ships with women's names sway slightly in their berths, their hulls creaking with the movement of the tide. A faint salty breeze brushes against my skin, cool but gentle, carrying with it the unmistakable scent of seaweed and brine.

There's peace in the ocean's presence, but also a quiet awe, like standing on the edge of something far greater than myself. I wish Eleni was here to see it with me.

When I finally turn away from that unknowable expanse, I'm faced with another imposing sight. Set inside the city walls, a towering edifice of white stone stands proud above us. The Veridian palace.

The prince scans the entrances to the many aqueducts that empty into the ocean, his nostrils flaring. His shoulders dip with relief as he scents what he's looking for.

"This one," he says, pointing to the middle pipe. It's easily big enough for us both to walk through.

"How many tunnels are there?" I whisper in the darkness. The sight of the ocean still lingers, pressing on my thoughts.

"A few. But they're all guarded at this time of night, so I needed to choose the right path."

"What does that mean?"

His silver eyes catch the moonlight, glowing like an animal's. "The one guarded by Apex most likely to let us through and keep it to themselves."

My brow furrows. "Why aren't there any guards at the aqueduct entrances?"

One side of the prince's mouth pulls up into a half-smile. "No sense guarding a hidden entrance from the outside, is there?"

We slosh through the sodden pipe until Taran stops in his tracks. After a quick surreptitious glance in my direction, he brings his pointer finger up to his mouth. When he pulls it away, there's a drop of crimson glistening on the tip. He swipes it on the section of pipe, and a door shimmers into existence.

Blood magic. This is the work of the Veridian Guild. The key master's title takes on new meaning. Is he an Apex? How would he have escaped serving the Elite?

"Let me do the talking," Taran murmurs, then pushes through the mysterious door without waiting for my assent.

Two uniformed Apex leaning against a torch-lit tunnel jolt to attention as we step through. Taran quickly removes his hood, and their jaws simultaneously unhinge. He nods at them both. "Leylah. Ethan."

Leylah is an athletically built female with umber skin and blunt black hair. Her partner, Ethan, looks young to be in the guard, maybe sixteen or seventeen, with moonlight pale skin and copper hair that badly needs a cut.

"Your Highness!" Ethan drops to one knee, his light green eyes shining up at Taran in clear idolatry. Leylah looks to the heavens as if for guidance.

Taran grasps the young male's arm, pulling him up to standing. "No need for formalities, Ethan. I'm just passing through."

Ethan nods so forcefully that a copper wave covers his eyes. He blows it away with an audible puff. He looks like nothing more than a young puppy, over-eager to please.

I shrink further into my hood as Leylah's sharp gaze flicks towards me. Taran also notices where her attention has gone. The breath whooshes out of me as a large hand brackets my waist, tugging me up against the hard planes of his body. "Can I ask you both to keep this to yourselves?" His suggestive smile spreads slowly. "I'm trying to sneak in one last bit of fun before Samhain."

So that's how he wants to play it. Fine. Improvisation is my specialty. I rest my hand against the prince's broad shoulder and rise up on tiptoes to whisper loudly in his ear, "You promised me more than a *little* bit of fun, Your Highness." His grip on my waist tightens.

Ethan's pale face flushes tomato red, and he stammers out an affirmative. With a snort, Leylah gestures for us to continue down the passageway. Before we leave, the female Apex does something to the tunnel wall I can't see, and the door to the aqueduct closes behind us. I pause, marveling. The door is just as invisible on this side of the wall as it was on the outside.

"Lady Lynx," Taran murmurs, his hot breath tickling my ear as he tugs me along, "admire the palace engineering another time."

As soon as we're out of sight of the Apex guards, Taran drops his hold on my body and pulls the hood back up, shadowing his face. "Just in case," he tells me. "We shouldn't come across anyone else this time of night."

I take quick steps to keep up with his longer strides as we ascend the dimly lit tunnel. "Who built these?"

"They've been in place long before my father's rule. But he added the key signatures a little more than ten years ago."

I sneak a sideways glance at the prince. "Key signatures? Is that what you call the blood magic?"

I can't see his expression beneath the hood. "Yes. The tunnel doors are keyed to the royal family."

We climb a narrow, winding staircase before proceeding down another stone passageway. "Where are you taking me?"

"To your suite. It's right beside Maeve's." He turns his head and glances at me, but I stare straight ahead, ensuring all he sees is the side of my hood. "The Apex the guild sends tomorrow will have to sleep in your chambers. There's a smaller bedroom in the suite meant for your guardian."

I roll my shoulders. "Fine. Hopefully they send a female."

The prince stops dead in his tracks. "You didn't tell them to send you a female?"

"We told them what the Apex was for." I shrug. "I'm pretty sure they got the picture."

"If a male shows up tomorrow, you'll send him away," Taran growls.

I narrow my eyes at the face hidden within his hood. "No. It's not inconceivable that I would have a male guardian."

"It's highly unusual and would arouse suspicion," he shoots back.

"Can we cross that bridge if and when we get to it? Look, I don't mean to be rude, but you mentioned a bedroom? It's getting late, and I have a heist to plan tomorrow."

He stands there for a beat, as if wrestling with himself. Then, without another word, he turns and continues up the tunnel. With a muffled curse, I hurry after him.

At another uninterrupted spot of stone wall, he stops again, removing his hood and bringing his hand back up to his mouth. In the close quarters of the narrow tunnel, the copper tang of blood reaches my nose. I shiver, realizing his canines are sharp enough to pierce his skin.

A quick swipe at the wall—I truly cannot see he does anything beyond that—and another door magically opens. Taran's arm shoots out and holds me back while he enters first. I cross my arms with a huff and wait for him to poke his head in, scenting the room and presumably making sure it's clear.

Finally, he heads inside, and I follow.

The sitting area is massive, larger than our biggest room at The Spinning Top. Brocade curtains in shades of blue and ivory frame expansive picture windows that look out onto a darkened garden. Two indigo armchairs flank a low table positioned before the view.

I pull back my hood and peek into the main bedroom while Taran walks through the suite, lighting the candelabras. An ornate fireplace carved with waves and sea creatures sits across from a grand canopy bed, its gilded frame draped in layers of sheer, embroidered fabrics that cascade down like a waterfall.

I let out a low whistle. "This is the guest suite?"

Taran chuckles. "It's part of Maeve's wing." As if that explains everything.

Three more doors line the suite. One leads to a dressing room, its empty wardrobe crafted from polished dark wood. A pretty vanity table sits nearby, piled with crystal bottles and silver-topped jars. Another door leads to a sumptuous bathing chamber. I will be availing myself of this just as soon as the prince leaves. The final door is to the Apex guardian's chamber.

It's tiny—smaller than either the dressing room or the bathing room—and spartan. A simple cot with basic linens and a wooden stool beside it to serve as a bedside table. Set against the opulence of the suite, it's jarring, a reminder of Valenrae's forced hierarchy.

Taran comes to stand at my shoulder, a deep frown on his face. I wonder if he's imagining how this would have been his life if he'd been anyone else's son on the day he emerged. But all he says is, "I don't feel comfortable with a stranger sleeping in your suite."

"We won't be able to meet in front of them, that's for sure," I agree. "They'll absolutely be spying for the guild. No doubt that's why they agreed to it."

His silver eyes catch mine. "That's not what I meant."

A wave of exhaustion rolls through me. "I know we have a lot to talk about and plan, but can we save it for tomorrow? It's been a long couple of days." More like a long *month* at this point.

"Of course. I'll leave you to it." Taran strides back towards the sitting room wall. I trail him towards the tunnel entrance, but just as he's about to go through it, he hesitates, turning back around to face me.

"Do you mind?" I complain. "I'm fairly desperate to wash the smell of strider ass off my body."

The prince releases a surprised laugh. "You don't smell like strider ass."

I suppose he would know. "What do I smell like then? Wait! Let me guess, sewer water."

That ensorcelling smile creeps over his rough-hewn face, brighter than the candlelight. "I have something for you."

My brow puckers. "For the heist?"

"Sort of." His hand slips into his pocket, pulling out a velvet drawstring bag. "It's a longer chain for your lynx charm. My father is extremely observant. You'll need to keep it hidden, and I didn't think you'd be willing to part with it."

I'm struck dumb at his thoughtfulness. "You're right. It's...important to me."

His mouth curves higher. "I got that impression when you wouldn't stop fiddling with it. Try not to touch it in front of my father, alright?"

"Alright." I draw out the word, holding out my palm to accept the tiny bag. He gives me a small nod, then exits through the wall-door, closing it behind him.

I stare for a moment at the uninterrupted stone. Then at the velvet bag in my hand. With trembling fingers, I open the drawstring and shake the contents into my palm.

A delicate gold chain, long enough to tuck under my clothes and fine enough to be almost undetectable against my skin, spills into my waiting hand. My eyes widen at the small charm attached to it. Tiny encrusted diamonds wink at me from a beautifully wrought Shanterran lily. It feels like a fragment of home, here in this foreign palace. The constant ache in my chest lessens—just a bit.

It appears the Veridian king is not the only one who's observant.

Chapter 16

ALORA

I awake with a start to rapid knocking on the door to my suite. The heavy drapes have the bedroom dark as a tomb. I don't even remember letting them down last night, but there's no way I would have missed hearing a maid enter the room, no matter how bone tired I was.

The bath after Taran left was even better than the one after staking out Count Zhao's estate. At least the ambiance was an improvement—the bathing room is the biggest I've ever seen, with warm water flowing from the pipes like magic instead of me having to haggle over it with Shenmi.

After the stakeout, the pearls heist, then the journey to Ravenscrest, it's a wonder I managed to make it under the thick, luxurious covers before passing out. I snuggle deeper for a moment, just enjoying the warm, soft bed.

"I know you can hear me, Thief," Maeve grumbles beyond the heavy oak door.

I sigh and throw the covers off. So much for peace. Time to get to work.

I pause to grab a full-length white robe to cover the nearly see-through silk nightgown I found in the wardrobe last night. On its new longer chain, my lynx charm now rests between my breasts along with its partner, the lily. I finger them both. What did the prince mean by giving me that charm? The chain makes sense. The lily doesn't.

Maeve resumes her incessant knocking. It's like she's deliberately trying to give me a headache. I swing open the door.

"Finally!" Maeve rushes into the room past me in a cloud of lavender, fully dressed as if for an event in a lilac silk gown and a full face of makeup. Her vivid red hair cascades in thick curls down to the small of her back.

She tosses a heap of pale blue silk on the unmade bed, then strides to the drapes, flinging them open. The room floods with blinding light, and I squint. She spins around on her heel and surveys me critically.

"What?" I snap, defensive. She's just mercilessly woken me from my first good night's sleep in over a month.

"We don't have a lot of time." Her voice is low, even with the suite door closed. "Your lady's maid will be here shortly to get you ready. I've brought a day gown in the proper colors; it should fit you."

My heart squeezes. "The prince told you about Eleni."

She purses her lips. "He did. What clothing did you bring with you?"

I glance around, spotting my pack in the dressing room, only to discover the one dress I managed to bring is already hanging up in the wardrobe, the wrinkles starting to release. I offer silent praise to last night's Alora.

"That's all you brought?" Maeve shoves me aside none too gently and hangs the blue day dress beside Eleni's black-and-gold masterpiece. "You can wear that gown for the Samhain masquerade. But you'll need another for the queen's Starry Night Ball. I can make an appointment—"

"No." I cut her off. "Eleni promised to make it. But, uh, I could use a few day dresses." Maeve sends me one of her signature glares and I deliver one right back. "I told you, I brought *my tailor*. How was I supposed to know I'd have to trade her to the guild for *your* heist?"

"Oh, I don't know," she muses sarcastically. "Maybe because you're supposed to be a professional. The best, according to Taran. And yet you couldn't even be bothered to pack properly for a trip to the *royal palace*!"

Enough of this. "What is your problem with me?" I demand.

Maeve shocks me to my core when she fires right back with the truth. "I don't want you here."

"You hired me!" I sputter.

"Taran hired you," she corrects. "I was against bringing in a criminal who only cares about how much coin she can steal."

Alright, ouch.

"And I was right," she continues, her cheeks flushing with the force of her emotions. "He keeps accommodating you! Letting you make off with the pearls in Heshan, then bring your tailor, then go to the guild—which could have ruined everything, by the way." She shakes her head. "What have you done to him?"

I cock my head, studying the Elite. She's talking about Taran like he's in need of her protection—*her*, a petite human lady, protecting an enormous Apex with a stoneclaw for a creature.

"You care about him." Even I can hear the incredulity in my voice. "The beast prince."

"Don't call him that," she snaps. "He's my cousin. His mother practically raised me. He might as well be my brother."

"He's Apex. Maybe he was like your brother once. But now that he's emerged, he could go feral at any moment. He'd tear out your throat without blinking, Maeve. He wouldn't even recognize you."

Her eyes flare. "It would be his creature that didn't recognize me. Not Taran. And he shouldn't have to answer for something that may never happen. Something he can't control."

I stare at her. "How can you be so casual about this? He could kill you, Maeve." And now I understand Eleni's earlier reaction. What was I thinking, riling him like that? "Maybe you Elite don't get it because you think you have the guardians leashed and under your thumb. But Apex are deadly."

"You think I need you to tell me that?" She barks a short derisive laugh, her fists clenching and unclenching as though she's itching to slap me. "The woman who was more of a mother to me than my own—Queen Kora. She was ripped apart by a feral Apex creature. Her own guardian, Nadine, had a rare healing gift and tried to save her, only to die herself in the process. That female was like my aunt." Maeve tilts a stubborn chin up defiantly, somehow managing to make me feel as though she's sneering down at me even though I'm a head taller.

I jolt backwards at the gruesome story. "Then why in Jinai's name are you helping your Apex cousin steal from the king?"

Her mouth sets in a thin line, and she crosses her arms across her chest. "I promised Taran I would let him explain."

"Deferring to your beastly prince again, I see."

"Don't. Call. Him. That," she practically growls.

A soft, tentative knock at the door.

"Come in!" we shout in unison.

After a moment of hesitation, the door creaks open. An incredibly petite Shanterran girl enters, eyes downcast. I forget all about the fight with Maeve. What is this girl wearing?

"Is that supposed to be your Apex?" Maeve whisper-shouts. The girl freezes at Maeve's words before she even makes it halfway into the room.

She's wearing a guardian's uniform. She must be the Apex the guild sent.

But if she is, she's the smallest one I've ever seen. She has to be wearing a youth-size uniform; no chance an adult's would come close to fitting her. And with her stick-straight ebony hair, dark, fathomless eyes and ivory skin, there's no mistaking her heritage—she's Shanterran.

I walk over to the small female, softening my gaze non-threateningly and keeping my voice gentle. "Did the key master send you?" I ask in the common tongue.

She hesitates, throwing Maeve a cautious look.

I break into the warm, kind smile I use when I need to coax children. "Lady Ashbourne is assisting with our little project." I had hoped not to reveal her involvement, but that window has now closed. Maeve huffs in my peripheral, crossing her arms.

The girl nods tentatively, and something about the way she cocks her head as I approach reminds me of a tiny bird.

"I'm Lady Loriella Thorne. What's your name?"

"Meiling." She pronounces it the Shanterran way: *May-ling*. Her voice is barely above a whisper, but the sweet tone combined with her name has my stomach sinking.

"Meiling." I do my best to keep the smile fixed on my face. "Are you an auditory Apex?"

She nods.

"You have an ear for music?" I venture.

She nods again, more sure this time.

Maeve outright groans, and though I don't join her, I'd very much like to. I knew it. Meiling means *beautiful melody* in Shanterran. I've no doubt she has perfect pitch, that she could pick up any instrument and play an incomparable sonata.

It's a gift I would kill for, actually, since I'm completely tone deaf. I can speak in countless languages and can't sing in a single one.

The irony is not lost on me.

But as much as I can personally appreciate Meiling's gift, it's not one that helps us today. There's no conceivable world in which an Elite father would choose a tiny songbird for his daughter's personal Apex guardian, much less select that Apex to travel with her to the Veridian capital.

Taran was so concerned that a big male Apex would blow my cover; now it's about to be annihilated by the exact opposite. I fume silently, cursing the prick of a key master for mocking me by sending someone so clearly unsuitable.

"Meiling—" I start, but she must hear the dismissal in my voice. Her fine-boned face is suddenly fierce.

"The key master said I don't ever have to go back." Her voice is still quiet but firm. "I serve you, as your Apex, for as long as you need, and then he will get me home. To my family." Tears well in her eyes, but her voice never wavers. "I know I'm Shanterran, Lady Thorne, and small. But that means I've never been to court. None of the Elite will recognize me."

I examine this dainty Apex more closely. Dark circles shadow her eyes. She must have traveled half the night to get here in time, which means she's not from the capital. She's likely right that no one will recognize her. If being Shanterran in Veridia is anything like being Veridian in Shanterra, she's probably been treated as a second-class Apex ever since she arrived in this country, hidden from view, certainly not paraded before guests. The ache in my rib cage intensifies.

Well, that settles it. Meiling is staying. It's not like I have another Apex waiting in the wings anyway.

She visibly relaxes at the decision on my face, her frame loosening. As I'm pondering how to play this, Maeve steps up beside me, staring down at poor Meiling, who seems to curl in on herself at the Elite's presence.

"This isn't going to work." Maeve isn't being intentionally cruel, just brutally realistic. I think.

It comes to me all at once. "Poison."

"What?"

"We'll say she can scent poison. And mix them. Odorless, tasteless—she can detect them." My imagination spins more backstory. "My grandfather was an emissary to Shanterra. An emissary might be wary of poisoning, right? Might pick up an Apex as a gift on one of his trips."

Maeve considers for a moment. "That might work. Even better, all the other women vying for Taran's hand will assume you brought the Apex along to poison *them*."

My lips tip up at that idea.

"Mei." I purposely shorten the female's name. No need to risk anyone else speaking Shanterran and connecting the dots. "Why don't you settle into your room before we need to go down?" I gesture to the tiny, windowless bedroom.

She squares her slender shoulders and gives me a determined nod before heading to the guardian room and closing the door behind her. A moment later, the cot squeaks as she lays down. Guilt tugs at me—I wish I could give her more time to rest—but we'll need to be downstairs soon. Whatever Maeve has planned, my new Apex guardian needs to be by my side if we're to have any chance of pulling this off.

Speaking of—"What are you all dressed up for anyway?" I speak softly, cautious of the auditory Apex now in our midst.

Maeve's mouth tightens. "The queen is throwing a garden party. Taran will be there and will publicly acknowledge you. If you're spotted together in the future, it won't raise as many eyebrows."

I nod slowly. "Is there any more backstory I need to be aware of? Like where Lady Thorne hails from?"

Her eyes flick to the closed bedroom door. "Nostura. It's near enough to the Shanterran border that your foreign guardian will make some semblance of sense. It's also remote enough that no one from the capital would visit but still has a population of Elite. Most importantly, it's not within Lord Winters' territory."

Before I can find out who Lord Winters is or why it's so important my cover story doesn't overlap with his territory, another gentle knock comes at the door. Maeve opens it, revealing a pleasantly plump Veridian woman of middle age. This one must actually be the maid.

"Suvi." Maeve's relief is evident. "Thank goodness they sent you. Lady Thorne needs a *lot* of help."

I barely resist rolling my eyes. Dropping casual insults is like sport to this woman. Still, I can't deny her help is likely to prove essential to shoring up my cover.

Maeve and Suvi huddle together, whispering conspiratorially, while throwing me pointed glances. The twin looks on their faces have me taking an automatic step back.

"Loriella...can I call you Lor?" Maeve sounds downright gleeful.

"Why don't you try it and see?"

Her emerald eyes flare in challenge.

"Lady Thorne," Suvi cuts in more respectfully. "Lady Ashbourne mentioned that things were done a little...differently...in Nostura than we do here in the capital, is that right?"

It behooves me not at all to disagree with this statement, so I nod, not sure where she's going with it.

"And, Lady Ashbourne also mentioned"—Suvi approaches slowly, hands raised like she's trying not to spook a wild animal—"you're quite taken with His Highness Prince Nyxley and hoping to set yourself up to your best advantage with the royal family. Correct?"

I nod again. Also not something I can refute, given it's the backbone of my cover. But the delighted expression on Maeve's face has me highly suspicious. I have to physically hold myself in place as the lady's maid advances.

She takes my hand in two of her pale ones. If she notices we share the same number of calluses, she's professional enough to hold her tongue. Suvi looks up at me with earnest blue eyes and a kind face, which has the unfortunate side effect of reminding me of Eleni and bringing the ache roaring back to the forefront.

Perhaps that's why when she asks, "Do you trust me, Lady Thorne?"

I respond in the most foolish way I possibly could.

"Of course I do."

Chapter 17
ALORA

Hours later, I've been plucked, polished and shaved to within an inch of my life. The two women barely let me bolt down the breakfast brought to the room. Meanwhile, Maeve lounged on one of the indigo armchairs, "supervising" and making a show of choosing just the right strawberry to munch on.

Far from the dramatic, sultry trend in Shanterra, Veridia is apparently going through an "innocence" phase for its female set. My dark locks are arranged in thick curls, loose down my back as if I were a girl. Blush pink highlights the apples of my cheeks and lips.

The gown Maeve selected for me fits fairly well. It's a little short, showing off the pale blue matching slippers, but that just adds to its girlish appearance. What's not girlish at all is the generous dip of the gown's tight bodice. Combined with the corset they both vehemently insisted on, it completely undoes anything innocent about the ensemble.

When I brought up this hypocrisy to the women I'm now thinking of as my captors, they both responded in unison, "Exactly!" and then laughed hysterically. I shut my mouth after that. You can't argue with crazy.

I touch Xinlei's shining hairpin, the only weapon I was able to wear with this ensemble. As usual, the day dress Maeve brought me had no pockets. A godsdamned travesty in my opinion.

Along with my lynx talisman, hidden with the longer chain, the hairpin provides some measure of comfort. This garden party is our first chance to cement my cover in front of the court. Maeve assures me that only the queen and Taran will be in attendance from the royal family—a fact that soothes my nerves. Slightly.

The late morning sun casts a soft, golden glow on the vibrant flowers and sculpted hedges that adorn the palace garden. As Maeve and I stroll through the gates, conversations hum around us, mixing with the delicate clinking of fine china and crystal to create a familiar symphony.

Almost immediately, I spot the queen holding court with her ladies at the heart of the revel. Queen Nyxley's gown is a cascade of pale pink silk, and it's an effort to tear my attention away from the glittering crown and array of jewels draped over her. All the extravagance almost hides her youthful appearance...almost. The mother of the crown prince of Veridia might be younger than I am.

She is sprawled on a checkered blanket beneath a white tent, surrounded by men jostling for her attention. A quick sweep of the party reveals no crowned man who might be the king. My shoulders dip in relief. I'd much rather get the lay of the land before being confronted with the mark.

Even though it's still before noon, servants are passing around sparkling drinks and many of the Elite in attendance look well into their cups. The queen gestures enthusiastically, sloshing the pale pink liquid in her glass. I'm sure it's no coincidence the drink perfectly matches her gown and the clusters of roses surrounding her.

At my side, Maeve appears unfazed by the debauchery. She casually swipes one of the pink drinks from a passing tray, though I notice she doesn't bring it to her lips. Meiling and Astrid trail close behind us.

Straight ahead, beneath the spreading branches of an apple blossom tree, a small group of female Elite are laughing together. I can tell at a glance these women are the ones to know, the most sought-after. Something about the way the others keep discreetly casting their eyes towards the little group—while the favored simultaneously preen at the attention and pretend they don't notice it.

Maeve visibly steels herself and starts chanting to me under her breath. "Remember, Mei is a poison detector. Your grandfather is a Shanterran emissary in Nostura. Your—"

I cast her an incredulous look and cut off her murmured tirade with a hand on her pale arm. She jumps at even that gentle touch. "Maeve." I catch her eye and nod encouragingly. "I've got this."

I have nearly infinite things to worry about in this palace, not the least of which is pulling off my and Meiling's cover in front of the fucking king of Veridia, who would undoubtedly torture me for pure pleasure should he discover what we're up to.

A handful of human Elite whose greatest gift is bullying other women they deem beneath them is not making the list.

Whatever Maeve sees in my eyes snaps her out of her anxiety. A haughty expression slides over her face. A mask, I recognize now, having seen this exact same expression directed my way when we first met.

She surprises me by tucking my hand under her arm and then casually strolls us over to the group under the tree.

"Lady Ashbourne, you're back." The speaker sounds neither surprised nor pleased Maeve has returned to court. But this is the world of the Elite—where every smile hides a motive, and every word is a delicate step in a dance of intrigue.

The woman addressing Maeve is striking, her fair coloring reminiscent of Eleni. But where Eleni's blue eyes hold warmth and are deep like the ocean, this woman's are icy and cool. Her voice, too, carries a chill that brings to mind the biting wind from the rooftop of Count Zhao's mansion.

"Ladies Winters, Pembrook, Holloway. " Maeve nods formally to each of the women, starting with the one who greeted her. My eyes widen slightly at the name—the mysterious Lord Winters' daughter, perhaps? "May I present Lady Loriella Thorne, recently come to court from Nostura."

"Nostura?" Lady Winters sneers. She's clearly the ringleader of this little band. The other two women stay silent, content to follow her lead.

I paste on a sweet smile. "Yes, my grandfather was an emissary to Shanterra." I'm careful to use the Elite pronunciation of the common tongue, ensuring my words show I've been educated in the ways of the court.

The lady's pale eyes slip past me to Meiling. I force myself to maintain my placid expression, hands loose at my sides. "*That's* your Apex?" she exclaims.

Well, better to get this out of the way. The ladies' own Apex guardians stand at attention behind them, all mirror copies of Astrid's strong stature. In comparison, the Elite women look dainty, petite.

And then there's Meiling. She looks like a child.

All of a sudden, I realize that I have grossly miscalculated. Even poison tasting is not going to be enough. I'm used to passing as an Elite in Heshan for a single evening, but this is the royal court at the Veridian capital, for Jinai's sake. Any Apex chosen to serve here are the cream of the crop—sharpshooters like Carter or physical marvels like Astrid.

Not to mention, I'm supposed to be here to pursue the country's most eligible bachelor. Even if Meiling *was* my Apex back home, surely my family would have chosen the most impressive one in our family's service to accompany me.

I'm frantically racking my brain on how to get out of this, but I'm starting to think my cover might be blown before the beast prince even makes an appearance.

"She can scent—" Maeve starts, already sounding defensive, and it comes to me in a flash.

"Lady Ashbourne," I scold quietly, cutting her off. "I asked you not to tell anyone."

The shift in tone has the desired effect. In spite of themselves, the ladies are intrigued. The plump brunette in a lemon-yellow dress, Lady Holloway, can't help herself.

"Can scent what?" she whispers excitedly. "Oh, surely you can't mean…"

"No, no, I really can't say." I let my smile falter, adding just the right amount of hesitation. "My grandfather was very clear about that before he gave me Mei to bring to Ravenscrest. She was a gift from a visiting Shanterran dignitary."

The ladies are almost rabid with curiosity—their faces hungry with it.

"Oh, come now, Lady Thorne," Lady Winters prods carefully. "We're all friends here. Lady Ashbourne can vouch for us, can't you?"

Maeve is clearly clueless about where I'm going with this, but she gives me an encouraging nod. "You'll find no greater friends at court than the four of us," she says with just a touch too much sincerity.

I wring my hands. "Well. Maybe just you three since you're Lady Ashbourne's friends. Can you keep a secret?"

They let out nervous laughs, even Maeve. Of course they can't keep a secret. Whatever I say now will be broadcast across the entire capital before lunch is served.

I lower my voice to a murmur, so quiet that the ladies have to bend their coiffed heads in close enough to nearly touch mine, their painted faces rapt with attention.

"Lies."

"Oh!" Lady Holloway lets out a gasp, then claps a gloved hand over her pink rosebud mouth, glancing over at Lady Winters and gauging her reaction.

But the ash-blonde is staring at Meiling with narrowed pale blue eyes. And not as if she doesn't believe me—as if she does. And now she's working out how to steal her for herself.

Smelling lies is an exceedingly rare talent. The way I've heard it described, it's not just that the Apex's sense of smell is so acute—it's that they can taste the veracity behind the words on their tongue. So, tasting lies is more accurate.

It's an almost legendary gift. Even if your Apex possessed it, you'd keep it to yourself, the better to wield it against your enemies.

But since Meiling can taste lies just about as well as I can, there's no reason for me not to spread this myth all over Ravenscrest.

It explains everything. Her short stature yet elevated position. Why my family would have chosen her to come with me. Why I think I even have a chance with the prince despite being from some no-name border town.

"Have you told Tare?" Lady Winters asks Maeve suddenly. Her use of the casual nickname, one his friends use, doesn't escape me.

"N-no," Maeve stutters. "I only just learned this morning. And Lady Thorne asked me not to tell anyone."

"Well, that's smart." Lady Winters' eyes are calculating. "Let's all make a pact right now not to reveal Lady Thorne's secret." She looks accusingly at her cohorts, and they pipe up quickly, confirming they won't say a word.

My lips tip up as if I'm relieved, but internally I'm a maelstrom of confusion. This is delicious gossip—why is she trying to keep it under wraps?

My answer comes in the very next moment as the prince himself strides into the garden, Carter in his wake.

The effect on Lady Winters is instantaneous. She pulls herself up to her full height—which is not much, I note snidely—tosses her beautiful platinum curls and lets a coy smile play across her pink-stained mouth.

This woman wants the prince. And she thinks if he knows I have an Apex who can taste lies, he'll be more likely to consider me as a match. I tuck that tidbit away for future use.

Taran makes a beeline for our little group, Carter in tow. I feel the weight of the queen's scrutiny on him from afar—he ignores her completely. Whispers erupt at his presence, filling the floral-sweet air with gossip.

The Elite ladies around me preen at his advance, fluffing their hair and rearranging their skirts. Too late, I realize I should do the same and half-heartedly smooth my borrowed gown.

The prince is dressed in a smart suit, black, of course, paired with a crisp white shirt open at the collar, revealing bronzed skin. No longer on the road, his facial hair is trimmed to a fashionable stubble that highlights his sharp cheekbones and square jaw. His unruly dark hair is tamed, smoothed back.

He looks like he did when we met in Heshan—an incongruent combination of rugged strength with polished Elite charm that somehow manages to quicken my pulse.

I begin to feel a small trickle of empathy for Lady Winters. Just a drop.

"Cousin. Lady Winters, Lady Pembrook, Lady Holloway." He bows to each one in turn before directing his attention to me.

Taran's gaze is heavy, like a physical touch, as it drags slowly over my body. I can feel the exact moment it reaches my deep bodice and the delicate chain that disappears beneath it. By the time he speaks, I'm breathless.

A slow curve starts up the right side of his mouth. "I don't believe we've met."

"Oh!" Maeve jumps as though she's only just remembered my presence. "Taran, this is Lady Thorne. My mother knows her family, but this is her first time at court."

"Lady Thorne, a pleasure." His rough, masculine voice, shaped by Elite elocution, rolls through me again, and it takes all my years of training not to physically react. Damn him *and* his beast. He's not even using my real name.

His eyes sweep over the Apex standing at attention behind us before lighting on Meiling, her contrast against the others. Thunderclouds of absolute rage darken the prince's expression. Mei's slender shoulders curve inward as if she expects him to strike her.

"And who is this?" he demands.

"My Apex." I can't help the defensiveness in my voice, not with that aggressive tone aimed at Mei. "My grandfather chose her to accompany me to Ravenscrest."

"She can scent poison," Maeve adds quickly, giving a meaningful look to the other women. Lady Winters' mouth curves into a sly smile.

Guess who Maeve's not fooling with that lie? The beast prince who can smell every Apex's creature and their gift. The other women must not understand the full extent of his power to think there's even a chance of keeping this under wraps around him. Possibly they think all he knows is that she's an olfactory Apex.

"Her grandfather was an emissary to Shanterra and himself the target of poison," Lady Winters cuts in. "Clearly, he's just looking out for his beloved granddaughter."

I almost laugh at Lady Winters lying on my behalf—selling the original cover I came up with, no less—and nearly miss Taran's building rage. Just like they did in the clearing, his silver eyes have shifted to glowing gray storm clouds. He stares, unblinking, at my petite guardian.

Shit.

Carter thumps his charge's shoulder once, breaking Taran out of his menacing trance. "I'll have a chat with our royal guard about this then, shall I?" his guardian suggests.

"Come now, Your Highness." Lady Winters boldly lays a delicate gloved hand on Taran's forearm. He looks down at it as though he might bite it off, and she quickly snatches it back. "We're in the palace gardens. No Thalassarian pirates are coming to steal us away. Poison *is* the more likely assault."

Maybe I *would* be better off with a poison detector for an Apex. I'm starting to think that would be this woman's weapon of choice.

"That's exactly right, Lady Winters," Maeve says in a decisive tone that means the argument is settled.

Lady Winters seizes her opportunity to change the subject. "Your Highness, I heard the queen is throwing a ball in your honor. We must know all the details."

The other women jump in to cajole him. He's visibly frustrated, thrown from his warpath, answering their excited questions in gruff monosyllables.

I gather the young queen is well known for her revels. Now that the prince is back from Shanterra, there's sure to be one nearly every night.

I can't decide if this is an advantage or a disadvantage in our search for the amulet. On the one hand, the Elite will be distracted nearly every evening, drinking until the early hours, then hungover all day.

On the other hand, apparently Taran is the only one who can find the amulet, *and* from this conversation, it sounds like he'll be a guest of honor at every single revel. I'm not sure how we get around that.

"Lady Thorne, will you accompany me on a turn about the gardens?" Taran's gravelly voice interrupts my scheming. Lady Winters' lips turn down into an almost comically sour expression as though she's bitten into a large lemon.

"I'd be delighted," I reply.

The prince inclines his head towards the maze of hedges. Instead of offering me his arm, his hands slip into his pockets, a subtle acknowledgement that he's not a regular Elite. The muscles on his right forearm tighten. He's clutching that same hidden object I spied on our journey to the capital. A talisman of some kind? A weapon?

"Oh, don't worry about her, Victoria," I overhear Maeve assure Lady Winters—whose first name I've now learned. "You know Tare. Tends to get all distracted by the shiny new thing. He'll come back to his senses soon enough."

Does he now? What a lot I'm learning about my new client. And what does she mean, "Come *back*?" Do he and Lady Winters have a history? That would explain her proprietary behavior around him. I feel multiple gazes on my back, following us as we disappear into the labyrinth.

Taran waits until we're out of sight of the party, then nods to Carter, trailing behind us with Mei. The guardian pulls up immediately, grasping Mei's arm and forcing her to a standstill, while we continue on into the garden. So we won't be overheard, I realize.

I can't hear or see anyone else nearby, but Taran doesn't drop cover, strolling along at a leisurely pace. Pretending to examine a particularly fragrant lily, the prince murmurs with barely repressed irritation, "The guild sent you a songbird?"

Interesting. I knew Meiling was auditory and had an ear for music, but I've never instinctively known someone's inner creature before. Well, besides the beast in front of me, but I'm trying to pretend that never happened.

"I told the ladies she can taste lies."

That's enough to temporarily shock him out of his building anger at the Veridian Guild. And turn it on to me. Whoops.

His quicksilver eyes flare. "You what?"

"I told them she can taste lies, but my grandfather said to keep it a secret. Lady Winters seems quite keen to assist me in hiding it. Do you two have some sort of history I should know about?"

His brow creases. "We grew up together. Her father is one of the king's closest advisors, so Victoria believes a match is inevitable. And Maeve has fueled that fire with the false rumor about changing the law for me."

There's an unpleasant dip in my stomach, and I'm not sure why. So what if the rumor that provides my cover was planted? They shouldn't make an exception for Taran, and even if they did, it would have no effect on my life. And I'm certainly not noticing that he called Lady Winters by her given name. Not. At. All.

"Maeve mentioned a Lord Winters," I say in a neutral tone.

He tenses. "What did she say?"

I raise my eyebrows. "Just that it was important my fictitious home not be located in his territory."

The prince's broad shoulders uncoil. "She's right. They were always close, but ever since my mother died, Simon Winters and my father have been inseparable. If you draw his attention, you draw my father's."

"What about his daughter's? How do I not draw her attention?"

He gives me a rueful look. "That was always inevitable. She's going to view any beautiful woman as competition."

My cheeks heat at the casual compliment. "So you two never..." I trail off suggestively.

An arrogant smirk curls Taran's full mouth. "Jealous, Lady Lynx?"

"Hardly." I sniff. "I'm supposed to be her competition. I'm just asking so I know whether *Victoria* is going to try to murder me in my bed." Fine. Maybe I did notice.

His expression turns abruptly serious. "Don't underestimate her. Victoria's expectations may be completely out of touch with reality, but that just makes her more dangerous if she thinks you're going to get in her way."

I really don't need him to tell me that. "You still haven't answered my question."

"We were betrothed. Our fathers arranged it when we were children, well before I emerged. Obviously, after that, the contract was considered moot. With the rumor of the announcement..." He rubs a big hand over his stubbled jaw. "An unfortunate side effect is that she falsely believes she has a chance to reinstate the match." His gaze sharpens. "Now, stop trying to distract me from the real issue, which is that liability the guild saddled us with."

"*She* can hear you. And *she* has a name. It's Meiling."

"Beautiful melody? That figures," he scoffs. I try to hide my surprise that the prince knows Shanterran. "And no, she can't, by the way. Her Apex sense tends more towards precision than distance. She can probably remember every note of every song she's ever heard, but she can't hear you from this range." He glances back to where we left our Apex shadows.

"Well, I couldn't pick out a melody if you were singing right in my ear, so I guess we all have our talents," I respond without thinking.

"You're tone deaf?" He looks positively delighted, and I experience instant regret. I don't know what possessed me to reveal that to the prince of all people.

"No need to look so pleased about it."

"It does give me comfort. I feel like I've yet to find something you can't do." He pauses. "Kind of intimidates me, if I'm being honest."

I snort. Sure, the royal stoneclaw is intimidated by *me*. "And what have I done that's been so impressive?"

He begins to tick off accomplishments on his long fingers. "One, you convinced the guild to let you operate in their territory. Two, you secured an Apex, albeit a minuscule one, within twenty-four hours to shore up your cover. Three, you came up with an excuse for said mini Apex that fooled even Victoria—"

I wave my hand to cut him off. "I get the picture. Things any thief worth her salt could do. They don't really compare to being able to sense the exact range of Meiling's auditory gift." I bite my bottom lip, my innate curiosity nipping at me as usual. "How did you learn how to use your gift once you emerged? It's just...it's unique. And—"

"And it was even more of a shock coming from an Elite," he finishes with a wry smile. "That's a long story, and unfortunately, you need to get back to the party before we set too many tongues wagging."

Taran's lips start to curve at my irritated expression before another thought must occur to him that wipes the almost-smile clean away. "Do *not* tell my father that Meiling can taste lies."

I huff. At some point, we switched over to hushed Veridian. My tongue flows nostalgically over the fluid words. "I don't know when you think King Nyxley and I will be chatting about my Apex, but fine. I'm not planning on telling anyone else that story anyway. I just needed Lady Winters to sell my cover to the rest of the Elite."

His nod comes slow, a measure of respect in his expression. "I'll walk you both back to Maeve and Astrid and then I'm getting out of here. I fucking hate these things."

I roll my eyes. Of course he's going to dip out on his own family's party while I have to stay here pretending to fawn over Lady Winters and her cronies. In a corset.

My breath stalls as Taran's hand moves without warning, catching my chin between his thumb and forefinger, his mouth dropping close against the shell of my ear. "I saw that. Not very ladylike behavior, Lynx."

His husky voice, a vibration more than a sound, is nearly impossible to withstand. My thighs clench together involuntarily, and my pulse flutters at the illicit touch.

I bat him away, and he lets me, leaning back with a satisfied smirk. His eyes glint, reading far too much into whatever he sees on my face. Or worse—whatever he smells from my body. Gods.

"Meet me in the library as soon as you can," he says, the commanding notes edging back in. "We should have privacy there, especially while the party is going on."

I sigh heavily for performance and glare up at him. "What now?"

A real smile splits Taran's face. "Now, we get to work."

Chapter 18

ALORA

Getting to work has to wait, however. At least for me. Taran doesn't even do me the courtesy of walking us all the way back. He exits another way, presumably to escape his stepmother and adoring fans.

Coward.

Of course, my little promenade with the beast prince hasn't gone unnoticed. The second I show my face back at the party, Maeve and Lady Winters' exclusive circle surrounds me.

"What did Taran say?" Maeve asks breathlessly, her enthusiasm just shy of believable. She's pretending to be excited for me and my fictional quest for his heart.

"There are lilies all over Shanterra." I shrug nonchalantly. "I mentioned I'm partial to them because of my grandfather. Prince Nyxley was just showing me Veridia's blooms."

Rule Number Three: The best lies are mostly true.

If anyone was spying on us—though I doubt they could pull that off—it fits what we were doing.

Apparently, I misstepped, though. Every one of the ladies' jaws drops. Every. One. We were in a godsdamn garden. Showing me flowers shouldn't be this surprising.

Then I'm rescued by the unlikeliest of saviors.

"Lady Thorne?" A servant in the queen's livery bows at my elbow. "Queen Nyxley requests your presence."

Every pair of eyes shoots to the queen's tent. She has her back turned to us, her strawberry-blonde hair arranged in a complicated updo that sparkles with gemstones. It's like she wants us to know she's important enough to summon me *and* ignore me if she chooses.

"Well." Maeve clears her throat. "I'm sure Lady Thorne would be delighted. I'll introduce you." And only her tight grip on my arm reveals her nerves.

I pat her hand reassuringly and say brightly to the other women, "Such an absolute pleasure to meet with you all today. I feel as though we've been friends forever." I'm laying it on a bit thick, but these are egos that need to be stroked. Lady Winters has already proven what an asset she can be in shoring up my cover.

Queen Delilah Nyxley appears slightly older than I thought at first glance—maybe just my age—but barely older than some of the debutantes fluttering around the edges of the gathering. Her pale pink skirts are spread out to good effect on the black-and-white checkered blanket beneath the snowy white tent. Potted pink roses frame the area.

Clearly, this queen adores a theme. The men sitting on or standing round her blanket also wear pink roses in their lapels; her four ladies are in various shades of blush.

I'm no expert in court politics, but it's not too different from spying or thieving when you get right down to it. The more information you gather, the better you can wield it to your advantage.

Rule Number Seven: Information is power.

"Ah, Lady Thorne, Lady Ashbourne." The queen shakes me from my reverie. Maeve and I both drop into graceful, perfect curtsies. Mine because my training gives me catlike reflexes. Maeve's because she's been doing this since she was in leading strings.

Queen Nyxley eyes us both. She's clearly been indulging in her signature pink cocktail. There's a rosy hue on her cheeks and a slight haze in her moss-green eyes.

"I hear you're from Nostura?" she prods, then hiccups daintily. She waves her hand at a servant, and they quickly fill it with a glass of ice water.

Heard from who? News does travel fast. Though, any of the surrounding Apex could be auditory.

"Yes, Your Majesty." My voice is demure, deferential. "Lady Ashbourne was so good to let me come join her in the capital. Truly, the Elite gatherings I've attended pale in comparison to this affair." I let my eyes grow big like I'm a simple country girl, overwhelmed by the grandeur of the palace.

As anticipated, the queen preens. I've hit on something she takes pride in.

"This is nothing," she boasts. "I'm hosting a ball that will be like nothing anyone here has ever seen."

"The queen is famous throughout the land for the elegance and artistry of her revels," a male voice booms. I turn in surprise to see a middle-aged man with ashy-blonde hair coiffed to perfection and snapping pale blue eyes approaching the blanket. Like the queen, he's draped in jewels, his clothes finely made. He has a haughty, stark kind of a beauty.

The queen magnanimously extends her hand, and he bows over it, depositing a kiss upon the many jeweled rings. "You're late," she scolds the man in an indulgent tone.

"My apologies, Your Majesty. You know how I tend to get lost in my research." He rises from his crouch and appraises me with a frank look, gaze lingering a moment too long on the low dip of my bodice. "Another new lady at court? How many is that now?"

The queen pouts. "It's ridiculous. Wherever is this gossip coming from?" She gives a pointed look around the party, stuffed to the brim with Elite ladies of marriageable age, drawn to court by Maeve's false rumor. What must the king think of this impromptu marriage mart for the son he disinherited?

Maeve interjects smoothly, "Perhaps they are here to experience one of your balls, Your Majesty. Just as Lord Winters said, they're all anyone talks about."

My gaze flicks back to the man—Victoria's father and the king's closest advisor. His hands gleam with rings, and a large, gold-plated emerald hangs around his neck. My fingers twitch with the urge to relieve him of some of his finery, but I tamp it down. There's only one amulet I'm here to steal, and Lord Winters isn't wearing it to a garden party.

Rule Number Eight: Stay silent and observe.

But now the queen has turned her attention to me, naked boredom in her green eyes. She snaps her fan in my direction. "Tell me, are you here to chase after my stepson, Lady Thorne?"

"I'm more excited to attend my first royal ball, Your Majesty." I pretend to sneak a peek at one of the lords lounging on her blanket. "I can't wait to dance with all the eligible young *men*. Assuming they ask me, of course."

A measure of satisfaction slips over the queen's face when I emphasize the word "men." Even if Taran hadn't told me about his disinheritance and the bigotry behind it, every Elite is certain in their place of human superiority over the "animals" they've tethered.

What's more interesting is that Lord Winters has the same reaction. I wonder how he feels about his daughter's obvious interest in an Apex, even one that happens to be a prince.

Queen Nyxley claps her sparkling hands. "You and Lady Ashbourne must come join me and my ladies for afternoon tea tomorrow," she commands. The ladies-in-waiting nod enthusiastically like little trained puppies.

I groan inwardly. I need to be focusing on locating the king's amulet and gaining access to the guardian records, not buttering up naive young queens. I only wanted her to like me enough not to actively undermine me in my task—not enough that she'd invite me to fucking tea.

"Oh, excellent!" Maeve answers for us both. "Queen Nyxley, that is *too* good of you. Perhaps you can share more details with us about the ball during tea?"

The queen waves her hand good-naturedly in dismissal, already moving on to her next distraction. Maeve and I take our leave with more deep curtsies, promising to join Her Majesty tomorrow morning. Thankfully, Maeve guides me towards the exit rather than back to the revelry, a familiar mask on her face.

She drops my arm the second we're back inside the palace.

"Thank Lumos that's over," she mutters.

"You did well."

Maeve raises one perfectly groomed eyebrow at the praise. "Shouldn't I be the one telling you that?"

I shrug. "You're the one who knows the landscape. It's actually more difficult for you. You have to carry the deceit."

"It sure felt like I was carrying something." She rolls her shoulders as if to relieve the tension. "I didn't expect it would be that much harder than it normally is."

"You're normally lying to everyone?"

She laughs without humor. "Everyone is lying to everyone. All the time."

Well, that's...sad, really. "Would it make you feel better if I said you're really good at it?"

The ghost of a smile. "Maybe."

We continue down the hallway, Astrid and Meiling trailing behind us. I can't be sure if their careful distance is typical or if Astrid is doing it on purpose so we can't be overheard by Mei. At least it means the tiny Apex has a semblance of a chance of keeping up with Astrid's long strides.

"That's why Tare can't stand these things, you know," Maeve confides under her breath. "All the lying."

"I would think he'd be used to it," I reply coolly.

Maeve stops me with a hand on my arm. "I know you think you know him, but you don't."

I blink. "I don't need to know him." I can tell she wants to say more but is restraining herself. Fine by me—I'm ready for this conversation to be over. "Speaking of our beastly prince, he said to meet him in the library."

"Don't call him that," she scolds. But she does lead me to the library.

"Be careful," she murmurs, with a pointed look at Mei, hurrying up the hall to meet us, taking three steps to every one of Astrid's. "You must keep Taran's involvement secret from the guild."

As Astrid and Maeve take their leave, I peek down at the Veridian Guild spy, who cannot, under any circumstances, see me scheming with the Veridian prince waiting for me inside those doors.

Splendid.

I fix an easy smile on my face. "Mei, I think you should head back to the room. Get some rest while you can."

Her brow crinkles. "I thought I'm meant to stay by your side at all times? As your personal Apex." Her protest is hesitant and carefully worded—this is not a female used to questioning authority. I can work with that.

"They're all still at the garden party," I reason. "If anyone sees me alone, which is unlikely, I'll tell them you took ill or something."

She twists her fingers in her oversized uniform. "Apex don't take ill, My Lady."

"They don't? Not ever?"

She shakes her head vigorously.

Taran was right. I would have been caught in a matter of seconds if I'd tried to pass as an Apex. Besides their danger, I know very little about them. "I'll think of something else. Lying is sort of my business, after all."

Her dark eyes dart to the large wooden doors of the library, their engraved vines curling like the ones in the garden. "The key master said..." she whispers but trails off.

I widen my eyes as if I don't know exactly what that prick told her to do—to shadow my every move. "I won't tell him if you don't."

Her hands twist tighter in the sleeves.

"Mei, I'm just going to the library to get a book. You're welcome to follow me in, but I'd really prefer you take the time to rest. There will be all-night revels, and you'll serve me—*and* the key master—better if you can keep your eyes halfway open for them."

The reasoning seems to reach her even if her uncertainty lingers. "Alright, My Lady," she finally acquiesces. "But please wake me when you come back to the rooms."

"Of course," I promise.

With one last wary glance, she leaves in the same direction as Maeve and Astrid. Fingers crossed she can find her way back to our suites.

With that taken care of, I push open the heavy doors and go inside to meet the beast prince.

Chapter 19

ALORA

The library ceiling arches above, supported by vaults inset with colored skylights that let in the natural light. Amber chandeliers lend a softened glow to the wall-to-ceiling bookshelves, comfortable armchairs, and big wood tables. The comforting smell of books fills the air, unmarred by the musty dust tang of neglect—the room is kept in pristine condition.

Whatever else can be said about the Veridian Elite, their palace was designed by a master.

As promised, the place appears abandoned. Almost. There's an older woman sitting at a massive desk, a librarian, I assume. She doesn't so much as glance up from her book.

I stroll towards the back, scanning the titles as I pass as though I'm here to pick out a book. I've always thought the guild's collection impressive, and perhaps their books are rarer, but the sheer size and breadth of this library puts theirs to shame.

The farther I go, the tighter the knot in my stomach grows. I've been wandering the labyrinth for several minutes, no closer to finding the prince, when my mind starts racing with what-ifs. What if another Elite finds me? Demands to know where my Apex is? But before I can spiral further, his head pops out from behind a door, and he gestures for me to hurry in to join him.

The room is small, meant for research, with a heavy wooden table at its center surrounded by shelves that curve into the walls. Open books spread out in chaotic piles across the desk, and at its head sits the prince. Although the wooden chair is a normal size, it looks like it was made for a child with the enormous Apex parked in it. He peers up at me from beneath tousled dark hair. I go to shut the door, but he barks out a "No!" with one hand outstretched to stop me.

I raise my eyebrows.

Taran lets his hand fall to the desk. "Sorry, can you keep it open, please?"

I look to the open door leading out to the library, then back at the clandestine meeting with the Elite prince, then back out to the open library, confused. "Aren't you worried that someone will see us alone together? I know there's the ruse of the announcement, but the law is still very clear—"

He leans back in his chair. "There are no other scents in this library besides ours and Mrs. Belgrade's. She's a reclusive human and not one for gossip. Plus, she's too far away to hear us."

I purse my lips. "Your gift is weirdly useful."

One side of his mouth kicks up into a lazy half-smile.

Leaving the door open, I plop down in the armchair across from the prince. Unlike his, it's plenty roomy for me. "Alright, Your Beastliness, what's so important I had to come straight here to meet you?" I roll my shoulders, the corset digging in. "You might have let me change out of this torture device first."

He peruses my dress with that same heavy gaze that's like a hand trailing upon my skin, though he doesn't move a muscle. "And miss getting to sit across from you wearing it?"

Before my lips can fully settle into a deep frown, he's already holding up his hands in surrender. "Truly, I didn't realize Maeve wouldn't let you change first." He gestures at his own attire—more casual, perfectly comfortable.

"Not all of us can just waltz out of the queen's garden party whenever we feel like it," I grouch.

"Touché." He shifts in his seat, gaze dropping to my neckline. "I see you're wearing the chain."

"You were right. It's more subtle." My fingers run along the golden necklace, his gaze following the motion. It's on the tip of my tongue to ask about the lily, but—

"How did you lose your shadow?" he asks.

"The poor thing is exhausted; I told her to lie down. Also, I get the impression she's used to ceding to Elite authority. Even though she knows I'm not a real lady, the response is too ingrained."

"Enjoying the advantages of our new cover, are we?"

I shrug. "The guild can't learn about your involvement." And not just for the sake of the prince's heist. It's my and Eleni's guild memberships on the line if they do.

His eyes narrow. "Indeed. So we'd better get this over and done with as soon as possible." The prince picks out one of the books on the table and hands it to me.

I finger the gilded lettering on the front cover of the heavy volume. It looks like a book of fairy tales or legends. "*The Gods of Valenrae*," I read aloud.

His brows arch. "I gathered you had an ear for languages but I didn't expect that extended to old Valenraenian."

"It doesn't," I answer honestly. "I had to study it. Dead languages like this one are harder to learn."

"I see. Something else that any thief worth her salt can do, I imagine?" My lips twitch and he responds with a teasing smile so brilliant, I have to pretend to examine the book in my hands.

He clears his throat. "Well, as you read, this is the history of the gods of Valenrae."

"And?" I prompt. This is the longest I've ever had to wear a corset before and the boning is digging into my ribs. I shift uncomfortably, trying to find relief.

"And I think it holds the key to how you can help me find the amulet."

Now we're getting somewhere. "Thinking you have god-like powers, Apex?"

He ignores the jab, holding out one large hand for the book. I hand it back, less than graciously. He turns it over, visibly steeling himself to reveal whatever it is he's brought me here to tell me.

"Spit it out, Prince."

"I'm just deciding where best to start. First, you need to know this—I can scent the amulet."

He pauses for a reaction, but I stare back, nonplussed.

"I thought you'd have some feelings about that," he mutters, almost sulking.

I shrug. "This is meant to be Faunera's amulet, right? The one she gifted her human consort, Calyx?"

His shock is extremely gratifying. I try very hard to keep the smirk off my face, but I don't think I manage it. "It's not that hard to guess, Prince Nyxley. You hand me *The Gods of Valenrae*. You're looking to steal a super special amulet. Maeve says you're the only one who can find it. It makes sense you would be able to scent it. If you believe the tale, the amulet is practically the genesis of the Apex race."

"Do you believe it?" he asks curiously. "The legend of the amulet?"

"Do I believe Apex inner creatures emerge because a mystical goddess imbued an amulet with her power so she could gift the heartbeat of nature to her human consort?" I scoff. "No, not really."

His face doesn't so much as twitch, completely impassive. Whatever reaction he's having is locked away.

"But..." He nods encouragingly, and I continue. "If you're saying you can sense it, there must be *something* to its origins. I just don't believe it has anything to do with why Apex emerge."

"Why do you think we emerge then?" His voice is thoughtful.

"What do you care what I think about it?"

"It's been a long time since I've had the chance to ask a new person their theories on the subject."

I stare at him. "You are…"

"What?"

"Different, I guess. Than I thought you'd be." He's talking like he's a fair-skinned scholar who spends his days buried in books. Not the enormous physical specimen in front of me, muscled and bronzed by hours spent outdoors fighting and tracking down Apex for the Veridian military.

"I'd say I'm happy to surprise you, but I fear your expectations of me were so dismal I couldn't help but do that." His voice is quiet.

A prickle of shame drips through me, unwelcome. Maybe that's why I ask, "Why do *you* think Apex emerge?"

His gaze drops to the book in his hands. "After I emerged, that question haunted me. You can't imagine what it was like. One moment being sure of who you are, of your place in this world, and the next—" His eyes finally lift to mine; they hold a rawness that presses against the ache already throbbing in my chest. "My mother told me that Apex inner creatures emerge when we're ready to live in harmony with them. For some people, their natural gifts and inner creatures never align. And so their senses stay dormant. Untouched. It is the soul's own instinct that brings them to life." He shakes his head as if to clear it. "I don't know if she was just trying to make me feel better, but I haven't come across a better explanation. You're correct that we're going after Faunera's amulet. Or Calyx's, if you prefer. And, as I said, I can sense it through my gift. For whatever reason that is." He gives me a small smile. "But what I've found in this book, what I *think* I've found, is a way you may be able to sense it, too."

He opens immediately to the page he wants, as if the book's bindings have contorted to allow easier access to this much-traveled section. He starts to hand it back, then pauses.

"Would it be better if I read it to you?"

I don't sense any mocking from the prince, and in truth, I'll follow it far better, so I merely nod. As he starts reading the old Valenraenian text aloud in his gravelly voice, I close my eyes so I can let the tale roll through me.

"The time came for Faunera to leave the Elysian Forest and make her journey around the world to bring new life to her creations. Yet, in the quiet recesses of her heart, Faunera harbored concerns for Calyx's safety in her absence.

"Even the stoneclaws, Faunera's four fiercest guardians bound to protect her consort, couldn't quell the goddess's worries. The treacherous nature of divine politics whispered fears of Calyx being targeted by envious gods who might exploit Faunera's vulnerability through her mortal love.

"Determined to safeguard her cherished consort, Faunera attempted to forge a divine connection with Calyx, an ethereal connection that would allow her to temporarily share in her gifts. Time and again, beneath the boughs of the Eternal Redwood, they intertwined their energies. And for a time, the heartbeat of the realm resonated within Calyx, a testament to their boundless love.

"However, the transient nature of the connection left Faunera unsettled and unable to alleviate the gnawing anxiety that gripped her heart. The risks remained, and her divine responsibilities to the creatures of Valenrae beckoned her away."

Taran sets down the book. "The rest is the story, you know. Faunera creates the amulet so Calyx can be forever protected and she can leave to do her duties to her creations." He pauses, studying me. "Do you know, when you frown, you get this little line—" He reaches out and touches lightly between my brows. "Just there?"

I let my frown drop into a full-fledged scowl, and he chuckles. "What's the matter, Lady Lynx?"

"Why have I never heard that part of the legend before?" I tap my thigh in an agitated rhythm. "The guild has access to more rare books than the Veridian palace, surely."

"Ah, but do any of the guild obsessively study Faunera's amulet?" Carter's perpetually cheerful voice breaks our tense little bubble. I start, glancing again at the open door, but Taran seems unperturbed. Of course. He must have sensed Carter as soon as he entered the library. Useful indeed.

Carter saunters in and drops a plate of tea sandwiches on the table. I snatch one up without hesitation. He sends me his crooked smile, the one that had Eleni so bashful. "Thought you might be hungry. I'll never understand why the kitchens make so much food for the queen's parties when none of the Elite are going to eat a bite anyway." He leans over and taps the top of the book. "Tare's been researching this one topic exclusively. And he has the coin and resources of the Veridian palace behind him. I'm sure one of the guild even secured this volume for him."

Taran bristles. "They did not. I located and purchased this one myself." Carter rolls his eyes at his prince.

I swallow another bite of the cucumber sandwich. It's delicious. "So...you think you can somehow share your power with me long enough that I can find the amulet? That sounds like a stretch."

"Wildcat, this whole endeavor's a stretch," Carter retorts, leaning against the wall.

"I'm just saying we should try," Taran coaxes me in an earnest tone. "If it doesn't work, we're no worse off than we started. But if it does..."

"You could just give me a general location, and I'd be able to go in there and steal the amulet myself," I finish for him. The thought is tempting—a picture of simplicity compared to this convoluted plan. It would give me control and this heist a far better chance of success. But—"Where would we even start?"

Taran taps the text, repeating it word for word. "*Time and again, beneath the boughs of the Eternal Redwood, they intertwined their energies.* We have a royal redwood grove in our forest, a kind of shrine where kings and queens used to go to pray. And there's an enormous tree right in the very center of it."

"*Used to* go to pray?" I ask, reaching for a second sandwich.

"Considered very pagan now," Carter remarks conversationally. "Communing with the gods, outside in nature. Faunera herself is quite out of fashion. King and Queen Nyxley take their prayers in the royal temple of Lumos."

Of course the mother of nature and Apex is out of fashion with the Elite. And is it any wonder their king prefers to worship the arrogant male sun god?

But I push that thought aside. It's time to do what I do best—pressure test this fledgling plan by poking as many holes in it as possible.

Rule Number Two: The first thing is first.

"Faunera was a goddess. You're just an Apex."

"Not just an Apex." To my surprise, it's Carter who responds. "The most powerful Apex to ever emerge."

My head snaps to Taran, who shrugs. "My gift is sensing other Apex's power levels. As far as I know, no one else comes close." His tone isn't boastful, merely matter of fact.

I take my time chewing my last bites of sandwich, hesitant to share my primary concern. But it can't go unsaid. Now really is the best time to address it, before we go too far down this path.

"Faunera and Calyx were joined already. They shared an emotional connection before Faunera was able to gift her powers."

Taran blows out a breath. I can see he's thought of this already.

"You're right, that's the biggest unknown. And the hardest to overcome. But I still think it's worth a try. I'll have to be seen at every revel from now to Samhain, and this is the only way I can think of that you can search for the amulet, too."

His silver eyes meet mine, and a current sparks, hot and electric, as though he's reached across the table and struck me with a lightning bolt. I rub at the ache in my chest, or maybe it's my bruised rib cage beneath the corset. "I'm not saying I necessarily believe this, but if this amulet is indeed a magical artifact, does it have any...properties...I need to be aware of?"

Taran and Carter tense in unison. It's unnerving, like two coiled predators poised to strike. I swallow, wishing I had a drink to wash down the sandwiches.

"I know you don't trust me," I continue, dry-mouthed. "And you don't need to. But right now, our interests align. I shouldn't have to explain to you the risks I'm taking for this heist. What will happen to me if I'm caught by the king of Veridia. Or even just the guild, for that matter." A muscle tics in Taran's jaw. "If the amulet could...do something to me...I need to know."

Taran draws in a sharp breath. "Faunera's amulet forces humans to emerge as Apex."

I rear back, all the blood draining from my face. The shock is on par with when I sensed his stoneclaw for the first time. We all know Apex are dangerous. The only saving grace is that they're rare. "What?" I choke out.

Carter's gaze flicks to Taran before it meets mine. "It never works as intended. The new Apex goes feral before they can find the balance with their inner creature."

"The balance..." I repeat faintly, Taran's words from earlier coming back to me. *My mother told me that Apex inner creatures emerge when we're ready to live in harmony with them. For some people, their natural gifts and inner creatures never align.* If a human were instead forced to emerge...

I gasp. "Is that how your mother died?"

It's Taran's turn to start backwards, his eyes wide as saucers. "What?" he whispers. My heart squeezes, and I deeply regret my insensitive words.

Carter's eyes thin, his arms cross over his chest. "Who told you that?"

"M-Maeve," I stutter. "She said a feral Apex k-killed the queen. Then the queen's Apex died trying to save her."

Taran exhales a long breath, shutting his eyes. Carter rests a hand on his charge's shoulder. "Yes," he answers for the shaken prince. "After the amulet turned the poor soul feral, the Apex turned on the queen. Queen Kora was a tender-hearted woman to the end. She thought she could bring the Apex's humanity back."

We lapse into an uncomfortable moment of silence. I remember Maeve saying the queen was like her mother. Now I understand why she's so committed to this heist.

Rule Number Four: Everyone wants something.

"Why would the king use the amulet to turn humans?"

Taran's eyes fly open, and he gives me a hard look. "You really have to ask that question?"

My brow furrows as I grasp at potential theories. "For more guardians? The Elite don't have enough protection?"

"Not protection, Wildcat." Carter's tone is grim. "Offense."

I drag in a sharp breath. "He's building an army."

"Trying to." Taran's words are coated in bitterness. "Faunera be damned if they all go feral."

I twist my fingers in my blue skirts. "What does the king do when they turn feral?"

Taran's shoulders drop as if the weight of the world is weighing on them. "The Apex paces a dungeon cell for two days, clawing at the bars, until Lord Winters deems the experiment a loss and they're publicly executed. Keeps the human populace terrified of Apex and dependent on the Elite who leash them."

My heart is pounding. In my rush to solve my own mysterious past, I've stumbled headfirst into a political nightmare, maybe more dangerous than the heist itself. But there's still one thing that selfishly scares me more than the king and his advisor's plans for the kingdom. "You're saying if I touch this amulet..."—my voice cracks—"I'll become an Apex? And likely...go feral?" I can barely get the words out.

Carter's brows slash. "I don't know that a simple touch would do it. They typically hold the amulet to the subject's body until it...marks them."

"Marks..."

"Burns a brand into their flesh, Lynx," Taran finishes. "Faunera's sigil."

As if pulled by the same strong force, all our gazes drop to the open book on the table, Faunera's tail and horns staring up at us.

I swallow hard. "Be that as it may. I believe I'll wear gloves." My feeble attempt at humor falls flat. Another thought occurs to me. "If they're trying to hide that they're forcing humans to emerge, does that mean the Apex records will be more securely kept, too?"

Carter's mouth dips down into an atypical frown. "Taran told me about that, and I don't think you understand the gravity of the ask. Simon Winters keeps them under lock and key in his lair."

I can't help the gasped laugh that slips out of me despite the serious subject matter. "His what?"

Carter's lips twitch. "It's a subterranean office near the dungeons. Wait until you see it. Lair is the appropriate word."

Taran fixes a steely-eyed look on me across the table, his mouth tightening. "You won't see it. I'll handle the guardian records; you'll handle the amulet. As we agreed."

"That's ridiculous. You're the only one who can sense the amulet," I point out. "And I am perfectly able to break into any 'lair' to steal the records. You promised me those *before* Samhain, need I remind you." I study the prince's stony expression. "I'm not going to take off once I have the records, you know. I would never not follow through on a deal."

"I'm not worried about that," he says. "I trust you to be a professional. I know your guild membership is important to you."

Implied is the threat that he'll ensure I lose it if I leave him high and dry. He needn't bother—Xinlei would strip me of it himself. "So what are you worried about then?"

His face is inscrutable. "Let's try the linking first. See if I can share my power with you. Then we can discuss the best path forward."

"Right now?" For some reason, my stomach twists with nerves.

Taran shakes his head. "Tonight. After Mei is asleep, so we can be sure we won't be caught together." He glances at Carter. "Can you walk Lady Lynx back to her suite?"

I bite my lower lip, and the prince's silver eyes zero in on it. I quickly release it. "What are people going to say when they see the prince's Apex guardian at my side?"

He blows out a breath. "Less than they'd say if they saw the Apex prince at your side. Carter will trail you like he's keeping an eye on you."

"I can walk myself back," I point out.

Carter bows solemnly. "Less suspicious to be trailed by a palace guardian than flitting about on your own, My Lady." The wink he throws in takes the sting off the honorific.

"Fine," I grumble. At least I can finally take off the godsdamn corset.

As we walk through the palace back to my suite, Carter trailing behind me as promised, I glance at the portraits lining the walls. The king stares back from multiple stages of his life—crowned in youth, austere in age. His new queen is present also. And the young crown prince. Even Taran is immortalized in oil at various points. But there's no Queen Kora.

Not a single portrait.

As if she never existed at all.

Chapter 20

TARAN

I stand in the passageway outside the Lynx's suite for far too long, bracing myself. It's not enough that I had to sit in that tiny research room with her, albeit with the door open, thank Faunera. Now I have to somehow get through the linking in the hollow of the tree where her scent will be even more potent.

For the tenth time, I consider abandoning this plan. Continuing the search for the amulet alone. Letting her go after the guardian records instead. As she clearly prefers.

But trying to do this alone is what got us into this untenable situation in the first place. Every time I think I catch a whiff of the artifact, my father or Simon Winters or his fucking daughter manages to waylay me, and by the time I can check it out, it's disappeared. Meanwhile, it's been years of pretending to be the king's loyal commander, executing feral Apex at his behest, as if I don't know exactly how they got that way. I can't risk Samhain resulting in yet another failure. My heart can't bear it.

It's more than that.

In the dim light of the passageway, with only my thoughts and my creature for company, I can admit it to myself. I don't want the Lynx anywhere near

Lord Winters. As long as he believes she's Elite, he'd never risk turning her. But if he was to catch her stealing...

An instinctual need to protect the little thief roars through my veins. I've been fighting the invading feeling tooth and claw since the day we met. But like all the battles of my life, it seems I'm doomed to lose.

I check my watch. An hour past midnight. I've waited long enough.

I brush my right pocket—a quick, superstitious check. Then my canines are elongating. I raise my finger to my mouth. A drop of crimson wells before I swipe it across the warded stone. The wound is already healing as the wall opens to her suite.

A dark apparition is within, incongruent in the lady's sitting room. Hidden in a black cloak, clad in dark pants and boots that seem to blend into the room's shadows, the Lynx looks every bit the professional thief I hired. Without a word, she sweeps into the passageway, her scent licking me on her way past. She pads up the tunnel on silent feet before pausing and turning back and facing me. I can't see her face in the deep hood, but the message is clear: What are you waiting for?

I square my shoulders and snatch up the unlit lantern, closing the hidden door behind me before catching up with the little thief. The tunnel is just wide enough for us to walk abreast, and I automatically shorten my strides. "Mei?" I murmur.

"Asleep," she answers in an equally low voice. We continue in silence, the Lynx following my lead. As I promised, most of the passageways are empty this time of night, but as we make our way to the exit, I catch the scent of a few guards. A ghost of a touch to her lower back is all it takes to redirect her.

She doesn't shy away from my touch, though it's not on her bare skin like it was in the garden. I suppress a shiver at the memory of my fingers brushing the soft skin of her face. I don't know what came over me, even secluded as we were.

As the prince, I've never lacked for female companionship. Even after I emerged, I was already familiar with the Apex guardians from training. If anything, they were more enthusiastic lovers than the court ladies I'd bedded in the past. We certainly shared more in common— similar interests, our heightened senses, and the companionship of our creature always thrumming beneath the surface.

But since the day I emerged, I've been caught in between two worlds—unable to pursue a real relationship, if I even desired one, which I don't. What would I do with a vapid courtier who genuflects in person only to smear me behind my back the moment I'm gone? It would never occur to me to touch any female that intimately in public, much less an Elite lady.

And yet.

When she rolled her eyes—something else no female would ever do in my presence these days—I didn't even think. Just reached out, clasped her chin, teased her as if we were two normal people from a less complicated time in my life. I didn't second guess how it would be perceived or interpreted if anyone might be watching. And that is a dangerous precedent.

For both of us.

But her reaction? That was the bigger shock. The responsive deepening of her scent, the musk of her arousal made me want—

I pull up sharply, and the Lynx mimics me at my side, her hood tilting in question. I mime putting a finger to my lips, and she nods.

Because the scent of arousal that tickles my nose now isn't the woman standing next to me. It isn't mine, either.

It's two Apex I know very well.

And they're blocking the only exit to the wooded forest.

Chapter 21

ALORA

I tilt my head to the side, trying to listen for whatever the prince is scenting around the upcoming corner. I may not be an Apex, but even a human can train their senses to fire more acutely. Xinlei taught me that. My eyes slip shut to concentrate. At first, I hear nothing, but then—muffled moans, heavy breathing. My eyes fly open.

Taran's expression is torn. He clearly knows who is having a secret rendezvous in the tunnel ahead and is debating whether to disturb them.

"Can we go another way?" I whisper, though I'm not sure whoever's over there would hear us over their…activities.

His brows knit. "We risk running into other Apex patrolling. And they're blocking the exit we need."

"We could wait?" I suggest. He scowls, and sure, I want to wait in this corridor while whoever is up ahead finishes their tryst as little as he does, but I'm not sure what our alternative is.

He winces. "They won't be quick." A quiet laugh bubbles out of me before I can stop it.

He glances at me sidelong.

"Sorry," I murmur, pressing my hand to my mouth, still trying to tamp down the giggles attempting to escape.

The corner of his mouth twitches. "Alright," he mutters, "let's brave it out. Make sure your hood is covering you." He pulls up his own hood and wraps the hand not clutching the lantern around mine.

My breath catches as the prince tugs me up and around the corner.

What greets us is...about what I expected.

A tall male guardian has a dark-haired Apex pinned to the stone wall, her bare umber legs wrapped around his waist. Her skirt bunched around her hips, his shirt untucked. The male's head turns for only a moment as we approach, tawny eyes flashing, before he goes back to thrusting with renewed vigor.

"Carter," Leylah gasps, no doubt sensing our approach. Her head tilts as if to glance our way, but Carter's mouth dips to cover hers, effectively blocking her view of us with his body. We slide past, Taran pulling me along, avoiding the tangled pair. Leylah's smothered moans and Carter's low grunts chase us to the end of the corridor. Taran drops my hand and unlocks the hidden door. He ushers me through, and we rush out into the dark woods.

My heart rate immediately slows and my breaths come easier in the night air. After a pause to ensure we're alone, Taran quickly lights the lantern. Barely slowing, he leads the way through a darkened wood. In the lantern's flickering light, impossibly tall, skinny trees with tufted green tops disappear into the dark night sky. A crisp scent of—

I whip my head to the giant male next to me, padding near-silently through the forest despite his size.

"What?" he asks in a low voice.

"Nothing."

But I drag in greedy breaths of the Veridian pine trees that line the path.

Eventually, Taran slows to a stop and lifts his hood. I copy him, certain he would be able to scent if anyone was nearby. He's deliberately not looking at me, his attention on the enormous trees with reddish bark that form a sort of semicircle. In the center, one of the trees is hollowed out to create a natural cave.

Now we've reached our destination, I can't hold it in any longer. I clap both hands over my mouth, but it's not enough to completely silence the laughter that shakes my body.

A snort from Taran, and then he's joining me in smothered laughter, disturbing the silence of the Sacred Grove.

I wipe a tear from my eye. "Didn't you tell him we'd be doing this tonight? He couldn't have chosen a different corridor?"

A boyish grin paints Taran's shadowed face. "Possibly she was guarding the exit, and he thought to, uh, distract her."

I press my lips together to keep another round of laughter at bay. "Are they together?"

He shakes his head. "Apex guardians must prioritize their Elite charges first. True relationships between guardians are...strongly discouraged."

All my amusement evaporates. "Will they get in trouble then? If they're caught?" I'm surprised to find that I'm worried about the Apex guardians I hardly know.

"Uh, no. No one minds if they do *that*." Taran pulls on the back of his neck. "The life of a guardian is a difficult one, with very little choice. Even the Elite recognize that after training and fighting, some...outlet is required. Besides, all Apex take the contraceptive tonic from the day they emerge."

The blood drains from my face. I sway on my feet, the ache in my chest reverberating.

"Lynx?" The prince reaches as if to steady me, then thinks better of it, folding his hand into a fist at his side. "Are you alright?"

"They...all take the contraceptive tonic?"

Silver eyes study me beneath a furrowed brow. "It is required. Because emergence is not hereditary, nothing is allowed to interfere with an Apex's duty."

That doesn't mean my parents weren't guardians, I decide, my jumping pulse finally slowing. Just because Apex are meant to take the contraceptive tonic and eschew permanent relationships doesn't mean some wouldn't rebel against the rules. It does mean that they would have had to keep my birth a secret. Or perhaps only my father was Apex and their relationship was forbidden. Or both my parents were, and I was smuggled out of Veridia after being deemed human. I sneak a glance at the Apex prince, proof positive emergence doesn't run in families.

I need to get those records.

I run my hands along the bark of the hollow tree, worn smooth as if many hands have touched it just this way, hoping for good fortune. "It's so quiet." My own voice is hushed, not wanting to disturb the peaceful serenity of this place, shielded even from the moon goddess by the trees' canopy. "So, how do we do this exactly?"

Still holding the lantern, the prince pulls a small book from his cloak, thinner and less ancient-looking than *The Gods of Valenrae*. "I'm not sure entirely," he admits. "But it may feel a little strange at first. There's another part I didn't get a chance to tell you yet."

"What is it?"

The prince shifts uncomfortably, noticeable in its difference to his typically solid stance. "To push my power out to you, I'm going to need to connect closely to my own creature and its powers."

"So?" Does the prince have a problem with his stoneclaw?

"So, I'm probably going to feel more driven by my creature's...instincts."

My stomach plummets, an icy wash of anxiety rolling over me as my hands tremble. "You mean you might go feral?"

"No! No, nothing like that. I would never ask you to attempt this if I thought that was even a remote possibility. Just—" He huffs. "I might...act differently. More instinctually. And if it works, you'll feel similarly."

"Is there more about the linking in that book?" I incline my head towards the slim volume he's gripping tighter in his large hand.

"Ah. This is my, uh, journal." I've never seen the prince bashful before, his cheeks darkening in the dim light. He clears his throat. "It contains my notes compiled from various books. References from *The Gods of Valenrae* and other texts that discuss the linking. I've tried to put them all together into a list of steps for us to try."

I'm trying very hard not to care about the contradictions of this male. I'm here to do a job, get some answers, and get Eleni back—preferably with a mountain of gold for our troubles and our guild memberships intact.

But in spite of all that, my blasted curiosity wins out again. "How long have you been working on this?"

"Eight years, give or take."

"*Eight years?*" I thought he was going to say eight months, maybe.

"I've been researching the general subject since the day my mother was killed." Taran's silver eyes hold mine, shining faintly in the filtered moonlight. "That's when we learned of the amulet, what it can do. Neither the king nor Lord Winters is aware that we know. I've been able to keep the secret by playing along as his dutiful son and commander. After my mother—" He chokes off. Takes a deep breath and tries again. "The new queen enables my father's worst impulses. His bigotry. His belief that the Elite have a right—even a duty—to control the Apex population and bend them to his will. Lord Winters has always been a power-hungry prick, whispering into the king's ear, but my mother...she was a steadying force." A small, wistful smile graces the prince's full mouth. "She was too kind for this world."

"I see. So, um, what's the first step?" My voice is too loud, too blunt for the moment, but I manage to rein in my wince.

Thankfully, Taran also seems eager to change the subject. "Step one. We need to go inside the Eternal Redwood."

"That makes sense." I keep my tone neutral, but my heartbeat quickens.

The tree is enormous, it's true, but so is the prince. As soon as we enter the hollowed-out trunk, my pulse begins to race. It's like being in a closet together, shielded from the outside, so deathly quiet we can hear each other's breaths like they're our own.

"Now what?" My voice is hushed.

Taran sets the lantern on the ground between us, then reaches out with one crooked finger and brushes my jaw. My breath hitches as he gently tilts my head up to meet his gaze, gray storm clouds swirling through the silver. "Try to maintain eye contact. Unless—" His finger drops from my chin, and

I take a too-shallow breath, the sound embarrassingly sharp in the confined space. He checks his little book of notes. "Unless you need to close your eyes to concentrate."

"Closed," I blurt out. "I can focus better if my eyes are closed."

"Alright. Let's both close our eyes for a moment then. First, you're going to clear your mind while I connect to my creature. Try to focus on my breath, on the natural world around you. Just observe."

Dutifully, I close my eyes and try to do what he asked.

The problem is, this already feels too intimate, and we've barely even started. I'm hyper-aware of the small space and the unfairly gorgeous male in front of me. Add in the fact he has a magically heightened sense of smell, and...

There's no way I'm going to be able to do this.

Eyes screwed shut, I drag a full breath in and let it out slowly. Like I did in the corridor, I let my other senses dominate, concentrating on the sound of each of our breaths. His, steady and controlled. Mine, getting there. The slight rustling of the leaves as the wind skips through the trees. The mingling scents of pine and Taran, so closely entwined I can't tell them apart. I start to imagine I can even hear our hearts thumping at the same steady pace.

Taran's voice is tight when he asks, "Are you ready?"

"I'm ready."

"Can you open your eyes and keep a hold of this state of mind?"

"I'm not sure, but I can try." I crack open my eyes to find Taran's glowing silver ones trained on mine, the unmistakable glint of a stoneclaw peering out from behind them.

The hole in my chest flares like someone has lit a match to it. A pained grunt forces its way out of my throat, and I immediately drop out of that peaceful, meditative state.

I can tell the moment Taran does the same, the strain leaving his eyes. "Are you alright?"

"Sorry." I rub my chest where the pain hasn't yet dissipated, my breaths still shallow. I don't know why I'm apologizing. Maybe because he's too close, too big, and the dark of the hollow is too still, amplifying everything. Even his rough, godsdamn alluring voice.

"Hey, that was great. You did well." He cocks his head, an uncertain twist to his lips.

I surreptitiously wipe my hands on my pants, trying to will my breathing under control. My chest throbs. "Maybe you should tell me the next steps ahead of time first. So, I know what to expect."

He hums in agreement. "That's a good idea. I should have thought of that."

"And...not in here. Let's go back outside." I step out of the hollowed tree, and he grabs the lantern and follows me, bemused.

As soon as we're outside the tree, I attempt to inhale a deep breath, but it's the same strong pine scent he exudes, so it doesn't even help. At least out here, it's slightly less intimate. Very slightly.

"Are you alright?" Taran sets down the lantern and steps closer.

I shake out my shoulders and jump up and down a couple times. The ache is a persistent problem, shortening my every breath. "Fine, I'm fine. Did you connect with your, ah, creature?"

I stop myself from saying "stoneclaw" just in time.

"I did," he confirms.

The dam of curiosity bursts, and the questions come pouring out. At least it distracts me from the drumbeat of pain. "Can everyone do this? How often have you done it? Do you have to be in the grove for it to work?"

He chuckles and holds his hands up as if to stem the flood.

"Yes, I think any Apex could do this if they were given the knowledge." His tone is thoughtful. "I can connect with my creature and amplify my power anywhere now, though that wasn't the case at first. It took me two years of research to discover this was possible."

"Can Carter do it?"

"He can. But we can't share our powers," Taran answers.

I nearly forget about the throbbing hole in my rib cage. Nearly. "You've tried linking with Carter?"

"Of course," he answers, puzzled. "Carter and I have been together since he emerged. I thought if I could connect with anyone, it would be him."

"Are you..." I wave my hand suggestively.

"Are we what?" Taran sounds as if he's trying not to laugh. He's going to make me say it.

"You know what I mean. Are you involved?"

A slow, distracting grin pulls at the prince's full mouth. "Should I be flattered you keep asking after my relationship status, My Lady?"

I snort—a decidedly un-ladylike sound. "You should not, Prince. This is purely academic."

"And Victoria?"

I frown at her name. "That was self-preservation."

"Whatever you need to tell yourself, Lady Lynx." He parrots my own words from days ago back to me. "I think it should be obvious after tonight's demonstration that Carter prefers females."

My cheeks heat. I rarely blush, and the fact I've done it twice now in the prince's presence is infuriating. "Just because he likes Leylah doesn't mean he can't also enjoy the company of men. And *you* said Apex are always needing an...outlet." I swallow hard as I realize for the first time that Taran may have been including himself in that statement.

"That's true," he admits, amusement still tinting his voice. "Though if he's open to male companionship, I have yet to see the evidence of it. And as you've just noted, Carter is not exactly subtle with his partners."

My cheeks burn hotter.

The prince takes pity on me and deftly brings the conversation back to the original point. "I've tried linking with Maeve and Astrid, too. Didn't work, either."

That makes my lips curve despite the dull ache still pinging in my chest.

"What?" he asks.

My smile widens. "You thought you'd be able to link with Astrid?"

"She's powerful. And female."

"And also an uncrackable safe," I point out. "I bet you couldn't get her favorite food out of her, much less power-share with her creature. And what does her being female have anything to do with it?"

He shrugs. "Faunera was female, as was her human consort." He studies my face. "If we can't get this to work, you should try linking with Astrid."

I can't stop the snort that bursts out at that. A bird in a nearby tree takes flight as the noise breaks through the quiet.

"What's her power?" I ask like I'm actually considering it.

"Night vision."

"Oh. Wow." That actually could really come in handy.

"Let's try it with you and me first, though, shall we, Lady Lynx?"

I nod, chastened. But damn, night vision. Astrid must be positively lethal.

"So, you wanted to know the next step. I'll be pushing my power out towards you. My creature and I are already linked. In theory, you're just...joining in."

"In theory?"

He pushes out a breath and the warmth of it fans my face. "Well, like I said, this is as far as I've gotten. Carter, Astrid and I have been able to connect to our own creatures but not push our power out to one another."

I'm silent for a moment, thinking. "What does it feel like to you? When you connect with your creature."

"First, my Apex sense of smell is intensified. That's how I find the connection in the first place."

I nod. "That makes sense. By dimming one sense, closing your eyes, for example, the others would get stronger."

"Yes." He clears his throat. "It's...like I said, it's quite intense." His brow furrows, and he starts flipping through his little book again. It looks like a doll's book in his large hands.

Just another intriguing contradiction that keeps reeling me in against my will.

"Here it is—'our eyes are the windows to our inner creatures'—a quote from the personal journals I found from one of the earliest known Apex. That's why I thought it would be better to maintain eye contact."

"Let's try again," I urge.

But no amount of staring into each other's eyes from inside a sacred tree helps us form that divine connection. By the third attempt, when Taran instructs me to open my eyes, the resulting pain in my chest is so great I can't speak.

"Lady Lynx?" Deep lines bracket Taran's frown. "Are you alright?"

"Fine," I gasp out.

His eyes narrow. "Don't lie to me."

My heart feels as though it's being squeezed. The ache reverberates through my whole chest as though it's cleaving apart, my lungs collapsing beneath it. Stars appear in the corners of my vision.

Just before I fall, I imagine a ghostly gray stoneclaw leaping towards me.

Chapter 22

TARAN

My hands are reaching for her of their own accord—I couldn't stop if I tried—when she stumbles forward, clutching her chest. Her fall is so sudden, she nearly kisses the ground, but I'm already in motion. One swooping reach, and I've got her. She's in my arms, eyes squeezed shut, face contorted into a grimace.

"Lynx?" I choke out. She doesn't respond. Her body stays locked in its tense position—she doesn't even seem to realize I'm holding her.

My stoneclaw is frantic, and I'm not far off. It must be something to do with the linking or this tree. Maybe if I took her outside—

I secure her body closer to my chest, her scent nearly suffocating—too much, too sharp—and stride out into the velvet night. It's a relief to be in the fresh air, but it has no effect on the Lynx. Her breath comes out in short pants, one hand still pressing on her chest.

I scent another Apex.

A snarl rips out of my throat, and the Lynx moans.

"Easy. It's just me." Astrid's eyes reflect the moonlight as she approaches. Of course, I scented her earlier and I knew she'd be keeping watch for us outside the tree. I'm hanging onto my control by a very thin thread that could snap at any moment. Astrid attempts to come closer, but my involuntary growl—more creature than male—stops her in her tracks.

Her head drops in supplication, though it hardly helps. "What happened?" she murmurs.

"I don't know! She just collapsed." I can hear the panic in my voice. "Lynx. Can you hear me?"

Her only response is a pained whimper. My canines punch into the inside of my bottom lip, and I taste copper.

"Lynx," I try again, my stoneclaw a thrashing maelstrom inside me. Then, in desperation, the false name she gave—the little name Eleni called her. "Lor!"

"Taran," she gasps, her eyes fluttering open, and my name has never sounded sweeter. A shiver snakes through my entire body.

"What's happening? Are you hurt? What can I do?" I know I'm acting the opposite of how you're meant to when talking to someone recently injured, but my heart is pounding in my chest, and a dull roar crashes against my ears. Dimly, I'm aware of Astrid studying us with that enigmatic look on her face.

The Lynx winces, still rubbing her chest. "It's...it's nothing. Just a little painful."

"Nothing?" I explode. "Nothing?! You just crumpled to the ground. You would've broken your nose if I hadn't caught you."

The little thief looks around and seems to realize where she is. "You can set me down now."

My arms tense, the muscles bulging. I grit my teeth and attempt to wrest back control. She's alright—she just said she's alright.

"Taran?" Amber orbs peer up at me in the moonlight, framed by heavy dark lashes. Gods.

I inhale a deep breath through my mouth and set her down, one hand splayed across her lower back to steady her. That she doesn't fight it lets me know exactly how "fine" she really is. I do my best to keep my tone non-threatening but as usual, my next words come out more growled demand than gentle. "What happened?"

She blows out a breath. "Any chance you'd be willing to chalk it up to a weird side effect of the linking and leave it at that?" She peeks up. I don't answer. My hard expression must speak for itself, and she sighs. "Thought not."

"She should sit down," Astrid remarks.

"I'm fine," the infuriating woman protests again, but I'm already steering her to a fallen log nearby, its surface worn smooth from the many worshippers who've rested here. Once she's settled, I sit beside her, reluctantly removing my arm now that she's stable. Astrid passes her a waterskin, and she takes it gratefully.

I let her sip the water slowly, but my patience is wearing thin. "Lynx," I warn.

"Could you get the lantern, please? I realize Astrid can see just fine but it's a little awkward sitting here in the pitch dark."

"You're stalling," I grumble, but I do her bidding anyway. By the time I'm seated back beside her, a calculating look has overtaken her face. A hand still rests against her chest, but the pain has clearly lessened. Good. My stoneclaw's patience—always in short supply—has reached its end.

"Let's have it, Lynx."

She pulls in a deep breath. "I don't remember anything before the day the Shanterran guild master found me wandering around Heshan in a daze. I was fifteen. I knew my given name but not my surname. I knew my age and how to speak my mother tongue—Veridian—but I had no idea where I hailed from. Nothing of my family or how I ended up in Shanterra."

Astrid sends me a pointed look, and the Lynx doesn't miss it. "You don't believe me." She sighs.

"We believe you," I tell her. A barely there widening of Astrid's eyes is her only tell. "Go on," I urge.

The thief gives me a skeptical look but continues. "Ever since then, ever since I can remember, I've had this...ache in my chest. It feels like a hole. Like a piece of me is missing."

I unconsciously lean towards her. "You feel your missing memory?"

"Maybe," she answers, but I can tell that's not what she thinks it is. But then, what is it?

After a moment's hesitation, she pulls the chain from beneath her shirt, holding up the lynx charm. Finally seeing the diamond lily I bought her hanging there around her neck shouldn't fill me with this level of satisfaction.

But it does.

"This is why I need the guardian records. When the guild master found me, I was wearing this charm. It's my only clue to my past. I thought…maybe one of my parents…"

This is why she reacted so strongly when I told her about the rules against Apex relationships. I foolishly thought—never mind what I thought. "What does that have to do with you collapsing?" My tone is too brusque, the words too blunt. I know it immediately, but the damage is already done.

Her expression closes off again. "The ache has been getting worse."

I frown. "Since you came here?"

She shakes her head. "Before that."

Realization dawns. "This is why you agreed to come to Ravenscrest. To help us."

Her mouth twists. She hates revealing this to us; the guild has taught her to hide her motivations at all costs. "Yes."

"So when I tried to share my powers…"

She buries her face in her hands. "It felt like my chest would break apart from the force of it. Every time you told me to open my eyes, it was stronger—"

"Why didn't you *tell* me?" I shout. Her head snaps up, a familiar scowl fixed on her face, but it's too late—I'm already lost to the rage of my stoneclaw. I feel my eyes shift and know they're glowing silver-gray fire.

"Why didn't I tell you that I have no memory before the age of fifteen? Oh, I don't know," she mocks. "Maybe because you're my *client*, and an *Elite*, and a fucking Apex besides! Why in Jinai's name would I reveal something like that to *you* of all people?" The words lash through me, sharper than claws. It would've hurt less if she'd hit me.

"No," I bite out through gritted teeth as I restrain my stoneclaw's reaction. "I mean, why didn't you tell me the linking was hurting you?"

Her lips part, but no sound comes out.

"It sounds like we should get those guardian records," Astrid cuts in. "Especially if the Lynx can't attempt linking until we determine what's causing the...ache."

"He promised me them anyway," the little thief grumbles. "*Before* we go after the amulet."

I rake a hand through my already unkempt hair, trying to pull my fraying emotions back under control. "I'll talk it over with Carter and Maeve."

"I want to be involved in the planning," the Lynx says. "I'm the professional here. This is what you brought me to Ravenscrest for. I need to know where you've already looked for the amulet, where exactly Lord Winters keeps the records. And then—"

"And then?" I prompt, although a part of me doesn't want to know.

She winces. "And then I need to meet the mark."

Faunera save us all.

Chapter 23

ALORA

By the time I collapse into my bed, there's barely an hour left before dawn will light the sky. Once again, I'm awakened far too soon by a very elegantly attired, very angry royal.

Maeve's emerald eyes, set off by her Veridian royal green gown, are flashing with annoyance. Her brilliant red hair is arranged in an intricate updo.

"Why aren't you ready?" she snaps in my face, then whirls around and faces an anxious Mei, who must have let her into the suite. "Why isn't she ready?" Maeve demands.

Suvi peeks around the Elite, a concerned expression on her face, and it hits me—the queen's tea. I whip my head to the picturesque windows, the shades flung wide, and oh, no. The sun has risen much higher than I expected.

I fling myself out of bed like it's on fire.

Suvi springs into action, bustling me towards the bathing room. My nightgown hits the floor as she ushers me into jasmine-scented bath water in record time.

She's already tugging my hair out of its messy braid when Maeve sweeps into the room, her eyes thin. "Start scrubbing," she commands, tossing a washcloth that smacks me in the face. I don't argue. Maeve looks ready to throw me in boiling water herself if I don't move fast enough. I scrub with alacrity, water sloshing around me as Suvi pushes some kind of powder into my hair.

At least the sharp pain from last night has lessened to its former dull ache. Suvi starts to arrange my long hair in a braided coronet while I'm still cleaning myself.

Maeve watches on, as though each second I waste costs her years off her life. If she wasn't so enraged, I would laugh at the absurdity of this moment.

Suvi's barely finished before they're pulling me out of the bath and shoving me into a dress colored the same as Maeve's. "Sit," Maeve barks, forcibly pushing me into the vanity chair. She slaps matching slippers into my hand. I carefully slide them on as Suvi dabs light makeup on my face, smoothing over the freckles that pepper my nose.

Maeve taps one slippered foot, her mouth tight, but despite her obvious impatience, she never once takes it out on the lady's maid. Instead, she waits—barely—for Suvi to be the one to pronounce me "ready" before she physically grabs my arm and drags me to the door.

The whole ordeal could not have taken longer than five minutes.

I throw a sincere "thank you" over my shoulder to Suvi, who only purses her lips in response. Mei is waiting for us in the hallway, dressed in her guardian's uniform. Someone, somehow, has found the time to get it tailored to her body overnight. Her ebony hair is pulled back into a smart ponytail, and I notice she's been given sturdy black boots like Astrid wears.

"You look nice," I murmur softly to Mei as she drops into step with Astrid behind us. Maeve has taken my arm in an outward show of friendship that in actuality services her need to drag me along at top speed.

Maeve sends me an arch look. "I don't know how you thought it would be alright for your Apex to show up to the queen's tea looking like she was wearing some novice's castoffs."

"Thank you, Maeve." My gratitude to her is no less heartfelt than the one I just gave Suvi. She sniffs in response but almost imperceptibly slows her pace so that Mei and I maybe have a slight chance of keeping up.

"Where is the tea?"

"In the queen's own suite. It's an incredible honor to be invited to join her."

"Anything I should know?" My question is soft, under my breath. Meant only for Maeve. And Mei, I suppose, with her Apex hearing.

Maeve nods in greeting to a couple of courtiers we pass, unsmiling. She's got her "above-it-all" mask firmly in place.

"She's bored and she wants to try and wring some gossip out of you. Don't speak unless spoken to, and try to absorb everything you can," she instructs me, non sotto.

Very well, then. *Rule Number Eight* it is. *Stay silent and observe.*

I can tell the precise moment we enter the queen's wing. Pink rose bushes line the walls, manicured into matching spheres, each one perched in pristine white ceramic pots—exactly like the ones framing the queen's blanket at the garden party. The overwhelming sweetness of their scent is cloying in the enclosed hallway.

A footman in royal Veridian colors stands at attention outside a set of grand double doors, which must lead to the queen's suite. At our approach, he swings them open wide and announces our arrival with a formal, "Ladies Ashbourne and Thorne, Your Majesty."

"Finally!" The queen claps.

Maeve and I drop into low curtsies, our eyes on the ground. I sense Mei and Astrid folding over into matching bows behind us.

"Rise," she commands.

I lift my head, taking in a sitting room large and grand enough to be a ballroom. The back wall, as with the rest of the palace, is lined with enormous windows, framing a view of the shimmering ocean. Glass doors lead to a balcony decorated—naturally—with more of those pink rose bushes. The room itself is a blinding mix of white and gold with multiple chandeliers, seating arrangements, and even a pianoforte.

Queen Nyxley sits in a wide white armchair at the head of a low table, a fizzing pink drink held carelessly in one hand. Her gown is the palest shade of green. Her strawberry blonde hair sparkles with pink sapphires the size of plums intermixed with diamonds. Her makeup makes the most of her delicate face and light moss-colored eyes. Her ladies, in various shades of sage, are arranged on white benches on either side of her and also seem to be eagerly partaking of the rose bubbly drink. Even the tiny cakes in tiered trays on the table are iced in green, white, and pink.

The queen gestures to the open white loveseat at the foot of the low table. Maeve quickly sits, pulling me down beside her. Astrid and Mei start to slide back and join the other guardians against the wall; the queen stops them with a raised hand. "I don't believe I've ever seen a guardian that size before. Come closer."

Mei steps forward hesitantly as the queen polishes off the rest of her drink. Before she can even gesture to the servant behind her, the glass is refreshed. "Turn around. Let me get a look at you."

Mei rotates in place. I clench my fingers in the fabric of my skirts.

"Shanterran as well..." After a pause, she waves dismissively in Mei's direction. I catch the Apex's relieved face as she hurries back to stand beside Astrid.

Maeve brings a delicate teacup to her lips, unruffled as ever. "Lady Thorne's grandfather was an ambassador to Shanterra. He was given her Apex as a gift during his travels."

"And what gift does your Apex have?" The queen's question barely manages to contain her ravenous curiosity, and it may as well be a command. No doubt, my diminutive guardian has been the subject of much speculation in court, and she's fishing for gossip.

I hesitate, unsure which lie is the right one to tell. Taran's warning echoes in my mind. *Don't ever tell my father that Mei can taste lies.*

I don't yet understand the relationship between the scheming king and his flighty young queen, but I can guess which lie Taran would want me to share right now.

"She's a poison catcher," I blurt out.

The queen leans back, clearly disappointed. It's still a rare gift, to be sure, but not an especially exciting one for the gossip mill.

"You remember Lady Song, of course," Maeve interjects suddenly.

The queen visibly perks up at the name. "Yes...that mysterious illness...such a tragedy."

Maeve nods meaningfully. The queen's ladies trade sly smiles.

"I heard Lady Song was much admired by the bea—by the prince," the queen remarks. Whoever this Lady Song was, her name alone has turned the mood of the queen, and thus the room, completely around.

"My cousin has confided in me his fear that Lady Song's death could have been foul play," Maeve whispers theatrically.

The queen's small close-lipped smile is one of vindication. *This—this* is the intrigue she was hoping for by inviting us to her gathering today. I don't know how Maeve knew to play into it but I'm learning that she's never one to miss a volley.

"Who could have been behind it?" one of the ladies, a petite raven-haired beauty, asks breathlessly.

This is the question the queen was waiting for. "We all know who can't seem to leave my stepson alone, even after his...condition...became apparent." Her every word drips with disdain. Is she implying that Victoria poisoned some other courtier just because Taran admired her?

"Oh, Your Majesty, you can't mean...?" Maeve acts the part of stunned courtier to perfection, a pale, manicured hand flying to her breast.

"Oh, but I do," she declares. "Simon is beside himself. With the king's favor, Lady Winters could make an elegant match, and instead, she clings to the past."

"Is it true the beas—um, Prince Nyxley—took you to see the lilies in the garden to allay your homesickness?" This from a starry-eyed lady with burnished brown skin and thick black hair braided into a complicated weave down her back. Now that we're closer, I realize all the queen's ladies are equally as stunning and young as their mistress. With the roses all around and their gowns the color of growing things, they're like a garden of exquisite flowers themselves.

"His Highness knew I'm partial to lilies from my grandfather's time in Shanterra and wanted to show me the ones you had in your garden, yes." I'm loath to repeat the lie that went down so poorly yesterday, but when all the handmaidens sigh dreamily in response, my shoulders dip. It seems Lady Winters is not the only woman at court keen to overlook the prince's "*condition.*"

The queen gives them a quelling glare. "My ladies are prone to romantic fantasies." Frowning, she turns her attention to me. "I do hope you aren't making the same mistake, Lady Thorne."

I wrinkle my nose. "Respectfully, I came to court to find an Elite man. Not a—" I cut off abruptly, but my meaning is clear. Maeve tenses at my side, but the queen smiles, mollified.

"Splendid, my dear. Though it does seem you may have turned the bea—my stepson's head." Her gaze travels over Mei, standing resolute in the corner with the other Apex. "Careful how you tread. Especially in Lady Winters' company."

Maeve pats my knee consolingly. "Never fear, Lady Thorne. Your Apex guardian's gift will serve you well in this particular game." Considering my so-called guardian is more qualified to serenade us on that pianoforte over there than protect me from Lady Winters' misplaced vengeance, my answering smile is brittle.

"Your Majesty," Maeve simpers, "could you tell Lady Thorne the tale of how you won King Nyxley's affection? I believe it may serve as powerful guidance to her as she seeks her own match."

"Oh!" I gasp as if positively enraptured with the idea. "I would be *so* honored if you would deign to share, Your Majesty."

The ladies add their cajoling to the chorus until the queen really has no choice but to oblige us.

"I had only recently come to court," she begins, preening at being the center of attention. "After the death of the king's first wife, you understand." We all make sympathetic noises.

"His Majesty was positively distraught, of course. To have his queen taken from us by that brutal animal!" She sniffs. "And so soon after his own son was revealed to be one of them." The handmaidens are following this tale like it's a riveting play and at this dramatic plot turn, they all gasp. Hidden beneath the folds of my skirt, I let my nails bite into my palm.

"His Majesty told me that no one else understood his grief at that time. But I, who had lost my own mother to a feral Apex, knew his pain like it was my own." She places her hand on her chest, her kohl-darkened eyelashes dipping, fluttering over her rose-tinted cheeks.

Even here, in her own sitting room, surrounded by sycophants practically sighing on cue, she's ever performing.

"You all but saved the nation!" Maeve declares. "Why, who knows what might have happened to Veridia had the king remained lost in his grief. Instead, you gave him—and all our citizenry—hope again by delivering us a new crown prince."

The queen waves, feigning modesty, though her cheeks are pink with pleasure. And the drinks. "It was only my duty as a loyal citizen of Veridia. It's hardly as if the beast prince could sit the throne after what happened."

"What happened?" I can't stop the words coming out of my mouth.

The queen looks stricken. If she hadn't been downing fizzy cocktails all morning, she likely wouldn't have slipped. "Well...after he emerged, of course." An unconvincing laugh. "Elias would never stand an Apex on the throne."

"Nor would we!" Maeve always seems to sense exactly when the queen needs her support and be poised to supply it. "After both you and the king lost so much to their savagery."

The young queen nods enthusiastically, visibly cheered. "Exactly. It really is a generosity, our care of those animals. They would all be howling at the moon without the Elite to keep them in line!" Her ladies laugh, and Maeve summons a tight smile. The best I can do is hold my neutral expression.

Never having known one personally, I haven't given much thought to Apex before. To me, they were just another obstacle to work around during a heist. As someone who was constantly considered an "other" due to my Veridian heritage, I never used or enjoyed hearing the slurs rolling so easily off the queen's tongue. But I did always accept the essential premise of Valenraenian law that with their superhuman healing, strength and powers, Apex are too dangerous to the populace to be left to their own devices.

And yes, Taran is still intimidating, and Astrid makes my heart rate tick up every time she so much as catches my eye, but the more I get to know the Apex as people, the less fair it feels that they are pushed under the thumb of the Elite, whose only power comes from born privilege.

I shift in my seat as I consider something else. My own parents may have been Apex—or at least one of them. Taran's words from the library play over in my head: *My mother told me that Apex inner creatures emerge when we're ready to live in harmony with them.* Told in that way, it sounds like a beautiful gift rather than something to be feared or corralled. Close to divine, as Eleni said.

The queen is speaking freely, spouting her venom, in front of her *own* Apex, standing stiffly around the room, intermixed with the potted plants. Thinking their greatest use is guarding her Elite person inside the safety of the palace walls.

Rule Number Ten: Maintain control.

I drop my gaze, fingers trembling as I pluck a tiny cake and set it in front of me. The queen is continuing her bigoted rant, lost in her cups and the fawning attention of her ladies. I mentally stuff my emotions into a tight metal box and slam the lid shut.

The rest of the tea passes uneventfully. Maeve and I don't take a sip, while the queen and her ladies grow more boisterous and inebriated by the hour. Finally, when one of the women has passed out on her fellow's shoulder, snoring lightly, the queen announces she has an engagement to attend to and waves us out the door.

We pass through the hallway, thick with the cloying scent of roses, in silence. Blessedly, Maeve heads straight back to our rooms, and I do nothing to gainsay her. Maeve sweeps into her rooms, and I follow right behind. Then turn to shut the door—and close it firmly in Mei's—and unfortunately also Astrid's—faces.

Maeve's eyebrows arch. "What?" She sweeps into her vanity chair and begins to pull off her heavy jewelry.

Since this is my first time in her chambers, I let my gaze wander. Her suite is of a similar size and setup to mine—a main sitting room with large windows looking out onto lush greenery plus doorways to the bathing room and presumably Astrid's small room.

But just as the queen's wing reflects her style, Maeve's room bears her own signature. The colors are soothing, the textiles a blend of neutrals and off-white. The pleasant scent of dried lavender relaxes me.

"I wanted to apologize again. For making us late."

Maeve sighs. "I know it wasn't really your fault. Taran kept you out too late. He's completely obtuse when it comes to court politics and single-minded about finding the amulet."

"Thankfully, you have that particular expertise in spades. You were really good in there."

As usual, Maeve waves off the compliment. "Queen Delilah is easily handled by anyone with half a brain for politics."

"Who's Lady Song?" I keep my voice as neutral as I'm able, but Maeve still shudders at the name.

"An Elite courtier. From Shanterra." I gathered that much from the lady's surname, but Maeve goes on without my needing to prod her. "It was a couple of years ago…Taran and Jia were just friends, but Victoria—" She uses the Shanterran pronunciation of the name, *Chyah*.

"You know Mei can't actually sense poison, right?" My voice has gone high and panicky.

"Calm down," Maeve reassures me. "It's never been confirmed that Jia's death was from poisoning or that it was Victoria who did it. And even if it was, she would never be so stupid as to use the same method twice."

Never in the history of *calm down* has anyone ever calmed down by being told to *calm down*. "You're sure about that?"

She gives me a level look. "The story the queen told is true. About how she met the king. What she didn't tell you is that her father and Victoria's houses are rivals for the king's favor. The queen's father, Lord Aquilon, runs the territory that includes the coastline and has access to the sea trade. Very profitable, though less so recently with the Thalassarian pirates making a nuisance of themselves. Victoria's father, Lord Winters, has been close to the king since childhood and his province holds all of Veridia's mines. Also very profitable. That's why Queen Delilah drapes herself in precious gems." She waves dismissively. "Overcompensating. When Tare's mother passed, all the lords in favor immediately sent for their daughters of marriageable age. They were ravenous to attach their respective families to the throne. Queen Kora wasn't from a prominent house." Maeve's eyes shadow. "They say it was a true love match."

"A *love match*?" I can't contain my incredulity. "With *King Nyxley*?"

Maeve finishes divesting herself of her jewels and peers up at me. "The queen's past personal experience with Apex gone feral, her hideous prejudice...it appealed to the king. They were quickly married, and later, Queen Delilah with child. On Prince Leo's name day, he was immediately designated heir and betrothed to the child of one of Lord Aquilon's Thalassarian allies. Lord Winters was furious. The Aquilon family was now properly ensconced within the royal family *and* the line of succession."

"Which leaves the beast prince," I say, understanding finally dawning.

"Don't call him that. Taran still has a strong claim to the throne upon King Nyxley's death, plus the military supports him." She shrugs one delicate shoulder. "Why do you think my uncle and his queen are so eager to fan the flame of hatred for Apex in this country? They want to *ensure* the people will never accept an Apex on the throne."

"But would the Elite? Lord Winters?"

"I mean, I'm sure he wouldn't *want* to. Of course he'd prefer Taran were human or that Victoria would shift her focus to a real match."

I almost feel sorry for Lady Winters caught up in this political game of crowns and matches and broken hearts. Almost, but not quite.

"But then why allow Taran to command the armies at all? For that matter, why don't they just strip him of his Elite status?"

Maeve is smirking at me, and I'm not sure why until I realize what I just said. The prince's given name. I frown, crossing my arms over my chest.

She takes pity on me and lets the slip go past. "It's a thorny path for Their Majesties. The king still relies on Tare's Apex power and military sway to intimidate Veridia's enemies *and* its allies. And although he is an Apex, his mother was beloved. He grew up in the public eye; the citizens thought he would be their king. Taran keeps playing along, acting the part of a dutiful son. The king can't risk engendering sympathy towards the Apex by casting him out, or arranging an 'accident.'" Maeve doesn't mention family ties as a reason to not want his son dead, and indeed, I can't imagine that's really the king's main concern.

"If he wasn't so horribly prejudiced, Lord Winters would give in to Victoria, ask the king to make an exception and reinstate the betrothal so he could wrest power from the Aquilons. But apparently, even Lord Winters' ambition ends when it means his only daughter would have to marry an Apex." She shakes her head. "Maybe he still would if he thought Taran would be willing to work with them. But lucky for him, Tare can't stand Victoria. Not least because of what she allegedly did to Jia."

He should still consider the match. At least to myself, I can admit that Lord Winters would make a powerful ally. I picture Taran and Victoria together—light and dark—two powerful Elite, assured of their place in this world.

My mouth drops into a deep frown.

"The queen's ball is tomorrow night." Maeve's voice interrupts my dark musings. "You said your tailor would be making your dress?"

Shit. "I have to get word to her. She's supposed to bring the dress to the palace and take the rest of the payment back to the guild."

She scoffs. "What are we paying for again? A tiny Apex who only creates more gossip?"

"You're paying them for their silence," I reply evenly. I shut my eyes, thinking. "I'll send a message with Mei."

"You're sure she can make a gown that quickly?"

No. "Of course I'm sure."

But when I head back to my room, there's no trace of Mei. Maeve's response when I rush back to her room is a heavy sigh. "She must be training with the other Apex."

I bite my lip, picturing tiny Mei sparring with Astrid. Poor girl. "Do I really need to attend this ball?" It would be the perfect distraction while I lift the records from Lord Winters.

Maeve sends me an incredulous look. "We just sat through the queen regaling you with every minute detail of the event planning. You told her that attending her balls is the sole reason you're at court."

Right. I was so distracted by the disgusting Apex rant and the new emotions it stirred up that I had a hard time listening to the rest of the queen's monologue. Xinlei would be incredibly disappointed in me.

There might still be a way to bend this to the mission's advantage. "I need to talk to Taran. Would he be at the training as well?"

"They'll all be there, but—"

I cock my head. "But what?"

"They're *Apex*," she emphasizes. "What's your excuse for being there?"

"Where do they train?"

"The yard, obviously," she snaps, then pauses, a calculating look entering her emerald eyes. "It's just on the other side of the gardens."

My mouth curves. "Fancy a promenade?"

Chapter 24

ALORA

Holy goddess.

Maeve needn't have worried about our standing out near the practice yard. A gaggle of Elite ladies and lords have already clustered at the edge of the gardens to ogle the guardians, Lady Winters and her cronies among them.

I can't say that I blame them.

My mouth goes dry at the sight of the Apex prince, tanned chest on display in the fall sunlight. He's locked in a battle with Carter, also shirtless, his umber skin glistening with sweat. Strong biceps swing heavy swords, muscles rippling as they trade good-natured insults back and forth. Naked hunger flickers across Victoria's face as she watches, and I fear my own expression is not much better.

I'm not one to be turned by a pretty face. Not anymore. Not since I gave my heart too easily in Shanterra, desperate to fit in, only to overhear the bastard bragging about stealing "the foreign whore's virginity" to his posse of friends. I wish I'd had the courage to confront him, but instead, I hid, heartbroken and ashamed, until Eleni found me.

It took me over two years to sleep with someone else after that. By then, my shame had morphed into cold acceptance. Men are good enough for a diverting night—an *outlet*, as Taran called it—but that's as far as I'm willing to go.

The prince lifts one bare, tree-trunk-sized arm for a sharp downswing of his sword. I swallow hard, remembering the feeling of those strong muscles wrapped around my body after I came to in the grove. The tension that rippled through them when I told him to set me down. He keeps getting under my skin in a way I thought I'd long since guarded myself against.

I drag my focus from the forbidden display and search the yard for a tiny, ebony-haired Apex. She appears to be working on conditioning with Astrid—their height difference a comical study in contrasts.

I stride confidently towards the females, ignoring the gasps from the gathered Elite at my back. Out of my peripheral vision, I catch Taran freeze mid-motion, Carter barely pulling his swing in time.

"Mei!" I call out in an irritated tone. Her mouth drops open at the sight of me moving across the training yard, and she stands there, paralyzed. Astrid pushes her forward, and she nearly falls to the ground, Jinai save me. The spy recovers just in time, hurrying forward to intercept me while Astrid strolls lazily behind her.

"My Lady?" she gasps, out of breath.

"I need you to instruct my...seamstress to bring me my gown for the queen's ball tomorrow night. She can bring it to my room at the palace, and I'll pay her upon receipt."

"Now, My Lady?"

I fix an annoyed look on my face. "Yes, right now." I gesture dismissively, like the queen. "What are you waiting for?"

Mei bows. "Of course." She rises, then bows again. "Right away, My Lady." One last bow, and she rushes off.

Astrid watches her go, the same enigmatic expression on her face. "Her obvious lack of training is going to be a problem," she mutters.

I nod slightly, the barest movement of my head to indicate I've heard her and will deal with it. Then I spin on my heel to head back to the gardens and come face to face with a heaving chest of bronzed muscle.

"Mind telling me what you're doing here, My Lady?" the prince asks with barely concealed annoyance. A droplet of perspiration drips down his broad chest to one tight, hard nipple. I'm momentarily at a loss for words.

"Up here," he drawls, and my eyes snap up to meet blazing silver.

Rule Number Ten: Maintain fucking control.

I lift my chin, emulating Maeve's haughty aura. "Not that it's any of your business, but I had an errand for my Apex."

Far from being dissuaded, the corner of Taran's mouth twitches with amusement at my playacting. "It's not safe for you here. Some of the Apex are new and still learning to control their gifts."

My attention shifts to the assembled Apex, curiosity flaring. I catch Ethan, the young guard from the aqueduct entrance, launching arrows at a target more than two hundred and fifty yards away. He hits the bullseye every time.

"Far-sight," Taran says in answer to my unspoken question. "He can see that target as though it was right in front of his face."

"He looks young to be in the guard."

I feel the weight of the prince's gaze on me. "He's sixteen. We emerge during puberty. Though I happen to know the boy writes letters home every week. Are you planning on taking in another stray?"

I finally turn my gaze back to the prince, suppressing the urge to cross my arms over my chest. "What do you mean another one?"

"Your tiny guardian. Don't think I haven't noticed how protective you've been over her." He cocks his head. "It's unusual for an Elite. To say the least."

Warning heard and received. "Were you all that young when you emerged?"

"Carter was the same age, sixteen, when he came to live here in the palace."

My stomach twists uncomfortably. "Carter was just...forced to leave his home? His family?" The tragic past seems so incongruent with the cheerful guardian.

Taran steps closer, the musk of his exertion mixed with rain-soaked pine washing over me. "Yes. I have tried to be a brother to him in their stead, but emergence leaves its mark upon us all."

Curiosity nips at me again. "How old were you?"

"Nearly a year older than Carter. He'd already been brought to the palace to serve as my guardian when I emerged." A self-deprecating laugh. "Not sure whether I would have warranted one otherwise."

We stare at each other for a moment and I'm not sure what to say.

"You two are causing a bit of a scene." I whip around at Carter's low voice behind me and am caught off guard by a black tattoo of Faunera's tail-and-horns sigil on his right pectoral, exactly where it would be on his uniform, marking him as Apex. I suck in a sharp breath.

Carter's brow furrows, and then he follows where my attention has gone. His tawny eyes glow liquid gold in the sunlight.

"Is that..." I breathe.

"It's just a tattoo, Wildcat," he answers quietly. "Every Apex bears this mark." So they can never hide from their fate.

I drag my gaze from his bare chest to Taran's. No tattoo—at least not where I can see, and there's a lot of naked flesh on display. I swallow and raise my eyes to meet the prince's. "I need to talk to you."

His eyes flick to the distant Elite voyeurs. "Can it wait?"

"Of course. I came here to talk to Mei. You accosted *me*." I step back, sliding my condescending Elite mask back on.

"That's uncanny," he mumbles. His eyes narrow. "I don't like it."

"You're the one who wanted me to act more ladylike." I drop into a mocking curtsy. "Your Highness."

He erases the distance between us with a single step. A heartbeat before I realize what he's about to do, the prince's large hand clasps mine, slowly drawing it to his mouth. His soft lips dust over my knuckles. "My Lady," he murmurs, his silver gaze fixed on mine. I can't hide my slight tremble, and I know his Apex senses mean he doesn't miss it.

"Not helping," Carter points out.

Swallowing, I snatch my hand back and whirl towards the waiting Elite. Head held high, I swan back through the staring Apex, straight to the gardens.

Maeve is waiting for me with a rictus smile pasted on her face. She has to be ready to murder me. "What happened?"

I exhale a long sigh, keenly aware that every Elite within earshot is holding their breath so as not to miss my response. "My Apex's knowledge of poisons may be second to none, but she would forget her head if it wasn't attached to her body. She's loath to miss training, but it's a fitting punishment for not completing her task earlier."

"And the prince?"

I scoff. "He wanted to know if I would be attending the ball." I feign a shudder for good measure. "I know he's your cousin, but I just don't think I can dance with an Apex, Lady Ashbourne. It's unnatural."

"Don't worry, Lady Thorne," Victoria simpers, her words laced with icy malice, "a nobody from Nostura has no need to fear a dance invitation from royalty."

My answering smile is sharp as a blade. "The beast prince is all yours, Lady Winters."

She steps close enough to share breath, her voice dropping low so that none of the gossiping courtiers can listen in. "Yes," she hisses. "He is."

Chapter 25

TARAN

I shouldn't have touched her again. Especially in front of an audience. I know it. Carter knows it. Fuck, even the Lynx probably knows it. But I can't seem to help myself where she's concerned. When she throws that mocking *Your Highness* at me, my canines *ache* with the need to sink them into the tender flesh where her shoulder meets her neck. My hands curl into fists as I imagine bringing her to ruin beneath me, until the only words out of her pretty throat are pleas for more.

I bite back a groan. This overwhelming desire—bordering on instinctual—is unlike anything I've ever experienced. And certainly never in relation to a human. Even if she didn't despise me for being Elite, for being Apex, for putting her best friend in danger. Even if our being together wasn't forbidden by every country in Valenrae. Even then, I could never trust my stoneclaw with her. Every piece of my being shies away from risking the little thief's safety. But that's exactly what I'm going to have to do to save this kingdom from my father's and Lord Winters' machinations.

"You alright?" Carter murmurs.

"No," I respond truthfully, watching that delectable ass saunter away from me. Again.

He clears his throat, his grin edged with sympathy. "Need to work out some of that, er, tension?"

A low chuckle escapes me. "I absolutely fucking do, but I don't think fighting is going to help."

Carter nods towards the tall blonde sparring viciously with Astrid. "I'm sure Sophie would be willing to oblige if you asked her."

I tilt my head, considering, but my stoneclaw erupts at just the thought of another female. Fuck me, this is bad.

"I've got to get out of here," I mutter. "Take over, will you?"

Carter's mouth twists in concern. "Of course."

I stride in the opposite direction from the temptress, towards my rooms. I haven't had the chance to talk through the disaster of the linking with Maeve and Carter yet. Astrid was right—we have to get those records and see what we're dealing with. Maybe her lack of memory and the pain that comes with it has something to do with an Apex parent. Those records cover every Apex in our kingdom that ever emerged, plus their gifts. Even if there's no lynx on record, there might be a gift associated with memory.

I haven't heard of one before, but if it was from her parent, they would have emerged decades ago. I'm not worried that Simon might not have kept old records—he's obsessed with his "research." No doubt he holds on to everything and keeps it all close to hand in case he needs to reference it.

That's why I know, bone-deep, that despite my continued failure, the amulet sits somewhere within the castle walls, waiting for me to find it. They use it too often for it not to be. I've lost count of the number of poor souls I've had to ferry out of this world as they try—and fail—to recreate what has only worked once, as far as I know.

"Your Highness!" I suppress a groan as a page rushes towards me. "Your Highness!"

"What." The word comes out clipped.

"His Majesty requests your presence." The boy's voice trembles. No doubt worried the ferocious beast will rip him limb from limb.

I smother a sigh and gesture for him to lead the way. Too soon, we arrive at the doors to my father's council room. I tense as I see the two guardians posted outside.

My father's Apex, Vorrick, is a massive brute with one of the strongest senses of sight I've ever perceived. Only Carter's is stronger, something I will never reveal to my father. Vorrick throws the ax slung across his broad back with deadly accuracy. Right now, though, he looks bored stiff, his brown eyes flicking over me without interest. Vorrick's inner creature is a wolf and he'd rather be on the move and fighting in battle than stuck guarding palace corridors.

It's the Apex standing beside him that gives me pause. Rhegar. Simon Winters' guardian is tall and slim, with the same pale coloring as his Elite charge. A powerful auditory Apex, he's a master of whispers, which makes him more dangerous to me than Vorrick. He tilts his head and stares at me, unblinking, like his owlish inner creature, as I sweep past.

Inside the council room, it takes every bit of my limited control to keep my lip from curling in distaste at the sight of Lord Winters. My hatred for this man is superseded only by the absolute loathing I feel for the one sitting beside him.

"Taran." My father's face, an older replica of my own but for Maeve's emerald eyes and streaks of white peppering his dark hair and beard, breaks into a wide smile.

I force my face into something resembling polite interest. "My king."

"Always with the formalities." King Nyxley shakes his head. I curl my fingers into a tight fist behind my back to keep the tension out of my expression.

"What can I do for you, Your Majesty? I'm in the middle of training." Never mind that I was on my way back to my quarters to slake my uncontrollable lust with my right hand—the only way I've been able to think somewhat straight since the day I trapped the beguiling thief. One heartbeat in the presence of these two has managed to kill any remaining hard-on.

Lord Winters' pale lips turn down. "Unfortunately, our scouts have caught another feral Apex."

I grit my teeth, rage pounding from the stoneclaw beneath my flesh. But my voice stays even. "Another one? How many is that this month?"

"Too many." The king sighs, as if he's not responsible for every single fucking one of them.

"At least we have managed to catch them all before any humans came to harm," Lord Winters interjects smoothly.

"Indeed, Lord Winters. Where did they find this one?" I can't help but needle him, but his placid expression remains unchanged.

"On the edge of the city. It was quite a close call. You've done an excellent job at training them, My Prince."

My vision begins to shift, the gray bleeding in, and I purposefully look at the rolling sea outside the window until I've got my emotions in check.

"A public execution, I think, Taran. In the town square," the king commands. As if there was ever any other way this would end. Despair wells in my chest, and I ruthlessly tamp it down. If the gods have any mercy at all, this will be the last execution of my kind I ever have to do.

"Of course, Your Majesty. I'll attend to it immediately." I tilt my head in the barest approximation of a bow, then turn to leave.

"Oh, and Taran?"

I school my expression and swing my attention back to the true monsters in this kingdom. "Yes, Your Majesty?"

"Your stepmother requires your presence at her ball tomorrow." He sends me one of those piercing looks he's known throughout Valenrae for. "You will not disappoint her."

The king's advisor stiffens at the mention of my attendance at the ball, and a smirk quirks my lips in response. He can't stand Victoria's unlawful obsession with an *animal*. Well, that makes two of us.

I direct my next words right at Simon. "I wouldn't miss it for the world."

Chapter 26
ALORA

I'm enjoying having my chambers all to myself while the guild's spy is off on her errand when my wall opens on its own.

I look up from sharpening Xinlei's stiletto hairpin with my dagger to find Taran, Carter, and Astrid filing into my sitting room, the prince holding some kind of scroll. Astrid strides immediately to my chamber door, opening it to admit Maeve. The Elite quickly claims the armchair by my side with a rustle of her skirts.

Carter rubs his hands together. "At last. The team has assembled." My face falls as I remember not every member of the original team to steal the amulet is here.

The prince's expression is equally troubled. I'm not sure what happened between training and now, but he appears...burdened by something. Likely our fleeting timeline for this heist. "I informed the others of how the linking went. Everyone is in agreement that we need to secure the guardian records as soon as possible."

Finally. "I can steal them tomorrow during the ball."

But Taran shakes his head. "Not you."

"I'm the thief!" I protest.

The prince rakes a hand through his damp hair. His pine scent wafts towards me, and I have to fight not to inhale it greedily. "If you're caught, that's it. The amulet heist is blown. There's no excuse for you to be in Lord Winters' office."

"Lair," Carter corrects helpfully.

"Not to mention, the queen is expecting you at that ball tomorrow," Maeve chimes in. Damn me. Caught in my own web of lies.

"Then who's going to steal them?" I study the towering Apex prince skeptically. "You?"

He sighs. "I am also expected at the ball tomorrow. And I can't be seen to be anything but my father's dutiful son ahead of Samhain." His eyes darken with some inscrutable emotion.

"Then it's either me or Astrid," Carter says. "Maeve has no excuse to be in his lair, and she's never been down there."

Maeve worries her lower lip. "Astrid, what do you think?"

My eyes widen. She's asking her Apex's opinion?

"Although I am infinitely more subtle than the overlarge bird, his gift lends itself better to criminal activities," she drawls.

Carter huffs a laugh. "What a winning endorsement. Thank you, Astrid."

My curiosity practically explodes. "Alright, now I have to know. What's your gift?"

Carter passes his prince a questioning look and, still frowning, he nods in answer.

Then, right before my eyes, the Apex guardian disappears.

My mouth drops open.

"Can't say that I mind that look on your face, Wildcat," comes Carter's voice—*behind me*. I whip around to find him standing by the front door to my chambers.

"You just...you were here and then..." I sputter. I rear back as he reappears at my side. He uses one long finger to carefully close my hanging jaw.

"I can jump distances," he explains, far too nonchalant for someone who just *broke reality*. "Though only to a spot I can see—it's tied to my Apex vision. So I can't jump through locked doors."

"Oh, only that?" I ask in a sarcastic tone, still shaken. "Who else knows you can do this?"

He rubs the back of his neck. "The king. Lord Winters. The lord who runs my home territory. That's why I was commandeered as the prince's guardian."

With a gift like that... "Couldn't you escape, then? If you wanted to?"

Taran tenses, but Carter only lets out a chuckle. "Not with my bloodhound brother over here." He shoves his charge good-naturedly. "Besides, where would I hide? I would never want to put my family in danger. No, if I can't be home in Belmara, there's nowhere else I'd rather be."

I'm starting to realize there's not much daylight between the prince and his Apex guardian. They seem to read each other's thoughts, anticipate each other's actions, the way only people who have been close for years can do.

Watching them is...fascinating. I've never had the chance to witness Elite–guardian relationships up close before. I suppose I get to see Maeve and Astrid too, but Astrid is such an enigma, it's far less satisfying. With Carter and Taran, I'm up on that rooftop again, lost in the drama of other people's lives.

I cock my head. "So you can move quickly, but not through walls. How are you going to pick the lock?"

A crooked grin that must have been responsible for many a female swoon lifts Carter's mouth. "I was hoping you'd teach me, Wildcat."

My eyes narrow. "And you think you'll be using *my* lockpicks?" It's possible Carter doesn't understand the personal nature of the favor he's requesting.

His smile widens. "We're a team."

I groan. "Don't remind me."

"I'll let you know what to look for," Taran informs Carter.

I frown. "Wait, I don't get to look through the records myself?"

"We can't risk Lord Winters finding them missing," Taran explains. "Carter will have to review them and put them back in place."

"But—"

"Lynx." He closes his eyes briefly as if trying to get his emotions under control. "The amulet is the priority. It has to be."

Rule Number Nine: Leave no trace. My least favorite rule. In this case, it means *not* stealing something.

"Fine," I huff. If Carter can't find what I need, I'll break into that lair myself.

Taran unrolls a long scroll and spreads it out over the low table in front of me. It looks like some kind of—

"You have the castle blueprints?" I blurt out.

"We do. For all the good it's done us," Taran replies, his tone bitter. "Every time I think I've found it, its scent disappears."

I drop to my knees and examine the blueprints, my fingers tracing the intricate drawings. "Could they do that? Hide the scent somehow?"

Taran sits on the floor and studies the blueprints with me. "In theory. If there's some kind of ward around it. But they'd need an Apex gifted in setting them and I haven't detected any."

I blink. "But you have wards at every entrance to the castle."

"You mean the key signatures?" Carter asks.

"Yes, key signatures, blood magic, wards—it's all the same. Who set those?"

Taran growls, frustration radiating off him. "I don't know. My father contracted a man to come in and set them."

"Not a man," I point out. "A male."

"No, I meant what I said. I had already emerged when they were set. I would have detected him if he was Apex."

"Unless he can ward himself," I muse. Taran falls silent at that, a slightly stunned look on his face. "Do you remember what he looked like?" I ask, a theory forming.

"It was ten years ago," he protests. "But..."

"But?" I coax.

"I remember his eyes. They were unusual, especially in a human. They were yellow brown. I haven't seen eyes like that except in an—"

"Apex," I finish for him. "I'm almost certain you're describing the guild's key master. You said the Elite here contract with the guild for security, right?"

"Yes." Carter answers for the prince, who is lost in thought. "The king and the other Elite have brought them in countless times to secure valuables. The guild is an open secret in Veridia."

"Eleni," I interject suddenly.

Maeve's mouth purses. "The tailor? What does she have to do with this?"

My eyes catch Taran's. "She's coming here tomorrow. To bring my gown for the queen's ball. She's been working with the key master."

Taran blows out a breath. "It's worth a try. See what she can find out. Or what she might already know."

"I'll, uh, need another purse of gold for the guild, by the way." He waves his hand in acknowledgement, and I go back to examining the flawless blueprints. "In the meantime, show me where you've already looked."

We narrow down three potential places in the palace where I think the amulet is most likely to be based on their information and where they've already searched. Maeve and Astrid excuse themselves, and I spend the next hour teaching Carter how to pick a lock.

He's a fast study, but I still keep throwing glances at my closed door, worried Mei will be back any second.

"Wildcat." Carter snaps his fingers in front of my face, winning back my fickle attention. "Taran will tell us if she gets close, don't worry."

"Easy for you to say," I grumble. "You'll just jump away." I tilt my head, considering. "Have you ever tried—"

"Bringing someone with me?" He flashes that crooked grin. "Of course. Hasn't worked yet, but if you want to hold on tight, I'm willing to give it another go."

A low growl rumbles from the wall where the prince is leaning, arms crossed, as he monitors our little lesson.

I snort. "You are an incorrigible flirt."

Carter winks. "Only with the pretty ones."

"Alright, I think the Lynx has given you enough of her expertise," Taran cuts in. "You can practice the rest on your own time."

Reluctantly, I relinquish my lockpick kit to Carter. "I'll give it back," he promises me, tapping his pocket reassuringly.

"With zero damage," I hiss.

He raises both hands in surrender. "With zero damage."

Right before he disappears through the wall, I call out, "And Carter?"

He turns his head, waiting.

"Plan thoroughly, but when you're in the moment...act swiftly."

His mouth kicks up into that crooked smile. "Will do, Wildcat." And then he's gone.

"I don't like this," I inform Taran.

"What?" A distracting smirk pulls at his lips. "Not being the one in control?"

"No." Yes.

His gaze catches mine. "You're still in charge. Your role is just a little different for this heist. You're the distraction."

I think that over a moment. "The distraction, hmm?"

"Yes, the sleight of hand while Carter reviews the records." His smile fades. "I have something to ask you."

"What?"

"You're not going to like it," he warns. "But please take a moment to consider its implications for the heist—*your* heist for *your* prize."

I cross my arms over my chest and stare at him, unblinking.

His voice is a low rasp that curls my toes when he asks me, "What's your real name?"

"You're right, I don't like it. And I'm not answering that."

His brow furrows. "Any detail from your past could help. You say you don't remember your parents' names or your surname or where you hail from. But perhaps, your given name—"

"The answer is no." My voice drops to a murmur. "You already know too much about me."

"Funny, I don't think I could ever know too much about you." His voice is deep and rich, a quiet rumble. He's watching me with those swirling silver-gray hunter eyes. He reaches out, fingers brushing my temple as he tucks an errant lock of hair behind my ear. Goosebumps explode down the back of my arms, a shiver I can't suppress.

"What about you?" I manage to ask, my voice not as steady as I'd like.

A gentle smile. "You already know my true name."

I raise my chin. "But not much else."

"What else do you want to know?" Despite the openness of the words, his tone is guarded.

"Why don't you have a tattoo of Faunera's sigil like Carter?"

His eyes darken. "My mother wouldn't allow it."

I finger the chain he gave me. "What was it like? Emerging?"

He gives me a sharp look. "You really want to know?"

I nod.

"It was both the most wonderful thing and the most terrible thing to ever happen to me." One corner of his mouth lifts half-heartedly. "Wonderful because Eleni was right. An Apex's connection to their inner creature is like nothing else. It's as if one part of your soul was always missing but you didn't know until you found it. You're...complete. Whole. In a way that previously felt out of reach."

I've unconsciously leaned in towards the prince, caught up in the magic of his words. *Whole. Complete.* As someone out of place for all my life—at least the life that I can remember—with a gaping, broken place inside of me, feeling whole is all I've ever longed for.

One large hand slides up and cups my face, the pad of his thumb swiping my cheekbone. Once. Twice. Try as I might, I can't force myself to pull away.

"And the terrible part?" I whisper.

"I think the very worst part of emerging as an Apex might be happening to me right now," he murmurs back, eyes locked on mine. His other hand sweeps out and brackets my waist, pulling me closer. He leans down, close enough that I feel his breath ghost over my lips and—

His head snaps up, the hands cradling my body dropping away. Without a word, he snatches the blueprints from the nearby table and bounds through the open wall to the passageway. The door closes behind him as I blink, still frozen where he left me, staring at the stone wall.

What is happening to me? I should be cringing at his touch, not leaning into it. What is it about this prince that keeps pulling me in like a tether I can't escape?

"My Lady?" At least Mei's quiet presence explains Taran's rushed exit. "I did what you asked," she tells me proudly. "The tailor will be by with your gown tomorrow. In fact, she had already started work on it. She is to return with the coin the guild was promised."

"Of course," I mumble distractedly. "Nice work, Mei."

Her cheeks pinken with pleasure, but her head is tilted like her inner songbird. "Are you quite alright, My Lady?"

"You don't have to call me that when we're alone," I remind her. "You can call me Loriella." Even though that's not my name.

She purses her lips, and I know she's not going to do it.

"Mei," I blurt out suddenly. "Do you have a Faunera sigil tattoo?"

She blinks. "Yes, of course, My— Yes, I do. It was given to me the day I emerged." A flicker of pain crosses her delicate face.

"How did you end up in Veridia?" I ask in a gentler tone.

"I was a part of my lady's retinue when she wed a Veridian lord," she answers. I flinch at the words, delivered in such a matter-of-fact tone. Maybe it's because she's so unusually small, maybe it's her harmless gift, but when I look at Mei, I see a person. Not a dangerous Apex who deserves to be shipped off to a foreign land, far from friends and family, because she happened to be bestowed the gift of song.

The ache in my chest sharpens. "The guild promised to get you back home, is that right?"

She nods, her dark eyes wary, like she's afraid to hope too much.

"How will you hide your power?"

She looks down at her feet, long lashes brushing her ivory cheeks. "It won't be easy. I'll never be able to use my gift, which will be physically painful. My family will need to move—everyone in the town knows I'm an Apex."

"They do?"

"It's considered a shame on the family to emerge as Apex." Her words come out in a cracked whisper. "No one expected it." She gestures to her petite frame. "I have a younger brother who would be thirteen now. It's been four years since I've seen him. I'm sure they're all watching him, waiting to see if he's going to emerge as well. When someone is revealed to be Apex, their neighbors say—" She chokes off her words, overcome.

I stay silent. Just listening. I wonder how many people she's been able to share this story with before. Not many, I'd wager.

She visibly gathers herself. "They would say that the mother must have been seduced by an Apex. Or the god Jinai." The god of tricksters and liars.

I snort. "Always the woman's fault. The prince is proof enough that emergence isn't hereditary." A tear slips down her cheek, and that's enough to make me add, "Besides, I heard that an Apex's inner creature emerges when the person is ready to live in harmony with them. And nobody can harmonize like you, Meiling."

She lifts her tearstained face to meet mine. "Thank you, My Lady."

"Please"—I reach out and clasp one of her tiny hands in both of mine—"call me Lor."

Chapter 27

ALORA

The sight of Eleni outside my chambers, clutching a large white box, is enough to make my heart burst. I snatch her by one arm and tug her into the suite, slamming the door shut behind her. Without hesitation, I throw my arms around her slender neck.

"Wait! You're crushing the gown!" she shrieks through laughter, but I don't let go.

"I missed you," I murmur fervently, feeling like this hug is cracking open something inside of me. She's safe.

"I missed you, too. Now please let me put this down before you ruin all my hard work."

Sighing, I give in. She hurries over to the low table, sets the box down, then spins around and envelops me back into a tight embrace.

"How are you?" I ask once I finally release her.

"I'm good. Really I am." Her deep blue eyes shine with the truth of her words, and something in my stomach that's been tight since the day I was forced to leave her unravels. "I'm learning so much. The guild is testing my limits with their requests and my skill is improving every day."

I give her a level look. "Is that prick key master keeping his distance?"

A breathy laugh slips from her lips. "Not so much, but he's harmless. He's really talented at what he does." She cocks her silvery head to the side. "You two are actually a lot alike. If you could get over your inane pissing contest, you might even get along."

I can't help but roll my eyes at that. "At least he let you bring the dress."

She brightens. "Not just the dress. I'm going to get you ready for the ball." She squeezes my arm. "It'll be just like home."

A genuine smile takes over my whole face. "I have so much to tell you."

"I can't wait. But first—" She rushes over to the box, flings the cover off and triumphantly reveals an iridescent yellow-gold masterpiece. The gown shimmers with an otherworldly radiance, as if it's spun from threads of sunlight itself. Delicate embroidery traces patterns of blooming roses and intricate lace. This isn't just a dress; it's a vision in gold, crafted by fairy hands.

My breath catches. "Len...it's incredible."

She beams. "Harlan told me the queen is obsessed with her themes and the royal family is devoted to the sun god. So I thought, what better gown for a celestial ball than a tribute to Lumos himself?"

My brows knit. "Is that the theme?"

"Lor," she scolds. "Rule Number Eight."

"I know, I know." I shake my head, disgusted with myself, especially since I'm sure the queen regaled me with every detail.

Her eyes fill with concern. "It's unlike you to miss something like that."

"I've had a lot on my mind," I murmur, the image of flashing silver eyes burned into my brain.

"Well, now's your chance to tell me all about it," she declares.

I brighten, then replay her earlier words. "Wait, who's Harlan?"

A flush creeps up her entire face. "Um. The, uh, the key master."

My eyes narrow. "You two are on a first-name basis now?"

She shrugs. "We're working together. What did you expect?" Then she gestures towards the dress, deftly changing the subject. "Do you want to see how the skirt pulls away?"

I sigh. "No need. My only role tonight is to be a distraction." My gaze rakes over the shining gown. "And it looks like I'm going to fulfill that role perfectly, thanks to you."

"It's a full skirt. Your leggings will still fit underneath. Just in case."

"You have no idea how tempted I am to do just that. But I'll be in heels, and I might even have to dance. I don't want to risk them showing."

One fist shoots up into the air. "Finally! Oh, Lor, this dress is *made* to be danced in. Layers of satin and tulle—when you spin, it's going to be gorgeous."

"At least it matches my hairpin," I grumble.

She smiles slyly. "And hides your thigh dagger."

I grin back. "That, too."

She looks around the pretty sitting room. "Where can I hang this?"

"Oh, in the wardrobe. This way." I lead Eleni into the dressing room and help her hang her masterpiece. She oohs and ahhs about the luxurious furnishings, then hurries over and examines the tiny pots of cosmetics lining the small vanity.

"My Lady?" Mei's quiet voice pulls me around. She's standing in the doorway, dressed in her guardian uniform. "I'm just heading down to training. Hello, Miss Katsaros."

Eleni waves merrily from her place by the vanity table—they must have met at The Painted Mask.

"About that." I pull out the lynx charm, rubbing it between my fingers. I need Mei to stay away from training, but I also need to be able to grill Eleni in peace about the key master. "I have another task for you." I cast around the room and my eyes catch on the heavy purse Maeve dropped off this morning, grumbling all the while. "I need you to bring this gold back to the guild. Eleni is going to be some time getting me ready for the ball, and the Viper won't want to wait."

She blinks. "Very well, My Lady." I drop the coin purse into her waiting hands and send her on her way with instructions to be back in time to accompany me this evening. For a heartbeat, I consider that she might run off with it but quickly dismiss the idea. Even with a mountain of gold, she couldn't hope to be smuggled back home without the help of the guild. They're offering her something far more precious—she would never betray them.

Which means as much as I feel sorry for Mei, I can't trust her, either. The only person I can trust is Eleni, who's eyeing me speculatively right now. No, she's looking at my necklace, the charm still caught between my fingers.

"What's that?" she asks, coming closer and peering at the tiny lily. She gasps. "Are those real diamonds?"

"The prince gave me a longer chain so my lynx charm wouldn't be noticed."

A teasing smile lights my best friend's face. "Not just the chain, it appears."

"The lily was already there when he gave it to me." I hold it in my hand, and we both examine it. "Maybe it came with the chain. He must have bought it in Shanterra."

"I wonder when he would have had time to do that. Tell me, were there lilies in the ballroom the night the two of you met?"

"You mean the night he trapped me?" I correct, my tone bone-dry. "I'm sure there were. It was in Shanterra, after all. Why?"

"No reason!" she trills. "Let's get started, and then you can tell me why you made up that lie to get Meiling out of here." She pushes me towards the vanity chair with surprising strength.

I bite my lip, unsure how to start now Eleni's revealed her camaraderie with the key master. She begins to twist my long hair with ribbons to set the loose curls the Elite are so fond of.

"We think the amulet might be...concealed somehow. Warded, actually." I watch her expression in the mirror, but her eyes stay focused on her task.

"And you're wondering if Harlan had anything to do with it," she guesses.

"Yes."

"It's possible. Actually, it's more than likely." She shrugs, starting on another section. "I told you, he's tremendously talented. If anyone could set something like that up, it would be him."

"Do you think he's Apex?" I ask.

She finally meets my gaze in the mirror. "I don't know," she whispers. "I've never seen his eyes glow like the prince's or his guardian's. But the things he's able to make..." She shakes her head. "I just don't know how they would be possible without magic."

"Does he have a tattoo of Faunera's sigil on his chest?"

Her face flushes beet red. "How would I know the answer to that?"

I arch my eyebrows. "How do you think?"

She puts both hands on her hips. "Well, I don't know!"

"Alright. Sorry I asked."

With a sniff, she goes back to twisting my hair. "Does the prince have a Faunera tattoo?"

I shift on the stool. "How would I know?"

She pauses, her eyebrows raising to her hairline.

The corner of my mouth twitches. "No, he doesn't."

Eleni gasps, clapping one pale hand over her mouth. "Alora!"

I break into helpless laughter. "Relax. I just saw him shirtless in training, along with half the court."

She hums in acknowledgement. "What did he look like without a shirt on?"

My mouth goes dry. "Oh, you know. Like a—" I was about to say beast, but the word feels stuck in my throat.

"Mmmmhmmm. That good?"

I reach out and pinch her waist.

"Ouch!" she complains, but a genuine smile plays on her lips. "So, are you excited? To finally get the records and your answers?"

"Nervous," I admit, my stomach twisting. "And I hate that I won't be the one to lift them."

Her brow furrows. "Who's doing it?"

"Carter."

"Wow," she responds, drawing out the word.

"What?" I ask.

"Never thought I'd see the day where the Lynx allows someone else to run the op."

"He's not running the op," I protest. "He's just more familiar with the territory. And I can't afford to get caught before the amulet heist. Rule Number Five."

"Secrecy is your most valuable asset," she agrees, finishing my hair and starting on the makeup. "How high are these heels you're supposed to wear?"

"Too high," I mumble. I may have well-trained grace, but that doesn't mean I would choose to waste it on impractical footwear.

"Are you sure you'll be able to dance with the prince in heels? Wait a second, do you even know the dances?"

"As long as they're similar to what the Elite do in Shanterra, yes. And I won't be dancing with the prince. I've convinced the court I'm repelled by his Apex nature."

She brushes powder across the bridge of my nose. "And are you? Repelled by his Apex nature?"

My fingers twist in my skirts. "I should be," I murmur.

Eleni meets my eyes with a frank look. "Just be careful, alright?"

"I don't think he's as dangerous as we thought he was," I blurt out.

She tilts her head. "He's not, *not* dangerous."

"I don't think he'd hurt me." Oh my goddess, I sound like Maeve.

"Maybe not," Eleni allows. "But the king would. Or the queen. Or anyone else who discovered you breaking the law with an Apex."

"I know," I reply in a small voice.

She goes back to brushing cosmetics on my face. "Is there any truth to the rumor that they might grant an exception for the prince?"

"None. Maeve made it up as a cover to bring me here." I drum my fingers on my lap. "But unfortunately, it's also introduced another problem. There's a lady at court the prince used to be betrothed to before he emerged. She's still interested in him, and I'm gathering that she's the jealous type."

"Then it's a good thing you aren't planning on dancing with him tonight."

I look at my reflection in the mirror, slowly transforming into an Elite. "Good thing," I echo.

Len rests her chin on my shoulder and meets my gaze in the mirror. "Concentrate on getting the answers you need, alright?" I nod. "And, Alora?"

"Yes?"

"Make sure to dance tonight. Even if it's not with the prince." A smile she can't contain spreads across my best friend's face, her bottomless blue eyes shining. "Because I made that dress to *move*."

Chapter 28

TARAN

As always, her wild jasmine scent teases me well before she enters the room. I didn't think anything could be more enthralling than that. Until I finally catch sight of her.

She glows like candlelight, an amber flame lit from within. Off-the-shoulder sleeves frame a tight bodice that hugs her curves in golden fabric. My chain winks around her neck, disappearing down the gown's neckline where I know the charms hide. A little smile plays on her plush mouth; her eyes, framed by kohl-darkened lashes, look more liquid gold than amber. Loose chestnut curls spill down her back, and I long to wrap them around my fist and pull her close, just to inhale their scent. My hands flex at my sides.

"Careful, you're drooling." Carter's voice is filled with amusement, but his warning is real. I can't be caught staring at her. But how the hells am I supposed to look away? Half the lords in this room are turning their heads to admire—

"This is fucked."

Carter's attention snaps from the Lynx to me, his frown immediate. "What do you mean?"

I can barely grit the words out through clenched teeth. "I'm going to kill the first man who talks to her."

My friend laughs, but it dies when he realizes I'm serious. "Stop staring," he urges me under his breath.

I can't. My eyes are locked on her, my beautiful thief. *Mine.* Minute trembles rush down my body, and the tiny hairs on the back of my neck stand on end.

Carter steps into my line of sight, blocking my view of the dangerous creature, and an involuntary low rumble starts up in my chest.

"Shit. Tare, you've got to pull it together. Your father can't see you like this with her, do you hear me? It's for her own protection."

The rising growl tapers off as I blink out of a possessive, lust-filled fog. "Her protection?" I repeat slowly.

"Yes." Carter's words are low and urgent. "If any of them see you go berserk over the wildcat, the first thing they'll do is look into her. The king, Lord Winters—hells, Victoria will try to poison her tonight if you so much as dance with her."

My eyes squeeze shut unwillingly. They want to drink their fill of her, then strip that golden gown off her luscious body and—

"Fuuuuuck." I push out a breath and force myself to take small sips of air. It doesn't help—her scent laces everything, even across the packed grand ballroom. My fingers slip into my pocket, curling over the talisman secreted there.

My eyes fly open. "Get over there."

"What?" Carter looks genuinely worried, which is an expression I don't often see on him.

My hand shoots out, gripping his bicep hard enough to make him wince. I immediately lessen the hold, but the urgency in my voice is razor sharp. "Get over there and make sure no one talks to her."

"How the fuck am I supposed to manage that?"

"Carter," I growl, my eyes starting to warm, my voice deepening.

"Fuck! I'm going alright?" He yanks his arm free and rubs at the spot, glaring at me. "Go...go get yourself together or something. Remember, this is for her protection, alright? You're keeping your distance for her."

I know he's right. But I don't have to like it. I clench my jaw hard enough to break. "Get. Over. There."

After one last pleading look, he obeys me. Even letting *him* get close to her is physically painful. Especially when he fucking smiles at her—

"Your Highness."

I turn blazing eyes on the unfortunate page trembling before me. His voice tight with anxiety, the page chokes out, "Um, the uh, I mean, His Royal High—I mean, His Majesty..."

My head whips to the royal dais and I take in my so-called family. Vorrick and Tazira, the queen's guardian, stand to one side in matching formidable stances. The king and queen sit in the two large central thrones. To their right is the crown prince; beside him is an empty chair.

The queen is her usual bedazzled self, her face alight with the triumph of the event. My gaze softens when I see my half-brother. Understandably bored, the little prince is lounging so deep in his chair he looks in danger of falling to the floor.

I always wanted a sibling. Mine was a difficult birth, and my mother was unable to carry more children. That was one of the few bright spots of my emergence—Carter. Another new Apex grappling with how emergence had irrevocably changed his life. Training beside me, sitting with me in lessons—it felt like being gifted a brother. As my parents' relationship continued to deteriorate, he was a lifeline.

But there was guilt, too. He'd been ripped away from his own parents, his own siblings, all because of a gift from a goddess that must have felt more like a curse. I know it did to me. And that was before my mother—

I shake my head to ward off dark memories.

At least the melancholy trip down memory lane has wrested me from my creature-induced trance. I deliberately turn away from the source of that distraction and stride towards the dais, the relieved page scrambling behind me.

"Your Majesties." I dip my head in the barest approximation of a bow and slide into my seat on the other side of the crown prince. Prince Leo straightens, visibly mimicking my posture, which makes me smile and his mother frown.

"Glad you could make it, my boy," the king booms. I manage not to cringe at the endearment. Here we are, just one big happy family. My stomach churns with rage. Every day it gets harder to hide my true feelings.

I spy Lord Winters, deliberately stepping into my line of sight, an unsubtle move to block his daughter from my view. A cruel smirk lifts my lips. At least tonight has its uses.

But unfortunately, Victoria is on her way to accost another guest of the ball, and once my gaze has found her again, I'm riveted. The Lynx's eyes shine, not like an Apex, but with anticipation. She's eager to get her answers.

I very nearly kissed her last night.

The thought still burns through me, equal parts frustration and self-loathing. I'm so close—so godsdamned close—to getting the thing I've wanted for *eight years*. The only thing that's kept me going. And I almost threw it all away, acting like a schoolboy unable to control himself.

She's already proven her worth—with the blueprints, connecting the wards to the key master. For the first time in a long time, I feel a flicker of something I thought I had lost.

Hope.

I can finally end my father's secret reign of terror. Finally secure my vengeance.

What would I have done if she left? Especially once she gets those records tonight, there'll be nothing but her honor to stop her from taking off. And why did I think she'd be open to advances from the beast?

I wasn't thinking. That was the problem then, and it's the problem right now because, try as I might, I cannot tear my gaze away from her in that golden gown.

"Lady Thorne dressed for the occasion," my stepmother remarks, tone nonchalant. "It seems she has taken my advice to heart."

"What advice was that, my sweet?" the king asks.

"How to win an advantageous match," she simpers. "She may be from a little no-name border town, but if she plays her cards right, Lady Thorne will do quite well at court, I believe. As long as she keeps her priorities in line."

My eyes shift with the strength of my stoneclaw's emotion, and I still can't seem to rip them away from the Lynx. Especially as Victoria approaches her and Maeve, a calculating look on her face.

The king chuckles. "She could find no better tutelage than yours, my dear." The queen squeals, and I know he's grabbed her without bothering to look. He married the young Aquilon girl almost scandalously soon after my mother's gruesome death, and he's been foisting himself on her ever since. It's a wonder I have only the one brother. I'm sure they'd love to knock me further from the throne if they could.

"Let's have Lady Thorne over here so I can get a look at her," the king decides. It's enough to break my attention, my gaze swinging to my father. My stepmother pouts. She doesn't like competition.

"She's nobody important, My King," the queen whines.

"Nonsense. She has the queen's favor. We'll see that she makes a match befitting that gift."

And I try, I honestly try with every scrap of my remaining humanity to suppress the growl that slips from my throat, but I can't quite manage it. My father's emerald eyes narrow.

He snaps his fingers, and a page runs to his side. "Get Lady Thorne over here," he commands. "Now."

Chapter 29

ALORA

At first, I'm nearly overwhelmed by the grand ballroom. Glittering courtiers, most in varying shades of night, mill about, diamonds twinkling like stars on their persons. The decor is a reflection of the courtiers—rich velvet curtains the same deep indigo as the night sky outside contrast with the vaulted ceiling sparkling with star-like crystals hanging from elaborate chandeliers.

But it's the lavish dance floor that truly captures my attention. Circular and laid with a glossy obsidian surface, it reflects the crystals hanging above. At its center, the orchestra plays enchanting music, though no one is yet dancing. White roses lace the air with the queen's telltale perfume.

Maeve joins me, her bright hair cascading loosely down her back, a delicate silver tiara atop her head indicating her royal status. It winks with tiny diamonds, just like her twilight-colored gown.

"Maeve," I breathe.

"Yes, yes." She dismisses the compliment before it can form. She's staring at something, a determined look in her green eyes. I follow her gaze to a platform where four thrones rest, two guardians flanking them. I sneak a quick glance at them—the female has the same athletic build as Astrid, with ebony hair shorn close to her scalp. The male is huge with brown hair and eyes and an enormous battle-ax peeking out from behind his back. My stomach twists with nerves, and I quickly move on to humans atop the dais.

And then I see him—the mark. The man responsible for Taran's mother's death and that of countless others: King Elias Nyxley.

Scrutinizing the king, I understand for the first time why no one ever insinuates Taran's mother slept with an Apex or the god of tricksters and liars. The king is an older version of Taran. The same dark hair, mixed with ebony and dark brown, only threaded with silver. Deep-set eyes beneath heavy brows above a strong, square jawline. The only noticeable differences are the king's lighter skin tone and the brilliant, piercing emerald of his eyes that match the crown prince's.

"Are you related to the prince on his father's side or his mother's?" I ask Maeve.

She grimaces. "The king's side. The eyes give it away, don't they?"

I nod, distracted, caught up in examining the mark. I have to admit he's intimidating. Not as enormous as Taran, given he's human, but he's still imposing. Despite his age and privilege, he hasn't let himself go like other rulers might. He's in trim, fighting shape. He uses it all to his advantage of course—his looks, his stature. It's all part of the authority that drives his anti-Apex propaganda. My lips press together at the thought.

"Uh-oh," Carter comments, suddenly sipping champagne by my shoulder. "That's a dangerous look."

I tilt my head, considering. "What did it look like?"

"Like you've finally let the lynx out to play. And we should all be wary of your claws."

My mouth twitches. "You should be."

He chuckles. "Already was, Wildcat."

"Lady Thorne. Lady Ashbourne." Victoria's cool greeting pulls my attention away from the royal family, and Carter steps back.

If Maeve is beautiful tonight, Lady Winters is devastating. She's a starlight princess in glittering silver. Her platinum locks appear to be twinkling with actual diamonds. I remember Maeve saying Lord Winters oversees Veridia's mines.

"Lady Winters," I gasp. "Are those real diamonds in your hair?"

Her pink lips turn up into a smile that doesn't meet her eyes. "Of course." Her hand clamps my arm, tight enough to bruise. "Lady Thorne, you must tell me who your seamstress is."

"Oh." I laugh lightly. "I brought this gown with me from Nostura. There's a talented seamstress over the border—she's much in demand." A kernel warms in my chest at being able to boast about Eleni's talents, even here.

"You simply must give me her name. Now that we are such *close* friends." Lady Winters begins to drag me away with her grip on my arm. "Have you tried this evening's special cocktail? The queen designed it herself."

My mouth opens to protest—I'm not drinking anything this lady gives me—when, out of nowhere, a page appears at my side. "Their Majesties request your presence, Lady Thorne."

Lady Winters is far too refined to growl but her face says she badly wants to as she reluctantly releases my arm. I notice it only in the abstract because my pulse has kicked up, and my stomach is twisting with dread at having to present myself to the king. I take small sips of air, trying not to hyperventilate. A helpless laugh floats from my lips. It sounds slightly deranged.

A small hand slips into mine. Maeve's. She squeezes once, fortifies me with a subtle nod and pulls us to the dais where the royal family waits. Both rulers are in midnight blue, diamonds twinkling on their crowns amidst silver-wrought vines and roses. Sitting beside them is a young boy with curious beetle-green eyes and his mother's strawberry hair. I hardly get a look at Taran on the end except to note he is pointedly ignoring me, a chilling mask on his face. I understand it. Of course I understand it, but it still feels...wrong somehow.

We drop into simultaneous curtsies and hold them for a long, anxious moment.

"Rise." The king's voice booms. Aggressive. My eyes snap to his face, along with most others in the ballroom. "Niece, introduce us to your new friend."

To Maeve's credit, she never wavers. She lifts her chin as if she's a queen treating with a fellow ruler. It helps to steady my roiling stomach more than I would have thought possible.

"Your Majesty, may I present Lady Loriella Thorne from Nostura."

The king's penetrating gaze flicks to me. My earlier bravado has forsaken me, leaving behind an unsettling void where confidence should be. I can't put my finger on what it is that inspires such trembling anxiety in his presence—except, of course, I can. I know exactly what it is.

This man would have me put to death in an instant if he knew who I really was. This man could command his guardian to cut off my head using that battle-ax right here on the dais, as easily as breathing. I wonder distractedly if they would bother to clear my body from the ballroom or just dance around it.

The king's oily gaze traverses the silky clinging fabric of my gown. "I hear you are lucky enough to have caught my queen's attention, Lady Thorne." Out of the corner of my eye, I catch Taran's grip on the arms of the throne tighten. The king's attention narrows in on me. "I also hear you have a tiny poison catcher for an Apex."

"Yes, Your Majesty." I manage to speak without my voice cracking. A feat in and of itself. At that exact moment, the string quartet finishes their song. Anyone in the ballroom who wasn't watching this exchange is rapt with attention now.

"Unusual eye color. And you're tall for a woman." His tone makes it clear that neither of those observations are compliments. "It's almost as if *you* are the Apex and your guardian is the Elite." Silence hangs heavy in the ballroom, and I'm barely breathing. To be called an Apex by this man is no small insult.

Suddenly, the king laughs. It's not a pleasant sound. And just like his voice, it resounds out across the room, echoing off the mirrored floor and high ceilings. The queen, the young prince and the rest of the Elite join in. The quartet finally starts playing again.

The king's mouth is twisted into a cruel smile that doesn't touch his eyes. That laugh was pointedly at my expense—a performance meant to humiliate.

But I've known worse. I'm well acquainted with the insecure swagger of a bully who knows exactly where his weak spots are and is terrified someone will find them.

My eyes flick to Taran. His face is a perfect mask of boredom, as if he can't be bothered. His only tell is the white in his knuckles where he clenches the arms of the throne. It must be a trick of the ball's strange lighting, but the tips of his fingers look darker by comparison, almost disappearing into the wood.

The king tracks my gaze to Taran. But before he can continue his needling, the prince rises gracefully. He doesn't look at me. He doesn't look at the king. He stalks away...right towards Lady Winters, who has been watching this audience with a look of pure elation on her beautiful face.

Taran bows at the waist and extends his hand to her. "May I request the pleasure of your company for the first dance?"

She looks directly at me when she purrs, "I'd be delighted, Your Highness."

They sweep off to the dance floor, and I'm powerless not to watch them, along with the rest of the court. As I expected, they look lovely together. Her petite, shimmering form contrasts perfectly with his large, muscled, dark one. The way they move, his strong hands guiding her, is enough for whispers to erupt in their wake, courtiers casting glances between them and the dais.

I turn back to the king, who is watching the couple with an inscrutable expression, my presence completely forgotten. I was never the audience for that little demonstration anyway. Just a prop.

"Elias"—the queen smiles up at him sweetly—"are you going to show Prince Taran how this dance is properly done?"

It's precisely the right thing to say. Without even bothering to dismiss us, King Nyxley takes the queen's hand and leads her out to join the swirling crowd. Maeve grabs my arm in a death grip and slowly backs us up to where Carter stands, eye on his charge as the prince and Lady Winters glide across the dance floor. I glance around for Mei and find her shrinking against the wall with the servants and most of the other Apex guardians.

I take what feels like my first breath since the page beckoned us over.

"That could have gone worse," Carter notes.

"Absolutely." Maeve's already pale face is ashen, her brilliant green eyes standing out in stark contrast.

It abruptly occurs to me that I may have only half escaped this evening's gauntlet. "Where are *your* parents, Maeve?"

The lady swipes a champagne glass from a passing tray and downs half of it in one gulp. Color starts to return to her cheeks. "Back at our family seat in Rivermoor. My mother and father are spineless sycophants who prefer to use their connections to the crown to line their pockets from afar rather than stay and have to witness the obvious immorality of this court—an immorality they'd never have the courage to do anything about anyway."

"I'm sorry." It's woefully inadequate, but I'm not sure what else to say.

"Don't be. The late queen was more of a mother to me than my own ever was."

I watch Lady Winters laugh at something Taran said. They certainly don't look like enemies, twirling in perfect rhythm. Both Elite, no doubt trained in these dances since birth. A far cry from my checkered past.

"I'd dance with you if I could." Carter knocks my shoulder with his own.

"This isn't really my kind of dancing."

Carter snorts. "Mine neither." He casts me a sideways glance. "You know why he asked her to dance, right?"

"I don't care."

"Suit yourself."

But as the second song starts up, and Lady Winters remains clasped in Taran's strong hold, I have to admit to myself that I do care. But it's only my pride that's hurt.

At least, that's what I tell myself.

As niece to the king, Maeve is in high demand and has long since abandoned us. I'm a little miffed that no one has offered me at least one turn about the floor, but then I catch Carter visibly baring his teeth at a potential suitor. The Elite lord makes an abrupt about-face, skin blanched.

I elbow the captain in his nonexistent gut.

"Ow!" he complains. I know it can't have hurt.

"What the hells? When I said this isn't my kind of dancing I didn't mean I don't know how."

"I know you can dance," Carter assures me. "You forget, I was at the pearls heist. I've seen the way you move."

"Then why...?"

He grimaces.

"Lady Thorne?"

I swing my head to meet the gaze of a middle-aged man with pale blonde hair, festooned in broaches and rings and necklaces. My pulse picks up. "Lord Winters. How are you this evening?"

He smiles. "Very well, thank you. May I have this dance?"

My hand trembles as I extend it to meet his. "I'd be delighted, My Lord."

As we make our way out onto the dance floor, I shoot a look over my shoulder at Carter, but he's already gone—off to find the records. My role as a distraction has officially commenced.

A waltz starts up, and Lord Winters' hand finds my waist. I lift my voluminous skirts and rest my opposite hand in his. It's easy enough to follow his lead, and I paste a demure smile on my face, waiting for him to speak first. There's no way he asked me to dance for my sparkling personality; there's always a motive.

Rule Number Seven: Information is power.

His frost-blue eyes study mine—with my heels, our gazes meet easily. "My daughter tells me you're from Nostura."

An innocuous start to an interrogation. "Yes, My Lord. My grandfather was a Shanterran dignitary, so we have always lived close to the border." He sweeps us around a turn, and as promised, the skirt of Eleni's gown billows around me, the golden fabric catching the light and scattering it in a thousand tiny sparks.

"Ah, I presume that's the source of your Shanterran Apex guardian, then?" he asks in a carefully nonchalant manner.

I keep my face relaxed. So Mei is the impetus for this conversation. Has Victoria told him she can taste lies? More than likely. My heart quickens for just a beat as I worry he might inform the king. But what can they do to her? She's already an Apex.

"Yes, my grandfather was gifted Mei by a visiting friend." We spin into another turn, and the layers of satin and tulle whisper against each other in a delicate symphony.

"That's a powerful thing to give away," he remarks. I fight to keep my hand in his relaxed.

I laugh, a courtier's laugh for show, tossing my long hair. "If I'm being honest, My Lord, I believe a wager may have been in play. You know how men are."

He smiles politely. "Of course. How long has the Apex been in your family's service?"

I smile back, buying myself time to think. "Well, I believe that—"

"Excuse me, Lord Winters." A gravelly voice, tight with repressed irritation, breaks into our conversation. Lord Winters and I come to an awkward stop amidst the still-twirling Elite. My eyes lift to meet glowing stormy gray.

"May I cut in?"

Chapter 30

ALORA

"Of course," Lord Winters replies smoothly, dropping my hand.

"B-but," I protest.

The lord sends me a pitying look. "We'll continue our conversation another time, Lady Thorne." He bows (noticeably only to me) then strides off the dance floor.

I'm in Taran's arms and moving again before my mind can catch up. But when I do—

"What. The. Hells," I hiss.

He's watching me with an equally dark expression, his eyes flashing brighter than I've ever seen them. "I was saving you."

"From what?" I demand in a harsh whisper. I twist in his grasp, craning to look around his massive frame to see where Lord Winters has gone. But the prince only tugs me closer, effectively blocking my view with his towering form.

"From Simon. He was doing what he always does, inserting himself where he doesn't belong." His hand around my waist grips tighter.

The heat of his palm burns through layers of fabric, and I fight the urge to shove him off. "The only one inserting themselves where they don't belong is you," I seethe, every word under my breath. "I was distracting him while Carter went for the records! Or have you already forgotten?"

The song comes to a close, and the couples around us separate, their polite applause drowning out the music's final notes. Taran doesn't let go. Instead, he steps even closer so that when the next song begins—another, slower waltz—he's able to sweep me right into it. His hold is possessive as he expertly leads us across the floor. Our every word is hushed, but this entire conversation is still a gamble.

"Your Highness," I start, which earns me a low growl. But what else does he expect me to call him in the middle of the dance floor? "I'm not even supposed to be dancing with you. I told the queen I find you repellent."

His head dips close enough that his breath fans my face. "I couldn't stand it, alright? Is that what you want to hear?"

My brow puckers. "Couldn't stand what?" He swings me out into a turn, and appreciative murmurs erupt as my dress floats around me with the movement, sending refractions of light bouncing across the obsidian floor.

"You," he snaps as he reels me back into the cage of his body. "In someone else's arms."

My mouth parts, but no words come out.

The fire in his gaze banks for a solitary heartbeat and something about his softened expression reminds me where we are and sends me into abject panic.

Reality crashes back in. I drop the prince's hand and duck beneath his arm, easily breaking the hold. I back up quickly, like the night I tried to escape out of Count Zhao's window, until I feel stone beneath my feet. Then I whip around and start pushing through the courtiers. I'm not sure what the expression is on my face, all I know is that I need to get out, out, out before I make even more of a scene we can't afford.

"My Lady." A smooth voice I recognize but can't immediately place is at my side. I seize the offered arm gratefully and let him guide me through the throng. We're finally out of the crowd, climbing a large stone staircase, when I sneak a peek to my right and stop cold.

"*You.*"

The key master winks. "Don't stop now, My Lady, we're almost there."

"Where?" I demand, refusing to move another inch until he answers.

"Somewhere we can't be overheard," he murmurs, gesturing up the stairs. "Now, if you please?"

I send him a menacing glare worthy of Maeve, then gather my skirts to climb the stone steps. At the top are double doors leading out onto an enormous wraparound terrace, wide enough to be another ballroom. A few courtiers linger, taking in the night air, but the wind whips their words away from us.

The key master guides me to the terrace edge, far from the other Elite. As I step closer to the edge, the wind snatches at my thin dress. The key master passes me a sympathetic look.

"My apologies. I chose this spot because I knew the wind would make it more difficult for us to be overheard. I forgot you'd be wearing…" He gestures to my elaborate gown. "This."

"I'm fine," I reply, but then my teeth clatter and betray me.

"Here." He shrugs off his black formal coat and holds it out to me. I want to decline it, but I don't. Unlike a real lynx, I don't have fur, just yellow-gold silk.

I slide it on and cross my arms over my chest, eyeing the key master with suspicion. "What do you want?"

His eyebrows arch. "Straight to the point."

I pull in a steadying breath. "I'm in the middle of an operation that you promised not to interfere with and I'm not clear what you're doing here."

"That's fair." I stiffen as he reaches forward into his coat pocket and slides out a cheroot cigarillo and a matchbook. "I'm not here to interfere," he assures me as he lights it. "More to…keep an eye on things. This is my territory, after all."

"I thought it was the Viper's territory," I counter sweetly. "And you already sent someone to keep an *eye* on things."

"Ah yes, the Shanterran." He shrugs. "I was under a time constraint. Meiling is not the most ideal asset. Untrained. Easily swayed."

"Did you send me a tiny songbird on purpose to try and scare me off?"

He smiles around the cheroot. "Maybe I thought you'd appreciate the challenge." He exhales the smoke out over the terrace half wall, and my nose wrinkles at the acrid scent. "Or perhaps, I was looking for an excuse to send the little songbird back to her people. Who can say?"

My lips turn down at that last bit. It never would have occurred to me that this man—or male—wanted to help Meiling. "Just trying to do your part for a fellow Apex, then?" I say in a casual tone.

His focus narrows on me. "Careful, Lynx. You speak of things that don't concern you."

"I disagree. I've learned about a few *key* signatures put in place by a certain local *consultant* that could be critical to my finishing this operation and going *quietly* on my way."

"And who's been telling you tales of key signatures, hmmmm? The king's niece, perhaps?" He takes another puff.

"Sounds like your asset is more valuable than you give her credit for."

"She has her uses." He cuts me a sideways glance. "Perhaps if you would share what it is you are looking for, I *may* be willing to assist. For the right price, of course."

"Of course," I murmur back.

"And for your silence," he continues in an even tone. "Naturally, once you are finished with the operation, there'll be no need for you to stay in Ravenscrest, and no need for you to speak of anything that occurred here. Or for anyone else to, for that matter." He levels me a hard look.

"Naturally," I agree.

"I'll give you a bit of time to talk it over with your...associate." I tilt my head, considering. If I didn't know any better, I'd say this criminal is concerned about Maeve. "But don't take too long, Lynx. Your house of cards is eminently close to collapse. Speaking of—" He takes one last pull of the cheroot, then crushes the nub beneath his boot. "Looks like you may have gotten a bit more than you bargained for with the beast." His strange yellow-brown eyes rake unashamedly over my figure. "Next time, ask the little tailor to tone it down a bit, yeah?"

"What do you mean?"

A terrifying snarl ripples through the night air. Both our heads snap to the terrace entrance. Courtiers scatter like pigeons, falling over themselves to rush back into the building, dodging the source of the threat.

The Veridian prince's glowing eyes are fixed on us as he stands across the terrace, his broad shoulders tense. He doesn't move. Watching. Waiting. He's giving the witnesses a chance to leave. Astrid stands just behind him, helpfully holding the door open for the distressed courtiers to file through.

"He had his guardian warning off anyone who tried to dance with you. Or so much as approach you." The key master eyes the prince speculatively. "I do hope you make up your mind quickly because I doubt you'll be maintaining that cover for much longer, even with the Elite lady's help. Good luck, Lynx." His lips curl into something that isn't quite a smile. "Jinai willing, you manage to keep your head. The tailor seems rather fond of it."

Without sparing me another glance, the key master walks with unhurried strides past the prince to the ballroom entrance, pointedly ignoring the seething glare cast in his direction. As soon as the key master disappears through the door, Astrid moves to block it with her body.

The terrace has been emptied of revelers. And now the door is blocked.

A menacing stoneclaw stalks towards me.

Chapter 31

ALORA

"Who the fuck was that?" the prince demands the moment he reaches my side.

I lift my chin. "The key master."

Taran casts a glance back to the terrace doors where Harlan has already disappeared. Except for Astrid standing sentry, we're alone.

When his gaze returns to mine, a guilty expression has replaced the fuming Apex. He opens his mouth as if to respond, then abruptly freezes, his entire body going preternaturally still. Slowly, so slowly, he cocks his head to the side in that predator way he has, silver-gray eyes thinned to slits, his nostrils flaring.

"Are you wearing his clothing?" His low growl raises the hairs on the back of my neck.

At first, I'm not even sure what he's talking about. And then it hits me. Harlan's coat. "Yes. I was cold," I snap.

The prince pulls in a deep breath as though attempting to gain control. "Lady Lynx, I recognize that you are rightfully angry with me. I know we need to talk about what happened in the ballroom—"

"You mean what *you* did in the ballroom—"

"But," he continues over the top of me in an even tone, "at this moment, I feel as though I am holding on by the very tips of my fingernails and you are rapidly shredding what remains of my resolve. Would you please, for the love of all the gods, *take that coat off*."

My eyes narrow. "Is this an Apex thing?"

"Yes. It is...an Apex thing."

I throw my hands in the air. "Fine." Shoving the over-large coat down my shoulders, he reaches out to help. In two heartbeats, the suit coat is off my body and in his hands.

With absolutely no warning, he hurls the key master's coat over the balustrade as if it's on fire. It catches the air like a black bird, fluttering down out of sight. We both stare after it, the prince dragging down gulps of the icy air as though he's surfaced from deep water.

I raise my eyebrows.

Taran takes one last deep, calming breath in—and screws up his face like he's smelled a decaying rat. Lip still curled in distaste, he shrugs off his own formal coat and drops it over my shoulders. The prince's familiar rain and pine scent envelops me along with the borrowed warmth of his body, and the tension eases slightly from his expression.

He steps into my space, pulling his enormous coat closed by the lapels. "Better?" he asks in a low rasp that makes me shiver, though not from the cold.

I meet his smoldering gaze. "Shouldn't I be the one asking you that?"

Instead of answering, he maintains his grip on the coat, crowding me with his huge frame and backing me up along the terrace edge. "My dear Lady Lynx. You have the most intoxicating scent I have ever experienced. Like an explosion of jasmine, hot in the sun. But the combination of his and your scents together..." My back hits the cold stone of the turret wall, and my eyes widen. The prince continues to invade my personal space, leaning closer until his hair brushes the skin of my neck. His hot breath grazes the shell of my ear as he murmurs, soft as a lover, "It makes me want to kill him."

A gasp sneaks out of my throat, whether due to the shock from his words or the rumble of his tantalizing voice that close to my ear, I can't tell.

"I am feeling an almost undeniable instinct to follow that criminal's scent down those stairs and rip him apart with my bare hands." He leans back only enough to make sure I can see the flash of his savage smile. "Or maybe my teeth. Probably both, frankly."

His words should scare me. I should be running away in terror of his stoneclaw's overly possessive temper. I should absolutely not, under any circumstances, feel this taboo thrill, this illogical instinct driving me to push him further. But here I am, anyway. "I'm not wearing his clothing anymore," I point out. "I'm wearing yours."

His eyes heat. "Yes, you are."

"You're unhinged," I complain, but my traitorous voice is breathy.

He finally drops the lapels of the coat, staying close enough to touch. "Never claimed not to be."

I shift against the wall, the cold of the stone seeping through the fabric. "That didn't sound like an apology."

His eyes darken to silver-gray storm clouds. "I'm sorry. I shouldn't have asked you to dance. I shouldn't have cut in when you were trying to distract Lord Winters. I abandoned the plan we all agreed to, and I'm sorry for it," he repeats.

"Why did you?" My words are soft, easily lost to the whipping wind, but he hears them anyway.

Taran braces his hands on the wall on either side of my head, caging me in as he searches my face for something. "I think...it might be the linking. The books did say it would bring my instincts to the surface. Make them more intense. And mine are—protective."

I shake my head. "We only tried it a few times." I wave at his too-close body in illustration. "And I believe you mean *possessive*, not protective, as the bigger danger here is clearly your murderous impulses over my choice in dance partners."

"I danced with Victoria because I didn't want to draw any more attention to you than I already foolishly had," he says in a complete non sequitur, raking his hand through his coal-black hair until the waves are deliciously mussed. "I thought my dancing with her and not you would get Victoria and my family off your back. Keep you safe. It's the same reason I couldn't stand to see you with Simon." He finally retreats, giving me some much-needed breathing room. "I'm barely restraining myself from ripping a man's arms off because you wore his coat for probably five godsdamn minutes."

"We need to stop this, whatever *this* is. Whatever the linking is doing to us, I don't want it." And now my voice is the one that sounds reedy with desperation, but I can't help it. It's not only his instincts that are worrying me.

"I think you're right, Lady Lynx." His worried expression is a mirror of my own. "The linking is obviously bringing too many of my creature's instincts to the surface. I'll resume the search for the amulet on my own."

"But that's the whole point of me being here!" I protest.

He buries his face in his hands, and his next words come out muffled. "I know."

With gentle fingers, I pull his large hands away, revealing his face. Silver eyes find mine, full of too many emotions for me to name. "Taran," I murmur, his bigger hands still clasped in mine.

He leans forward, hanging on my every word. "Yes, My Lady?"

It takes me a moment to steel my spine well enough to ask the question. "This doesn't make sense, but...is there something else it could be besides the linking?"

The prince jolts back, making me drop his hands. The cool night air rushes over my body as soon as he's no longer there to block it. "Why—why do you ask that?"

Because I'm not an Apex, but I've been feeling it, too. Because I've felt connected to you and unable to escape it since the moment I first heard your voice. *Because I sensed your stoneclaw.* "Just a feeling."

His right hand slides into his pocket. "There's something I need to tell you—"

The terrace doors bang open, and our heads swing to the entrance. Astrid is already closing them behind Maeve and Carter, who rush to join us by the turret.

I set aside this fraught conversation for another time. "Did you get to the records? Did Lord Winters catch you?"

Carter sweeps into an overelaborate bow, presenting me with my lockpick kit as though it's a crown. "Good as new, My Lady."

I snatch it back, a smile forming. "Thank you."

"I managed to waylay Lord Winters," Maeve cuts in with a pointed look at her cousin. "Carter got the time he needed."

My stomach feels full of rocks as, for the first time, I consider what happened in the ballroom after I stormed off. "Does anyone suspect...?"

"Running off was the best thing you could have done," she assures me. "Your cover is intact." She sends a sidelong glance at Taran. "Though His Majesty's interest in you is piqued."

A muscle tics in Taran's jaw.

"What did you find?" I practically beg Carter.

His eyes dart to the prince.

"You first, Lady Lynx," Taran insists. "What did you learn from the key master?" I turn a frustrated glare in his direction, but he's unmoved. "We need to be sure *all* of our covers remain intact," he reminds me.

"He knows about Maeve, but I don't think about any of you."

Maeve nods. "We knew that much after Meiling saw us together."

My heart pangs. I wish I didn't have to treat Mei like a foreign spy, but she's the guild's asset. I already knew, and Harlan just upheld it. "He didn't confirm that he's an Apex, but he didn't deny it, either." I pull Taran's coat tighter around my body. "He offered to assist. For the right price."

"This is becoming an expensive endeavor," Maeve mutters.

"It's more than worth it," Taran counters in a sure tone. "Anything else?"

"He wants our silence." I frown, thinking. "I can't be sure who he's most worried we'll tell his secret. And he wants me and Eleni gone when this job is done." With a start, I realize he only specified that *I* had to leave Ravenscrest. I'll have to worry about that another time.

"What's your opinion?" Maeve surprises me by deferring to me over her cousin. "Do you think we should take his offer of assistance?"

Reluctantly, I shake my head. "Not yet. We still have a bit of time. I want to try searching those places I picked out on the blueprints first. The key master is a last resort." My eyes find Carter's, the torchlight reflecting their glow. "Now tell me what you found."

He looks stricken. He keeps glancing at Maeve and Taran as if they'll relieve him of this responsibility somehow.

"Carter, whatever it is, just tell her. She can take it," Maeve says, surprising me for the second time in as many minutes.

He lifts his chest and refocuses on me. "First, I looked back at the older records. From when your parents might have emerged. Nothing. No lynx as an inner creature, no power having to do with memory manipulation—nothing that points to an Apex being your parent."

My heart sinks. For the first time, I consider there might not be any answers waiting for me here at the palace. Taran places a supportive arm around my shoulders, and I don't shrug it off. I'm too disappointed, and it feels too comforting.

Carter pulls in a deep breath. "But..."

I perk up. "But?"

"I remembered Taran said you were fifteen when you were found in Shanterra. And you told Maeve that first night on the road that you're twenty-five. So I checked the records from ten years ago."

My heart stops. Vaguely, I'm aware of the arm around my shoulders tensing.

Carter pushes out a loud breath. "There was a female who emerged. With a lynx as an inner creature. Auditory. Her gift was—"

"Languages," Taran breathes from beside me. All the blood drains from my face.

Carter nods. "And possibly even the ability to crack codes. There was a question mark written there; I don't think they had the chance to examine her."

Examine her.

Me.

My body is frozen solid, just another column of stone on the terrace.

"What else did the records say?" Maeve prompts, with a concerned glance in my direction.

Carter shoots me a pitying look. "That she was from Lord Temshal's territory. That the royal guard came to pick her up to commandeer her for the palace, but—"

"Go on," I rasp. I feel torn in two. As if I'm floating above, looking down at myself saying the words.

"But the girl had disappeared. Her parents were the only ones there."

"What happened to them?" Taran asks for me.

"Dead," he answers.

"Killed," I correct, my voice trembling. "For her disappearance." I can't bring myself to say *my*. I turn in the circle of Taran's arm and meet his conflicted gaze. "This can't be—it isn't true, right? I would know, *you* would know—"

"You smell like a human to me," he confirms. "I can't sense any inner creature or power level. But—" I raise my hand to stop him there, yet he plows on. "The ache you described, the feeling like an essential piece of you is missing. That's what it would feel like to be without your creature."

Maeve crosses her arms over her chest. "So what, someone somehow removed her creature and made her human again?"

Taran shakes his head. "No, that's impossible. If she's the one in those records, she's Apex. It must be...buried somehow. In hiding." He frowns. "I've never heard of someone losing the connection with their creature after emerging without..."

"Going feral," Carter finishes in a grim tone.

"You're sure that entry was about her?" Maeve jabs her head in my direction. "You said her scent is human. Her eyes don't glow. I understand the timing matches up, and there's the lynx thing, but still."

"There was something else," Carter admits. "Something that might confirm whether the lynx they're talking about is our Lynx or not."

I shut my eyes, unable to look at them as they talk through this impossible possibility—one that's somehow feeling more and more possible.

Taran's thumb rubs my arm in soothing strokes. "What is it?"

"I know you don't know your surname, but the entries are meticulous. They recorded everything. Even...even the first names. The name of the girl, the one who emerged with a lynx as her creature, was...Alora."

Chapter 32

TARAN

Alora. The name shoots through me like wildfire injected into my veins. My heart pounds so hard, it's a wonder the others can't hear it. And alongside each quickening beat, her name rings in my ears. Alora, Alora, Alora...

The Lynx—*Alora*—sways, and I automatically shift my arm to encircle her waist, propping her body against mine.

"Did she faint?" Carter asks, guilt shadowing his eyes.

"She did not," Alora replies, but her voice is tense and small trembles shake her body.

Maeve snorts. "She's a professional guild thief. The best in Shanterra. Of course she didn't faint." I shoot my cousin a grateful look, but her attention is hyper-focused on the girl in my arms. "Lady Thorne and I need to be getting back to our chambers if we're to have any hope of making it there unnoticed." Maeve's tone is purposefully unconcerned, as if Carter hasn't just dropped a massive bomb that changes almost everything.

"I'll walk you back," I respond immediately.

"You most certainly will not," Maeve counters. "If we escape tonight without scandal from your rash decisions, it will be a minor miracle. No, the thief and I will walk back through the ballroom together."

A low growl rumbles through my chest. "She can barely stand."

"She is right here," Alora interjects, pushing out of my half-embrace. "I'm fi—"

My eyes begin to shift. "If you try to say you're fine, so help me—"

"Alright, I'm not fine. Far from it. I don't know what to think or how to feel right now. But I want to be alone, and the very last thing I want is to blow my cover." And fear, real fear flickers across her face. It's the first time I've ever seen it. Sure, she's been anxious around me, occasionally intimidated. But it was always cut by that calculating, devious mind, seeking to turn anything and everything to her advantage. Never this naked panic.

"Shall we?" Maeve holds out one slender arm, and to my surprise, Alora hooks hers through it. "Wait," Maeve interjects. "Take off Taran's coat first."

Before my stoneclaw can object—which it wants to, emphatically—Alora slides the coat off and hands it back to me without meeting my gaze. I reach for her hand, but she pulls back quickly, already turning away with Maeve. Astrid opens the ballroom door and disappears through it behind them. I take a measure of comfort that the formidable guardian will be at their side, though there's little risk of anything worse than gossip in their path.

"Gods." Carter groans, rubbing his temples. "That was brutal."

My gaze is still trained on the ballroom doors. "I feel as if I've hardly processed it. They left in such a hurry."

Carter winces. "I think the wildcat preferred to be with another human after that news." His eyes widen. "I mean, a human. Faunera, this is confusing."

"I don't detect a hint of her creature or her power. But..."

"But?" he prompts.

"There's always been this undercurrent of *wild* to her scent. I'm not sure how else to describe it." I shrug.

He stares out at the dark night beyond the terrace. "Do you think the entry was really about her? That her name is Alora? She never confirmed."

I know it is. "Yes, I do. You saw her reaction when you said the name." Not to mention my own.

My friend's attention swings back to me. "How do you feel about that?"

"What do you mean?"

He snorts. "What do I mean? I mean, how do you feel about the fact that the Lynx is *also* an Apex and therefore not a forbidden human?" His voice drops, and he growls out what I assume is meant to be an impression of me, "'Get over there and don't let anyone talk to her, or I'll kill them.'"

I stiffen. "In truth, I'm conflicted. A part of me is incredibly relieved that maybe there's an explanation for why my creature has been so...possessive around her. Maybe it has something to do with her creature being buried and wanting to pull it to the surface."

Carter gives me a skeptical look. "Perhaps. And the other part?"

I sigh. "Even if she discovers her creature again and truly becomes an Apex, does that mean there are fewer obstacles in our path? She's not really an Elite. When she's done with this job, she'll need to leave the city or face the wrath of the guild. She might be better off as a human, able to return to her life in Shanterra as a guild member. Nothing to hide." My stoneclaw seethes beneath my skin at the thought. I catch my friend's gaze. "Would you choose to be Apex? If you had the choice to remain human?"

He cocks his head. "It's hard to even consider. I can't imagine giving up the connection with my gryphon for anything. It's an essential part of who I am."

I nod. "She doesn't know what that feels like. All she knows is that if anyone discovers she's an Apex, she'll lose her freedom overnight." And for a bold thief used to making her own way in the world, that would feel like the biggest loss of all. Of course she panicked.

"Still, she might be willing." One side of Carter's mouth pulls up as he gives me a pointed look. "If there was a prize to be had."

"I'm no prize. Apex aren't allowed relationships, remember? This changes nothing."

He grins. "Who said anything about a relationship?"

I level him a hard look, but he's already shifted back into his typical teasing nature. "Now that we know she's Apex, maybe I have a shot. What do you—ahhhh!"

I leap for him, arms raised, canines extended, but come up with only air. He's jumped using his power and is now behind me and doubled over with laughter. I snarl half-heartedly.

"Relax, Prince. I'm not going to take your girl. Though I could, just so you know. My powers of seduction know no bounds."

I reach for him, and he reappears behind me once again. I spin around, frustrated. "She's not—" I was about to say she's not mine, but I can't force myself to form the words.

Carter's laughter dies out. "I've never seen you like this."

"I've never felt like this," I admit.

"What does it feel like?" he asks, and if I didn't know any better, I would almost describe his tone as vulnerable.

"Like I'm being pulled to her by something beyond my control. Something I can't see, something I can't fight. Like I would destroy anyone who even thought about hurting her. Including myself, if I was the one who was going to hurt her."

He clasps my shoulder. "You won't, Tare."

I shake my head. "You don't know that." A shudder ripples through me. "It's happened before."

My friend's eyes darken at the memory. "Never again."

"Never again," I vow.

Chapter 33
ALORA

I can't force myself out of bed the next day. I tell Mei I drank too much at the party, and she fetches me toast and other bits of food that pile up beside my bed where they sit, ignored.

I wish I could sleep. Instead, I lie awake, staring off into nothing. The ache is still there, dulled now, smothered by the numbness of the fog.

Maeve storms in at one point, shouting at me, but I refuse to meet her furious gaze. Eventually, she gives up. Neither Taran nor Carter would risk coming in, not with Mei sat in the corner of the room on a stool, quietly embroidering.

And then, not so quietly. A hauntingly beautiful lullaby rises, and her sweet, clear voice washes over me. I remain frozen beneath my covers. But it soothes one tiny piece of my jagged soul.

It's enough that I can focus on Maeve's words when she returns hours later.

"Get the tailor," she commands. Mei jumps up and hurries out the door.

I miss her singing.

Maeve drags the stool over to the side of the bed I'm facing and perches on it, a scowl marring her heart-shaped face. "Tare searched two of the rooms you picked out on the blueprint. Both of them, nothing. But the third—he thinks he caught a whiff of the amulet."

I stare back at her, unblinking. My heart, so dulled, detached, doesn't so much as stir.

She huffs at my non-reaction. "It's the old throne room. The one used by the former queen and the king. Taran won't go in there because—well, I can't get him to go in there, but he agreed to walk closer than he ever has before, and he *thinks* he may have scented it." A note of cautious optimism creeps into her voice. "I believe we might have finally found it, Alora."

I close my eyes at the sound of that name on her lips. At the memory of how she learned it.

"I'm sorry this happened to you. That this is the truth of your past. Clearly, I cannot begin to imagine what you are going through right now. But we need your help." The warmth of her fingers closing over my ice-cold hand forces my eyes to blink open. "We need you to do what you came here to do and get. That. Amulet. *Please.*"

I pull my hand free, rolling over to face the other wall. A deep sigh, then the sound of the stool scraping tells me she's standing. Presumably to leave. Instead, there's a knock on the door to the suite.

"My Lady, you are required to attend to the front courtyard at once, by order of His Majesty King Elias Nyxley," a young voice calls, high-pitched. I don't recognize it.

"Very well," Maeve replies, but the other voice stops her.

"Lady Thorne must attend as well."

"Lady Thorne has taken ill and is asleep. Too much sparkling wine at last night's ball," she stage-whispers.

"You'll have to wake her, My Lady, and with haste. His Majesty was very clear. Every person in the castle is to attend immediately. Your Apex will be there already."

"What is the event?" Maeve sounds unsettled in a way I've never heard her before.

"I can't say," the voice replies firmly. "Now, I must go, My Lady. I need to inform the rest of the castle."

The door closes with a soft thud. Maeve turns on me, ripping off my covers. I roll over to meet her wild eyes.

"Get up," she snaps, before rushing out the door. She returns nearly immediately with a green dress the same shade as the royal crest, presumably from the dressing room. She tosses it at me, growling when she sees I haven't moved an inch. She strides towards the bed and hauls me to a seated position by my arm, her pale fingers digging into my flesh deep enough to bruise. "You need to be dressed and in that courtyard within five minutes. If you aren't, everyone will wonder what's wrong with you. And if they start looking into Lady Thorne from Nostura, her dignitary grandfather, and her tiny Apex who can allegedly taste lies—"

"Noted." My voice cracks from disuse. I slide off the bed, and she helps me fasten the dress, her fingers flying over the buttons. I locate a pair of black slippers and slide them on as she roughly drags a comb through my bedhead hair. She spares one final second to look me over, her eyes catching on the gold necklace with its two small charms.

"Tuck that into your bodice," she hisses. Her eyes, wide with anxiety, compel me to obey. Something has her spooked.

"Maeve. What is this?"

"Nothing good," she mutters. "Alright, this will have to do. Let's go." Just as she did last night, she hooks an elbow through mine, practically dragging me out of the suite. We meet a throng of courtiers, servants, and guardians, all streaming towards the front of the palace. My heart rate kicks up as the crowd's tense apprehension begins to break through the numb cloud that's enveloped me since Carter said my true name last night.

A wooden platform stands at the center of the courtyard, with a dais for the royal family extending out to one side. Whether by happenstance or design, the crowd has arranged itself in distinct groups. To one side are the guardians, eyes glowing and clearly on edge. On the other side, clustered between the platform and the royal dais, are the human palace staff—ladies' maids, gardeners, housekeepers and cooks. And positioned in the center, with a direct view of the stage, is a growing throng of Elite lords and ladies trading excited whispers.

Maeve heads straight there, and I can't help but tense, dragging my slippered feet to slow our approach. I spy Victoria near the front with her small posse, but not her father. My heart rate slows just a bit at his absence.

The royal family files in—or rather, just its human members. The crowd cheers for the king, and he waves good-naturedly before settling into his seat, his wife and young son following his lead.

"Where's—?" I begin to ask Maeve, but another roar of the crowd snaps my gaze to a well-dressed figure taking center stage.

The adulation for Lord Winters lasts longer than for the king, and he stands there, arms wide, soaking it in. I glance around in confusion. The Elite around me are eager—they know what to expect next and are ravenous for it. I open my mouth to question Maeve again, but the words die in my throat.

A figure in restraints is being shoved onto the platform. Snarling and snapping at the crowd. Every drop of courage I've managed to gather drains out of me. My knees nearly buckle, and it is only Maeve's arm in mine that keeps me upright.

It's Ethan.

The sweet boy, always with a smile peeking out from beneath overgrown copper locks, is nearly unrecognizable. His uniform is torn, and wounds cover his body, but he doesn't seem to notice them at all.

Instead, he's acting like a cornered creature, his face twisted into a menacing snarl, his eyes glowing with an animal-like sheen. A raised red mark peeks out from beneath his torn tunic.

And standing behind the wild broken boy that used to be Ethan, his tormented eyes fixed on mine, his gigantic silver sword at the ready, is the beast prince.

I don't know how he found me so unerringly, tucked within this crowd of bodies. The sword sags in his hands as I experience that same feeling again.

The one from when we first met. Where everything else falls away but the male looking at me from behind silver-gray stoneclaw eyes.

Lord Winters' voice breaks our connection. "People of Veridia."

Another roar greets this simple address, and it takes him a few moments to calm them again, an indulgent smile playing upon his lips.

"I come before you today with chilling news." He pauses for effect. "Another Apex has gone feral." The human crowd gasps and shouts. One woman near me actually faints. They are already primed for hysteria, like tinder ready to be lit.

"This was a promising Apex, promoted to the palace guard." Lord Winters' tone is dramatically regretful. The crowd boos, but the lord admonishes them. "No, no, it's true. Even Apex can serve their purpose. As long as we know who holds their leash!"

The cheers are deafening. Winters grabs his prince by the arm and shuffles him to the front. The symbolism is clear. Taran is the protector, the one able to scent and capture these dangerous creatures. But more importantly, he is one of the "good ones." An Apex tethered by his own Elite leash.

Taran's face is a block of stony rage. He speaks not a word. But it only serves to better complement Lord Winters' narrative of a savage species that needs taming. My gaze darts to the other side of the platform to see how this story is playing out amongst the guardians. All of their eyes are shining bright, and their expressions range from murderous to panicked to carefully masked.

"I give you your protector, the Apex hunter himself, Prince Taran Nyxley!"

The crowd goes wild. More Elite women faint. Excited murmurs of "The beast prince!" assault my ears.

It's entertainment, I realize dully. A twisted play, meticulously staged. And this lord is a master at directing it.

Winters gestures to the two guardians at Ethan's side, who carefully escort the hostile guard to the forefront. Carter wrestles with one of the boy's shackled arms, his eyes empty. I spot Leylah, eyes red-rimmed, dirt smudged across her face on Ethan's other side.

The lord sweeps out of the way, giving the crowd a full view of the spectacle. A cacophony of jeers explodes. Pages scatter through the Elite crowd, handing out rotten fruit and refuse for them to throw. Props for the performance. The projectiles rain down, pelting Taran, Carter and Leylah just the same, though none of them so much as flinches.

It's not until they're forcing Ethan to his knees that the truth hits me like a slap in the face. I'm about to watch this innocent boy be executed right in front of me. My breaths are coming too fast, my heart is pounding in my ears, and I'm desperate—*desperate*—to do something, anything to stop this from happening. But I can't. I *can't*.

I surge forward anyway, a futile instinct to intervene. Maeve anticipates me, holding me back with surprising strength and hissing commands in my ear. I finally sag, defeated, in her arms.

"Don't look," she murmurs. But that's impossible.

Bearing witness feels like the last thing I can give to this innocent child of circumstance, who will never shoot an arrow or blush cherry-red again. Despite that Ethan is well and truly lost to his creature—his snarling face holds no hint of a human soul—I keep my own eyes trained on his glowing pale green ones.

Until Taran raises his sword.

And cuts off Ethan's head in one brutal stroke.

Chapter 34
ALORA

I don't remember getting back to my room.

Maeve must have maneuvered our way out of the crowd and through the palace. I vaguely recall Eleni shouting at her—notable in its strangeness—before someone thrusts a glass into my hand. I automatically take a draw of the bitter liquid, then erupt into a coughing spasm.

When I've finally caught my breath, Eleni's worried face is peering up at me. She's kneeling in front of me as I sit slumped in one of the blue armchairs. Maeve is ensconced in the other chair, and Mei is wringing her hands in the corner.

I risk another sip of the brandy and manage to keep it down this time. I rarely drink, but this is steadying. I must have been in shock.

"I'm sorry," I mumble. I'm not sure why.

Eleni's eyes widen. "Are you alright?"

I open my mouth to tell her I am, but instead, to my absolute horror, a sob bursts out. She doesn't hesitate—she wraps me in her arms as I cry in earnest for the first time since that prick in Shanterra made me into a laughingstock.

It's all too much. Ethan. My own fractured self.

Ethan. The look on Taran's face when he saw me in the crowd.

Ethan. Caught between two opposing worlds when I want nothing to do with either of them.

And again, Ethan. Will his family ever learn what happened to him? Or will the letters just stop coming?

It takes me longer than I'd like, but I manage to reel in the emotion and pull myself back together. I wipe my face with the clean towel Mei hands me, her face stricken.

Certainly a crying jag is out of character for a notorious spy and thief. But letting go of the dam seems to have helped. I take a deep breath and, holding one of Eleni's slender hands tightly, ask Mei to please give us a moment.

Hurt stains her dark eyes, and I'm sorry for it, but I need to tell Eleni the truth of my past, and I can't do it in front of her.

Rule Number One: Trust in the Guild. And no one else.

"You can wait in my room," Maeve offers. "Astrid will be along shortly, I'm sure."

As soon as Mei's gone, I recount everything that's happened since Eleni left me last night, leaving nothing out. She stiffens and gasps and covers her mouth but remains, by and large, silent throughout, still clutching my hand.

And when I've finished choking out the entire story, my throat closing over, she rises to standing and envelops me in another hug. More tears streak down my face, and I wipe them away angrily. "I understand if you don't want to be around me anymore."

She pulls back abruptly. "What are you saying? You're my *sister*, Alora. In all the ways that count. I wouldn't care if you transformed into a real, live lynx with pointed teeth and claws."

"She won't," Maeve assures us. "I've been surrounded by Apex my entire life, trust me." There's something comforting in her no-nonsense, brisk manner in the face of all of this uncertainty.

I smooth a hand through my mussed hair. "But I *could* go feral. And hurt you. If I even want to, if I'm even *able to* get my connection to my creature back, it will be a torn, damaged thing." My jaw clenches. "When a sweet soul like Ethan can go feral, it means it can happen to anyone. Especially someone with a broken connection."

"Now you listen to me." Eleni grabs my face in both hands, staring into my eyes with a fierce look. "You and I are family. We had each other when we had no one else, and I'm not letting *anything* get in the way of that."

I shudder, pulling out of her grasp and looking away. "You didn't see it, Eleni. His humanity was lost. He wasn't even remotely present. He looked like a restrained wild animal."

Her eyes soften, empathy settling into her features. "A mercy to have it end then."

My head snaps up as her words register. A mercy. The only one Taran could give him by that point. A swift death.

For the first time, I am able to separate this horrible event from my own selfish worries and personal trauma to think about how the prince experienced it.

I catch Maeve's gaze. She nods imperceptibly. *I know you think you know him, but you don't.*

"How can he stand it?" I murmur. She knows what I mean. How can he serve as the figurehead for this reprehensible thing? How can he keep executing his own kind? For eight long years.

"He bears it because he must," she replies simply. "Because it's the only way to stay in the fight." She leans towards me, her tone even. "And it's why I must ask you again to help us. Every time he has to do this, I watch another piece of his soul chip away. I'm asking—" She chokes off. "No, I'm begging you. Help me save him before there's nothing left."

The wall of my sitting room swings open.

"Someone's ears were burning," Maeve mutters, but the prince only has eyes for me. He strides directly to my side, and Eleni jumps up, scurrying to Mei's former spot by the wall. To my utter shock, he drops to his knees before me, grasping my hand in both of his large ones. His face is wiped clean, but his military uniform is stained from the pelted fruit.

"I'm so sorry you had to witness that," he breathes.

My mouth pops open. "You're apologizing to me?"

His silver eyes are shadowed with what might be self-loathing. "You only just learned you're Apex, and you had to see one go feral. And watch me execute him in cold blood." He bows his head, wavy dark locks falling, covering his face. "If you no longer feel safe in my presence and want to leave Veridia, I understand."

Maeve makes an exasperated sound in the back of her throat.

I cut her a pointed look. "Maeve, Eleni, could you give us the room, please?"

"Where are we supposed to go?" Maeve protests, spreading her hands. "Mei is in my chambers."

Eleni grabs her hand and shuffles her awkwardly to my bedroom. "Take all the time you need," she assures us.

At the same time, Maeve snaps, "You have two minutes."

It's enough to quirk my lips, but Taran doesn't react. His face remains downcast.

I reach out with my free hand, lifting his chin until his eyes meet mine. A sharp breath escapes me at the sorrow that blankets his face.

"It's not your fault," I whisper.

Taran barks a short, mirthless laugh, and it's horrible. "Then whose is it? I'm the one who just removed an innocent sixteen-year-old's head from his body." I swallow a lump in my throat, and his hands tighten on mine. "You need to leave, Alora. You and Eleni. Get out of here while you still can, while you still—"

And all the rest of the numbness that's enveloped me since yesterday evaporates like steam. I lift my chin. "I didn't know any Apex before I came here. I believed the stories we were told." I shake my head. "I don't know if I'll ever find my creature again. I don't know if I *want* to. But I know it's not right that the Elite control the Apex. And that's not even taking into consideration the amulet." The words come out defiant, sure. Perhaps the king really did love the former queen. Maybe this misbegotten crusade is all to avenge the woman who was taken from him. But that doesn't make it right. All of my earlier malaise has left, leaving resolve in its wake. "I'm not leaving. We made a deal. You held up your end, now I'm going to hold up mine."

"I release you from our bargain," he insists. "Please leave, *please*. I can't—" He shakes his head.

"Can't what?" My voice is barely audible.

Silver-gray hunter eyes meet mine, and the anguish in them takes my breath away. "I can't let anything happen to you. Not again, not after..."

Oh, *oh*. After first his mother, then his friend—possibly lover—were killed.

"Nothing's going to happen to me."

"You don't know that. You can't know that." He drops my hand and starts to stand, but I stop him with a hand on his cheek. He freezes at the touch.

"Taran," I murmur. He shudders, a full-body shake that travels all the way down his large frame.

One of his hands reaches out and smooths my hair back from my face, gentle beyond what should be possible for this enormous male. His eyes, shining faintly with that predator glow, search mine for a long, silent moment. "I like it when you call me that."

"Better than 'Your Highness?'" I tease, but my heart is pounding, that invisible tether pulling tighter and tighter with every breath.

His eyes darken. "In certain instances, I could grow used to that, too. But I prefer it when you use my name." And in that moment, I know, down in my bones, that I'll never refer to him as the beast prince ever again. Almost tentatively, his hand reaches under the heavy curtain of my hair and cups the back of my head. He hesitates, then asks, "May I call you Alora?"

The sound of my true name on his lips when he's looking at me like that—the room suddenly feels stifling. I clench my thighs together against the pooling heat, hoping he won't notice my body's reaction. But his nostrils flare, and I know there's no hope of that.

"Yes," I answer—anything to break the cloying tension.

That beautiful smile takes over his whole face.

"I'm not leaving," I say again.

"Alora," he says, like he's tasting the sound of my name on his tongue and deciding how it feels. "Last night, when you asked me whether I thought this connection between us was something other than the linking—"

"So is she staying or not?" Maeve's strident tone cuts through the air, and we pull away from each other self-consciously. I catch Eleni's wide-eyed stare just beyond Maeve.

My cheeks heat. "Staying."

Maeve releases a breath. "Good. Good. Then we need to plan our next steps."

Before Taran can protest again, I say, "Maeve said you think you sensed the amulet."

He frowns, leaning back into a seated position on my rug. "Yes. Near the old throne room. It was faint but...unmistakable."

"How do you know what the amulet smells like?" Eleni asks frankly. "Have you ever seen it?"

"Once," Taran replies, which fires up my curiosity, especially since the king and Lord Winters believe he knows nothing about it, but his tone warns us not to interrogate any further.

Rule Number Six: Plan thoroughly, act swiftly.

I jump up and begin pacing. "I need to start surveillance. I need to see for myself inside that room to learn what we're dealing with in terms of security and begin to make a plan. No point in robbing the manor if there's no coin in the safe. But we can't tip anyone off, or they'll only make it even harder to get in." I turn to Maeve. "Is there something coming up? Some kind of social event for the court when I could slip in there unnoticed?"

Taran rises to standing and stops me with a hand on my arm. "I don't want you anywhere near the amulet—I'll do it."

"You don't need to worry about that anymore," I remind him. "I suppose there's one silver lining to my heritage; the amulet can't force me to emerge." The rest of the words get caught in my throat—the reason the amulet can't hurt me is because I already emerged as Apex. It doesn't feel real yet. It feels like something I can ignore and it will go away. The ache in my chest pangs as if to dispel my foolish state of denial.

"There's a hunt day for the lords and ladies in three days' time," Maeve cuts in. "If Taran said he was going, Victoria would go, which means Lord Winters would likely attend too to ensure he doesn't get too close to her."

"No," Taran growls.

Eleni tilts her head. "Alora may not be able to get into the room anyway." We all turn and stare at her, and her cheeks pink. "I mean, there's probably some kind of lock on the door that requires a key signature."

I slap my forehead. "Gods, I'm an idiot. You're absolutely right, Eleni. There must be some kind of ward dampening the scent if you've never noticed it before."

Taran clears his throat. "That's likely true, but that's not why I didn't realize it was in that room."

My and Eleni's brows furrow in unison.

"His mother died in that room," Maeve tells us in a soft voice. My face slackens.

Taran releases a sigh. "I don't go into that wing. Ever. For obvious reasons. Looking back now, it makes sense—that room would be an ideal place to hide the amulet, but—" He shakes his head. "I allowed my emotions about the...event to cloud my judgement." His tone is measured, careful not to reveal too much.

I school my expression, not letting any trace of pity show. "Then it's time."

"Time for what?" Maeve asks.

Now it's my turn to sigh. "Time to ask the damn key master for his help."

Chapter 35

ALORA

"I'm coming with you," Taran demands for the fifth time since he appeared through my wall this morning immediately after Mei left. Convenient, although, considering his gift, I suppose the timing wasn't by accident.

"You're not," I shoot back, not even bothering to look at him. I sift through my wardrobe, finally selecting the darkest cloak to drape over my navy belted dress. Despite the ladylike attire, I'm armed for anything: sturdy black boots, suede leggings, my thigh dagger, and another in my boot. I even cut a slit in the gown for easier access to the thigh dagger. Preparation is critical. "You're not coming for two reasons, both of which I've already explained to you."

I finally meet his frustrated gaze. "The first is my cover. I'm going into Ravenscrest, under the guise of a protected Elite, accompanied by my Apex guardian, to do a bit of shopping." I arch an eyebrow. "Do you frequently escort Elite women who want nothing to do with you on shopping trips into the city?"

I don't wait for an answer—and indeed, none is required. "The second is my and Eleni's guild membership. I don't know if I'll be able to return to the Shanterran Guild after this. But I'll make damn sure Eleni has that option. Which she won't if the key master even suspects I've been working a commission job in his territory. And he'll know that's exactly what I've been doing if you accompany me." For the final touch, I slide my shining golden hairpin into my dark locks.

Taran grinds his teeth, obviously wanting badly to continue arguing and having absolutely no grounds on which to do so.

"Now, if you'll excuse me, I have to go meet my carriage."

"Carriage? You're not riding into the city?"

I wince. "Mei can't ride." And as much as I would have preferred the fresh air, the carriage *is* the more appropriate means of transport for my cover.

My cover that feels simultaneously as fragile as a cobweb and more important than any I've ever had to maintain. I'm not just hiding the fact I'm a thief, which would be bad enough—I'm hiding that I'm an Apex. I don't even want to imagine what the royal family would do to me if they found out. An Apex masquerading as an Elite? Speaking with the king, taking tea with the queen? That level of insult would demand retaliation. I shudder just thinking about it.

"What?" Taran asks.

"You can't scent my creature, right?" I confirm again, needing reassurance.

"No," he answers firmly. "Never. And besides, no one else has my gift. Even if I did sense it, I wouldn't tell anyone."

"I know." It should be enough to assuage my concerns, but I don't think anything will until this job is done and I'm back in Shanterra. The hole in my chest throbs again. Coming to Veridia was supposed to be my homecoming, a place where I didn't stand out as other. Where I could find the answers to my past. Instead, the answers I longed for have only set me farther apart.

Can I even go back to Shanterra with this massive secret hanging over me? Xinlei's words from that final night in Heshan ring in my head: *There is no reburying the truth once uncovered.*

Taran is studying me with an inscrutable expression, and I fear my worries are playing out over my face. "Of course you're right about me not attending," he finally acknowledges. "Besides, this meeting is nothing any thief worth her salt couldn't handle. Much less the Lady Lynx."

My lips tip up into a half-smile. "I'll let you know if I secure the key master's help to enter the old throne room."

"*When* you secure it, tell Maeve, and she'll get word to me. She's already spread the word that I'll be attending tomorrow's hunt." He frowns, and I know he's thinking of Victoria.

"What's the prize?" I ask.

His frown deepens. "A black boar that gored one of my father's favorite horses."

"The ladies are attending a boar hunt?"

"No, no, of course not. The queen is releasing a snow-white hare as well. Probably matches whatever her inane theme is for the event."

I smirk. "I wouldn't have thought you even knew the revels had themes."

An answering smile tugs at his lips. "Maeve is attempting to tutor me in politics. Though she has proclaimed me hopeless, so I can't say for how much longer she'll deign to share her expertise." He tilts his head. "I rather enjoyed the celestial theme, however. Pass my and the court's admiration on to the tailor when you see her today, will you? Even the queen remarked on the gown."

"I will. She'll like that."

"You looked magnificent in it. Like a goddess made of sunlight. I don't know if I told you."

My breath catches. "No. I believe you were too distracted by my wearing the key master's coat." He scowls, and my lips twitch. "I need to get going."

"Of course." But his silver gaze holds mine a moment longer. "I haven't thanked you yet. For helping me find the amulet. For getting us closer than we've ever been to ending this."

"Thank me after the heist," I tell him. "With gold, preferably." If I can't go back to Shanterra, maybe I can convince Eleni to start a new life with our winnings. Somewhere far from Ravenscrest. The thought is so sharply painful, it takes my breath away.

It's nonsensical, the pull I feel to this male. Is it because my creature is in hiding and he can sense others' creatures? Does my lynx long to be discovered? That could explain the disaster of the attempted linking.

He cuts me a serious look. "Lady Lynx, if you pull this off, all the gold in the royal treasury won't be enough to thank you."

My lips curve. The nickname is growing on me. "But it'll be a nice start."

Chapter 36
ALORA

The key master meets us at the door of The Painted Mask, similarly ensconced in a dark hood. "Not here," he mutters, pushing past us into the street.

Mei and I exchange a confused look. It's not as if we're conspicuous. We left the carriage back in the tony shopping district and made our way here on foot. I glance back at the Veridian Guild headquarters, pained to miss seeing Eleni.

But Harlan is already striding away without bothering to check if we're following. With a growl, I chase after the key master, Mei fast on my heels. We wind our way through the cobblestone streets, passing stucco buildings painted various shades of blues, pale greens, and peach. Even with the chill in the air, greenery spills over the flat-topped roofs and from planter boxes. The palace is its own kind of mastery, but I prefer being here, exploring the city. I hope Eleni has had the opportunity to venture out more than I have, especially as we'll likely need to flee in haste once this job is over.

As the crash of waves against the docks increases in volume, I realize we're heading towards the marina. I pick up my pace and match strides with the aggravating key master. "Is this really necessary?"

"Yes," he replies shortly. We pass through an enormous gate, open wide, and under the high stone walls. The guards in city livery barely give us a passing glance, such is the volume of traffic heading in and out. To my surprise, Harlan makes a sharp right instead of continuing to the marina, making for the deserted shore where the aqueducts let out. The place where Taran and I first entered the palace under cover of night.

"Here we are." The key master flings back his hood, settling onto a stone, his face tilted to the warm sun glinting off the water.

I follow suit, removing my hood and glancing around at the deserted cove. "You're that concerned about being overheard?"

His strange eyes narrow. "You would be too if you had any sense."

"In the palace, of course. But among your own guild members?"

Rule Number One: Trust in the Guild. And no one else.

He shrugs but doesn't respond.

If this male really is an Apex, he's perhaps the sole person who understands my predicament—the only other one who's managed to maintain his anonymity and escape from servitude to the Elite. I still can't be sure whether he's Apex or even whether I am, but if it's true, we share something few, if any, do.

He stares back, content to remain silent, as any well-trained guild member would. I'm the one who asked for this meeting—it is on me to make the first play.

"At the palace...you offered your services, should I require them."

"I remember," he replies. "In exchange for you wrapping up this job with haste and leaving this country."

I start. "You said I needed to leave Ravenscrest."

"I've since decided that's not far enough." The sun reflects off his yellow-brown eyes, making them shine. "Also, I require your silence and the continued silence of your...colleagues."

"Lady Ashbourne, you mean." I decide to just say her name outright, in hopes of determining whether he suspects I'm working with anyone else.

"*Anyone* privy to your plans," he replies evenly, spearing a pointed glance at Mei.

"I won't say a word," she whispers, barely loud enough to be heard above the nearby surf.

"No, you won't. You'll be silent as the grave," he agrees, the threat clear.

"You promised to return Mei back to her family in Shanterra," I cut in. "Or don't you keep your bargains in the Veridian Guild?"

He scowls. "My word is good. As long as she holds her tongue, she'll be returned to her family upon your departure from this country."

That same ache throbs at the thought of leaving. The answers I longed for have brought me only more questions. How can I leave what might be my homeland without finding out more? The briny scent of the ocean, so different from the crisp mountain air, taunts me. How can I return to my life in Shanterra as a human thief when I might be a Veridian Apex? How can I stay, knowing discovering my creature means lifelong servitude to the Elite?

"What about Maeve?" I demand.

His eyes turn calculating. "How exactly did you wind up with the king's niece as an asset?"

"That's my business," I reply coolly.

"Unless she's your client," he counters. "In which case, the Viper will be *very* interested to learn that you are indeed operating a job within her territory."

"She's not." *Rule Number Three: The best lies are mostly true.* "As you said, she is an asset. Our interests...align. But you need not fear her speaking out of turn. And any deal we make would need to include her safety."

He studies me for a long moment. "Very well. But I will be watching. If I even suspect she has shared secrets with—"

I keep my expression purposefully neutral. "She won't."

"Then I suppose the only point left to discuss is my payment."

My eyes narrow. "I've already paid your Viper twice what her silence is worth."

"Ah, but can you truly put a price on silence?" A sly smile curves his mouth. "In any case, that coin went to the guild coffers. This deal would be directly with me. For *my* services."

My brow furrows. What kind of guild is this? I would never consider taking a job without Xinlei's knowledge or approval. Guild membership is its own form of protection and level of professionalism. For the first time, I consider that Harlan may have set those wards without the Viper's permission. That he may be the only one with the knowledge of the amulet.

"Fine," I snap. "But this is the last time."

"I expect the same amount you gave the Viper. Both payments."

I scoff. "Certainly not."

He spreads his hands, his confidence irritatingly smug. "What are your other options, Lynx? You said it yourself—no one else can give you the access I can."

I pretend to fume. I don't care about the gold—no doubt Taran's coffers are plenty deep. But if I were funding this venture myself, I'd at least attempt to negotiate. Appearances matter.

"I'll let you take the tailor with you when you leave," he offers, as if he hasn't just thrown around the safety and personhood of my best friend as a deal sweetener.

And now my outrage is real. "Why, you little—"

"You must know she adores Veridia," he cuts in. "Ravenscrest is just the kind of cosmopolitan city where a talented woman like her can thrive. The Viper is more than pleased with her services and would happily make her an offer to stay—if I proposed it." His lips kick up into a sneaky smile. "I'd be willing not to, of course. Provided we can come to an arrangement today."

His manipulation is no less effective for being obvious. Can I really take this opportunity from Eleni? The chance to stay somewhere her skills are valued, where her foreign heritage doesn't hold her back?

"It's her choice," I grit out. "You'll get your godsdamn gold, but it's her choice whether to stay in Ravenscrest." A plan begins to form. If Taran and Maeve can help secure passage on a boat to Thalassar, I'll have something else to offer her when this job is done. Something beyond returning to our ill-fitting lives in Shanterra. An adventure.

"As you wish."

I raise my hand. "Then we have a deal?"

He holds up one finger. "Not so fast. You haven't yet told me what you're attempting to access. I know it's not the palace—clearly, you have no problems getting in or out of there." He gestures to the aqueducts behind us, and I pretend to be confused.

"Is there a secret entrance to the palace? That might come in handy for my exit." Especially as the passageways empty out nearby the marina and beyond the city walls. There's no telling if Taran will be on hand to assist with extraction.

The key master's mouth tightens. "We'll discuss that possibility after you share the location you need access to."

I turn to Mei, guilt tightening my chest. "Mei..."

She ducks her head. "Of course, My Lady. I'll wait for you by the city gate."

She scrambles out of sight, Harlan monitoring her. "Still don't trust her, I see. Is that because she's an Apex?"

Little does he know. "It's because she's your spy."

"You're about to reveal the location to me," he points out.

I level him a direct look. "This is the location of my prize. The fewer people who know about it, the better. I expect you to keep this to yourself."

He nods, a measure of respect flickering in his eyes. "Very well. And the location?"

I extend my hand again. "First, promise to keep the location a secret from *anyone*. Including Mei and the Viper." And the king and the lord you set the ward for, I mentally add.

He rolls his eyes. "Fine." He clasps my hand, shaking it once firmly. "It's a bargain."

Without letting go, I murmur, "The old throne room."

That fast, the cool blade of his dagger kisses my throat. "Ah, ah, ah," he tuts. "Don't even think about it."

I hesitate, my free hand already on the hilt of my own weapon, tucked into my thigh sheath. Harlan presses the dagger harder into my flesh until blood trickles down my throat. With a huff, I release my dagger, raising both hands in the air. "You're making a mistake."

"Am I? Is your prize the amulet or is it not?"

My lips press into a thin line.

"Tell me what you know," he demands. "Why do you want the amulet?" His eyes narrow. "Who are you trying to steal it for?"

"I told you, this is personal—"

"Personal?" His laugh is a sharp, mocking bark. "Yes, yes, personal business. I've heard that song and dance before, but I'm afraid it's not going to work this time."

"It's the truth," I hiss. "Now will you help me get into the throne room or not?"

We hold each other's gaze. For a heartbeat, I think I see his piercing yellow-brown eyes glow with Apex luminescence, but it's gone before I can be sure it's not just a trick of the light reflecting off the water.

He finally lowers the knife. "Not. You're on your own, Lynx."

My heart skips, then speeds up doubletime. "But—"

"But nothing." A door slamming shut. "And not that you deserve my advice, but I'll give it to you anyway. For free. Forget all about the amulet." His eyes turn haunted. "Nothing good will ever come from that cursed thing."

"Your silence—"

He pulls up his hood. "We made a bargain. The location of your prize won't cross my lips. But heed my warning, Lynx. Go back to the Shanterran Guild and your life as an infamous thief stealing pretty baubles from unsuspecting Elite. Pretend you never heard of that gods-cursed amulet." He pauses, his figure silhouetted against the crashing waves. "Your life may well depend on it."

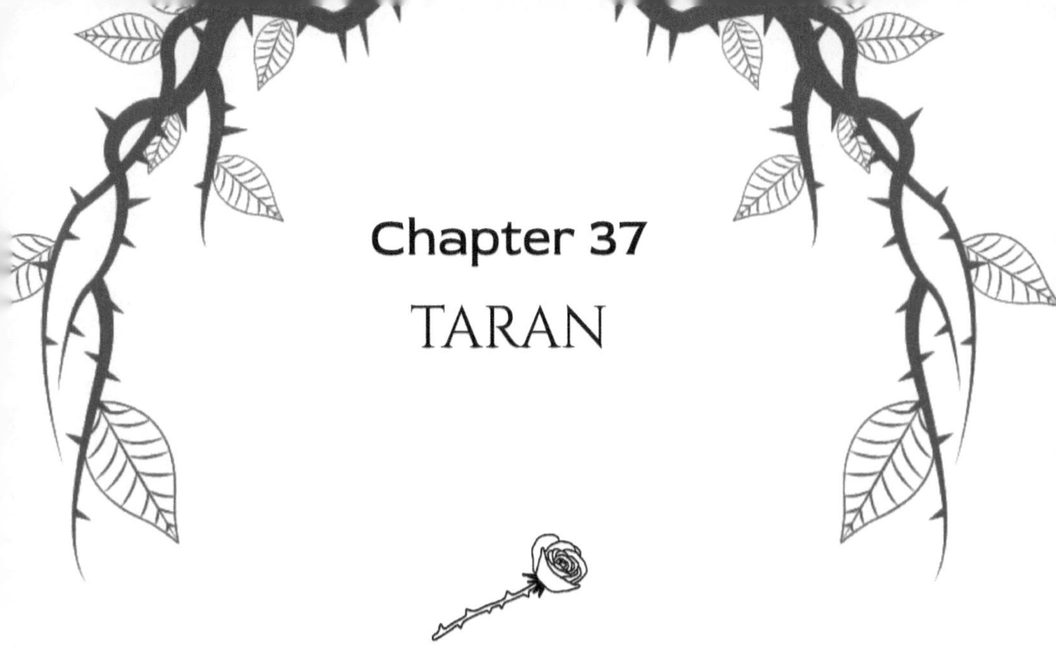

Chapter 37

TARAN

I take another swallow of whiskey, the burn doing little to calm my anxious mind. First, I sparred with every Apex close enough to my level in training—bouts of intensity that helped not at all. The only one who can really keep up with me is Carter. He could easily best me, if he was free to reveal his gift. Which, of course, he isn't. After a few hours of exertion and a much-needed bath, Carter convinced me to try drinking.

"She's fine," he says again. "The wildcat can more than handle herself."

"I know that." I gesture for him to refill my glass for the fourth time. I might be feeling a slight effect? Probably, I'm just imagining it. I've never been able to feel so much as tipsy, so I typically avoid alcohol altogether. What's the point? But right now, I'm on a mission to shut down my churning thoughts in any way possible.

Letting her swan out the doors of the palace without me was excruciating. Holding my stoneclaw back, snarling to go after her. But when I saw the fear flicker across her beautiful features, I knew—godsdamnit—I knew letting her go alone was the right thing to do. She needed my support, my belief in her abilities just then, not my stoneclaw's irrational coddling.

"It's not that I don't know she can handle this on her own. Of course I do." I snort. "She's infinitely better at this than I am."

Carter refreshes his own drink. He's only on his second, and I get the feeling he's really just here so I don't have to drink alone. "Then why hasn't your leg stopped moving the entire time we've been sitting here?"

I still my jiggling limb self-consciously. "It's my stoneclaw. I told you, my creature can't stand the idea of seeing her hurt. Or in danger."

"Or not in your line of sight," he drawls.

I sigh. "That, too."

"I get why you had me break into the guardian records and not her. But, Tare, on the night of Samhain, she'll need to complete the heist. On her own. None of the rest of us have the skills to do it. That's what you brought her here for."

I bury my head in my hands, the same way I did when Alora said nearly the same thing to me on the balcony. "I know."

"She'll be in far more danger during the heist than she is right now."

I lift my head. "*I know.*"

"Then do you mind telling me what's going on?"

I jump to my feet, the whiskey forgotten. "I wish I knew. Truly." My head snaps to my chambers' door a moment before a soft rap announces my cousin's arrival. Finally.

But when I swing the door open, the scent of blood—her blood—floods my senses. My hands curl into fists, my eyes shift and my voice is barely above a growl as I demand, "What happened."

Maeve pushes me inside, and I have just enough wherewithal left to let her. She slams the heavy door shut. "What are you thinking?" she hisses. "Rhegar could be anywhere!"

Carter raises his glass. "Not sure if you've noticed, but our princely friend has not been doing much thinking at all lately. At least not with his head."

I snarl but don't take my eyes off Maeve. "You smell like her blood."

Maeve raises her hands. "The key master was...uncooperative. He refused to assist us."

"Is. She. Hurt?" I bite out.

"A superficial wound." She bats the air. "Apparently, he held a dagger to her throat to make a point. I just helped her clean it, and she's good as new. I didn't realize you'd still be able to scent it on me."

I think I'd still be able to scent her blood hours later, but I don't say that out loud. My family is already looking at me funny. So it helps not at all when I reply, "I'll kill him."

They exchange a concerned look.

"Tare—" Maeve starts.

"Don't try to talk me out of it, Maeve. That criminal was already on thin ice."

She blinks. "What did he do before this?"

"Talked to her, most likely. Maybe looked at her," Carter drawls.

Actually, he put his clothing on her. His *scent* on her. But I realize that doesn't help my case any.

"Moving on," she continues, oblivious to me internally losing my sanity. "She says he suspects the target of the heist is the amulet. She had to tell him the location of the prize so he could add her key signature. As soon as she mentioned the old throne room, he went berserk. Started threatening her."

A low rumble starts up in my chest.

Carter's tawny eyes alight. "That's excellent. It means the amulet really is in there. And that he's the one who set the wards."

Maeve purses her lips. "Yes, and now the key master knows we're after it. Or that Alora is anyway."

"So we kill him."

Maeve's and Carter's alarmed reactions to my pronouncement mean the smile curving my lips is just as deranged as it feels.

"The thief says no," Maeve informs me, and my smile wipes away. "She says he never mentioned you and it's unlikely he knows you're involved. They made some kind of a deal in exchange for each other's silence. He won't even inform the guild."

Carter claps my shoulder. "We may still need his services, Tare. At least stay your hand until we have the amulet."

The scent of her blood continues to torment me. Now I've been assured she's well, it no longer sends me into a murderous rage. Instead that same ache has started up in my canines. Faunera, save me from this madness.

"Another thing to consider," Maeve cuts in. "Without the key signature, you'll need to be the one to breach the former throne room tomorrow while the court is distracted by the hunt. I know you don't want to, Tare, but you're the only one who might have access." Because I share my father's blood.

My pulse kicks up into a panicked frenzy at only the thought of stepping into that room again.

"I'll come with you," Carter offers.

That's enough to snap me to a decision. Despite the fact it's completely illogical, I would rather face the trauma of my past alone than have her be the one in danger. I really am going insane. "No. No, I can handle it. You'll accompany Alora on the hunt."

"What?" they burst out in unison.

I sigh. "Mei can't ride. And you saw what that boar did to my father's horse."

"The ladies are hunting the hare," Maeve points out.

"It's less suspicious with just me anyway," I counter.

Carter frowns. "Except that the king and Lord Winters believe you have no memory of what occurred in that room, but you stay away because you were told that's where she died." I'd give nearly everything I have for that to be the actual truth.

"In the unlikely event that I'm caught, I'll feign that a flash of memory broke through, and I went to the room to try and remember," I suggest.

"That's not ideal. They might move it if they believe you're remembering."

"It's not, but I'll just have to do my best not to get caught. You said it yourself, I'm the only one who can get in there."

Their brows furrow into twin expressions of displeasure, but they know I'm right. There's no other choice.

Chapter 38

ALORA

The next day, Maeve turns up at my door with a gorgeous riding habit. It has a deep hood to keep out today's foggy chill, and it's made of a luxurious green velvet that would make her own emerald eyes sparkle. The high collar even hides the mark from yesterday's incident with Harlan. But best of all, it's split up the back in the Shanterran style so that I can ride astride.

"Naturally, you weren't going to be hunting sidesaddle," she sniffs, brushing off my gratitude for her thoughtfulness. "How else are you expected to win?"

"Win?"

Maeve gives me that look I've come to recognize as her political plotting face. She's proven many times over that she's the group's expert on this front, so I listen intently. "We need as many Elite as possible out of the palace while Taran tries to access the room with the amulet. We need Victoria and all her cronies to attend the hunt, even though Taran is bowing out. She's competitive."

"So you think if I challenge her, she'll be sure to stay," I reply slowly.

"Not directly," she replies, "or she'll be suspicious. But she's already jealous of you, especially after Taran danced with you at the ball."

One corner of my mouth kicks up. "I can do that." I don't love being the distraction—*again*—but if that's my role, I'm going to damn well succeed at it.

When we reach the stableyard, Maeve reveals another surprise: a bow, a fine set of gold-tipped arrows and a massive black stallion. She greets a lovely brown mare named Acorn with a feisty disposition who matches her lady's personality well.

"No striders?" I ask, running my hand along the stallion's strong neck.

"They're faster and better over long distances," Maeve admits as she adjusts Acorn's bridle. "But trained striders are rare, and there aren't enough for the entire court. The court settles for horses when they're more interested in spectacle than practicality."

It seems, though, that the entire court has decided to attend despite the gloomy weather. In the interest of parity in the competition, even the king and queen are upon horses rather than striders, surrounded by their retinue, though the young crown prince has been left behind. The queen, seated atop a pure white mare—of course, the better to match today's prize—remarks that servants have gone ahead to set up tents and refreshments at a clearing within the forest for lunch.

The king looks jovial, patting Lord Winters on the shoulder in response to something he's saying. I freeze at the glimpse of the lord—my first since I saw him on the execution platform. Carter said he's obsessed with researching Apex and their gifts. Meticulous records and his ongoing crusade with the amulet. How eager would he be to examine *me*, the one supposed Apex without a creature? I suppress a shudder.

"Borrowing the prince's horse for the hunt, My Lady?" My head swivels to Victoria, dressed in a pale blue habit. She's one of the few other ladies who've also chosen to sit astride. She means to win.

Clever of Maeve to gift me Taran's horse to get under her skin. "Surely, it's not against the rules?" I say, tone just sweet enough to sting. "I understood from Lady Ashbourne that he wasn't coming. All's fair in love and war, is it not, Lady Winters?" I can't help my cruel smirk, one aimed directly at her. I couldn't care less about today's so-called prize, but beating these Elite ladies? Especially this one? I can't wait.

"Of course, Lady Thorne," she responds through gritted teeth, wrenching her poor horse around to rejoin her cronies.

Carter appears at my side, leading a strider. "Taran would not be pleased you're antagonizing her."

I tilt my head. "It is possible that I have just a touch of a competitive streak."

An unexpected laugh bursts out of him, startling a few of our neighboring horses. I shoot a glare in his direction. "Stop scaring away my prize!"

He keeps chuckling, quieter at least. "Just as long as you're not going after the boar." He weaves his hands together and assists me in mounting the enormous gelding, big enough to support even the prince's towering frame. Then, he swings up atop his own mount.

I frown. "Why do you get a strider?"

That crooked smile pulls at his lips. "I am not part of the royal hunt and therefore not burdened by its rules. But fear not, Onyx is the next best option."

I pat his neck. "Are you going to help me win, Onyx?"

"Likely better if he doesn't," Carter points out.

I frown. "Why are you even here?" Shouldn't he be accompanying Taran, who is no doubt having to force himself into the room where his mother died?

"To keep watch over you of course."

I turn an outraged look onto the guardian.

"There's an enormous wild boar in these woods, and you don't have an Apex with you."

I bite back a curse. Mei's absence, due to the "illness" we had to fake, is highly suspicious. But what else could I have said? My poison catcher ate something bad?

"Then who's guarding the prince of the realm?" I hiss.

Carter groans. "Can we just skip ahead to the part where you agree? You're not going to win this one with him. I guarantee it."

I haven't seen Taran since we spoke in my bedroom before I left for the disastrous meeting with the key master. I'm a bit ashamed. He was so filled with confidence in me and my ability to pull this off—as he's been since the beginning. But this time I failed.

The sight of Lord Winters disappearing back into the castle wrenches me from my errant thoughts. I swing an alarmed look in Carter's direction. His grim face tells me he's seen it, too. The lord must have decided the hunt wasn't worth his time once Taran didn't show.

"Go after him," I urge under my breath.

Carter's expression is torn.

"Carter. I'll stay close to Astrid and Maeve. Please, he might be going to—" He might be heading straight to the amulet. Straight to Taran.

He spears me with a sharp look. "Stay close to Astrid," he commands. He dismounts quickly, handing his strider off to a confused stableboy and disappearing into the palace after Lord Winters. Hopefully, he can use his gift to catch up.

The distraction has cost me. The hunting party is already well on its way and Astrid and Maeve are lost to the thick forest.

I urge Onyx into the brush after them.

But I soon lose myself within the quiet forest, far from our competitors. Onyx makes his way steadily around trees and over fallen branches while I keep my eyes trained for Maeve's royal-blue riding habit. I'm scanning the surrounding forest when I catch the barest hint of snowy white tucked within a bramblewood bush. Even better.

I move slowly, drawing my bow. But just as I align the shot, two horses crash into the vicinity. The hare streaks off, a blur of white against the brown and green of the forest.

Cursing in Shanterran, I take off after the hare, ignoring my competitor and her Apex. Out of the corner of my eye, I spot the doe-eyed handmaiden from the queen's luncheon. The one who sighed about Taran showing me the lilies.

She's after me like a shot, her Apex trailing behind. I urge Onyx faster, and Taran's stallion easily outpaces the handmaiden. Soon, the Elite lady is lost to the forest, but so too is the hare.

"Woah, boy," I murmur to Onyx, patting his heaving neck and offering endearments in various languages.

A steady ache starts up in my chest, and my fingers fly to my breast. Apart from the beautiful beast beneath me, I'm alone.

Maybe I could try...

Maybe now, surrounded by the natural world and the adrenaline rush of the hunt coursing through me, I could connect to my lynx. It's reckless, foolish even, but the idea takes root before I can stop it.

I shut my eyes and allow my pulse to regulate to a steady thump. Just how Taran said he finds his connection to his stoneclaw, I train all my attention on my auditory sense. First, Onyx's heavy exhales find my ears, then, the wind whistling through the pine. The quiet rustle of small creatures making their way through the dead leaves that litter the forest floor. My heart swells with a momentary surge of hope, but then...

Something strange happens.

Instead of sound sharpening to Apex level, it's my olfactory sense that increases until I can smell the clean scent of the mist clinging to the nearby pine needles. It's disorienting enough to shake me out of the trance, and my eyes fly open.

Disappointment floods me. What did I expect? That I could just close my eyes and find my creature on my first attempt after ten years in hiding? Ridiculous. I rub my chest—has the ache lessened? Even a little? It's hard to tell.

All at once, a streak of white flashes in the corner of my vision, and Onyx and I are off again, chasing after the day's prize. We crash through the forest, just managing to keep it in sight.

"That's it, Onyx, you've got it," I coax.

The hare darts ahead into a small clearing. Afraid of missing it again, I draw my bow, notch an arrow mid-canter and send it flying. I miss spectacularly, but the hare freezes, its ears flat to its head, perhaps hoping to hide among tall grass.

Once again, I pull up the stallion.

This time, I'm ready. Bow in hand, I sit up straighter and focus. Inhale. Exhale. I listen to the rhythm of the forest—the wind, which way it's blowing. I notch another gold-tipped arrow and on the next exhale, release towards the speck of white hidden among the winter-faded bushes.

"Did we get it?" I ask Onyx quietly in Veridian. He huffs in response. "I can't tell, either."

I dismount and tread on silent feet to the spot at the end of my arrow's path. The prize hare is lying there helplessly, stuck with a golden-tipped arrow. But it wasn't a clean shot. It's not dead yet. Its eyes are wide and rolling with terror. Its muscles twitch with impending death throes. In silence, I watch the hare's breathing slow until at last, it stills forever.

To my dismay, a tear streaks down my face. I wipe it away, unsure where this feeling is coming from. I'm no stranger to hunting snowshoe hares—they're one of the more plentiful small game options in the Shanterran mountains. This one, sleek and well-fed, was obviously bred for Elite hunting games. Pierced with a golden arrow.

Then it hits me.

Ethan.

Seeing a dead animal, so close at hand, has brought me right back to the trauma of watching Ethan's copper head separate from his body. Another death the Elite are responsible for.

A noise startles me out of my melancholy, and I turn, resigned, expecting another hopeful lady who has found the hare too late.

Instead...

A massive wild boar—bigger than any I've ever seen—with hairy black skin and tusks larger than my forearm, starts running pell-mell across the clearing, heading straight for me.

A strangled scream escapes. And then I *run*.

I've got one dagger on my person, but it's not nearly enough to take on this huge beast. My bow and arrows are on Onyx, who is neighing madly, still at the entrance to the clearing. I spare an ungenerous thought that perhaps the boar will go after the stallion instead, but a quick glance over my shoulder shows that it's me the creature has in its crosshairs.

I put my head down and sprint like the god of the underworld is nipping at my heels. I make it across the clearing and, without slowing, leap onto a skinny pine tree, hands singing in pain as I scrabble at the rough bark and begin to climb.

The boar reaches me and, with a supernatural leap of its own, manages to sink its monstrous teeth into the flesh of my left leg.

A bloodcurdling scream wrenches from my throat, but somehow—by some small vestige of self-preservation—I manage to hang on to the tree with my arms and my remaining leg, refusing to let go. The boar shakes its head like a dog with a bone looking to pry me loose, and I cry out again as the white-hot agony of it nearly blinds me, every tooth cutting like a knife into my flesh. But I don't let go. I will not let go.

I'm going to lose the leg. Any second now, this vicious thing is going to chomp it clean off. I'll be left clinging to the tree with nothing but shredded muscle and bone. In the haze of the pain, a single thought rises above the others. If I can just hang on...if I can keep hold of this tree, maybe the rest of me will survive.

As the boar's jaws tighten, and before it can sever my leg for good, the roar of another beast echoes through the woods. Guttural, savage—a sound no human throat could ever produce.

A stoneclaw.

Chapter 39

TARAN

Rhegar stands outside the old throne room.

I don't scent his lord, and I can't tell exactly what he's doing in that particular corridor since I'm staying out of sight around the corner. But odds are, he's been tasked with guarding the entrance. The wild, unique scent of the amulet—faint but unmistakable—winds around me. It must be in there.

After a moment of internal fuming, I'm forced to admit that just because Rhegar is guarding the entrance doesn't mean that the key master has given us up. This might be a regular guard rotation for the Apex. Not that I would know, given I never come down here. Which means I still have no excuse to kill him. Pity.

I'm contemplating my options for approaching the throne room without completely destroying my cover, when Carter appears out of thin air at my side. I rein in my yelp and hold a finger to my lips, tilting my head towards the throne room. *Rhegar*, I mouth.

My friend's lips turn down. He tilts his head in the opposite direction of the corridor, indicating I should follow him. Bemused, I obey, wondering what in Valenrae he's doing here in the palace with me. Is the hunt already over? No, certainly not. The luncheon revelry would last hours on its own.

Was it cancelled and he's coming to bring me back before the other Elite return?

He dips into a servants' stairwell, and we clatter down the steps, bursting through a door out into the stableyard.

"What's going on?" I demand.

"Sorry, I don't know Rhegar's range. Didn't want to risk him overhearing." He's breathing hard from using his gift, followed by our mad dash out of the palace.

"Why are you here? Was the hunt cancelled?"

He winces. "Don't get upset..."

I take one menacing step towards him. "Is she out there alone?"

He raises both hands. "Lord Winters disappeared into the castle as soon as he saw you weren't attending. She told me to go after him! What if he was going for the amulet and caught you?"

"And was he?" I grit out. "Going for the amulet?" Maybe Simon was in the throne room and I couldn't sense him around the dampening wards. I could sense the amulet, though. Faintly, but it was there.

"Um, no. He's in his lair. Doing Faunera knows what. Writing notes, thinking up evil plans, I don't know."

My eyes shift to burning ash, the familiar heat surging behind them. "You left her?"

"Astrid's with her," he assures me.

I relax a fraction. "You left her with Astrid."

"Well, not exactly, but—"

I'm stalking towards the stables before he can finish his excuses. A strider waits to be unsaddled, a wide-eyed boy holding her reins. Presumably this is the animal Carter was meant to ride. Without a word, I swing up onto her back.

"Tare, I'll go. It doesn't make sense—"

But suddenly, I feel something I can't explain. Something I've never felt before. A tickle of my consciousness, a subtle tug on my power. I taste the unmistakable scent of wild jasmine. My creature roars to the surface, and my head snaps to the forest.

Without a word, I urge the strider into the woods. The animal easily breaks into a canter, flying through the trees, hooved feet nimble as a deer. In the corner of my eye, I catch a blur winking in and out of sight. Carter, using his gift to jump alongside me.

Then a faint sound breaks through the forest that freezes my blood. A scream. *Her* scream filled with fright. Followed by Onyx's frenzied neighing.

I urge the strider faster, Carter nearly disappearing as he follows, my eyes shifting with the force of my emotion.

Another scream, worse than the first, far worse. This one is soaked in raw, agonizing pain.

The bellow that roars from my chest in response is more beast than human.

I burst into the clearing, launching myself from the strider before it fully comes to a stop. A massive boar, as big as a wolf and twice as wide, swings around from where it has Alora treed across the clearing. My canines lengthen on their own, and a menacing snarl rips from my throat, challenging the creature.

The boar lowers its head, showing pointed tusks that could maul a grown stallion. The thought of their pointed tips sinking into Alora's flesh pulls another roar from my lips. Pawing at the ground, the boar sprints across the clearing towards me, the bigger threat.

A slow smile curves my lips as I spread my arms wide in welcome. My fingers lengthen, nails hardening into black stone claws. Out of the corner of my eye, I catch the curve of a dark, sharp horn.

That's new.

Too late, the boar realizes it has more than met its match, but its eyes are bloodshot, its sanity long departed. I relish every swipe of my hardened claws, every bloody puncture of my horns. But most of all, I cherish the moment I sink my canines into the animal's neck and with a violent rip, tear out its throat, drenching my beastly body in its lifeblood.

Chapter 40

ALORA

Thank all the gods, the boar releases my tattered flesh before swiveling to face the incoming threat. I chance a look over my shoulder as it charges away. Another roar shakes the clearing. It's clear my next move is to get down from here before the horrible thing comes back.

But just one slight shuffle of my badly scraped hands down the trunk has me panting through gritted teeth. The torment in my leg is nearly unbearable.

A sudden, gentle tug at my waist has me in panic, thinking the boar has returned to finish what it started.

"Stop screaming! Do you want it to come back?" Carter's harsh voice jolts me back to reality. I release the tree so fast that he barely manages to break my fall before we both tumble to the ground.

Carter groans and rolls out from underneath me. I just lie there, chest heaving, staring up at the gray sky. Terrible noises are coming from the wild boar dying behind me—awful squeals and harsh grunts.

I do my best to block it out and concentrate on watching the misty clouds drift past.

"Shit." Carter has finally gotten a look at my leg. He drops to his knees at my side and starts tearing his shirt off. He wraps the pieces around my torn flesh in a makeshift bandage. "I'm so sorry, Wildcat. I should have been here."

"My fault," I manage, breathing through my teeth. "I told you to go."

A snarl ripples through the air. Carter is pushed bodily aside. Silver-gray eyes, molten with Apex power, take his place.

"T-T-Taran." He shivers at the sound of his name but doesn't speak.

I'm not even sure he can.

He appears lost to a deathly rage. A rumble echoes from his throat, and in my muddled state, I see a stoneclaw looking down at me with burning eyes and elongated canines sharp enough to pierce flesh.

I blink, and the prince is back, his face painted with blood.

"My—my leg," I grit out. As though he's just realized I'm injured, Taran's head whips to my hastily bandaged limb. He pulls the shirt away none too gently and a whimper sneaks out from between my lips. He wraps it back up quickly, then scoops me into his arms and stands as if I weigh nothing at all.

He strides through the brush past the dead hare, back towards Onyx, who is astonishingly still in one piece and being held by the bridle by Carter, along with a strider.

There's an enormous black lump on the ground at the animals' sides, nearly the size of a bear, and it takes me a moment for it to click. It must be the mauled carcass of the boar. It's almost completely unrecognizable—reduced to a grotesque heap of gore.

For some reason, Taran's words from the night of the ball ring through my head. *I am feeling an almost undeniable instinct to follow his scent down those stairs and rip him apart with my bare hands. Or maybe my teeth. Probably both, frankly.*

"This is going to hurt." Taran finally finds his voice, half a second before he lifts me onto the strider. I bite my knuckle as the pain lances through me. The prince swings up behind, carefully cradling me against his body.

As soon as Carter's strider takes off, it takes all my concentration not to scream as my injured leg bounces. The strider's gait is smoother than a horse's, and Taran does his best to stabilize the leg, but that's no consolation. Whimpers and gasps spill helplessly from my lips. Taran's own are locked in a tight, grim line as we race back towards the palace.

By the time we pull up at the front courtyard, my barely suppressed moans have turned to all-out cries. Taran pulls the strider up abruptly. I don't even get a moment of stationary relief before he's got me off the animal and back in his arms, striding purposefully deep into the castle. He blatantly ignores the shocked faces of the skeleton staff left behind.

Despite being off the strider and in Taran's careful hold, the torture of the bite has somehow only deepened, splintering up my leg beyond where the beast bit me in jagged lines of lightning. I throw my arms around the prince's neck and bury my face in his jacket, attempting to muffle my shouts.

"Try to keep those curses to the common tongue, if you can." His voice rumbles against my cheek where it's crushed against his chest, my tears further marring the blood-soaked velvet. I let loose with a particularly nasty one aimed at him, but he just strokes a hand up and down my spine.

After what feels like an eternity, we reach a heavy wooden door. Taran doesn't give the occupant an opportunity to answer—he physically kicks it in with such force, it hangs precariously on its hinges.

I grit my teeth and lift my tear-stained face to a...

Well, lair does appear to be the accurate word for it. The subterranean room is crammed with countless vials and tinctures, workstations, and a table at the center big enough to hold a body.

Whipping around from a desk, a journal open in front of him, the surprise clear on his face, is Lord Winters.

I bite down on my tongue so hard I taste blood. No way in hell I'm sobbing in front of this man. But a fire is burning through my leg all the way up to my right hip now, and a harsh grunt forces its way out of my throat.

"My Prince?" the lord sputters.

"The antidote." Even in my scattered state, I can hear the ground-shaking fury lacing Taran's voice.

Lord Winters blanches. "Antidote, Your Highness?"

Taran lays me on the center table, more gently than I would have thought possible, cradling my head until the last possible second. I writhe against the cold surface, smothering my cries as best I can.

In the time it takes to blink, Taran is bent over the man's neck, looking for all the world like he's going to rip his throat out.

"You think I don't recognize bloodbane when I see it?" Rather than shouting, his voice is dangerously quiet, his every word clipped and vicious. "I don't know how you ensured your tainted boar would attack whoever killed that hare, but I hold no doubts this plan came from you and your *despicable* daughter. You won't get away with it this time, Simon. If Lady Thorne dies, I'll wipe out every member of your cursed bloodline down to the last tiny babe—saving you for last. So you can hear their screams echoing in your ears for the remainder of your very short life. Now. Give. Her. The. Antidote."

"I'm sure I don't know what—"

"Then there's no reason for you to live."

Taran's muscled arms move and clutch Lord Winters' head, preparing to snap the Elite's neck when the man bursts out, "Alright! Alright! Let me get it. I'll get it."

Taran releases him instantly, prowling behind the lord as he fumbles for the correct bottle. His hands shake as he fills a syringe and makes his way over to where I'm burning on my pyre. The makeshift bandage comes off, and he lets out a panicked breath when he sees the state of my ravaged leg.

"Your Highness..."

I'm sure he's about to say I'm too far gone. I feel too far gone, close to shattered, the blazing fire speeding towards my heart, my extremities already succumbing to numbness. I would welcome death at this point. Anything to stop this nightmare. I'm full-out screaming now, wordless.

Taran grabs the syringe and plunges the liquid into my thigh. The last thing I remember is the soft glow of troubled storm-cloud eyes.

Chapter 41
ALORA

TEN YEARS EARLIER

I'm barely past my fifteenth birthday when my heightened auditory sense
hits me like a blow to the head.

*Our cottage is set back, close to the woods, at least two miles from any other
dwellings. But that distance doesn't stop me from clutching my head in agony
at the screeching voices of our neighbors, the Skoies, as they fight about whether
or not to sell their old nanny goat. The Skoies are Thalassarian. They speak not
a word of Veridian, yet I understand every syllable as though it were my mother
tongue.*

*My father is beside me when it happens. He shouts my name multiple times
before realizing his mistake.*

*By the time the Skoies stop arguing and I can finally remove my hands from
my ears, he's figured out what is happening. What has happened.*

My emergence.

I come to with my head in his lap, his calloused fingers smoothing my hair.

*"Concentrate on the sound of my voice," he instructs in a low whisper. "Let
everything else fall away. Let it fade to a dull murmur."*

Two hours crawl by. He keeps talking me through it, infinitely patient. How does he know what to do?

"Can you feel your creature?" he asks finally. His voice is hoarse from the long hours of whispering.

Tears stream down my face. Half from relief, half from sheer joy at this beautiful, divine connection. I'm whole in a way I never imagined possible. The final piece of my soul slotted into place. "She's a lynx."

"Your lynx is your other half, Alora," he murmurs, his voice cracked. "Embrace her, and there is no end to how powerful you can be."

My father leaves me in the stables while he goes into the cottage to tell my mother. I think he hoped the barn walls and the animal bodies would muffle their conversation, but they don't. Even with straw pressed against my ears, I can still hear them.

My mother wants to turn me in to Lord Winters. My father wants to take me and run.

My mother is afraid. She knows what will happen if they attempt to hide an Apex from their lord. Especially a useful one who can speak languages and hear whispers from miles out. The beast prince has already emerged, and his ability to track down Apex is well known. She doesn't see any means of escape.

My father is worried about what will happen to me. A young female Apex enslaved to the palace or at our lord's house. He wants us to run, together, as a family.

My mother eventually agrees. But...it's a lie.

She must slip out to inform the lord's men after my father has gone to bed. In the wee hours before dawn, I am awakened by my father clasping a delicate chain around my neck. He tells me he loves me, shoves a pack in my hands, points me towards the Shanterran border, and says, "Run."

But I am fifteen. Too young. Too scared of the dark forest to run far.

When Lord Winters' men come for me, I am still close enough to see.

Close enough to see them slit my father's throat as he tries to tell them he has no daughter.

I take off running. But my auditory sense emerged only hours before, which means it is still unwieldy and sharp, so sharp.

I must be at least a mile away when they begin to torture my mother. They made a grave mistake. In killing my father first, they took away the one person who knew where I'd gone. So in their rage, they torture my mother for information she can't give.

I never stop running. And still, my mother's screams and pleas for mercy assail my ears over and over. The trauma of it breaks me, forces a dissociation—a fracture.

A black shroud envelopes my mind, my lynx fades from my consciousness, and I forget.

Chapter 42
ALORA

"**M**other." The word is croaked out from between my parched lips.

"Praise Faunera, you're awake." Mei's sweet voice brings me hurtling back to the present. Eyes squeezed shut, I cast around within my consciousness. It takes only a heartbeat to find the answer: My lynx is still gone.

A crushing wave of disappointment rolls through me. When Carter told me about that entry in the guardian logs, I wasn't sure I even wanted to find my creature, to be Apex. Half of me remained in denial, convinced the entry couldn't have been written about me. But now I've tasted what it feels like to finally be whole in my memory—I'm despondent to wake and find myself splintered once more.

I reluctantly open my sleep-crusted eyes to find Mei perched on a stool at my bedside. "Water," I whisper. She jumps up and returns with a small glass, which she guides to my lips. I drain it immediately, and when she pulls back, I gesture for more.

"Slowly," she cautions. "You've been unconscious for two days."

Two days! I lift the coverlet and examine my leg. It looks good as new; there's not even a bandage on it. I feel freshly bathed, and my nightgown is barely rumpled. Someone has been taking care of me while I've been out of commission, likely Mei.

Disjointed memories of before I passed out stream through my mind. Taran accused Lord Winters of using something called bloodbane. That must be why the pain was so torturous, why it kept getting worse.

I glance up to discover that Mei has disappeared somewhere, presumably to alert the castle I'm finally awake. I take the opportunity to make use of the bathing chamber, shuffling on unsteady legs. I'm washing up when I hear the door bang open, and then—

"Where is she?" I'm surprised to hear Maeve's voice.

"I'm here." I step out of the bathing room and hold the wall for a moment, fighting dizziness.

"What are you doing?" I close my eyes against Maeve's shriek, and she immediately lowers her voice to a whisper-shout. "Get back into bed! They said you were on death's door. We didn't know if you were going to make it."

I am feeling pretty weak, despite the lack of pain, and so I allow the two of them to bustle me back into bed. Maeve sweeps into the stool at my side in a rustle of lavender taffeta.

"What happened?" I direct my question to the Elite lady, knowing she'll give me a direct answer.

Instead, she swings her attention to the spy in our midst. "Mei, will you go down to the kitchens and fetch some food for Loriella? I'm sure she's starving."

I start to protest, but my stomach makes itself known, and Mei is gone before I can get the words out.

"You asked what happened, but you likely know more than me." Maeve arches her eyebrows. "I came back from the hunt to find you barely alive, Taran in an absolute state. As soon as I'm sure you're well, I'll go tell him you're awake. He's been beside himself."

"I need to speak with him, too," I murmur. About a lot of things, but most of all, how I can connect to my lynx again. My stomach twists. He has to help me. Surely, he will?

"He'd be here if he could, but…"

Right. He can't show that much interest in an Elite lady who's supposed to be off-limits.

My heart quickens with the worry that this setback may have further shredded my already tenuous cover. "How did he explain what happened to the court?"

"He said he was out riding his strider and scented the boar. Then he found you injured and rushed you back to the palace for care." She purses her lips. "Their Majesties were quite put out that he killed the boar from atop a strider. Said he, 'Ruined the spirit of the competition.'" She shakes her head. "Of all the inane things to focus on."

Rule Number Three: The best lies are mostly true.

If they're focusing on whether Taran cheated during their hunt, they're not focusing on what he was doing before he found me. "And what of Lord Winters? That's who Taran took me to. He said something about bloodbane and then injected my leg with a serum."

Her emerald eyes darken. "Tare maintains they got the antidote into you in time and that's how you survived the poison. But both Winters are keeping a rather low profile after their attempted subterfuge went awry."

I huff. "Their attempted murder, you mean. Nothing will happen to them?"

She sighs. "They claim to have had nothing to do with it. In fact, His Majesty suggested that you owe the lord your gratitude for having saved your life."

"What?!" I yelp.

"You should have seen Taran's reaction to that," she confides, her smile full of satisfaction.

I twist my fingers in my thin nightgown. "He shouldn't have reacted at all."

"I know," she sniffs. "He's hopeless. A complete waste of my tutelage. But everyone knows how upset he was over Jia. I've been fueling the gossip mill around that and the scandal of another poisoning. With any luck, the court will believe his reaction is in relation to that instead of—"

"Indeed," I murmur. Instead of whatever this is between us that called him to my side in the hour I needed him most.

"Mei will be back shortly with the food, and I have to tell you about the amulet. Taran is certain now that it's being held in the old throne room. He's been surveilling and said there's a rotation of Apex guards posted outside at all times, usually Rhegar, Lord Winters' Apex. He's an auditory, master of whispers, and quite powerful."

"Great," I mumble weakly.

She reaches out and gives my hand a squeeze. "I know you've just been through something horrible, on top of the cruel shock you received days earlier. But we are running out of time, and we need your guidance now more than ever. Taran's only ideas these days seem to be to kill everyone."

"For Jinai's sake."

She shrugs one delicate shoulder. "You can't really blame him. I was also ready to kill Carter when I heard he'd left you alone to be gravely injured."

"I told him to!" I protest.

"And I'm thankful you did. I can't imagine the repercussions if the lord had caught Tare." She meets my eyes with her own green gaze when she says, "Thank you."

My mouth pops open.

"I know I was not the most...accommodating...when you first came here. I didn't agree with taking the risk of bringing in an outsider. It seemed more likely to result in us all being caught. Yes, we've been able to keep our true motives a secret all these years, but that's resulted in our becoming more and more cautious. Perhaps too cautious, in hindsight." She squeezes my hand again, then releases it. Lifting her chin, she adds, "We are closer than we have ever been, and I can't help but think that is due to you. Perhaps introducing a little risk was what this mission needed after all."

I can't find the words, so I just nod. All my life, I've only had Eleni and Xinlei. Now it seems I can count a few more friends in my life, and one of them is a royal Elite lady. Will wonders never cease?

A soft thud of the door announces that Mei is back. She enters my bedroom holding an overloaded tray that makes my mouth water.

"I'll go let—everyone know you're awake," Maeve announces, rising from the chair. "Don't eat too much or it'll all come right back up."

And with that dire pronouncement, she sweeps out of the room. I stick out my tongue at her back, and Mei chuckles softly. "She's right, you know."

"I know." I sigh. "If you ever tell her I said this, I'll deny it with my last breath, but she usually is."

I manage to keep myself to sips of the soup and bites of the warm, soft bread, though I stare longingly at the fruit tart. My stomach is full almost immediately, though. Two days without eating or drinking will do that. But I know I need to keep up my strength so my body can continue to heal.

Mei is silent throughout the meal, perched on her little stool. But once I've accepted this is the best my stomach can do and I'm resting back against my pillow, she finally speaks. "Miss Katsaros doesn't know what happened. That you were injured, I mean."

My brow puckers. "She doesn't?"

She shakes her head. "No. I didn't want to leave until you awoke." A beat of silence, then, "The key master doesn't know, either. And he won't, My—Loriella. I'll keep your secrets."

Tears prick my eyes. I don't know what I've done to earn this female's loyalty beyond treating her with the bare minimum of human kindness deserved by any living being.

I reach for her small hand. "Mei, you do whatever you need to do to get back to your family. If that means telling the key master of my injury, then you do it."

Her gaze darts to my unmarked leg, covered by the soft blankets. "I don't think that's such a good idea, My—Loriella."

I stiffen, releasing her hand. Of course. The antidote may have saved my life, but this level of healing in such a short time would only be possible with an Apex. Mei washed my body, tended to me in my recovery. Surely she saw the advanced pace of healing with her own eyes. My breath catches in my throat. My lynx...? But no, my creature still slumbers, our connection severed by trauma. My stomach hollows out at the loss.

But in that moment, reaching for my lynx and power and finding them gone, I finally recognize something else.

The persistent ache I've carried with me for the past ten years has...disappeared. I inhale a full breath for what feels like the first time in my life.

"Mei—" I start, but the slam of my chamber door flying open cuts me off. Our gazes swing to the bedroom door where the towering frame of the Veridian prince appears. His clothes are rumpled, his facial hair overgrown and dark circles shadow his eyes as though he hasn't slept.

My jaw drops. "Your Highness," I choke out. "Wha—what are you doing here?"

"You're awake," he breathes.

"Um, yes. Yes, I am." Conscious of my thin nightgown, I pull the blankets up to cover my chest.

He hardly seems to notice, his gaze roaming over me, searching out any injury. I brush a finger across my throat and find only smooth skin—even the cut Harlan gave me has disappeared. It hasn't scabbed over; it's gone as though it never occurred.

Taran sucks in a full inhale, nostrils flaring. Did he just scent me?

Mei's gaze bounces back and forth between us. Taran finally rips his gaze from me, settling on my pretend guardian. "Mei, is it?" he asks in his gravelly voice.

The poor thing blushes pink to the roots of her dark hair. "Yes, Your Highness," she confirms.

"Thank you for caring for Lady Thorne," he tells her, his tone sincere.

Her dark eyes dart to mine. "It's my duty, Your Highness. As well as my pleasure."

"I would like to grant you a boon, if I may. In recognition of your steadfast support."

Her petal-pink lips part. "That's not necessary—"

"A gold purse wouldn't go amiss," I cut in. She'll need funds for her trip north and to care for her family while in hiding. The corner of Taran's mouth twitches.

"Oh, I couldn't possibly—" she starts.

"Done," he interrupts. "I'll have it brought to your room tomorrow. Please accept it with my gratitude. Now, if you don't mind, I'd appreciate a private word with the lady."

She casts a quick glance in my direction—am I alright with that? My heart swells at this tiny Apex willing to oppose the Veridian Guild and the prince of the realm on my behalf. I give her a subtle nod and, after a quick bow, she departs. Leaving me alone in my bedroom with a prince who's looking at me like he can't stop.

Chapter 43
ALORA

Taran shuts the door behind Mei with a soft thud, and I try valiantly to keep my breathing steady. Why couldn't I have thrown on a robe when I was up earlier?

"You shouldn't be here," I whisper, even though I trust Mei to keep it to herself.

My bed dips as he settles his weight onto it, ignoring the tiny stool. "I couldn't help it. I needed to see you. I had to see for myself that you weren't hurt."

"Surely Maeve told you...?"

"How's your leg?" he cuts in.

My brow furrows. "It's good as new. Completely healed. I don't understand it."

He closes his eyes for a brief moment. When they reopen, there's a softened quality to them. "I can answer that. Just after I injected you with the antidote, your eyes glowed amber."

I gasp. "Like a—?"

"Like an Apex," he confirms. "I believe your creature surfaced to save you from the bloodbane."

"Did Lord Winters see?"

"No. No, I don't think so," he assures me. "It was hardly a moment before you passed out on his table. I've told him and the court the antidote must have reached you in time. But, Alora, in that moment, I saw…"

"What?" I lean forward, caught up in his words.

One of his hands finds mine, a calloused thumb running along the top of my palm in soothing strokes. "Please don't be upset."

"What did you see?" I demand.

"Your lynx," he breathes. "Looking out at me from behind your eyes."

I freeze.

"I scented it too," he continues. "But that's gone now."

"I remembered something while I was unconscious. About…my lynx. About…the day I emerged." In starts and stops, I reveal the whole sad tale, leaving nothing out. He watches me with that steady gaze the entire time, his big hand tight on mine.

"The ache is gone, but my lynx is still missing and so is my power. I want to connect with my creature again, to bring her back," I finish. "Please, will you help me? Teach me as you taught Carter and Astrid?"

"Gods, Alora." He gives me a sad smile. "You don't even need to ask. I'm so fucking sorry that happened to you."

"I understand why she did it," I murmur. "My mother, I mean. Now that I've met Lord Winters and the king and seen what they're capable of…she was frightened. And she'd been taught that turning in Apex was the right thing to do. That they are—that *we* are—dangerous. I thought the same of all of you when we first met." I drop my gaze, ashamed. "I called you…" I'm unable to say it.

"I understand. Emergence leaves its mark upon us all," he reminds me, and the words hit deeper this time. "You'll find your balance, Alora. You'll bring your lynx back—I know you will."

"There's something else." I draw in a deep breath. Here goes. "You said you saw my lynx looking out at you."

His mouth tightens. "Yes, that's right."

"Has that ever happened to you before? Is that a part of your gift?"

"No, never. Usually, I can scent the creature, but to feel it—no, that's never happened to me before."

"Me neither. Except...except the night you found me in Count Zhao's study."

He leans back, an uncertain expression on his face. "What are you saying?"

My eyes close. As if I can keep it from being true if I can't see him.

"Eyes on me, My Lynx." His husky command has me automatically obeying, unwillingly opening my eyes to collide with his. To find his creature looking out at me behind stormy silver gray.

In a voice scarcely louder than a whisper, I admit, "I sensed your stoneclaw."

"What?" The prince jolts backwards, his jaw slack, hand dropping mine. His reaction is so reminiscent of Xinlei's when I told him that it might have made me laugh if this all wasn't so fucking scary. "When I saw you for the first time, I could see your stoneclaw looking back at me."

I didn't think it was possible to stun him still further, but I've managed it. His mouth works, as if trying to form words and failing. He rakes his hands through already tousled coal-dark hair. "You know my creature."

Not a question, but I answer it anyway. "Yes."

"No one knows my creature," he says under his breath, almost to himself.

My brow furrows. "No one?"

"Almost no one," he amends. "No one who would have told you. And no one who would talk about it so that you could have overheard." Which means, he knows I'm telling the truth. He spears me with a piercing look. "Has this ever happened to you before?"

"No! No, of course not. Well, except for Mei, I suppose. I guessed hers might be a songbird."

He huffs. "Not a terribly large leap. But you didn't say you 'guessed' my creature. You said you sensed it. Immediately."

My voice drops back down to a murmur. "Yes."

Taran's silver eyes widen. "This is why you were so anxious when I found you under the desk. I could scent it on you. I thought it was because of the pearls, but…"

"I also had never been caught before," I point out, a little bitter, even now. The corner of the prince's mouth quirks. "But yes, I didn't understand what it meant, and your creature is straight out of a godsdamned legend. It didn't make sense to feel this…connection to someone I'd never met. Much less an Apex."

I'm not sure what it is that gives him away. Some slight movement of his eyes—darting away as if he can't fully hold my gaze. The automatic clenching of his jaw.

"Taran?" My tone is heavy with suspicion.

As if in answer, his hand slips into his pants pocket and closes around something there. My pulse flutters. He's finally going to show me what he's been carrying around all this time.

His nervous intake of breath warns me before my mind even realizes what it is it's seeing.

There, catching the dim light from its place resting on his outstretched hand, is a lynx figurine made of amber.

My calling card.

I lean back almost instinctively, and when I speak, my voice shakes. "Where, where did you get that from?"

"Atop Count Zhao's jewelry case. I could lie to you and say I took it so you wouldn't get caught stealing the pearls. That's what I told Carter and Maeve." He inhales another rasping breath. Like he's having trouble getting air down. "But I don't want to lie to you anymore. I *can't* lie to you anymore." My gaze is fixated on the amber lynx, worn in places from being held in a warm hand. I refuse to think about what that means.

"When I first caught your scent, it was like nothing I'd ever sensed before. I felt…intoxicated for the first time in my life." He shakes his head with the memory. "You smelled like paradise." His hand closes around the tiny lynx, and he pockets it once again. "Like home."

He leans closer, and I mirror his movements. His eyes are swirling silver shadows, burning with his power and the strength of his emotions. "I stole that lynx because I couldn't stand for anyone else to have a single piece of you. Even then." One hand reaches up and cups my face, the other splays across my lower back, pushing me closer. The forgotten blankets pool on my lap. "I kept it all this time because I needed something of yours to hold on to. Something to clutch when the urge to claim you was riding me so hard, I was ready to give up everything, *everything*, for just one taste."

"And now?" I breathe, heart pounding doubletime.

"Now, I've watched you nearly die in my arms. Now, I've learned you feel the same undeniable pull. Now, I know you've seen the truth of me—the beast at the very heart of my being. And you're still here." His voice is almost wondering. "You haven't run."

My mouth tips up into a smile. "I may still."

His next words are little more than a rasped breath against the curve of my lips. "Then I'll catch you." And he captures my mouth with his.

I won't deny I've wondered what it would feel like to kiss the beast prince. Even before I discovered the kind male lurking within the beast, I was drawn to his dominating presence, my body alight with the desire to close the distance between us.

But reality surpasses every expectation. Every distrustful thought, every worry that's plagued me since embarking on this treacherous journey eddies from my mind.

Because all I can concentrate on is how incredible he *tastes*.

My tongue dances with his stroke for stroke, and it is, gods, it is licking creamy vanilla ice cream chased by after-dinner liquor. All my senses are firing so intensely that when my ears pick up his quiet groan, I lose all sense of control—if I ever had any to begin with.

My hands spear into the soft waves of his dark hair and his long arm winds tighter around my waist, tugging me flush against him. I melt into the embrace, my nipples pebbling at the friction as my chest brushes his.

Every hungry thrust of his tongue shoots another shudder of throbbing need between my legs. I'm growing light-headed from lack of breath and all I can hear is the thundering of my own heart in my ears. A steady drumbeat of more, more, more. Please more.

"Gods, I love hearing you beg me," he rasps in my mother tongue. His impossibly deep voice sounds even huskier than usual, the melodious words scraping against gravel. My mind stutters—did I say that out loud? But I forget all about it when his hand slides back to tangle in my hair.

His grip is firm, angling my neck, exposing it to hot kisses under my jaw, pausing only to nip at my ear and drag in a long inhale. A gasped whimper escapes, and he responds with a low growl, tightening his grasp on my hair almost to the point of pain, and I still want more.

My stomach clenches, my core heats, and I'm starting to think I'm finally going to get what my body is so desperately craving when the prince pulls back. We're both breathing hard, his hand still twisted in my hair, my nightgown askew.

"I need to leave," he grates out. "I don't trust my creature around you. Especially not in this room, in this bed practically coated in your scent. If I let myself lose control...I'm afraid of what might happen."

"That's why you wanted to stop attempting the linking," I murmur.

He hums in agreement. "That night in the redwood, it was all I could do to keep my hands to myself. Your scent was...potent." My throat tightens as I remember how intimate it felt inside the tree. How I ended up in his embrace that night anyway.

My lips turn down in a pout, and he releases my hair, swiping a thumb across the protruding lower lip, eyes hooded with lust. "Fuck me, these lips," he breathes, fusing his mouth to mine once again. His tongue sweeps the seam before he nibbles gently on the bottom curve. "Softer than I imagined."

But the mention of the linking reminds me. "Taran, how did you find me the day of the hunt? How did you know I needed you?"

He leans back, his eyes unfocused as he searches his memory from that day. "I was already on the strider, planning to come after you. Carter told me he left you alone."

"I told him to," I interject.

"Hush, Lady Lynx, he told me that, too. I was going to let him take the strider himself when I felt something I can't explain. A tug on my power. I tasted your scent in my mouth." He shrugs helplessly. "I was racing through the forest when I heard you scream."

My hand finds the lynx charm my father made me. "Before the boar found me, before I shot the hare, I was trying to find my lynx. Focusing on my auditory sense. I thought I felt a stirring of something, perhaps, but then my olfactory sense took over and I lost it."

His head cocks to the side like his creature. "What are you saying?"

"Taran, I think, just maybe...the linking worked."

Chapter 44

TARAN

"We have two days until the Samhain masquerade," Alora states. Her dark hair swishes, and her burgundy dressing robe flares as she paces Maeve's sitting room in the candlelight. She looks like the wildcat Carter often calls her. "During which time, Taran and I need to cement the link so I can access his power. We need to find a way for me to breach the throne room door, and we have to determine a plan for getting past Rhegar."

Alora, Maeve, Carter, Astrid and I are conducting this planning session under the cover of night. Alora seems convinced that Mei is on our side, but I won't take the risk. I'm already taking too many risks with her.

"Also, you can't be seen outside your room before the ball, as you should still be recovering from the boar attack," Maeve chimes in.

Alora looks down at her perfectly healed legs as though she's just realized she's pacing.

"We could push the heist back," Carter offers. "I know Samhain is a good opportunity, but there will be more."

My jaw clenches. On one hand, I've been waiting for this night for *eight years*, and after Ethan, I can't take another execution. On the other hand...my gaze meets Alora's. We haven't yet discussed what will happen after she steals the amulet.

Mine, my stoneclaw growls.

"I can't stay," she admits, eyes stuck to mine. "The key master was very clear—his vow of silence only extends for so long. He wants me out of the country when the job is done, and so does the guild master. Eleni already gave the guild our timeline in our first meeting."

My muscles bulge with the force needed to contain my reaction. "Where will you go?" I bite out.

She winces. "I can't go back to the Shanterran Guild. Not after connecting with my lynx and showing obvious signs of being an Apex. That would be a poor thanks to give my mentor for his years of support." She rubs at her breastbone, a habit. Since she awoke, memory restored, the pain has yet to return. "Eleni has always longed to see Thalassar, her homeland. I hoped you might be able to help with passage for us both the night of the heist?" Her big amber eyes turn pleading, and it slices right through me.

Maeve shoots me a concerned look. "The Thalassarian pirates aren't only rumors. It would be a treacherous journey."

Alora's chin drops. "I have nowhere else to go," she says in a small voice and damn if it doesn't pierce me to my core.

Stay here! I want to shout, to bellow at the top of my lungs. *Stay here with me.* But how can she? She's right. As soon as she accesses her lynx, her days at the palace are numbered. As a recently emerged Apex with barely any control over her gift, there will be no hiding it. I've already piqued the court's interest in her—piqued *my father's* interest in her—through my own inability to suppress my feelings. It will be a miracle if this ruse can hold the two days more until Samhain.

"I might know someone," Carter admits.

Astrid snorts. "Of course you do."

"He's a Thalassarian captain. Well, smuggler is more accurate. He docked yesterday. If we make it worth his while, he *might* be willing to wait until Samhain to depart. You'd be as safe as you can be traveling with him."

The Lynx's head snaps up, her expression alight with hope. "You can give him my payment for the amulet. That is, if I can get an advance?" Her gaze darts to me.

"We'll take care of it," Maeve answers after a long pause in which it becomes obvious that I'm incapable of speech.

"Thank you," Alora breathes. Though she speaks to all of us, her attention is still snagged on me. "I'll send Mei to make Eleni the offer." A note of vulnerability enters her tone. "Hopefully, she'll choose to join me."

Maeve frowns. "The tailor? Why wouldn't she?"

A shadow passes over Alora's face. "The key master said she loves Ravenscrest. That it's a proper place for her to pursue her talents." She twists her hands in her dressing gown. "She may not want to brave pirate-infested waters to leave it."

"She will," I tell her, my voice guttural. "Eleni loves you. She won't want to leave your side." We stare at each other for a long, silent moment.

Maeve clears her throat. "Shall we get on with the planning then? Time is of the essence."

"We can attempt the linking tomorrow night," I suggest.

Carter frowns. "That's cutting it close."

I shake my head. "I can't be seen going to her room again, and she can't be seen leaving it. Smuggling her next door to Maeve's sitting room in the middle of the night is one thing, getting her across the palace into the Sacred Redwoods is another."

"It will work," Alora says, her voice sure. "And it's a nice-to-have, really. Taran's already identified the room the amulet is in." She gives me a tentative smile. "You can also show me how to connect to my lynx. It might not happen tomorrow, but at least I'll be able to get the basic foundation down so I can practice on my own."

Actual physical pain cracks my ribcage at the reminder that she's planning to leave. How am I supposed to accept this?

"Taran?" Her tone is uncertain.

"Yes, of course," I grit out. "For getting into the room, I have an idea." I nod to Carter, who reveals two tiny glass-stoppered vials from his pocket.

"I snatched these from Lord Winters' lair before he fixed his door." He grins. "Taran can fill them with his blood, and you can use that to get in."

A measure of relief washes over her face. "Excellent. Now all that's left is the guard."

I scowl. "Rhegar. I don't want you anywhere near him."

Maeve tilts her head. "It might not be him on duty. That's why we're planning it for Samhain. He should be with Lord Winters in the ballroom."

"Could we ensure that somehow?" Alora asks. "Give him a reason to feel vulnerable and want his guardian at his side? A reason for him to be on time to the masquerade?"

Maeve cuts me a sidelong glance. "The only thing I know that motivates Lord Winters is protecting his daughter from Taran."

Alora's eyes darken with what might be jealousy, and my heart leaps in response. One side of my mouth kicks up. "I can work with that. I'll play the role of the distraction this time, Lady Lynx."

"She'll still have to get past another Apex," Astrid points out. "They won't leave the amulet unguarded no matter how big a distraction you pull off."

"Leave that to me," Alora responds, that clever mind already at work. "Talking my way past guards is something of a specialty of mine."

"We don't know what you'll encounter in the room itself." Maeve's mouth sets into a grim line. "It's a complete unknown."

"You're not wrong. But that's where my training comes in," the thief assures us. "This is what you hired me for."

That night in Count Zhao's study feels like a lifetime ago. Once more, she's planning to run, and once again, I want nothing more than to chase after her.

An idea forms and takes root. *Yes,* my stoneclaw growls approvingly. "Very well, Lady Lynx, we'll defer to your expertise."

"How will I get the amulet to you once I've stolen it?"

"You can use my blood to access the passageway." I think for a moment. "The closest entrance will be two doors down from the old throne room in the far wall. It's a sitting room my parents used to use for private meetings. If it's even in use anymore, it should be empty that time of night, with the masquerade going on."

"I'll wait for you there," Carter tells her. "I can take the amulet and lead you to the ship. Tomorrow morning, I'll secure your and Eleni's passage with Captain Ataxas. Maeve can tell you once it's in place so you can send Mei to the guild."

"A thorough plan," Alora says, but her uncertain expression belies her confident words.

I rise to my feet. "Let's get you back so you can rest."

"I feel as though that's all I've been doing," she complains.

Maeve shakes her head. "Need I remind you that you were knocking on the door to the underworld mere days ago?"

I lean out of Maeve's chambers, quickly checking the hallway for foreign scents.

The tantalizing smell of jasmine winds around me. "Taran, I—"

I give her a reassuring smile. "Don't worry, Lady Lynx. We'll talk more tomorrow night. For now, you need your rest."

After another moment of hesitation, she follows my direction, slinking to her own suite. My eyes track her until she's safely ensconced in her own room, then I stride back to my friends.

"Are you alright?" Carter asks me in a quiet tone. Maeve and Astrid wait for my answer, their expressions pitying. Have I been that obvious? I snort inwardly. Of course I have.

"Better than alright," I respond, a wide grin taking over my whole face. "I'm going with her."

Chapter 45

ALORA

I know I sounded full of conviction when I told them the linking wasn't necessary. And sure, *Rule Number Two: The first thing is first.* Access to Taran's Apex sense isn't strictly needed when I already know the location of the amulet.

But when you're facing a difficult heist, every bit of leverage you can swing to your advantage becomes consequential. Which is why, after over eight straight failed attempts, I find myself once again in the hollow of the Sacred Redwood Tree, staring into the quicksilver hunter eyes of the prince of Veridia.

"This isn't working." I break Taran's gaze and throw my hands in the air. "We've been at this for hours, and we're no closer than we were before." Worse, there's been no sign of my lynx, which really *would* be an advantage tomorrow night.

Taran sighs deeply but doesn't disagree. He taps his foot, thinking. I take the opportunity to drop into my stretching routine, my body stiff from standing in the misty chill for so long.

"What about a change in scenery?" Taran asks suddenly.

I pause mid-lunge. "I thought we needed to be within this extra-special holy tree or whatever your book said?" I'm being snide, but in my defense, I'm cold, stiff and filled with eight attempts worth of stifled tension.

"Well, ideally, but that's not the actual situation we're going to be doing this in, is it?"

I finally break out of my routine. "No..."

"We're going to be far from each other, not looking into each other's eyes." Taran warms to his subject. "And definitely not inside a supposedly sacred tree."

"I just thought..." I blow out a breath. "I thought we would make the connection here and then hopefully be able to replicate it under more difficult conditions tomorrow." The idea is even more pathetic when said out loud. "This is hopeless."

"No. No, I wonder if—" Taran's eyes catch mine, and there's a determined expression in them that's new after hours of failure. "Do you trust me?"

I cough. "What?"

"Do you trust me?" he asks again.

There's a pregnant pause. Do I? I shouldn't. It's quite literally the first rule of the guild. But he's been there every time I've needed him, even putting himself at risk in favor of my safety. He's made no secret of the fact that he's drawn to me, apparently since before we even met. The idea of him betraying my trust like that boy in Heshan feels laughable.

When the silence drags out and it becomes evident his question is not actually hypothetical, I finally admit, "Yes."

"Come with me. I want to show you something." I barely have time to blink before he grabs one of my hands and starts tugging me along.

We make our way back through the palace passageways, hidden inside our hoods, backtracking to avoid any night guards that Taran senses. I have no idea where we are when he finally swipes his finger against the wall (I cannot wait until I finally get to do this myself) and opens a door into...his chambers?

He drops my hand immediately, hurrying into his bedroom. I follow more slowly, taking a moment to examine my surroundings.

The bedroom is large, as befitting a prince, but other than big clear skylights, it's more of an inner fortress, lacking the big windows overlooking the sea from his sitting room. It feels dark, secretive.

At the center stands the prince's wooden sleigh bed—enormous. Big enough for the giant stoneclaw of a man and possibly two partners. My pulse kicks up at the thought. It's tastefully decorated with dark gray bedding. Masculine.

Taran finds whatever it is he's looking for in a chest of drawers and whips around triumphantly. When he sees where my focus is, a teasing smirk curves his lips, but he stops short of saying anything.

Instead, he crosses the room in two giant strides, holding out a miniature portrait of a beautiful woman with dark ebony hair and deep, liquid eyes.

"My mother."

So this is Queen Kora. I examine the portrait more carefully, looking for signs of her son in her features. For all that Taran is King Nyxley through and through, there is something of the prince there in the queen's devastating smile. In the bronzed tone of her skin and the slight waves of her midnight hair.

"You have her smile." My eyes lift to meet Taran's, questioning. Why has he shown me this?

He clears his throat. "Yes, Maeve says much the same. Will you sit?" He gestures to the bed behind us, the only place to sit.

I manage to nod and sit beside him, my back ramrod straight.

He blows out a deep breath, still clutching his mother's portrait in his hands. "I think, perhaps, we need to...talk."

"Talk?" I can't hide my overt skepticism.

"Yes. My creature—" He takes another breath and starts again. "My stoneclaw seeks to protect me. I imagine your lynx is the same."

He takes my silence for acquiescence and continues. "Can I ask you something? Something personal."

"You can ask. I can't guarantee I'll answer."

"That's fair." Taran sets the portrait aside and takes my hands in his. "You didn't ask me to come with you and Eleni to Thalassar."

My lips part. "That didn't sound like a question."

"I need to know. Is that because you wanted to get away—from me?" There's no way for him to ask this question without revealing his emotions about it. My eyes jump up to meet Taran's, and the vulnerability in them hurts my heart. I open my mouth to tell another mostly true lie, and I just...can't.

My throat closes on the words like my body won't allow me to speak them. Whatever I say next, it will be the truth.

"When I lived in Shanterra, my life never quite fit. Now I know why of course—why I always felt out of place, broken. But it was more than missing my creature." I sigh, embarrassed to share this story but knowing it's the only way he'll understand. "I was...teased for my Veridian heritage. Never truly accepted by the other guild members. I didn't have it as bad as Eleni, but it compounded with the feelings I was already experiencing from being without my creature. You told me one time I couldn't imagine what it was like—one moment to be sure of your place in the world and the next—"

His hands squeeze mine. "Of course you knew what it was like. That was foolish of me."

My words are coming out all wrong again. Why do the perfect lies slide easily from my tongue while the truth gets caught in my throat? "No, it wasn't. I didn't even know the truth of my past then. Anyway, in Shanterra, I kept searching for a way to belong—to feel complete, you know? There was this boy." I sigh. "I thought he loved me. He said all the right things. But after I—gave myself to him, I overheard him bragging about it to his friends. About stealing the foreign whore's virginity. It was all a lie. A prank meant to mock me."

Taran grazes a knuckle over one of my reddened cheeks. "Don't you dare feel embarrassed for even one solitary second over that idiot. You gave your heart willingly. That takes courage and is nothing to ever be ashamed of." He pauses. "What's his name?"

"Why?" I ask warily.

He shrugs one shoulder. "I'm going to kill him."

My lips kick up at the corners. "Let me finish first. You have here in Veridia what I've always wanted. A home. People who love you. Carter, who is like your brother. Maeve, who is like your sister. Astrid, who is..."

"Astrid," he finishes with a smirk. "But I take your point."

"Being here, with all of you these past weeks, I've felt more at home than I did the entire time I lived in Shanterra." I shake my head. "I can hardly believe it, but it's true. I would never ask you to leave that for me. Never."

His eyes soften. "My turn?"

I nod.

"You already know I've been fighting this connection to you since we met. When I first emerged, I had little control over too much power and a creature that wouldn't be contained." His jaw clenches. "I've been holding on so tightly for so long that I'm not sure if I know *how* to let go. Everything in my life is lies on top of secrets, secrets on top of lies, and I'm terrified that the few people I still have left will be hurt if I can't maintain them all. I still worry about the power of my stoneclaw around you, especially while you're apart from your creature and your own power. Maybe I always will. But, My Lynx—" He cups my face. "In this one area, I am done fighting. I want to be with you more than I want air to breathe. More than I want my kingdom. More than I want that fucking amulet I've been chasing for eight long years." I suck in a sharp breath. "Alora, I thought I needed that amulet to avenge my mother, but if you knew her, you would know vengeance is the very last thing she'd ever want me to devote my life to. If she was here right now, I know exactly what she'd tell me to do."

"What?" I whisper, captivated by his words, my gaze holding his, taking in every single thing about him.

"Go with you."

My eyes widen. "What about—"

"I don't want to leave the others in danger. We should still do everything we can to get the amulet tomorrow. And when you do, because I know you will, we'll take it with us across the ocean, far away, so it can't hurt anyone in Veridia ever again."

"I can't ask you to do that—"

His lips curve into the devastating smile his mother gave him. "We already established that you're not asking me." His smile falters. "Although, if you don't want me to—"

"I do," I interrupt. "I do."

We stare at each other, just basking in the glow of that potential future.

"Let's try the linking again," I say impulsively. "Right now."

His hand drifts down from my face to clasp mine again. "If you're sure that's what you want...?"

"I'm sure."

Eyes screwed shut, I take a full breath in and let it out slowly. I concentrate on the sound of each of our heartbeats, like I did in the redwood. But this time, instead of trying to clear my mind and be open for the prince to share his power, I turn inward, the way I did on the hunt. To my own creature. To the lynx that's hidden from me for ten long years. The part of my soul still trapped inside an invisible cage.

I hyperfocus on my hearing, trying to amplify it the way an auditory Apex would be able to. The sounds sharpen. My heartbeat. Taran's. The blood pumping through our bodies. His steady breaths, the slight catch that means he's found his own connection. I can easily pick out the strain in Taran's low voice when he asks, "Are you ready?"

"Yes," I murmur.

We open our eyes.

The first indication it's worked is the overwhelming rush of his scent—pine and rain. Then, other scents flood in: the wood of the bed frame, gods, even the tang of dust motes in the air.

But this time, the connection holds.

A surge fills me as Taran's power merges with mine, and I moan out loud, Taran echoing me. My shoulders push back as I feel the strength of a stoneclaw fill my limbs.

I could take on monsters and win.

I gasp, and as if the sound is a trigger, Taran lunges towards me, close enough to draw breath, grasping my face firmly with both hands.

"Say my name." He bites out the harsh command.

And the sweet smell of his breath fanning my face makes me murmur back, unthinkingly, "I want to taste you."

I try to lean forward, but he holds my face frozen in his grasp. "First, drop the link."

"What?" My mind is muddled.

"Drop the link, Alora." His voice is tight, and his hands, where they clutch my face, tremble slightly. "Please."

It's that vulnerable "please" that ultimately breaks me out of the trance that I'm caught in. The connection severs, and the overwhelming scent and feelings of power ebb until it's just me in my own head.

Taran's hands drop from my flesh like it's on fire. "That was…" He shakes his head. "I don't have words for what that was."

It was intense.

And suddenly, I find myself saying, "We should try again. Make sure it wasn't a fluke."

His face slackens.

"What? You don't agree?"

"No, I absolutely do. I'm just surprised you want to. It was…intimate. To say the least."

I crack a smile. "Still want to hear me say your name, Your Highness?"

He stares at me, unblinking, like he can't believe I just said that. But then his lips kick up into a smirk, and he purrs back, "Still want to taste me, Lady Lynx?"

I swallow. Hard. I'm sure the answer is plainly written across my face. And probably just as easy to read in my scent.

The prince drops my hands suddenly, jumping to a standing position. "Maybe we should try standing this time. And, uh, not looking at each other. See if we can still manage it."

My mouth curves, and I rise to stand a few steps away from him. "Like this?"

That muscle feathers in his jaw. "A little farther."

I huff and take two mockingly long strides away from him. "Better?"

"That's fine," he says, but his voice is tight, and his hands are clenched. *It was all I could do to keep my hands to myself.*

Since it worked this way before, I shut my eyes and concentrate on my auditory sense. Despite the relative physical distance between us, an immediate connection to Taran, combined with the orgasmic rush of his power, fills me. I can't help the moan that floats from my lips at the delicious feeling.

"I have something in my chest of drawers. Tell me what it is," Taran challenges.

I intentionally focus my borrowed olfactory sense on the chest, letting Taran's own overwhelming scent fade into the background. I sniff experimentally, then—

"Chocolate? You keep chocolate in your bedroom?"

His grin widens. "Midnight snack."

But now he's spoken, my focus automatically shifts back to the prince, and my mouth starts to water with the need to taste. Not the chocolate. His scent turns deeper, muskier. I wet my lips.

"Alora." He speaks like he's in pain. "I'm going to drop the link."

My eyes track his mouth as it forms my name. "I like the way you smell."

He shuts his eyes, and then all at once, I'm pushed almost violently back into my own body, his power once again draining out of me. I sag with the loss of it, shaking my head to clear away the fog. Slowly, I peek up at him from beneath my lashes, a bit embarrassed at getting so carried away.

He's breathing heavily, his quicksilver eyes alight and fixed on me where I still stand across the room.

"Tare?" I venture.

As if my saying his name snapped something in him, Taran eats up the distance between us with two long strides, pulls me close with one hot hand against my back, cradles my head with the other and crushes his mouth to mine.

He tastes just as good as I thought he would. Even without the link.

Chapter 46

ALORA

I part my lips slightly, and his tongue slips in, deepening the kiss to something edged with desperation. As before, the taste of him floods my senses. Will it be like this every time?

When his big hand at my lower back slips down and palms my ass, I forget anything but the heat of his mouth on mine. He makes a low groaning noise in the back of his throat, and the sound shoots a line of fire straight to the now throbbing spot between my legs.

He backs me up to the wall, still ministering bruising kisses, then uses his hand on my ass to lift my leg around his waist. He lines our hips up, grinding into me with his hard length. My eyes squeeze shut with the sheer pleasure of it.

"Fuck," he pants, finally pulling his mouth from mine and trailing kisses along my jaw, down my neck.

"Fuck," he says again when he reaches the swell of my breasts. With only one hand, he rips my tunic down the middle as easily as if it were paper. He peppers more kisses on the newly exposed skin, punctuated by little nips of his teeth. I tangle my fingers into his soft waves, holding him there.

His helpless swearing is turning me on even more, if that's possible. Everything this male utters seems to fall like honey on my ears. He thumbs a hard nipple and I arch my back against the wall, giving him better access, letting the remains of my tunic slide off my shoulders to the ground.

My breaths are already coming in mortifyingly loud pants when he puts his mouth close to my ear and rasps, "I have to taste you. Now."

I make a sound so needy it will no doubt embarrass me later. With both hands, he lifts and carries me effortlessly from the wall and deposits me roughly on the nearby bed. He kneels between my legs, using his knees to knock them apart, denying me the friction I'm desperate for.

"Are these clothes important to you?" His already deep baritone has gone guttural.

"Whaa—?" I'm not very eloquent after he just touched me like that.

"Are these clothes ones you brought with you from Heshan? That Eleni made," he clarifies. A little late to ask, considering he just destroyed my tunic.

"No, but—"

He doesn't wait for me to finish. He rips the rest of my clothes off as if he had claws, flinging the shredded cloth to the stone floor. I glare up at him, but it's completely lost on Taran.

He's staring down at my naked body as if I'm the goddess Faunera come to Valenrae.

Well, two can play at that game.

I surge upwards, capturing his mouth with mine, using the distraction to rip his shirt open, buttons flying. He smiles against my mouth. I bite his bottom lip in response, earning myself a low, rough laugh that sends goosebumps trailing up my bare legs. With jerky movements, I manage to pull his shirt off, then lie back to admire the view.

Gods, this male. He's miles of bronzed skin over rock-hard muscles. I drink in the sight as I wanted to that day in the training yard, leisurely raking my eyes over his luscious biceps, down to his hard abdomen and the deep V that disappears down his pants to the impressive length straining against them. My mouth goes dry.

His smirk is all smug male satisfaction. "Like what you see?"

Before I can retort, he's already captured the hard bud of one of my nipples in his mouth, his calloused hand roughly toying with the other. I let out a cry, tightening my legs around his knees, trying to find some relief from the building ache between my thighs.

One hand snakes down and spreads me wide, splaying out against my inner thigh. I buck my hips off the bed, desperate for him to move that hand to where I need it. He ignores me, lavishing rough kisses intermixed with tiny nips on my breasts until I'm so worked up and desperate, I try to take matters into my own hands.

"Naughty lynx," he chides, circling both wrists in one huge hand and pinning them to my other inner thigh. My legs are spread wide for him, my breasts pushed together by my arms, as I writhe on the bed.

His nostrils flare, and a savage hunger flickers across his beautiful face. His pupils are blown wide with lust, just a thin band of glowing silver ringing them. He leans down, running his nose lightly against my center, then breathes out over the sensitive flesh.

"Knew you'd be like this. The most delectable bouquet."

"Taran, please."

"Mmmm, remember, I like it when you beg. Please what, My Lynx?" A tiny part of me wants to rebel against this small claiming me as his—not the first time he's done it—but it's quickly drowned out when he blows another cool breath against my throbbing core.

"Touch me." I'm whimpering now.

He rubs his stubble against the sensitive flesh of my inner thigh, and my legs tighten against his hands and my own.

"With my hand?" he muses. He releases one thigh and runs a featherlight touch where the ache is becoming unbearable. My hips buck involuntarily, chasing those fingers and the relief they can deliver.

He chuckles darkly, pushing down the other thigh with the hand still holding both of mine in a firm grip, keeping me pinned. Another couple of featherlight touches on that bundle of nerves, using just the one finger, wring a garbled plea from my lips.

"Or with my mouth?" At the first flick of his tongue, my eyes shutter.

He stills. Confused, I open my eyes. He's waiting for an answer. I clamp my lips together, refusing, but he just brushes me again with the tip of one finger, and I cave.

"Your mouth. Gods, taste me, Taran, please."

They're the right words. The best words. They make him release my wrists in an instant, hooking both hands around my thighs, lifting my ass off the bed and guiding the apex of my thighs to his hot mouth.

And then he feasts.

In barely any time at all, I'm a gasping, pleading mess, my hands buried in his hair, simultaneously desperate to tug him closer and push him away; the pleasure is so intense. When he slides one thick finger inside my entrance, I cry out, squeezing my eyes shut.

"Keep those amber orbs on me, My Lynx," he admonishes, stilling once again, letting me know he's serious. My eyes fly open, and I keep my gaze trained on his while he goes back to his meal.

He growls in appreciation, the vibrations divine. My legs start to stiffen in his hands, my release shimmering.

I close my eyes without thinking, and he stops. Again. I open them quickly, but he's already pulling his finger out, leaving me achingly empty.

"Don't stop."

He rubs his nose against my center lightly, then groans. "You are the most divine thing I have ever tasted."

"Tare," I pant.

"Mmmm." Another light rub, this time with his mouth. "Say my name again."

"Taran, please."

"Please what, My Lynx?"

"Taran!"

"Please fuck me with your fingers, Taran?" He drives two fingers inside me, curling them to hit a spot that makes me see stars. His arms knock my legs wider as they try to close on their own against the intensity. The build starts up again, faster than before, already nearing the precipice.

"Please lick my heavenly wet cunt, Taran?" He buries his face back between my thighs, lashing me with his tongue while his fingers keep up their steady pace. My legs are shaking violently, and I'm almost scared of what's coming.

"Taran, I...I'm—"

"Come for me, Alora," he commands, then curls his fingers again. And with my name in his mouth and his eyes fixed on mine, I break.

I scream as the most powerful release I've ever felt rips through me. His mouth descends back between my legs, licking and biting and drawing out the pleasure until I'm almost sobbing with it. Still he holds me open wide, never letting me have any relief. I nearly black out before he finally slows, lapping me up almost lazily, then licking his fingers clean.

I finally let go of my death grip on his hair and press a hand to my mouth, utterly speechless. I've never experienced anything like that. I didn't know it *could* feel like that.

He starts kissing his way up my body. Soft, tender kisses that create tiny pulsing aftershocks, especially when he pauses at my breasts and gives them extra attention.

"You." He punctuates each word with a kiss. "Taste. So. Damn. Good. Alora."

His weight settles over me, and he dips his head to draw my mouth into a deep, leisurely kiss. I taste myself on his tongue as it strokes mine. By the time he pulls back, I'm breathless again.

I feel raw, shaken. And also like I want him to lose control under me this time.

My fingers trace the deep V of his abdomen, then run lightly along the waistband of the pants he's still wearing and his eyes, already lit, burst into silver-gray flames.

"I want to taste you, too," I admit, almost shyly.

He groans, then to my utter dismay, falls backwards onto the bed and lies at my side, an arm flung over his face. I make a noise of protest as his weight lifts off me.

His voice is muffled when he says, "I want that, too. You have no idea how much. But we can't. *I* can't."

I roll over until I'm leaning half on top of him, toying again with his waistband.

"You can't?" I drop my hand down and boldly cup him over his pants. He lets out the sexiest groan, thrusting into my hand like he can't help himself. The sound, combined with the impressive feel of him, has my desire ratcheting up faster than I would have thought possible after the mind-blowing pleasure he just gave me.

Every time I get a taste of this male, I only end up wanting more. I'm starting to wonder if I'll ever be satisfied where he is concerned.

"It appears you can," I tease.

But the prince captures my wandering hand with his own, bringing it up to rest instead against his face. We lock eyes, and amidst the copious lust and desire, there's something else there. Something that makes my heart race.

His eyes flick down to my bare breasts. "You need clothes. Unless you're ready for my stoneclaw to claim you?" He sighs deeply at my wide-eyed expression. "I thought not."

Before I can respond, he's vaulted off the bed, pulled on one of his signature black shirts and is returning with another for me. I hold out my hand resignedly (my own clothes are certainly in no condition to be worn), but instead of placing the shirt there, he slips it on me himself.

It's so large, it hangs down to my knees, like a robe. He does up the buttons slowly, breathing through his mouth, avoiding taking in the full scope of my scent. When he's done, he leans back and admires me in his shirt, a blatantly possessive look on his face.

My eyes narrow. "You like this."

That devastating smile overtakes my whole vision. He leans forward and kisses me breathless.

"Yes," he finally breaks off to murmur against my neck, his breath tickling my ear. "Yes, I like this."

I can't help my giggle. I feel his smile against my neck.

"Do that again," he murmurs, capturing my lips and swallowing the sound.

"Do what?" I gasp out.

"Laugh. I love your laugh. Every time you laugh, I want to taste it." His tongue strokes mine, and instead of laughter, a whimper slips out. Wrapping his arms around me, he pulls me down to the bed. I rest my head on his broad chest, and he begins stroking my hair. If I could purr right now, I would.

"What did you mean about your stoneclaw claiming me?" My infernal curiosity won't let it lie.

He hesitates for only a moment, then goes back to raking his fingers through my hair. "I want to tell you, but I'm worried about scaring you off just when I've finally gotten you where you belong."

"A reasonable fear." My pulse is already thumping. "I can't promise you won't, but—I want to know."

His arm around me tightens. His soft lips brush against my forehead, and it's so...sweet...after the inferno of earlier.

His calloused fingertips graze a light, teasing trail along the flesh where my neck meets my shoulder, firing up every nerve ending along the way. "I'm desperate to bite you right here. My canines ache to mark you as mine."

I swallow. "What would happen if you did?"

"I don't know. But I'm not willing to gamble with your safety to find out." His voice is as grim as I've ever heard it. "And I refuse to hurt you. Bad things happen when my stoneclaw is in charge."

An icy chill snakes down my spine. "Has that ever happened before? During...?"

Gently, he tilts my face up to his. "You're the only one I've ever felt this pull towards. My stoneclaw craves you as much as I do. I've slept with human women and Apex, but I've never been so...crazed for someone before. Nearly feral." He whispers the final word like the dangerous taboo it is.

My irrational jealousy spikes again at his mention of other women. "Not even with Victoria?"

He chuckles, running his thumb along my cheekbone. "I never slept with her, my vicious lynx. It was always a business arrangement between us. But I also haven't slept with a human woman since I emerged, and I won't experiment with the person I'm most desperate to keep safe." I frown. "You'll find your lynx, Alora. I know you will. But until then, I can't risk it. Risk *you*."

Tentatively, I press a kiss to his neck. At exactly the point where he said his stoneclaw longs to mark me. He groans, pulling me tighter, and I feel his still rock-hard length against my hip.

"This is...the sweetest torture," he grates out, palming my bare ass under his shirt and squeezing. I grind against him automatically, and he sucks in a breath.

I continue to trail kisses along his collarbone. "How do you think I feel? You basically said that it's only your stoneclaw that wants me."

He catches my chin in his fingers and raises my gaze to his. "That is not what I said." A soft kiss, the barest brush of his lips to mine. "I said I don't trust my stoneclaw to be careful with you." He holds my chin for a beat longer before letting me look away. "I should let you go. If I was a better male, I would let you sail away from me to Thalassar tomorrow. But the thought of losing you..." Another sigh. "I can't. You've hooked your claws too deep in my soul."

I drag in a breath and meet his swirling silver eyes. "You've done the same to me."

His answering smile sets the room ablaze. "You won't regret bringing me with you. I promise you. I won't ever let you regret it."

"Are you still sure you want to? You'll have to leave Carter and Maeve and—"

He cuts me off with a kiss. As his mouth dips down to meet mine, I throw one bare leg over his, pushing my body against him.

"I promise," he gasps out between kisses. "I promise."

Our caresses grow more frenzied, wild. One big hand tangles in my hair, pulling slightly so my neck is wrenched back, my lips where he wants them. The other tugs me harder against him as I writhe against his length, increasingly desperate to have it thrusting inside me. A moan wrenches from my throat.

Until he stops us. Again.

"This is getting old," I complain.

A bashful half-smile. "I should probably walk you back to your room. You need your rest for tomorrow. And I'm nearly tapped out on restraint." His eyes dip down to his oversized shirt wrapped around my naked body, rucked up to my waist. The hand on my hip flexes.

"I can sneak back myself. Better they think I was with some other human lord than see us together."

He growls, tugging the shirt down to cover my bare ass. "Fuck that. You'll be walking with me."

My heart pounds every step of the silent journey through the passageways back to my chambers. I don't even want to imagine the consequences if we're caught. My completely healed, bare leg would be the very least of it.

Outside the secret door, the prince gives me a whisper of a kiss, murmurs, "Sleep well, My Lynx," and then he's gone.

Chapter 47

ALORA

I rush into my suite and slam the wall door shut with my whole body, closing my eyes and leaning against it to catch my breath. My mind is running so fast, I can't keep up. Connecting with Taran. Feeling his power rush through me, his stoneclaw at the other end. Taran's hands on my body. Taran's mouth on my body. His plea to sail with us to Thalassar. To stay by my side because he can't stand not to be there.

My eyes fly open at that last thought.

And land on Maeve.

She's sitting across the room in one of the armchairs, her eyebrows to her hairline. A barely there laugh, hardly more than a hard breath, reaches my ears and my eyes snap to Astrid, standing at Maeve's side, looking more amused than I've ever seen the guardian.

Underworld, take me now.

The traitorous thought that at least neither of them can scent Taran on me burns my cheeks. Or maybe it's the way Maeve is staring at my bare legs.

I cross my arms over Taran's shirt and try for bravado. "Can I help you with something?"

A full-out grin breaks out on Astrid's face. It's so unbelievable it almost distracts me from the mortifying situation I've found myself in.

Almost.

Maeve blinks slowly. Her mouth opens and closes a few times before she finally gets a word out. "Where did you just—no, *who* did you just—" She seems to take a better look at the very big, very black shirt I have wrapped over me and evidently answers her own question.

"Yes, well," she says primly, even going so far as to fold her hands in her lap. "There's no time to discuss that now. We have an emergency. Meiling is missing."

There's almost nothing else she could have said that would have overcome my embarrassment right now.

"What?" I can hear the panic in my voice. "What do you mean missing?"

"She was supposed to meet after dark in my chambers to review her exit plan for tomorrow. We thought it would be a good distraction while you were attempting the linking with Taran. She never showed."

"After waiting for an hour, I searched the castle but couldn't find her," Astrid adds.

"So we came back here," Maeve finishes. "When you weren't back yet either, we hoped she was with you, but..." Clearly, Mei wasn't with me.

"We need to alert Carter and Taran," Astrid says. "Immediately."

"Yes." I nod, thankful to have someone else taking charge because I feel completely incapable of it at this moment. "Yes, let's tell Carter and Taran."

"Ahem." Maeve eyes my attire, or lack thereof, meaningfully. "Perhaps you want to put on...something else while Astrid fetches them. And do something about your hair."

My hand flies to my hair, tangled beyond repair from Taran's grasping hands and my own writing against the bed sheets. Oh gods.

Despite the terrifying situation with Mei, Astrid makes that almost-laugh sound in her throat again before disappearing to find the males. Maeve's eyes stay trained on the door for a long moment after she's gone.

"Do you know," she remarks to me conversationally, "I don't think I've ever heard her make that sound before. Was it a laugh, do you think?"

I cover my face with my hands and give myself one full breath—inhale and exhale.

Rule Number Ten: Maintain control.

I square my shoulders and head to the wardrobe for some underwear.

By the time Astrid returns with a grim Carter in tow, I'm dressed in an unassuming tunic and loose pants set, my hair smoothed back into a ponytail. And my nails are well on their way to being bitten to the quick, my mind racing with all the things that could have happened to Mei.

"I couldn't find her either," Carter announces without preamble. "I didn't want to ask anyone else and alert the other guardians that she's missing."

"What could have happened to her?" I'm nearly frantic.

"She could have run," Maeve offers. "I gave her the purse of gold earlier as Taran instructed."

But that doesn't feel right. I know Mei wants to get home to her family, but there's no way she'd attempt it without the guild's help. And leaving us stranded on the eve of the heist doesn't fit with what I know of her character.

"No." Astrid's voice is unequivocal. "No. She was taken."

"By whom?" Maeve asks. But none of us has the answer. Until my wall opens and spits out Taran.

"Lord Winters has her," he says.

I start trembling.

"How do you know that?" Carter demands.

"There's no other explanation."

"Lord Winters has her?" All my scattered fears about what could have happened to her crystallize into this one, sharp, focused terror. "But that doesn't make any sense. She's already an Apex!"

The room plunges into an awkward silence, during which I begin to realize there's another secret they've been keeping from me.

I stare stonily at the prince I trusted with my body and my heart only an hour earlier. "Taran. Why Mei?"

He squeezes his eyes shut. Like he can't bear to look at me.

"Wildcat," Carter starts.

"I asked *His Highness*." Taran visibly winces, either at the return to his title or my harsh tone. "Why?"

When he finally opens his eyes, the look in them is so bleak, it would take my breath away if I had any left in my lungs.

Finally, he says, "I can taste lies, Alora."

And the ground drops out from underneath me.

He starts speaking, quickly. As if he's afraid I won't let him get the words out. "Faunera's amulet. It doesn't just turn humans into Apex. For Apex, it can further enhance our connection with our creatures and our ability to draw power from them. But just like with humans, it doesn't work. The balance is off, and the creature takes over. The Apex goes feral. That's what happened with—"

"Ethan." I thought Ethan going feral meant it could happen to me, someone already at an imbalance with her creature. Maeve heard me express that worry to Eleni. She *let* me think that. My head feels like it's floating. Like this moment isn't real. I watch Taran's lips move in a sort of haunted detachment.

"Yes. My guess is they chose Ethan because of his age. That close to emergence, maybe the balance would be easier to find. But it never is. They always go feral. Except...when Winters used the amulet on me, it *did* work as intended. I don't know why except perhaps my power level. The amulet magnified my sense of smell to the point where I can scent, or taste, lies."

"Wait." I hold up my hand. "Lord Winters used the amulet on you? How did your father allow that? How did your *mother*—"

"My parents' relationship had already deteriorated beyond repair by that point. The strain caused by my emergence...they were barely speaking." His jaw clenches. "My father is the one who called me into the throne room, at a time when Carter was unavailable to accompany me—they had obviously planned it in advance. I don't know how Winters convinced him, but my father was likely ready to be rid of me as heir anyway and wouldn't have seen a downside to failure. Vorrick and Rhegar restrained me before I knew what was happening. My stoneclaw…it did take over initially. I don't know how to describe what happened next. It was a mental fight between us for control. But during that time, I was completely feral, lost to my creature. My mother burst in and I—"

"His creature killed his mother." I think Maeve finished the tale for him out of kindness. It *is* a kindness to say his stoneclaw was responsible and not him.

Bad things happen when my stoneclaw is in charge.

But as I stare at the prince, unable or unwilling to keep the horror off my face, I know he doesn't blame his creature. He places the blame for his mother's death where he always does. On his own two shoulders.

"When I finally came to, I was chained to a wall in a dungeon cell. I called out, and Carter was there on the other side of the bars looking as though he'd seen a ghost."

"I thought he was lost forever. We all did." Carter's voice is numb with remembered pain. "The only reason the king hadn't executed him yet was because the kingdom was in mourning for the queen. Taran was lost to his creature for nearly two full days."

I suddenly remember his face after the boar attack in the clearing. The mangled corpse of the animal. "Your teeth, your…"

"Yes." I can feel Taran's eyes on me, watching for my reaction, though I keep my gaze averted. "My stoneclaw has always given me strength, but now, the physical gifts grow even more pronounced. Not just glowing eyes but stone-hard claws and elongated canines. Horns."

My canines ache to mark you as mine.

My thoughts are tripping over themselves, and a cold hard rock sits at the base of my stomach. My next words are directed at Maeve. "You said Apex don't turn into their animals. You told Eleni she had nothing to worry about when she was *in danger*—"

Taran pushes out a sharp breath. "Maeve didn't lie. I've never known another Apex to shapeshift into their creature. There's only one instance of that happening. Only one time when the amulet worked as intended. Me. My father and Lord Winters have been attempting to recreate it ever since."

"Neither the king nor Lord Winters know that Taran can taste lies," Carter tells me solemnly. "They saw Taran's claws, his teeth. They thought the amulet created the physical transformation and a strengthening of his power, not an entirely new gift. He feigned amnesia. Said he didn't remember anything that happened to him and didn't know how his mother had died. The king and Lord Winters believed it because he's the only one who's come out the other side. Why would they question it?"

"Mei." It hits me now—why Winters wanted her.

Taran nods, his lips pressed together in a hard line. "Victoria must have told him she can taste lies. Her father would have been giddy to use it on her. To see what more the amulet might bring out. How that gift might be strengthened."

The absolutely debilitating guilt that crushes me like a boulder is the only thing that could supersede the betrayal of him keeping this secret from me. I curl in on myself, almost falling to my knees. "This is all my fault."

"What? No!" Taran's voice feels like it's coming from very far away. "If this is anyone's fault, it's mine for not warning you."

"But you did warn me," I respond miserably, the guilt eating me alive. I feel like I might be sick. "The very first day in the palace. You said, 'Don't ever tell my father Meiling can taste lies.'"

"But you didn't tell him. Victoria did," Taran counters.

"Because I told her!" I shout back.

"Before I warned you not to!"

I close my eyes. "I brought Mei here," I tell them, my voice dull. "I put her in danger in the first place. I made up the lie that got her taken." I drag in a shallow breath. "Do you think they've already used the amulet on her?"

"There's no way to know." Carter's voice is gentle. "But...she might make it through. She's a fighter."

Taran nods. "And more importantly, she's in harmony with her songbird. Her creature is less likely to battle for dominance."

Another terrible thought occurs to me. "But...if her songbird gives her enhanced powers or if there's a physical transformation..."

It's clear Carter and Taran thought of this exact thing the second they learned Mei was taken. Winters will know immediately he's been lied to. And it won't take him long to realize Victoria isn't the one who knowingly lied.

"We're going to get her back, Lady Lynx," Taran vows.

"If she hasn't already been lost to her creature," I reply, my tone hopeless.

"Even then," Carter promises.

We end up strategizing until just before dawn lights the sky, working out how to both seize the amulet and save Mei. My eyes feel gritty, like there's sand in them.

Maeve tells me I'll be spending the remaining hours until the heist in her room so Astrid can keep an eye on both of us. In her typical high-handed way, she instructs me to gather everything I'll need for tomorrow and bring it over to her suite.

They're all leaving when I quietly ask Taran to stay for a moment. He nods once, sharply, his posture tense, hands held rigidly behind his back. He's never looked more like the soldier he is.

"What do lies taste like?" I wonder aloud.

True panic races across the prince's face, and he drops his stiff position. "Lady Lynx—"

"They must taste of the sweetest nectar," I muse. "You said earlier that *I* was the most divine thing you had ever tasted, but that can't be true, can it?"

"Alora..." His voice breaks on my name.

"I imagine lies must taste sweeter still. Because you are well and truly addicted to them."

He stares back at me, the anguish stark on his face.

"You told me I'd seen the beast at the heart of you and chosen not to run. But you never gave me the full truth."

"I was selfish," he breathes. "You had only just started to look at me like I was worth something. Like I wasn't the beast everyone calls me behind my back. I knew if I told you the truth, you'd never look at me like that again."

"And after I revealed my own truth? After you learned the secret of my past and my lynx that no one else knows? After we—" I choke on the words. "Did you ever plan to come on that boat tomorrow, or was it all just a ploy to get a hold of the amulet?"

"What? No! No, Alora. Everything else I said is true. You must believe me." He reaches for me, and I flinch back. His hands fist at his side.

"Must I?" I muster a mirthless laugh. A mockery of the ones he claimed to love. "Because I seem to remember just hours ago, you promised me I would never regret choosing to let you join me. Choosing you. But you were about to send me out on that heist without even informing me of the real danger!"

"It's not just my secret to keep. It's a secret that protects the entire realm. That protects the Apex species. My father and Winters already won't stop and they don't even understand the full so-called benefits of the amulet's effect on Apex. Imagine if even more people knew what was possible." He hangs his head, raking hands through wild dark hair.

"But I'm only talking about one person knowing what was possible. Me. The person you asked to trust you, and who, against her better judgement, did." The pain in my chest now has nothing to do with the loss of my creature and everything to do with the Apex standing in front of me, head bowed. "Don't worry, Your Highness. You are free to taste your fill of sweet, decadent lies. Because after tomorrow, I will never again have to hear them."

His head snaps up. "What are you saying?"

"Don't be on that boat tomorrow. I don't want you there."

"Please, Alora—"

I step closer, holding his gaze. "This is *my* choice. Once the amulet is in your possession the bargain is done. *Don't be there.*"

His face goes blank. "Very well." He reaches into his pocket and for a moment, I'm so afraid he's going to hand me back my amber lynx he stole that I stop breathing. But when his hand opens, it reveals white, shimmering stones that shine with an otherworldly light.

The pearls.

I try to suppress my confusion. "You said—"

"I said you couldn't give them to the Guild. But you will need them to barter your way into Thalassar if—if I am not there with you." I hesitate, and he forcibly places them in my hands, closing my fingers around them. His gaze bores into mine. "They were always yours," he murmurs. "A prize skillfully won."

I snatch my hands back, clutching the buzzing stones, and turn away quickly before he can see the heartbreak on my face.

But not before I have to see the devastation on his.

Chapter 48
ALORA

The sun is well on to rising, its watery rays breaking through the sides of the dark curtains when Maeve finally snaps. She sits up suddenly on her side of the massive featherbed with an enraged shriek.

"Go. To. Sleep!" she orders.

I need to, desperately. My head aches, my eyes burn, and tonight promises to be the biggest heist of my life. But no matter how much I toss and turn, I can't relax enough to allow sleep to claim me.

There's no safe harbor from the barrage of shameful thoughts. I not only put Mei in mortal danger by selfishly enlisting her as part of my cover, but it was also my own foolish lie that got her taken—her humanity likely already stripped forever.

Every time I start to drift off, I picture Mei looking like Ethan as I last saw him—eyes wild and rolling, snarling—before her head tumbles to the ground, freed from her delicate shoulders by a shining sword. The weight of my guilt compounds until it threatens to smother me.

"Is it Taran?" In the darkened bedroom, I feel rather than see Maeve's shrewd gaze on me.

No, I want to reply. But that's not true, either. Whenever my anxious mind takes a momentary break from watching Mei's imagined execution, the prince rises to haunt my thoughts.

"What did you say to him after we left?" As usual, Maeve is direct in her questioning.

I let loose a weary sigh. "Nothing."

"I doubt that. You looked ready to stab him."

I stare unblinkingly at the shadowed ceiling. "He betrayed me."

"What?" Maeve's voice in the darkness is shocked. "How?"

"He lied." Maeve makes a clear noise of disagreement. I cast her a narrow-eyed gaze she can't see. "He did. He...killed his own mother, Maeve. And then lied about it."

"Well, I can't imagine why." Her voice is icy sarcasm. "Given your immediate understanding of it *not being at all his fault.*"

"I'm responsible for my parents being killed too, Maeve," I say quietly into the darkness. "Also through no direct fault of my own. But when the time came to tell him the story, I told it truthfully."

That's what really hurts, I realize. After being viciously betrayed by that boy in Shanterra, then rediscovering the same happened with my own mother, someone who was meant to care for me and put me first unconditionally—it's no wonder I'm slow to trust. Slow to share my story.

I can respect Taran for not wanting to tell me. What I can't respect is that when I finally did open up to the Veridian prince, he couldn't do the same.

I feel Maeve's eyes on me in the dark as she sits by my side, taking that in. "I don't know your story," she starts slowly, "but I do know Taran's. And it has *destroyed* him. He's kept this secret for eight years. The fact he is even considering opening his heart again is a miracle sent by Faunera herself. You said you wanted to go to Thalassar and he *didn't even hesitate.* He told us that night he was leaving all of us, his family, his home, to be with you." She sniffs. "The worst part of it is that's exactly what his mother would have wanted. She was the most loving, big-hearted person you'd ever meet. If she was still alive, she would want Taran to go with you. Even if it meant leaving her behind. *That's* how Aunt Kora loved. Selflessly."

My breath catches as the weight of what she's saying takes hold. If Maeve is right, then when Taran revealed his biggest secret, the worst thing he's ever done, I treated him exactly as he feared I would. Just like everyone else has treated him since the day he emerged.

Like a beast.

I manage to snatch a couple hours of sleep. The result is that Maeve and Astrid are bathed, dressed, and ready to leave by the time she manages to shake me awake.

"Don't leave the room," Maeve warns me seriously. "I ordered you some breakfast. Don't open the door for anyone but Suvi."

I take in her instructions with wide eyes and no small amount of trepidation.

Apparently, it doesn't go unnoticed. Even Astrid gives me a gruff "You'll be fine" before following her charge out the door. We'll meet again tonight as we prepare for the ball together, then I'll peel off to secure the amulet while Maeve and Astrid head to the ball to support Taran's distraction they still refuse to tell me the details of.

I'll be on my own for the heist. It's what I'm used to, but a small part of me balks at losing the comforting presence of...can I call them friends? At least teammates.

I snort as I recall Carter's original welcome to me in the Shanterran mountains. The team to steal the amulet. The name still needs work.

After breakfast, I fall asleep in the bath, waking only to ice-cold water and excited female voices coming down the hall. I'm out of the tub and dressed in one of Maeve's silk dressing gowns, a bandage wrapped around my leg by the time their owners tumble into the suite.

I barely, and I mean barely, keep a stoic expression in place when Victoria fucking Winters glides in behind Maeve, trailed by her Apex guardian, Astrid, Suvi and two maids I don't recognize—the latter loaded with what appear to be the Elite women's gowns for the evening's festivities.

"What's this?" I ask, a careful smile fixed firmly on my face.

"Oh!" Maeve giggles unconvincingly. "Victoria heard we were getting ready together—"

"Don't blame Maeve, Lady Thorne," Victoria cuts in, batting her eyelashes innocently. "I couldn't help but invite myself. It's so much more fun to get dressed up with girlfriends, don't you think?"

"I couldn't agree more." I force my fake smile to widen. "Lady Winters, I'm dying to see the dress you've chosen for tonight. Nothing could top your silver one from the Starry Night Ball."

"Oh, call me Victoria, please." She winks. "And you're right. That dress was a knockout. But wait until you see tonight's!"

The theme of Queen Delilah's Samhain Masquerade is "Wild Animals," which is either unforgivably obtuse or purposefully cruel. None of us have been able to work out which. Not even Maeve, which is saying something.

Victoria snaps her fingers, and one of the maids hurries to lay out the pale blue-and-yellow frothy confection. There are gauzy strips coming out of the back with wrist straps.

"Wings?"

A smug smile curves the lady's pink lips. "Yes, and!" Triumphantly, she unearths a headpiece with two bobbing antennae.

"A butterfly," Maeve supplies. "How lovely, Victoria."

I clamp my lips together tightly so nary a chuckle can slip out. The theme, absurd as it is, is wild *animals*, not bugs.

"Where's yours, Loriella?" Victoria asks, confident she has the better costume.

My pulse picks up. "Um, it's a surprise." In truth, I didn't plan a costume, certain I wouldn't be stepping foot in the ballroom.

Maeve sweeps in to save me. "I'm a swan, a black one. The feathers are quite dramatic. Let's get started, ladies!"

We arrange ourselves around the vanity mirror. Champagne, berries and tiny sandwiches are delivered while the maids work their magic, and the whole affair takes on the tone of an impromptu party.

I'm pretending to sip the alcohol and join in the giddy fun, excusing myself to the bathing room to dump my drink whenever I can. I have no idea how I'm going to get out of this. I need to be clear across the palace about to enter Queen Kora's throne room when the distraction takes place. Plus, I'll need at least a moment to wrangle getting past the guard. I feel the hours slipping through my fingers like so many grains of sand.

By the time the maids are helping us into our gowns, I'm a nervous wreck. Thankfully, Eleni's gown I brought from Heshan is already stocked with all my lynx tools, including my custom lockpick kit and the pearls. All that's required is to slip into the bathing room to pull on my leggings, strap on the hidden daggers and swap my heels for practical soft black boots. Carter dropped the rest of my things at the boat earlier.

I still don't know if Eleni will be waiting for me on it or not and that alone has me in a state. Before she was taken, Mei assured me she delivered my note. I keep reminding myself that it's her choice. Either she'll be on the boat, or she won't.

There are too many variables, too many things out of my control. And now, this snake-in-the-grass lady. There's no conceivable excuse I can come up with for me not to accompany them to the ballroom. By the increasingly alarmed glances Maeve and I keep exchanging behind Victoria's back, I can tell she hasn't thought of one, either.

Just as we're readying ourselves to leave, a knock at the door makes my heart leap with hope. Carter. Or Taran. Astrid must have gotten word to them somehow and now they're going to—

Suvi opens the door to admit the Veridian prince, and my heart sinks when I catch his blatant surprise at finding Victoria in Maeve's chambers. He's dressed in his typical black, the dark mask that covers his face shot through with silver embroidery, the better to offset his quicksilver eyes. He looks devastatingly handsome, and I fear my expression reflects that.

"Lady Winters." He clears his throat. "What a surprise."

"Your Highness." She drops into a low curtsey, and we all copy her. "But where is your costume?"

He grins wolfishly. "Surely the beast prince has no need for a costume for the *Wild Animals* Masquerade Ball?"

We're all momentarily speechless, jaws slightly agape. I've never heard Taran speak openly about the infamous moniker the courtiers call him behind his back.

His eyes land on me and drag over the length of Eleni's black-and-gold gown. "But, Lady Thorne, you will need a mask and gloves, I think." He produces a delicate black mask from his coat pocket, threaded with white around the eye holes and with gold patterning like a...

"A lynx?" The words come out in a whisper. I cannot believe his audacity.

With gentle hands, Taran ties the lynx mask to my face, carefully avoiding Xinlei's shining hairpin. He comes back around and examines the effect. "You're only missing the tufted ears." He fingers one of my own rounded curves, and a tremble shivers through me.

For the final touch, the prince hands me a set of long black gloves and murmurs, "As requested." Right. Because now I know that being Apex doesn't afford me any protection from the amulet. My stomach clenches.

"Your Highness, will you escort all of us to the ball then?" Lady Winters cuts in, attempting to pull his focus.

He shoots me a rueful look before turning away to answer her. "Only you, Lady Winters. Maeve, didn't you need a moment to gather the rest of Lady Thorne's costume? We'll see you both at the ball."

To her credit, Maeve keeps the relief off her face, though it's still palpable. But my own stomach sinks. Taran is about to leave us. This is goodbye forever, and with Lady Winters now taking his arm, her Apex falling in behind them, there's no chance to repair what's broken.

Before I can even catch his eye, the prince is gone. Just as I turned away from him last night. Without a second look.

A lump forms in my throat. But at Maeve's pitying expression, I quickly swallow it down. The maids file out behind them, including Suvi, leaving me, Astrid and Maeve just as planned.

"We don't have much time," Maeve urges. As promised, she embodies every inch the fashion drama of the Shanterran Elite with her dark feathery swan mask and gown. She could almost pass as Apex with her brilliant emerald eyes ringed in black.

Impulsively, I throw my arms around her narrow shoulders. The Elite lady stiffens at first, but then she cautiously returns my embrace.

"I'll miss you," I whisper, meaning not just Maeve but all of them.

She clears her throat. "You too, Thief."

I smile, then pull back to turn to Astrid. The intimidating Apex crosses her arms over her chest in clear refusal.

"If you ever make it to Thalassar, come find me," I tell her. "We can go night hunting."

Her lips twitch, which I count as a win.

"It takes me ten minutes to get to the ballroom," Maeve reminds me. "As soon as I walk in, Taran will start the distraction."

"You're still not going to tell me what it is?"

A sly, foxlike smile curves the lady's painted mouth. "Carter can fill you in later."

I huff. "Fine. Keep your secrets."

A tinkling laugh. "I always do." Then—"You should leave first. Get a head start."

I go to remove the lynx mask, but she stops me with one black-gloved hand. "No, keep it. If you're spotted on your way, you can say you're headed to the ball."

I nod, secretly relieved not to have to give up Taran's final gift. I'll take it with me, I decide. He already has one of my lynx figurines; the remaining one is secreted in a pocket of Eleni's gown. So we'll each have a token to remember each other by. My heart squeezes at the thought.

Maeve's shrewd green eyes watch me too closely. "Good luck, Lynx. We're all counting on you."

Her words are enough to jolt me back to the present. I square my shoulders and sweep out of the room just as Taran did. Without looking back.

I have a heist to pull off.

Chapter 49

ALORA

I slip through the shadows of the palace corridors, my heart beating faster with every step. The vial of Taran's blood secured in my pocket should allow me to breach Queen Kora's throne room, then access the passageway for my escape.

Just before I turn the corner to the throne room, I pause, slinking to a shadowed corner. Despite linking with Taran and sharing his stoneclaw's power, my lynx remains elusive. It's worth trying again before approaching the guard. I shut my eyes, concentrating on my breathing, trying to reach inward—but the sound of approaching footsteps has my eyes flying open. The second whoever that is comes into view, the clock starts.

Rule Number Six: Plan thoroughly, act swiftly.

I step out of the shadows and force a sweet, nervous smile just in time. A fraction of me relaxes when I don't recognize the guard—this isn't the guardian I've seen shadowing Lord Winters. But his uniform indicates he's still an Apex. A burly male with a sharp-angled face hewn from stone. I approach him with the same timid demeanor Mei first showed.

"Excuse me, sir," I say in the common tongue, my voice trembling slightly. "I seem to have lost my way to the ballroom. Could you help me?"

He looks me up and down, recognizing my dress and mask as belonging to an Elite courtier. His posture eases, his eyes flicking to my bodice neckline. "Certainly, Lady..."

"Thorne," I tell him.

The effect of my cover name on the guard is instantaneous. His face drops into an angry scowl, his arms extending to grab me. Internally cursing myself to the deepest pits of hell, I swiftly pull my dagger from its sheath on my thigh and slice it through his throat, cutting off his yell before it can form. I dance away quickly before his blood can spray me. It soaks into his dark tunic instead and he drops with a heavy thud.

Fuck.

I look around but there's nowhere to stash the male's body nearby, and he's enormous. I settle on pulling him into a seated position up against the wall and dropping his head to his chest to hide the bloody throat, his cap pulled down over his unseeing eyes. By the time I'm finished, I'm breathing heavily as I examine my handiwork.

It's fucking terrible. An absolute mockery of *Rule Number Nine: Leave no trace.*

I'm trained for manipulations and nuanced subterfuge, not godsdamn assassinations. But I've already wasted too much time. As soon as anyone sees this body, I'm as good as caught.

I stride down the hallway and get my first break of the evening. The guard I dispatched was the same one patrolling the throne room. I pull off one of my gloves and shake a drop of Taran's blood on my bare index finger. I have only to swipe the door with my finger and it opens on its own. Thank Jinai. The next unknown is whether an alarm will be even now alerting someone to come to the guard's rescue.

Rule Number Two. The first thing is first.

The air inside is cool and still. I scan the crowded space, taking in the countless jewels and necklaces that glint under the dim light. It's a dragon's hoard—piles of treasure and overflowing boxes intermixed with portraits of the fallen queen. So this is where they stashed them all. I count over ten potential amulets in just my first glance.

My pulse quickens—there's only one chance at finding the amulet among all these treasures in time. And it means mentally connecting myself to someone I have never felt farther from.

I shut my eyes and concentrate on my breathing. The deathly quiet of the throne room. My heartbeat.

I picture Taran. The way his silver eyes harden with determination. The way they soften when they settle on mine. His pine scent that haunts my dreams. I search with my mind, trying to find the connection.

Nothing.

The minutes tick by, but still, I can't reach him.

My breaths are coming faster now. Any second, those doors could burst open and—

Rule Number Ten: Maintain control.

This time, I keep my eyes open while I picture his stoneclaw.

Watching me from within. Calling to me from the first second we met.

Alone, surrounded by glittering gems and mountains of gold, I let myself admit the truth. There has been a connection between us since the very beginning. Pacing impatiently. Waiting for me to let down the barriers I erected in the wake of my first lover's betrayal.

I was so traumatized from what happened in Shanterra, and the unknown break with my creature, then in a state of vulnerability, specifically taught not to trust again. *Trust in the Guild. And no one else.*

Every one of Taran's actions has shown me his devotion, his drive to protect me at all costs. Even his final lie was one meant to shield me from the burden he carries every day. My gaze settles on the portrait of his dead mother. She watches me with a gentle smile. Asking me to open my heart to her son.

And maybe...maybe I should have.

Suddenly, I'm flooded with Prince Taran Nyxley's famed Apex sense of smell. The scents of the room sharpen, and there—beneath the heavy odor of metal and velvet—I catch the distinct scent.

The amulet.

I can't explain how I know, but the same way as if it was Taran or Carter or Astrid, the amulet smells uniquely Apex. Wild.

I follow the alluring scent, moving quickly. Time is slipping through my fingers. My heart leaps as I spot a blood red circular stone resting on a silver plate set on one corner of a nondescript desk. I creep closer until I'm able to pick out the gold-wrought vines and plants circling the crimson gem. The scent nearly overwhelms me, and the power thrumming from it is almost visible. My fingers reach towards the artifact on their own, desperate to touch it.

Stop.

It's my own instincts that save me in the end, some sixth sense. My natural defense system screaming a warning.

Something's off. My gaze sharpens, and I see it. A faint, almost invisible shine to the plate. A trap.

"What was your mistake?"

The voice in my memory is Xinlei's.

I suppress a sigh. "I should have chosen the rock."

"They're both the same weight."

My eyes widen and I study the plate with renewed interest. "I don't see the sensor."

"It's designed by the Veridian Guild's key master." Xinlei crouches down and examines the mechanism, prodding it gently with a curved finger. "I think he's using blood magic."

Ignoring my internal ticking clock, I study the plate with greater care. As soon as the weight of the amulet is removed, an alarm will trigger.

Fate taps me on the shoulder, her whisper unmistakable.

This moment will define the outcome.

I find the secret pocket in my bodice. The one with the final amber carving. It should be an almost exact match in weight to the amulet. My fingers tremble as they remove my left glove. I place a single drop of Taran's blood onto the figurine.

Every movement feels magnified. I hold my breath as I delicately exchange the lynx for the amulet.

The trap doesn't spring.

No alarm sounds.

Pure relief washes through me, along with the overpoweringly lush scent of the amulet. It smells like every plant and every animal combined together in an overwhelming bouquet that is somehow intoxicating beyond belief. My eyes water. The plate must have been doing more than guarding the amulet—it must have been masking its scent as well.

And yet Taran had scented it anyway—through wards and walls. How powerful is he, truly, if I can scent it with just a link to his power?

I have no time to dwell on the thought. The same second I retrieve the amulet, the door swings open. I whip the hand holding it behind my back.

Rhegar.

This is no regular guardian like I met in the hallway. He's a fully grown Apex, one of the most powerful auditories out there, according to Taran. Before I can blink, he's racing across the room. I switch the amulet to my left hand and go for my dagger, but he's too fast. He's already got one beefy hand squeezing my wrist, making me drop the weapon, as he uses the other to press a soaked handkerchief to my nose. The world tilts and darkens as a sickeningly sweet smell fills my lungs and everything goes black.

Chapter 50
TARAN

Maeve sweeps into the ballroom, Astrid by her side. It's time.

"Are you ready for our announcement, my dear?" I ask the insufferable woman standing beside me, a glittering white mask concealing half her face.

Victoria gives me a simpering look. "Of course. I can't wait to tell everyone I'm going to be your queen, Tare."

I clench my jaw at the nickname on her lips. "Where's your father? I want him by our side when we announce our betrothal."

"Oh, he won't be able to make it. Something came up."

My blood freezes in my veins. I grip Victoria by both arms and stare down at what I can see of her scheming face.

"Taran, how inappropriate," she complains, but her eyes say she's thrilled by the contact.

"Where's your father? Why isn't he here?"

Her pink lips curve into a smug smile. "Not to worry, my love, we have his blessing. He's just taking care of a little something. Think of it as a wedding present."

My lungs are robbed of breath. "What. Did. You. Do," I bite out.

Her icy-blue eyes narrow. "This has gone on long enough, Taran. It was one thing to look out for her when we all thought she was an Elite lady. I understand you have your mother's protective instincts, in fact, I love that about you. But now?" She shakes her head, her ridiculous antennae bobbing back and forth. "That girl is a thief *and* an animal. She came here to steal from us, from your family!"

My blood roars in my ears. As if from outside myself, I watch my hands fall away from Victoria's pale arms. "Your father has her."

The deranged woman pats my chest. "He's likely using the amulet on her as we speak. I'm sorry, Tare, you've lost. My father and I have known for years that you and your cousin have been after the amulet. It's only due to *our* continued intervention that the king and queen don't suspect." Her eyes shine with a manic light. "Marry me, Taran, and you'll get your throne back, I promise you. Daddy understands. He'll back you with the other lords." She grabs my hand in a claw-like grip, nails forming crescent moons in my skin. "You'll be king, I'll be your queen, and our son will be your heir, just as it always should have been."

I rear back, horrified. My gaze darts frantically around the ballroom of masked courtiers, looking for the black of Maeve's feathers. The royal family sits atop the dias, clad in taupe masks and attire like a pride of lions. I finally catch my cousin's eye, and she starts towards me, her mouth tight with concern.

Victoria sighs. "Give it up, Taran. No one will hurt your precious cousin if you just accept your fate. We can put this ill-begotten rebellion to rest and concentrate on more important matters, like our future as the rulers of this kingdom."

"Taran?" Maeve appears at my side. "Lady Winters? What's going on?"

"Nothing that concerns you," Victoria sneers.

Choking down my disgust, I slide my arm around the lady's shoulders and begin to herd her towards the exit. Maeve follows on my other side, Astrid trailing us.

"Where are you taking me?" A note of caution has finally entered Victoria's voice.

"Somewhere we can't be overheard. You're going to tell my cousin what you just told me so she can help us take the throne."

Victoria relaxes at my words, allowing me to guide her out of the ballroom. "We can't take too long," she says, that fucking smug smile sliding back into place. "We have our announcement to make."

"What announcement?" Maeve interjects, feigning ignorance of the betrothal ruse.

"You'll see," she sings.

I practically push her into the first room I find, a small smoking parlor, blessedly empty. Maeve and Astrid follow us inside, Astrid closing the door behind us.

Victoria's smile widens, her eyes shining with victory. "Do you want to tell her, or should I?"

"I will," I say, and then in one quick movement, I wrap my arm around Lady Winters neck, cutting off her airway. She bats at my forearm with increasing urgency until her movements slow and I feel her body sag as she drops unconscious. Still, I hold on.

"Taran," Astrid barks.

Another moment of hesitation and I relent. Victoria's body falls to the ground with a thud.

Maeve jumps back about a foot, her mouth wide open with shock. "Lumos, Taran! What the hells was that?"

"He has Alora," I choke out.

"Who?" Astrid asks in an urgent tone.

"Winters. Victoria told me he's going to use the amulet on her. *They know*, Maeve. They know we've been trying to steal it all this time."

Maeve claps her gloved hands over her mouth. "Lumos save us."

I pull the second vial of my blood from my pocket and hand it to Astrid. Her jaw is set, but she maintains her steady gaze. "You both need to come with us. Grab gold and whatever you can carry and get to the marina. The ship is called *The Sea Witch*. Take the passageways."

Maeve's eyes are fixed on Victoria's limp body.

"She's alive," I grumble.

"Ought we...tie her up somehow?" For perhaps the first time in my memory, my cousin appears out of her element.

"I'll take care of it," Astrid assures me. "We'll meet you there. Where are you going?"

"To catch Carter before he gets caught trying to break Mei out. And then, to get my thief back."

Chapter 51

ALORA

My head is killing me.

That's my first thought when my eyes blink open what feels like hours later. My hands are numb where they've been shackled behind my back. I can't stifle the groan that slips out as I roll to my side, painfully wiggling them back to life.

"Ah, you're awake."

I squint through the dim light towards the sound of Lord Winters' voice. My brain is still muddled from whatever his guardian drugged me with, my senses not firing correctly. I've lost my lynx mask somewhere, and the amulet, of course, is gone, as is the dagger from my thigh, plus the one in my boot.

I'm on a stone floor, and iron bars are blocking my view of the lord. But if we're in the dungeon, deep below the earth, why do I hear the gentle chirps of a bird?

The lord's smiling face, framed by perfectly coiffed platinum hair, distracts me from the incongruous sound. "The Lady Lynx herself." He holds up a tiny amber figurine.

My mouth tightens.

"Yes, my dear, I know." His voice drips with condescension. "I'll admit, it took me longer to put it together than it should have. But after your miraculous healing from the bloodbane, it wasn't that far of a leap. You were too far gone when Taran brought you to me—unless you had Apex healing, that is. A quick look through the records, and I found what I was looking for. A missing female, roughly the same age."

I shut my eyes against the pounding in my head. With my vision shut off, my ears pick up that strange chirping sound again.

Winters sighs deeply. "I should have realized you were lying to Victoria about the songbird being able to taste lies. Her name is Meiling, for Lumos' sake."

My eyes fly open. Steeling myself against the pain of my stiff joints, I rise to a seated position on the cold stone floor. Nearly against my will, my head turns to the cell next to mine.

Mei looks nothing like I pictured.

Her dark eyes are unfocused, gazing off into the distance, her head tilted. Her delicate lips are the source of the pretty little chirps I heard. She may not be aggressive, but try as I might, I can find no trace of her humanity.

I can't help the trembles that reverberate through my whole body.

"How long?" I croak.

"How long what?" Lord Winters asks in a patient tone.

"How long since you used the amulet on her?"

He cocks his head to the side. "I suppose it's been a little over a day now."

I let out a silent breath. Not yet two days. So there's still hope.

"The king was quite displeased, as you might imagine." The lord's ice-blue eyes, twins to Victoria's, narrow. "When the songbird wasn't what my daughter had claimed." A cruel smile twists his mouth. "But you, on the other hand...once he has *your* talents magnified and in his grasp, he'll forget all about this little...mishap."

"And marry Taran off to your daughter?" I ask scornfully.

"The beast is a means to an end." His lip curls in disgust. "Ridiculous that that animal and his cousin thought they could outwit *me*. He's already asked her to marry him, you know. Now, you and I both know that was only ever meant to be a distraction while you completed the heist." His expression turns gleeful. "Too bad he'll have to go through with it now. My daughter will bear him a *human* son with a direct claim to the throne. Then Rhegar will take care of the mongrel."

Maeve was right. This man does want the throne. She was wrong about his ambition being curtailed by his bigotry, however. But I can't focus on that right now. I need to get myself and Mei out of this dungeon and onto that ship.

Unaware of my inner scheming, the lord holds up the amulet. "Lovely, isn't it? You might even say divine." He chuckles at his own poor joke. "I must admit, I'm quite keen to discover what your enhanced power will be. Translating codes and spying on enemies is already quite the distinction. Let's find out, shall we?"

Chapter 52

TARAN

I take the stairs two at a time, Carter fast on my heels. At least he's armed. I had no time to go back to my quarters for my sword.

But I'm never really without a weapon these days.

I slow my pace as we near the dungeons, taking a moment to scent the air. Rhegar. And two others I don't immediately recognize. No sign of my father or Vorrick. They must still be in the ballroom where I left them. I pray Victoria was telling the truth about keeping them in the dark.

I hold up three fingers to Carter and mouth, *Rhegar.* He nods, sliding his sword from its scabbard as quietly as he can.

My eyes shift, and I let my stoneclaw take over. My canines lengthen, my claws harden, and horns curl over my head, somehow bigger than the last time.

Carter's eyes, glowing with Apex power, widen at the sight.

But all I can feel is deep satisfaction. I'm going to rip them all to shreds.

Unable to wait any longer, I charge down the corridor.

Rhegar is waiting. Of course he is. He no doubt heard me coming. But the sight of me—more beast than man—freezes him just long enough. I inhale the tantalizing scent of his fear, basking in it but never slowing. He swings his sword, but it's like it's moving in slow motion for all it bothers me. I dodge with ease, swiping my claws across his back. His agonized screams echo, sweet and satisfying. Carter flashes back and forth at my side, battling the other two Apex simultaneously.

Rhegar manages to swipe his sword near one of my horns, and I roar as its sharp edge slices through the tips. He smiles, breathing heavily. "You fucking animal," he grunts. "I wonder what your pretty little lynx will look like with her own claws." He laughs hoarsely. "Think she'll still be pretty enough to fu—"

His taunt dies in his throat as blood dribbles out of his mouth. He looks down. My hand is embedded inside his chest.

My stoneclaw roars with victory as I wrap my claws around his heart, feeling its feeble, panicked beat, and yank it from his body.

Chapter 53

ALORA

My heart beats faster as the lord approaches my cell, the amulet held out before him like a talisman. He's taller and stronger than me, and my hands are shackled to the floor. All he has to do is touch me with that thing and my humanity will be lost forever.

But I have three things in my favor.

First, he cuffed my hands behind me. Normally, this would be a disadvantage—arms wrenched back painfully, escape nearly impossible. But a tougher position means the guild trained me harder. I learned how to wriggle out of anything.

Second, I'm wearing Eleni's dress.

The pockets are filled with various parts of my lockpick kit, including the thin iron rod Xinlei designed specifically for handcuffs in a slim, unnoticeable *back* pocket. The tool was in my hand almost immediately, and I've been fiddling away at the cuffs this entire time, all the while carrying on the conversation.

Third, he may be bigger than me, but I'm a fucking Apex. And he's about to learn what that means.

Inhale and exhale.

Inhale and exhale.

I concentrate on the beat of my heart. Then Mei's. Then the lord's as he approaches my cell.

In my mind's eye, a glowing amber thread occasionally pulses. At the other end of it, I feel that piece of my soul, the part of myself I denied so long ago.

An invisible cage keeps it trapped. *Maintaining control.*

It's time to let her run free.

In what feels like an hour—but in reality is only a few heartbeats—I tear through the once solid walls of her cage like paper.

And curled deep into the recesses of my mind, so close we breathe as one, I feel her. My lynx.

Tears spring to my eyes. It feels...sacred. Taran's description of the creature connection pales against reality. The bond between my soul and my lynx is divine, limitless. Something that will never—could never—be broken. How did I ever think it could be?

Everything feels absolutely and completely right in a way nothing else in my life has been since the day my mother tried to turn me over to the Elite. And I know now, no matter what comes next, this connection is unbreakable.

A rush of warmth blooms through me, like sunlight on my face. It feels like—love.

So when the lord starts chanting in old Valenrae over the amulet, I don't panic. Not even when it glows ember-hot in his gloved hand. Confident I'm shackled and chained to the dungeon floor, he opens the door to my cell, never pausing in his spell.

It happens in seconds. Like the Guild's *Ten Rules of the Spy Craft and Thievery*, it takes only ten.

One. I slide the unlocked cuffs from my wrists. They hit the floor with a resounding clang. Lord Winters' blue eyes widen, but he doesn't stop his chanting.

Two. I pull the shining hairpin, sharp as a stiletto. Heavy chestnut locks tumble to my shoulders. Winters stops speaking, triumph alight in his eyes. He's finished the spell. The front of the amulet glows red, like a branding iron.

Three. We lunge at the same time—he with the amulet outstretched in his right hand, my own right hand with the stiletto hairpin aimed at his left eye.

Four. Our arms collide, locking us into a battle of strength and will. I'm Apex, but he's a grown man with at least fifty pounds on me, and I've only just connected to my Apex strength. The red-hot amulet inches closer to the bare skin on my chest, exposed by the low neckline of my gown.

Five. I make a decision that will possibly cost me everything.

Six. I abruptly release the arm I've been staving off. As expected, he falls forward, slamming the blazing amulet against my chest, sizzling my skin with searing pain and infusing the air with the distinct smell of roasting flesh. I seize his moment of surprise, burying my stiletto hairpin in one icy-blue eyeball.

Seven. He screams. I scream. My knee slams into his balls.

Eight. He collapses to the dungeon floor. The stiletto winking gold from his ruined eye. The amulet still clutched in his hand, its mark seared permanently on my chest.

Nine. I dive after him. Yank the stiletto free. Swipe it viciously across his throat, hot blood splashing across my marred chest. His choked gurgles drown in the crimson pooling beneath him.

Ten. I gasp, each inhale pulling at the fresh brand. But my free hand lunges for the table, snatching a tiny amber carving...

And then I drop it.

My calling card.

Onto Lord Winters' fresh corpse.

My gaze locks on the tiny lynx, frozen. I barely register Mei's mad chirps from the adjacent cell.

I should get her free. I should, I should.

My gaze drops to the raised mark of Faunera's love for her human consort. The panic I pushed down earlier now rises in earnest.

Can I feel my lynx more than before? How long do I have before my creature takes over? I can't be sure.

Loud noises erupt in the corridor, startling me out of my daze.

Right. I need to get us both out of here.

I pry the now-cooled amulet from the lord's death grip. Just as I move towards Mei's cell, the dungeon door bursts open with a loud bang. Hairpin raised, I bare my teeth. If I'm going feral, these assholes will experience the full force of my lynx's fury.

But there, at the door, his clawed hand dripping blood, one horn missing its edge, his glowing silver eyes wild, it's—

"Taran?"

I stagger, and in three giant strides, he's across the room, catching me before my trembling legs give out.

"My Lynx," he murmurs. But his sharp intake of breath pulls me back as his gaze narrows to the brand on my chest.

"They know," I blurt out. I don't know how long I'll have the words to say this, and I need to get it out while I still do. "Lord Winters and Victoria." My tongue feels heavy in my mouth. "Not just about you, about Maeve too."

I press the amulet into his hands. He takes it automatically, sliding it into his pocket—the same pocket where he keeps my lynx figurine. Or did. Gods, I hope he still does.

"I know. Don't worry, they're all coming with us." Taran's eyes are frantic, but the thumb that sweeps my cheek is slow and gentle. Such a dichotomy, this beast who is also a prince. "I'm so fucking sorry, Alora. You were willing to share your true past with me and I still kept my own from you. I'll never lie to you again. Just stay with me, please. I need you."

The corner of my lips lift. "Need...me?"

"Every bit of you. Your clever mind, your sharp tongue." His eyes shine with what might be tears. "Your beautiful, hard-to-win laugh. I want it all, Alora. And I will be damned if I let anyone take you from me. Even your creature. Even a goddess."

I'm running out of time. "I found my lynx, Taran. She's—she's here."

His throat bobs. "I knew you would."

"This key doesn't work!" Carter's frustrated voice seems to reach me through a haze, muffled like he's very far away. He must be at Mei's cell door.

No, no, this isn't right. It's Mei who needs to get out, not me. This is all my fault. She just wanted to be with her family again.

"If you can't get us both out, take her," I croak. "Take her to her family. We owe her that."

A tear slips down his cheek. I want to brush it away but I can't seem to move my arm. "I'm coming with you. We are going to Thalassar together. Did you hear me? You belong with *me*, Alora. You need to find your way back to me. I'll be right here, waiting for you."

Words, always quick on my tongue, no matter the language, are now too hard to form. I can barely manage the final plea in my native Veridian, choked out weakly from where my lips graze the curve of his ear, "Promise me you'll save her."

And this time, Taran keeps his promise.

The next word out of his mouth is the unvarnished truth. Not a whisper of a lie.

"No."

Chapter 54

TARAN

As soon as the last word my lynx might ever hear me speak crosses my lips—an ugly, terrible truth—her eyes roll back in her head, and she collapses, unconscious, in my arms.

I rise, cradling Alora's prone body against mine. My claws have receded along with my horns.

I leave Alora's amber lynx resting on Lord Winters' corpse, a final symbol of vengeance, where it belongs.

"I don't believe this. You're really leaving Mei?" Carter grabs my arm. "Hey!"

I wrench away, unable to stop the snarl that rips out of me at another Apex getting this close to my female in her vulnerable state.

He stands unmoving with crossed arms and narrowed eyes, waiting for an explanation.

"There's no time," I grit out. "Any minute now, Alora could go full feral, and it's going to take everything I have to contain her. You'll be our only defense against anyone we encounter. I'm not even sure we're going to be able to get *Alora* out of here and onto that ship. We'd have to locate the key to Mei's cell—or break it open—then deal with a *second* Apex lost to her creature. My father or Vorrick could be down here at any minute. There's no time," I repeat, frustrated.

Carter tosses an anguished look at Mei, chirping softly to herself in her cell, completely lost to this world. He nods once, then holds out his hand. I prick my finger and swipe it over his so he can use it to open the passageway door for us.

"She'll never forgive you for this," he informs me as the dungeon wall closes behind us, unsheathing his sword as he walks.

"I know," I reply, walking as quickly as I can while keeping my hold on Alora. "I just have to believe she'll fight her way back so she can hate me for it."

As we walk, my gaze keeps darting down to the brand of the amulet that mars her chest, raw and red and standing out in stark relief against her bronzed skin. It's a twin to the faded white one on my upper thigh, and at the memory of the pain that accompanied its marking, my rage springs anew, imagining it inflicted on her.

Lord Winters was her kill by all rights, but godsdamn, I wish I could have made that piece of shit suffer.

I'm lost in vivid fantasies of all the ways I could have made him pay—for the boar, for today, for my mother, for everything—when Alora stirs, making soft growling sounds. We're less than halfway to the exit—farther than I thought we might get, though not as far as I'd hoped.

I stop, bracing myself, and open my mouth to warn Carter, but before I can get his name out, my lynx's eyes fly open, and she lets out an echoing hiss. At least Carter's aware now.

Her amber eyes are wild, rolling. They shine with the animal-like luminosity I've only glimpsed in them once before as she snaps at me. I snap right back, baring my sharp canines. She bucks against my hold, thrashing, trying to get away. I grapple but manage to keep a hold of her.

"Fuck," Carter swears. "What can I do?"

"Just keep watch," I tell him, capturing her gaze with a dominant glare.

She growls, low and angry, refusing to submit, refusing to back down.

"There's my wild lynx." I give her a little smirk and then, with no warning, lunge forward and bite down hard at the sensitive spot where her neck connects with her shoulder. She whines, a sound halfway between defiance and surrender. I let my canines press just deep enough to bruise, careful not to break her skin.

I hold her there, pinned by my teeth and arms, until finally, *finally*, her body relaxes. Slowly, I open my jaw and release her from my bite, leaning back to lock eyes with her again. Inch by infinitesimal inch, she lowers her gaze. I huff, my stoneclaw more than pleased by her creature's submission.

It takes every single shred of whatever humanity I still have left to hold myself back from tasting her right then. Audience be damned. I thought marking her would be enough, but now that I have, I'm increasingly desperate for more.

But I meant what I said earlier. I want more than this animalistic claiming, her lynx's surrender to my stoneclaw's dominance. I want all of Alora—*her* consent, not her creature's. I console my stoneclaw by admiring our mark on her neck, branding her as mine.

Carter stares at us, stunned, his sword slack in his hand.

"Thanks for keeping a lookout," I manage to snark, rearranging Alora's head to rest against my neck, tucking her limp body against my chest. She starts purring, actually fucking purring, and I wince as the vibrations go straight to my already painfully hard cock.

"Your relationship is deeply weird," Carter announces.

"You better thank Faunera I could dominate her enough to calm her," I retort. "It's the only chance we have of making it out of here."

"You're telling me. Most of the time, she dominates *you*." Carter seems to have gotten over his initial shock and has regained his usual careless humor. I glare at him over Alora's head, but the truth is, he's right.

Usually my lynx fights me tooth and claw—and I love every second of it. The only time she ever seemed to let me take over was in the bedroom. It's when her own natural instincts are more present, and she recognizes and even embraces the dominance of my stoneclaw. I had a hunch she might respond to it in this state, too. I'm just relieved it worked.

By silent agreement, we start moving down the passageway again, slower this time as I continue to balance Alora. She's like carrying dead weight. I'm strong enough to do it, but it's awkward. Plus, we're heading downhill, about to enter the deeper underground tunnel that lets out near the docks.

The scent hits me first. Apex.

I come to an immediate stop, and Carter mimics me as only someone who's followed my steps for a lifetime could do. We share a loaded look.

Guard? he mouths.

I shake my head, frowning. The scent isn't familiar. It's not a castle guard.

That can only mean one thing: These are Lord Winters' males, brought here to assist in his coup. The hard set of Carter's jaw and the way he renews his grip on his sword tells me he knows it, too.

Alora lets out an ear-splitting yowl. The element of surprise lost, Carter takes off for the enemy Apex, leaving me alone to contend with a vicious feral lynx in female form.

She arches her back wildly, and I finally lose my grip. She crashes to the ground hard, and her head strikes the rough stone floor.

"Alora!" I shout, diving for her. She's blacked out. As I cradle the back of her head in my hands, it feels wet and sticky. I check my fingers. Stained with her blood.

The scent—strong and metallic—sharpens my anxiety to a knifepoint. For a moment, I forget to breathe. I'm about to go ballistic when I catch her pulse beating at her neck, strong and steady, and am able to wrest myself and my creature into some sort of—not calm, nowhere close to calm, but at least not full-out panic.

Not yet.

Carter's already back, breathing hard, his blade in his hand. It looks hastily cleaned, as if on someone's tunic. "We need to go."

"I know," I bite out.

"What happened?" Carter bends down and examines Alora's head, grimacing when he sees the blood.

"I dropped her." The words are soaked in self-loathing.

Carter snorts. "You mean she pushed out of your hold and fell."

"Same result." I gently lift my lynx into my arms again, taking care to rest her injured head against my chest. I am filled with disgust at myself for letting her come to harm while she's unable to care for herself.

"There were only two." Carter doesn't sound happy about that—he sounds worried. Which worries me.

I push out a breath. "It doesn't matter. We need to get Alora to that ship. Let's go."

He nods his assent, and we hurry through the tunnel.

I do my best to avoid looking at the bodies of the too-young Apex as we pass. Carter wears a mask of indifference, but I know he's anything but. He's the one who trains the young ones, mentors them, rekindles their hope when they've been yanked from everything and everyone they know and love. He's the best of us in that way.

I hate that I've once again put him in a situation where he's having to fight against his own kind. Alora gives a soft whimper, and I tighten my grip. It feels like I put everyone in this position.

We come across a couple of Apex guards lying in wait. I catch their scent and alert Carter, who dispatches them efficiently. I stay back, holding Alora close. Carter wipes his blade on the tunic of one—a female, barely older than Ethan. If only we could wipe our souls clean so easily.

The waning light of dusk softens the familiar view of the marina as we exit the tunnel. Relief surges through my veins when I spy *The Sea Witch* still docked at port. I don't know what we would have done if Captain Ataxas had left without us, but I'm beyond thankful we don't have to find out.

We approach the ship's berth carefully, but it's dark and quiet. Alora is still passed out against me, her blood invisible against my black cloak, but its scent is stuffed in my nostrils. I can hardly think around it.

The crew is running about, performing last-minute checks above *The Sea Witch*. The captain is nowhere in sight.

Carter motions for me to stay put while he heads up the gangplank. I lurk in the shadow of the ship, my lynx held tightly against me, one hand cradling her injured head.

"What are *you* doing here?" At the sound of an unknown male voice, I'm immediately on alert, my stoneclaw snarling inside me. What the fuck is going on?

"I could ask the same thing of you," Carter retorts.

"Where's the Lynx?" the man demands.

I weigh my options. I'm running out of time to get Alora on board that ship and secured before she wakes up brawling again. Her steady breath is reassuring, but I won't be able to quell my unease until a healer looks her over—and if she wakes up too soon, that chance will be lost.

"Where's the captain?" Carter counters.

"I'm here, I'm here." The captain's voice gives me the confidence to make my way up to the ship. I'm running out of time. *She's* running out of time.

But when I come up the gangplank and see the scene on the deck, I immediately know I've made the wrong decision.

The Thalassarian captain looks frustrated but resigned, a curved, wicked-looking dagger held to his throat by a human male with russet-colored hair and piercing yellow-brown eyes. Carter has his back to me, both hands in the air. He glances over his shoulder, then groans when he sees me stupidly coming up the gangplank to join him in captivity.

A woman with silvery white hair and sea-deep blue eyes bursts onto the deck from below. "Harlan!" she admonishes. "What do you think you're doing?"

The man's mouth sets into a thin line, but he doesn't remove his dagger from the captain's throat.

I see the exact moment Eleni realizes who I hold unconscious in my arms. "What happened?" Her words are fast, panicked.

Alora suddenly shifts out of her stupor, moaning plaintively and turning her body, revealing the angry brand on her chest.

The man sucks in a sharp breath and he grabs Eleni by the shoulder with his free hand, halting her progress towards Alora. "They marked her with the amulet. She's been turned feral."

An involuntary snarl rips out of my throat. "She's *not* feral. She's battling with her creature. She'll find her balance, and then she'll come back to me." She has to come back. If I have to sell my soul to Zathis to ensure it, I will.

The hand with the dagger sags away from the captain as its owner studies me with an excruciating blend of pity and disgust. As if I've finally lost it. Maybe I have.

"Taran?" Maeve hurries onto the deck, changed from her costume, but her face still painted with dark shadows. Astrid is at her side and my gut uncoils a fraction. They made it. "Where's Mei?" she asks, her eyes widening at the sight of Alora.

Carter grimaces. "We had to leave her."

Maeve's hand flies to her throat. "No."

The ringing of the city bells cuts through the night air.

"Shit. Time to go," the captain announces. A crew member hurries behind me and draws up the gangplank. All across *The Sea Witch*, the sailors fly into action.

"She was lost to her creature," Carter is telling Astrid, who's examining a cut on his shoulder that's bleeding sluggishly. I didn't even realize he'd been hurt. "We had to flee. We couldn't get both of them out."

"So you left her behind." The russet-haired man sneers. "Fucking typical."

A rumble starts up in my chest. "Who the fuck are you?"

"Um, he's with me," Eleni pipes up, stepping around the man's body. He growls. "This is Harlan, the, er, former key master of the Veridian Guild."

"*You.*" I seethe. At least one good thing has come from this night—now I'll get to kill this bastard myself.

Eleni blocks the man—*male*—with her body, or at least she tries to, petite woman that she is. "He requested to join us." She pulls in a deep breath. "He's an Apex."

"I know," I reply, the words clipped, and Harlan jolts back a step.

"So you understand then? The king has been blackmailing him against his will, forcing him to do his bidding in exchange for letting him pass as human."

Harlan raises his hands as if facing a rabid animal. "I couldn't do it anymore. I couldn't help him conceal the amulet when I knew what he was doing with it."

"Well, we have the amulet, no thanks to you, and we're taking it the hells out of this country and far away from my father," I tell him. No bitter taste floods my mouth. It's not a lie. "So you can fuck right off."

But the ship is already leaving its berth, the crew urging *The Sea Witch* to top speed. The city I've lived in all my life disappearing into the night.

Maeve touches my arm. "Taran, surely you can understand wanting to escape the king's manipulation." Her emerald eyes catch on the blood matted in the Lynx's chestnut locks. "She's hurt."

"We met with trouble in the tunnels."

"I took the liberty of scuttling His Majesty's fastest ships," Captain Ataxas boasts. "There's no chance of them catching us once we hit open water." His face falls at the sight of Alora. "I'll get the medic."

Finally, I can focus on the female in my arms. I look down at Alora, and the wave of despair that washes over me is so powerful that I nearly fall to my knees.

A small hand on my arm has me staring despondently into steady, deep blue eyes. "Katerina says you need to get her down into the brig before she wakes up." Eleni's words are apologetic, sure I'm not going to like this.

But she doesn't know I've also been lost to my creature before. I know full well Alora will need to be restrained, and quickly. The need for tangible action shakes me out of my hopeless fog, and I start towards the hold.

I pause after two steps, looking over my shoulder to Astrid. "Watch him." She nods sharply, sliding over to stand beside the former key master, who passes her a dark look.

"I'll be back up for you later," the medic, Katerina, tries to tell Carter, but he immediately disobeys her and follows us.

"Not a chance, sweetheart."

Eleni peels away, murmuring something about getting fresh clothes and bedding for Alora. Gratitude rushes through me at her consideration. I should have thought of that.

There's another gut-punch moment when I see the cell. It's clean enough, but that's about all you can say for it. There's not even a bench for her to lie on. The manacles are heavy, iron. Sure to mar her beautiful skin.

"She's strong." Carter's voice steadies me as always. "She's just as strong as you."

"Stronger," I admit.

"Exactly. And you made it through, didn't you? In worse conditions than these, might I add."

I grimace at the memory. At least it serves the purpose of reminding me that conditions mattered not at all when I was lost to my creature. Just like Mei chirping to herself in the dungeon, I had no idea where my body was physically located while I was lost inside my mind.

"Why don't you sit down inside the cell while I examine her," Katerina suggests in a practical tone. "We'll wait until we absolutely have to before we put the manacles on."

I settle inside the cell, leaning against the wall. Alora is still cradled against me, muttering nonsense.

Eleni appears, along with Captain Ataxas, who assures us we've made it out of the marina and are heading for Thalassar. I lean my head back against the wall and shut my eyes, letting the adrenaline drain out of me.

I hear the quiet sounds of the others working—Katerina cleaning the blood from Alora's hair and bandaging the brand on her chest. Eleni undoing the full skirt of her gown, removing it to reveal the tight leggings that stunned me stupid the first time we met. Taking off her boots, unlacing her blood-splattered top to replace it with—

"Whose fucking shirt is that?" My eyes fly open.

Eleni rears back, her hands trembling as she clutches the fabric. "H-Harlan's, Your Highness," she stutters. "Katerina instructed me the shirt needed to button up and—"

Carter comes to her rescue by reaching in with his good arm to silently pass Eleni my extra shirt from his pack. Bemused, she trades him the key master's shirt and slides mine on Alora. As soon as she's covered in my scent, my lynx starts to purr again.

Misery overwhelms me, and I fight the prick of tears.

"Your Highness." Eleni addresses me in a gentle tone. It has a warmth that reminds me of my mother, which only makes the next words hit harder. "It's time."

I shudder, a full-body shake. The others have moved outside the cell, giving me some semblance of privacy. Gently, I shift Alora's prone body to the pallet Eleni prepared and tenderly clip on the manacles.

Immediately, she starts to thrash.

Eleni firmly ushers me out of the cell, and the captain locks it behind us with a resounding clank. Inside, Alora tosses in a fitful sleep, the iron bands already rubbing her skin red. Her rich chestnut hair is plastered to her head with sweat and the remnants of caked blood. The pain of her panicked whimpers reverberates in my bones.

Too late, I was too late.

"Your Highness." Eleni calls me over to where Katerina is cleaning Carter's wound, exchanging words with Captain Ataxas and Maeve in quiet murmurs.

"Taran," I croak.

The human looks alarmed but respects my wishes. "Taran," she corrects herself awkwardly. "The captain said he has something to tell us."

Captain Ataxas' sun-weathered face is serious. "I was just telling Lady Ashbourne that the threat of Thalassarian pirates is unfortunately quite real.

And I can't be sure what kind of reception you can expect from the royal family."

Eleni's big blue eyes sparkle. "And *I* was just about to tell the captain that Alora was wearing the dress I designed for her tonight."

We all stare at the tailor, uncomprehending. She lets out an impatient huff. "Which means I know where all the hidden pockets are."

From the blood-stained bundle of silk in her hands, she pulls out a necklace. Shining with an otherworldly quality, the luminescent pearls seem to reflect off her sea-blue eyes.

I can't help my hoarse laugh. The start of it all. The heist that brought her to me.

The captain's eyes are wide. "That's...that's..."

"The Pearls of Azure," I confirm. "I gave them to her last night." Four sets of eyes widen. "I wanted her to have them to barter her way into Thalassar. They were her prize, after all."

Carter shakes his head, a glimmer of admiration in his usually guarded eyes. But none of them know the full extent of the pearls' value and I have no intention of explaining now.

As the others talk in excited whispers, I wander back to Alora's cell, leaning my forehead against the bars. Her head tosses in panic, her eyes fluttering—she's locked fast in a mental battle with her creature.

I close my eyes, emotionally drained to the point of near collapse. But I know this is just the beginning of my vigil. And her struggle.

"Come back to me, Lady Lynx." My voice breaks, but I manage to choke out the rest. "I have one more truth to tell you."

EPILOGUE
ELENI

J ust before the sails come into view at the edge of the horizon, the
crewmembers take up the call. "Pirates! Pirates!" They scramble to trade
long scopes to better see the skull and crossbones flags, still undetectable to
my naked eye.

"We won't be able to outrun them." Captain Nikos Ataxas appears at my
side at the rail, his weathered face grim. "Best get ready to negotiate, Lady
Ashbourne." He hurries off, shouting orders at the crew.

Maeve exchanges a worried look with Carter. "I need Taran."

Carter shakes his head. "He'll never leave her. The ship could be sinking
into the ocean before he'd leave her side."

"It's the third day," Harlan cuts in, drawn by the commotion. Astrid,
his constant shadow since the prince gave her the command, trails behind
him. "It's time he accepts that she's not ever going to wake up," he says in a
matter-of-fact tone.

Maeve turns and faces the former key master, lifting her chin with an
imperial air. He smirks back, nonplussed.

"Do go fuck yourself," she tells him, her Elite enunciation crystal clear.
Then she spins on her heel and strides off, presumably to the brig, her
lavender skirts swishing behind her.

Carter's mouth quirks as though he'd like to smile but can't quite manage it. We've all been in a tense holding pattern since our escape from Ravenscrest, desperate for Alora to wake, terrified she won't.

"I've never heard Maeve curse like that before," Carter murmurs, as if to himself. "Didn't know she knew the word." His gaze slides to me and my pulse picks up, as it always does in his presence. "You'd better go after her."

My eyes widen. "*Me*?"

"The one chance she has of getting him to leave Alora is if you agree to stay there with her." He shrugs one shoulder. "He trusts you."

"He trusts *me*?" I squeak.

"Of course." Carter's brow furrows. "You love her." My heart squeezes.

"She's not going to wake up," Harlan mutters again.

"Say that one more time." Carter's eyes light with a menacing golden fire I've never seen from the guardian. "I fucking dare you."

"I'll, uh, just go after Maeve then," I cut in, taking two quick steps. But a moment of hesitation has me turning back to the males. "Behave yourselves. We're all on the same side."

"That remains to be seen," Carter drawls. But at my frown, he adds, "Go take care of the wildcat. I promise I won't kill your lover."

My cheeks flush hot. "He's not my lover!"

"Like you could," Harlan counters at the same time.

Carter takes a step closer. "Care to test that theory, asshole?"

"Carter," I admonish.

"Should have let Tare kill him," he mutters. He waves me off, turning back to stare at the ocean where the black-and-white of snapping flags is clearer every moment.

I hurry down the creaking stairwell into the brig where Alora has been chained for the better part of three days. The sounds of the prince and his cousin arguing assault my ears.

"What's the point of being by her side when this entire ship is going to be blasted apart by pirates?" Maeve shouts. "What was the point of any of this if you give up now?"

"You're not listening to me." The prince's voice sounds drained of all life, and when I reach the bottom step and catch sight of him, I can't help but gasp aloud.

He won't eat or drink unless Alora does, which means he's been surviving on the same little bits of broth and water we can dribble down her throat. His facial hair has grown bushy, and his eyes are hollow, set within dark black circles. It's only been a night since I've seen him, but he appears to be deteriorating ever more quickly.

"I didn't say I won't leave her. I said *I can't*," he continues. "We both know you're the better negotiator anyway."

"I need the prince of the realm at my side," she grits out. "The beast prince, infamous throughout Valenrae for his power, for his temper and for his bite. Not to mention, I don't even know what the pearls can do because *you haven't told me*. How am I supposed to negotiate when I don't understand what I'm negotiating with?"

Taran's eyes shutter. "I don't know what it is you expect from me. I just told you, I can't do it."

"I'll stay with her," I offer. The prince's eyes blink open and meet mine. Consciously maintaining a serene expression, I make my way further into the brig, keeping contact with his strange silver gaze. "I'll stay right here, beside her, until you come back." Without waiting for a response, I settle myself onto the pallet of blankets next to the cell and slide my hand through the bars to settle on Alora's.

Her flesh is hot to the touch, her hair matted and sweat soaked. She whimpers and snarls in her sleep, but at my touch, her face relaxes just a bit. The prince drops to his knees beside me, his gaze fixated on Alora. I stroke the top of her palm with my thumb, and her breathing slows. Her sleep is still fitful, but it's measurably improved.

I glance up at the prince, his sunken eyes kindling with what must be hope. Behind his back, Lady Ashbourne mouths, *Thank you.*

"Go help your cousin, Your Highne—Taran. I've got her."

He shudders, a full-body shake that I feel in my bones. "Call for me immediately if anything changes," he commands.

"Of course. Now, please, go. We'll be alright."

His gaze lingers on my friend, the look so laden with longing, it takes my breath away. Then, as if he has to physically force himself to do it, he turns away and strides up the stairwell for the first time since he brought Alora on this ship three days ago, Maeve fast on his heels.

"Wow," I murmur. I turn back to Alora, her breathing now even, the pained furrow gone from between her brows. But she remains asleep, locked in a silent world I can't enter. I sigh, leaning my head against the cell bars and shutting my eyes. Listening to the creak of the boat as it sways beneath me.

I wonder if anyone will ever love me like that.

"Oh, Eleni." Her voice is cracked with disuse.

My eyes fly open and meet my best friend's glowing amber gaze, clear and undeniably present, though shining with an animal-like luminosity. Through the tangle of her hair, her ears curve into delicate points, like the tufted ears of a lynx. And when she smiles, her canines are long and sharp.

My jaw drops open as Alora pushes herself up on shaky arms.

"Of course they will, my friend. No one could help but love you."

Dying to find out what happens next to Taran and Alora? Pre-order Book 2 *An Ear For Secrets* now!

PLUS

Villains deserve love too.

Get your exclusive copy of the prequel to *The Apex Kingdom* series, available only to email subscribers.

A Heart For Sacrifice is a short novella that takes place a few decades before the events in *A Taste For Lies*, and follows the whirlwind love match between the capital "R" rake King Elias Nyxley and the innocent courtier who falls for him and becomes queen.

PLEASE LEAVE A REVIEW!

Indie author careers are made when you share the books you love with the world. If you enjoyed *A Taste For Lies*, please consider helping other readers discover the magic of Valenrae by taking the time to leave a review on Amazon or Goodreads.

ABOUT THE AUTHOR

LC Whitehouse has been imagining fantasy worlds since childhood when she would sculpt tiny queens and angels out of modeling clay. She is a devoted minimalist and sometimes feels like the only girl on bookstagram without a trophy shelf.

LC lives with her own fated mate and their son on the central coast of California where wine country meets the sea. She is also a certified Nutritional Therapy Practitioner and a firm believer in the magically restorative powers of magnesium.

Join LC Whitehouse's Bookish Beauties Facebook Group

ACKNOWLEDGEMENTS

First, thank YOU for reading this book. It means the world to me that you took a chance on a new author's debut. I hope you loved the beginning of Taran and Alora's story as much as I loved writing it.

Thank you to my ARC readers and Street Team. Since my first post on social media, the entire Bookstagram, BookThreads and BookTok communities have been the support system of my dreams. It is scary to put yourself out there—to put your soul in art form out into the universe—and every share, every sweet DM, every comment cheering me on, and yes, every "like", made it just a little bit easier.

Thank you to my husband. Without you carrying the team, this book would have never been. You have always been 100% supportive of my dreams and whatever it takes to get there. Know that I do not take it for granted.

Thank you to my son. You were very patient with me and the time I had to devote to writing. I hope this "spicy book" does even a fraction as well as *Dragons Love Tacos*.

Thank you to my dad. For bragging on me to everyone. Your pride is palpable and it feels like wings. Thank you for supporting me so I could work with the editor of my dreams.

Thank you to my mom. For proving there is no "perfect" time in life to become an artist, all you need is a will to learn and an artist's heart. Thank you for sending my book to everyone you know.

Thank you to Laura Bonner. Who gave me the best advice at the very beginning: "Lean into the parts of the process you enjoy. Make friends. Enjoy the journey."

Thank you to Eileen LaGreca. Who created the incredible map for this book after she saw my first draft. I'm so glad no one else had to see it.

Thank you to my mother-in-law. Who agreed not to choose *A Taste For Lies* for her book club, but only under duress. Thank you for your support since day one.

Thank you to Chandler Bolt, Ramy Vance, Barbara Hartzler and the entire team at SelfPublishing.com. I thought author dreams were too big for me; you all showed me that no dream is too big. Thank you for the work you do.

Thank you to Shavonne Clarke at Motif Edits. From your sample edit when you suggested Alora be human to your monumental advice to insert the forbidden love trope, this novel has changed so much for the better because of you. You are truly gifted and I am fortunate to work with you and your team.

And finally, "to those who dream of stranger worlds". Write the damn book.